About the Authors

USA Today bestselling, *RITA*®-nominated, and critically-acclaimed author **Caitlin Crews** has written more than 130 books and counting. She has a Master's and PhD in English Literature, thinks everyone should read more category romance, and is always available to discuss her beloved alpha heroes. Just ask. She lives in the Pacific Northwest with her comic book artist husband, is always planning her next trip, and will never, ever, read all the books in her to-be-read pile. Thank goodness.

Barbara Hannay lives in North Queensland where she and her writer husband have raised four children. Barbara loves life in the north where the dangers of cyclones, crocodiles, and sea stingers are offset by a relaxed lifestyle, glorious winters, World Heritage rainforests, and the Great Barrier Reef. Besides writing, Barbara enjoys reading, gardening, and planning extensions to accommodate her friends and her extended family.

European Escapes

July 2023
Madrid

August 2023
Sicily

September 2023
Sweden

January 2024
Paris

February 2024
Prague

March 2024
Athens

April 2024
London

May 2024
Berlin

European Escapes:
Prague

CAITLIN CREWS

BARBARA HANNAY

MILLS & BOON

First Published in Great Britain 2024
by Mills & Boon, an imprint of HarperCollins*Publishers* Ltd,
1 London Bridge Street, London, SE1 9GF

www.harpercollins.co.uk

HarperCollins*Publishers*
Macken House, 39/40 Mayor Street Upper,
Dublin 1, D01 C9W8, Ireland

MIX
Paper | Supporting
responsible forestry
FSC™ C007454

NOT JUST THE
BOSS'S PLAYTHING

CAITLIN CREWS

To the fabulous Sharon Kendrick, who sorted out
what was wrong with an early draft of this book on
a long, rainy, Irish drive to and from Sligo town (and
an atmospheric tour of Yeats country) – both of which
amounted to a master class in writing for the
Mills & Boon Modern series.

And to Abby Green, Heidi Rice, Fiona Harper and
Chantelle Shaw, for our inspiring days in Delphi.

And to all the readers who wrote me to ask for
Nikolai's story. This is for you most of all!

CHAPTER ONE

TORTURE WOULD BE preferable to this.

Nikolai Korovin moved through the crowd ruthlessly, with a deep distaste for his surroundings he made no effort to hide. The club was one of London's sleekest and hottest, according to his assistants, and was therefore teeming with the famous, the trendy and the stylish.

All of whom appeared to have turned up tonight. In their slick, hectic glory, such as it was. It meant Veronika, with all her aspirations to grandeur, couldn't be far behind.

"Fancy a drink?" a blank-eyed creature with masses of shiny black hair and plumped-up lips lisped at him, slumping against him in a manner he imagined was designed to entice him. It failed. "Or anything else? Anything at all?"

Nikolai waited impatiently for her to stop that insipid giggling, to look away from his chest and find her way to his face—and when she did, as expected, she paled. As if she'd grabbed hold of the devil himself.

She had.

He didn't have to say a word. She dropped her hold on him immediately, and he forgot her the moment she slunk from his sight.

After a circuit or two around the loud and heaving club, his eyes moving from one person to the next as they propped up the shiny bar or clustered around the leather seating areas, cataloging each and dismissing them, Nikolai stood with his back to one of the giant speakers and simply waited. The music, if it could be called that, blasted out a bass line he could feel reverberate low in his spine as if he was under sustained attack by a series of concussion grenades. He almost wished he was.

He muttered something baleful in his native Russian, but it was swept away in the deep, hard thump and roll of that terrible bass. *Torture.*

Nikolai hated this place, and all the places like it he'd visited since he'd started this tiresome little quest of his. He hated the spectacle. He hated the waste. Veronika, of course, would love it—that she'd be *seen* in such a place, in such company.

Veronika. His ex-wife's name slithered in his head like the snake she'd always been, reminding him why he was subjecting himself to this.

Nikolai wanted the truth, finally. She was the one loose end he had left, and he wanted nothing more than to cut it off, once and for all. Then she could fall from the face of the planet for all he cared.

"I never loved you," Veronika had said, a long cigarette in her hand, her lips painted red like blood and all of her bags already packed. "I've never been faithful to you except by accident." Then she'd smiled, to remind him that she'd always been the same as him, one way or another: a weapon hidden in plain sight. "Needless to say, Stefan isn't yours. What sane woman would have *your* child?"

Nikolai had eventually sobered up and understood that whatever pain he'd felt had come from the surprise of Veronika's departure, not the content of her farewell speech. Because he knew who he was. He knew *what* he was.

And he knew her.

These days, his avaricious ex-wife's tastes ran to lavish

Eurotrash parties wherever they were thrown, from Berlin to Mauritius, and the well-manicured, smooth-handed rich men who attended such events in droves—but Nikolai knew she was in London now. His time in the Russian Special Forces had taught him many things, much of which remained etched deep into that cold, hard stone where his heart had never been, and finding a woman with high ambitions and very low standards like Veronika? Child's play.

It had taken very little effort to discover that she was shacking up with her usual type in what amounted to a fortress in Mayfair: some dissipated son of a too-wealthy sheikh with an extensive and deeply bored security force, the dismantling of which would no doubt be as easy for Nikolai as it was entertaining—but would also, regrettably, cause an international incident.

Because Nikolai wasn't a soldier any longer. He was no longer the Spetsnaz operative who could do whatever it took to achieve his goals—with a deadly accuracy that had won him a healthy respect that bordered on fear from peers and enemies alike. He'd shed those skins, if not what lay beneath them like sinew fused to steel, seven years ago now.

And yet because his life was nothing but an exercise in irony, he'd since become a philanthropist, an internationally renowned wolf in the ill-fitting clothes of a very soft, very fluffy sheep. He ran the Korovin Foundation, the charity he and his brother, Ivan, had begun after Ivan's retirement from Hollywood action films. Nikolai tended to Ivan's fortune and had amassed one of his own thanks to his innate facility with investment strategies. And he was lauded far and near as a man of great compassion and caring, despite the obvious ruthlessness he did nothing to hide.

People believed what they wanted to believe. Nikolai knew that better than most.

He'd grown up hard in post-Soviet Russia, where brutal

oligarchs were thick on the ground and warlords fought over territory like starving dogs—making him particularly good at targeting excessively wealthy men and the corporations they loved more than their own families, then talking them out of their money. He knew them. He understood them. They called it a kind of magic, his ability to wrest huge donations from the most reluctant and wealthiest of donors, but Nikolai saw it as simply one more form of warfare.

And he had always been so very good at war. It was his one true art.

But his regrettably high profile these days meant he was no longer the kind of man who could break into a sheikh's son's London stronghold and expect that to fly beneath the radar. Billionaire philanthropists with celebrity brothers, it turned out, had to follow rules that elite, highly trained soldiers did not. They were expected to use diplomacy and charm.

And if such things were too much of a reach when it concerned an ex-wife rather than a large donation, they were forced to subject themselves to London's gauntlet of "hot spots" and *wait*.

Nikolai checked an impatient sigh, ignoring the squealing trio of underdressed teenagers who leaped up and down in front of him, their eyes dulled with drink, drugs and their own craven self-importance. Lights flashed frenetically, the awful music howled and he monitored the crowd from his strategic position in the shadows of the dance floor.

He simply had to wait for Veronika to show herself, as he knew she would.

Then he would find out how much of what she'd said seven years ago had been spite, designed to hurt him as much as possible, and how much had been truth. Nikolai knew that on some level, he'd never wanted to know. If he never pressed the issue, then it was always possible that Stefan really *was* his, as Veronika had made him believe for the first five years of the boy's life. That somewhere out there, he had a son. That he had done something right, even if it was by accident.

But such fantasies made him weak, he knew, and he could no longer tolerate it. He wanted a DNA test to prove that Stefan wasn't his. Then he would be done with his weaknesses, once and for all.

"You need to go and fix your life," his brother, Ivan, the only person alive that Nikolai still cared about, the only one who knew what they'd suffered at their uncle's hands in those grim years after their parents had died in a factory fire, had told him just over two years ago. Then he'd stared at Nikolai as if he was a stranger and walked away from him as if he was even less than that.

It was the last time they'd spoken in person, or about anything other than the Korovin Foundation.

Nikolai didn't blame his older brother for this betrayal. He'd watched Ivan's slide into his inevitable madness as it happened. He knew that Ivan was sadly deluded—blinded by sex and emotion, desperate to believe in things that didn't exist because it was far better than the grim alternative of reality. How could he blame Ivan for preferring the delusion? Most people did.

Nikolai didn't have that luxury.

Emotions were liabilities. Lies. Nikolai believed in sex and money. No ties, no temptations. No relationships now his brother had turned his back on him. No possibility that any of the women he took to his bed—always nameless, faceless and only permitted near him if they agreed to adhere to a very strict set of requirements—would ever reach him.

In order to be betrayed, one first had to trust.

And the only person Nikolai had trusted in his life was Ivan and even then, only in a very qualified way once that woman had sunk her claws in him.

But ultimately, this was a gift. It freed him, finally, from his last remaining emotional prison. It made everything simple. Because he had never known how to tell Ivan— who had built a life out of playing the hero in the fighting ring and on the screen, who was able to embody those fights he'd won and the roles he'd played with all the self-righteous fury of the untainted, the unbroken, the *good*— that there were some things that couldn't be fixed.

Nikolai wished he was something so simple as *broken*.

He acted like a man, but was never at risk of becoming one. He'd need flesh and blood, heat and heart for that, and those were the things he'd sold off years ago to make himself into the perfect monster. A killing machine.

Nikolai knew exactly what he was: a bright and shining piece of ice with no hope of warmth, frozen too solid for any sun to penetrate the chill. A hard and deadly weapon, honed to lethal perfection beneath his uncle's fists, then sharpened anew in the bloody Spetsnaz brotherhood. To say nothing of the dark war games he'd learned he could make into his own kind of terrible poetry, despite what it took from him in return.

He was empty where it counted, down to his bones. Empty all the way through. It was why he was so good at what he did.

And it was safer, Nikolai thought now, his eyes on the heedless, hedonistic crowd. There was too much to lose should he relinquish that deep freeze, give up that iron control. What he remembered of his drinking years appalled him—the blurred nights, the scraps and pieces of too much frustrated emotion turned too quickly into violence, making him far too much like the brutal uncle he'd so despised.

Never again.

It was better by far to stay empty. Cold. Frozen straight through.

He had never been anything but alone. Nikolai understood that now. The truth was, he preferred it that way. And once he dealt with Veronika, once he confirmed the truth about Stefan's paternity, he would never have to be anything else.

Alicia Teller ran out of patience with a sudden jolt, a wave of exhaustion and irritation nearly taking her from her feet in the midst of the jostling crowd. Or possibly that was the laddish group to her left, all of them obviously deep into the night's drinking and therefore flailing around the dance floor.

I'm much too old for this, she told herself as she moved out of their way for the tenth time, feeling ancient and decrepit at her extraordinarily advanced age of twenty-nine.

She couldn't remember the last time she'd spent a Saturday night anywhere more exciting than a quiet restaurant with friends, much less in a slick, pretentious club that had recently been dubbed *the* place to be seen in London. But then again, she also didn't like to look a gift horse in the mouth—said gift horse, in this case, being her ever-exuberant best friend and flatmate Rosie, who'd presented the guest passes to this velvet-roped circus with a grand flourish over dinner.

"It's the coolest place in London right now," she'd confidently assured Alicia over plates of *saag paneer* in their favorite Indian restaurant not far from Brick Lane. "Dripping with celebrities and therefore every attractive man in London."

"I am not cool, Rosie," Alicia had reminded her gently. "You've said so yourself for years. Every single time you try to drag me to yet another club you claim will change my life, if memory serves. It might be time for you to accept the possibility that this is who I am."

"Never!" Rosie had cried at once, feigning shock and outrage. "I remember when you were *fun,* Alicia. I've made a solemn vow to corrupt you, no matter how long it takes!"

"I'm incorruptible," Alicia had assured her. Because she also remembered when she'd been *fun,* and she had no desire to repeat those terrible mistakes, thank you, much less that descent into shame and heartache. "I'm also very likely to embarrass you. Can you handle the shame?"

Rosie had rolled her extravagantly mascaraed and shimmery-purple shadowed eyes while tossing the last of the poppadoms into her mouth.

"I can handle it," she'd said. "Anything to remind you that you're in your twenties, not your sixties. I consider it a public service."

"You say that," Alicia had teased her, "but you should be prepared for me to request 'Dancing Queen' as if we're at a wedding disco. From the no doubt world-renowned and tragically hip DJ who will faint dead away at the insult."

"Trust me, Alicia," Rosie had said then, very seriously. "This is going to be the best night of our lives."

Now Alicia watched her best friend shake her hips in a sultry come-on to the investment banker she'd been flirting with all night, and blamed the jet lag. Nothing else could have made her forget for even a moment that sparkly, dramatic still Rosie viewed it as her sacred obligation to pull on a weekend night, the way they both had when they were younger and infinitely wilder, and that meant the exorbitant taxi fare back home from the wilds of this part of East London to the flat they shared on the outskirts of Hammersmith would be Alicia's to cough up. Alone.

"You know what you need?" Rosie had asked on the

chilly trek over from the Tube, right on cue. "Desperately, I might add?"

"I know what *you* think I need, yes," Alicia had replied dryly. "But for some reason, the fantasy of sloppy and unsatisfying sex with some stranger from a club pales in comparison to the idea of getting a good night's sleep all alone in my own bed. Call me crazy. Or, barring that, *a grown-up.*"

"You're never going to find anyone, you know," Rosie had told her then, frowning. "Not if you keep this up. What's next, a nunnery?"

But Alicia knew exactly what kind of people it was possible to meet in the clubs Rosie preferred. She'd met too many of them. She'd *been* one of them throughout her university years. And she'd vowed that she would never, ever let herself get so out of control again. It wasn't worth the price—and sooner or later, there was always a price. In her case, all the years it had taken her to get her father to look at her again.

Alicia had been every inch a Daddy's girl until that terrible night the summer she'd been twenty-one. She'd been indulged and spoiled and adored beyond measure, the light of his life, and she'd lost that forever on a single night she still couldn't piece together in her head. But she knew the details almost as if she could remember it herself, because she'd had to sit and listen to her own father tell them to her the next morning while her head had pounded and her stomach had heaved: she'd been so drunk she'd been practically paralytic when she'd come home that night, but at some point she'd apparently wandered out into the back garden—which was where her father had found her, having sex with Mr. Reddick from next door.

Married Mr. Reddick, with three kids Alicia had babysat over the years, who'd been good mates with her dad until that night. The shame of it was still scarlet in her, bright and horrid, all these years later. How could she have done such a vile, despicable thing? She still didn't know.

Afterward, she'd decided that she'd had more than enough *fun* for one lifetime.

"Sorry," Alicia had said to Rosie then, smiling the painful memories away. "Are you talking about love? I was certain we were talking about the particular desperation of a Saturday night shag...."

"I have a radical idea, Saint Alicia," Rosie had said then with another roll of her eyes toward the dark sky above. "Why don't you put the halo aside for the night? It won't kill you, I promise. You might even find you like a little debauchery on a Saturday night the way you used to do."

Because Rosie didn't know, of course. Nobody knew. Alicia had been too embarrassed, too ashamed, too *disgusted* with herself to tell her friend—to tell anyone—why she'd abruptly stopped going out at the weekend, why she'd thrown herself into the job she hadn't taken seriously until then and turned it into a career she took a great deal of pride in now. Even her mother and sisters didn't know why there had been that sudden deep chill between Alicia and her dad, that had now, years later, only marginally improved into a polite distance.

"I'm not wearing my halo tonight, actually," Alicia had replied primly, patting at her riot of curls as if feeling for one anyway. "It clashed with these shoes you made me wear."

"Idiot," Rosie had said fondly, and then she'd brandished those guest passes and swept them past the crowd outside on the pavement, straight into the clutches of London's hottest club of the moment.

And Alicia had enjoyed herself—more than she'd expected she would, in fact. She'd missed dancing. She'd missed the excitement in the air, the buzz of such a big crowd. The particular, sensual seduction of a good beat. But Rosie's version of fun went on long into the night, the way it always had, and Alicia grew tired too easily. Especially when she'd only flown back into the country the day before, and her body still believed it was in another time zone altogether.

And more, when she wasn't sure she could trust herself. She didn't know what had made her do what she'd done that terrible night eight years ago; she couldn't remember much of it. So she'd opted to avoid anything and everything that might lead down that road—which was easier to do when she wasn't standing in the midst of so much cheerful abandon. Because she didn't have a halo—God knows, she'd proved that with her whorish behavior—she only wished she did.

You knew what this would be like, she thought briskly now, not bothering to fight the banker for Rosie's attention when a text from the backseat of a taxi headed home would do, and would furthermore not cause any interruption to Rosie's obvious plans for the evening. *You could have gone straight home after the curry and sorted out your laundry—*

And then she couldn't help but laugh at herself: Miss Misery Guts acting exactly like the bitter old maid Rosie often darkly intimated she was well on her way to becoming. Rosie was right, clearly. Had she really started thinking about her *laundry?* After midnight on a dance floor in a trendy London club while music even she could tell was fantastic swelled all around her?

Still laughing as she imagined the appalled look Rosie would give her when she told her about this, Alicia turned and began fighting her way out of the wild crowd and off the heaving dance floor. She laughed even harder as she was forced to leap out of the way of a particularly energetic couple flinging themselves here and there.

Alicia overbalanced because she was laughing too hard to pay attention to where she was going, and then, moving too fast to stop herself, she slipped in a puddle of spilled drink on the edge of the dance floor—

And crashed into the dark column of a man that she'd thought, before she hurtled into him, was nothing more than an extension of the speaker behind him. A still, watchful shadow.

He wasn't.

He was hard and male, impossibly muscled, sleek and hot. Alicia's first thought, with her face a scant breath from the most stunning male chest she'd ever beheld in real life and her palms actually *touching* it, was that he smelled like winter—fresh and clean and something deliciously smoky beneath.

She was aware of his hands on her upper arms, holding her fast, and only as she absorbed the fact that he *was* holding her did she also fully comprehend the fact that somehow, despite the press of the crowd and the flashing lights and how quickly she'd been on her way toward taking an undignified header into the floor, he'd managed to catch her at all.

She tilted her head back to thank him for his quick reflexes, still smiling—

And everything stopped.

It simply—*disappeared.*

Alicia felt her heart thud, hard enough to bruise. She felt her mouth drop open.

But she saw nothing at all but his eyes.

Blue like no blue she'd ever seen in another pair of eyes before. Blue like the sky on a crystal cold winter day, so bright it almost hurt to look at him. Blue so intense it seemed to fill her up, expanding inside of her, making her feel swollen with it. As if the slightest thing might make her burst wide-open, and some mad part of her wanted that, desperately.

A touch. A smile. Anything at all.

He was beautiful. Dark and forbidding and still, the most beautiful thing she'd ever seen. Something electric sizzled in the air between them as they gazed at each other, charging through her, making her skin prickle. Making her feel heavy and restless, all at once, as if she was a snow globe he'd picked up and shaken hard, and everything inside of her was still floating drowsily in the air, looking for a place to land.

It scared her, down deep inside in a place she hadn't known was there until this moment—and yet she didn't pull away.

He blinked, as if he felt it too, this terrible, impossible, beautiful thing that crackled between them. She was sure that if she could tear her eyes from his she'd be able to see it there in the air, connecting their bodies, arcing between them and around them and through them, the voltage turned high. The faintest hint of a frown etched between his dark brows, and he moved as if to set her away from him, but then he stopped and all he'd done was shift them both even farther back into the shadows.

And still they stood there, caught. Snared. As if the world around them, the raucous club, the pounding music, the wild and crazy dancing, had simply evaporated the moment they'd touched.

At last, Alicia thought, in a rush of chaotic sensation and dizzy emotion she didn't understand at all, all of it falling through her with a certain inevitability, like a heavy stone into a terrifyingly deep well.

"My God," she said, gazing up at him. "You look like a wolf."

Was that a smile? His mouth was lush and grim at once, impossibly fascinating to her, and it tugged in one hard corner. Nothing more, and yet she smiled back at him as if he'd beamed at her.

"Is that why you've dressed in red, like a Shoreditch fairy tale?" he asked, his words touched with the faint, velvet caress of an accent she didn't recognize immediately. "I should warn you, it will end with teeth."

"I think you mean tears." She searched his hard face, looking for more evidence of that smile. "It will end in *tears,* surely."

"That, too." Another small tug in the corner of that mouth. "But the teeth usually come first, and hurt more."

"I'll be very disappointed now if you don't have fangs," she told him, and his hands changed their steely grip on her arms, or perhaps she only then became aware of the heat of his palms and how the way he was holding her was so much like a caress.

Another tug on that austere mouth, and an answering one low in her belly, which should have terrified her, given what she knew about herself and sex. On some level, it did.

But she still didn't move away from him.

"It is, of course, my goal in life to keep strange British women who crash into me in crowded clubs from the jaws of disappointment," he said, a new light in his lovely eyes, and a different, more aware tilt to the way he held his head, the way he angled his big body toward her.

As if he might lean in close and swallow her whole.

Staring back at him then, his strong hands hard and hot on her arms and her palms still pressed flat against his taut chest, Alicia wanted nothing more than for him to do exactly that.

She should have turned away then and bolted for the door. Tried to locate whatever was left of her sanity, wherever she'd misplaced it. But she'd never felt this kind of raw, shimmering excitement before, this blistering heat weighing down her limbs so deliciously, this man so primal and powerful she found it hard to breathe.

"Even if the jaws in question are yours?" she asked, and she didn't recognize that teasing lilt in her voice, the way she tilted her head to look up at him, the liquid sort of feeling that moved in her then.

"Especially if they're mine," he replied, his bright winter gaze on her mouth, though there was a darkness there too, a shadow across his intriguing blade of a face that she nearly got lost in. *Jaws,* she reminded herself. *Fangs. He's telling me what a wolf he is, big and bad.* Surely she should feel more alarmed than she did—surely she shouldn't have the strangest urge to soothe him, instead? "You should know there are none sharper or more dangerous."

"In all of London?" She couldn't seem to keep herself from smiling again, or that sparkling cascade of something like light from rushing in her, making her stomach tighten and her breasts pull tight. *Alive. At last.* "Have you measured them, then? Is there some kind of competition you can enter to prove yours are the longest? The sharpest in all the land?"

Alicia felt completely outside herself. Some part of her wanted to lie down in it, in this mad feeling, in *him*—and exult in it. Bask in it as if it was sunshine. As if *he* was, despite the air of casual menace he wore so easily, like an extra layer of skin. Was that visible to everyone, or only to her? She didn't care. She wanted to roll around in this moment, in him, like it was the first snow of the season and she could make it all into angels.

Her breath caught at the image, and somehow, he heard

it. She felt his reaction in the sudden tension of his powerful frame above her and around her, in the flex of his fingers high on her arms, in the tightening of that connection
that wound between them, bright and electric, and made
her feel like a stranger in her own body.

His blue eyes lifted to meet hers and gleamed bright. "I
don't need to measure them, *solnyshka.*" He shifted closer,
and his attention returned to her mouth. "I know."

He was an arctic wolf turned man, every inch of him
a predator—lean and hard as he stood over her despite
the heels Rosie had coerced her into wearing. He wore all
black, a tight black T-shirt beneath a perfectly tailored black
jacket, dark trousers and boots, and his wide, hard shoulders made her skin feel tight. His dark hair was short and
inky black. It made his blue eyes seem like smoke over his
sculpted jaw and cheekbones, and yet all of it, all of *him,*
was hard and male and so dangerous she could feel it hum
beneath her skin, some part of her desperate to fight, to flee.
He looked intriguingly uncivilized. Something like feral.

And yet Alicia wasn't afraid, as that still-alarmed, still-
vigilant part of her knew she should have been. Not when
he was looking at her like that. Not when she followed a
half-formed instinct and moved closer to him, pressing her
hands flatter against the magnificently formed planes of
his chest while his arms went around her to hold her like
a lover might. She tilted her head back even farther and
watched his eyes turn to arctic fire.

She didn't understand it, but she burned.

This isn't right, a small voice cautioned her in the back
of her mind. *This isn't you.*

But he was so beautiful she couldn't seem to keep track
of who she was supposed to be, and her heart hurt her where
it thundered in her chest. She felt something bright and
demanding knot into an insistent ache deep in her belly,

and she found she couldn't think of a good reason to step away from him.

In a minute, she promised herself. *I'll walk away in a minute.*

"You should run," he told her then, his voice dark and low, and she could see he was serious. That he meant it. But one of his hands moved to trace a lazy pattern on her cheek as he said it, his palm a rough velvet against her skin, and she shivered. His blue gaze seemed to sharpen. "As far away from me as you can get."

He looked so grim then, so sure, and it hurt her, somehow. She wanted to see him smile with that hard, dangerous mouth. She wanted that with every single part of her and she didn't even know his name.

None of this made any sense.

Alicia had been so good for so long. She'd paid and paid and paid for that single night eight years ago. She'd been so vigilant, so careful, ever since. She was never spontaneous. She was never reckless. And yet this beautiful shadow of a man had the bluest eyes she'd ever seen, and the saddest mouth, and the way he touched her made her shake and burn and glow.

And she thought that maybe this once, for a moment or two, she could let down her guard. Just the smallest, tiniest bit. It didn't have to mean anything she didn't want it to mean. It didn't have to mean anything at all.

So she ignored that voice inside of her, and she ignored his warning, too.

Alicia leaned her face into his hard palm as if it was the easiest thing in the world, and smiled when he pulled in a breath like it was a fire in him, too. Like he felt the same burn.

She stretched up against his hard, tough body and told herself this was about that grim mouth of his, not the wild,

impossible things she knew she shouldn't let herself feel
or want or, God help her, *do*. And they were in the shadows of a crowded club where nobody could see her and no
one would ever know what she did in the dark. It wasn't
as if it counted.

She could go back to her regularly scheduled quiet life
in a moment.

It would only be a moment. One small moment outside
all the rules she'd made for herself, the rules she'd lived
by so carefully for so long, and then she would go straight
back home to her neat, orderly, virtuous life.

She would. She had to. *She would.*

But first Alicia obeyed that surge of wild demand inside
of her, leaned closer and fitted her mouth to his.

CHAPTER TWO

HE TASTED LIKE the night. Better even than she'd imagined.

He paused for the barest instant when Alicia's lips touched his. Half a heartbeat. Less.

A scant second while the taste of him seared through her, deep and dark and wild. She thought that was enough, that small taste of his fascinating mouth. That would do, and now she could go back to her quiet—

But then he angled his head to one side, used the hand at her cheek to guide her mouth where he wanted it and took over.

Devouring her like the wolf she understood he was. *He really was,* and the realization swirled inside of her like heat. His mouth was impossibly carnal, opening over hers to taste her, to claim her.

Dark and deep, hot and sure.

Alicia simply…exploded. It was like a long flash of light, shuddering and bright, searing everything away in the white hot burn of it. It was perfect. It was beautiful.

It was too much.

She shivered against him, overloaded with his bold taste, the scrape of his jaw, his talented fingers moving her mouth where he wanted it in a silent, searing command she was happy to obey. Then his hands were in her hair, buried in her thick curls. Her arms went around his neck of their own volition, and then she was plastered against the tall, hard length of him. It was like pressing into the surface of the sun and still, she couldn't seem to get close enough.

As if there was no *close enough*.

And he kissed her, again and again, with a ruthless intensity that made her feel weak and beautiful all at once, until she was mindless with need. Until she forgot her own name. Until she forgot she didn't know his. Until she forgot how dangerous *forgetting* was for her.

Until she forgot everything but him.

When he pulled back, she didn't understand. He put an inch, maybe two, between them, and then he muttered something harsh and incomprehensible while he stared at her as if he thought she was some kind of ghost.

It took her a long, confused moment to realize that she couldn't understand him because he wasn't speaking in English, not because she'd forgotten her own language, too.

Alicia blinked, the world rushing back as she did. She was still standing in that club. Music still pounded all around them, lights still flashed, well-dressed patrons still shouted over the din, and somewhere out in the middle of the dance floor, Rosie was no doubt still playing her favorite game with her latest conquest.

Everything was as it had been before she'd stumbled into this man, before he'd caught her. Before she'd kissed him.

Before he'd kissed her back.

Everything was exactly the same. Except Alicia.

He was searching her face as if he was looking for something. He shook his head slightly, then reached down and ran a lazy finger over the ridge of her collarbone, as if testing its shape. Even that made her shudder, that simple slide of skin against skin. Even so innocuous a touch seemed directly connected to that pulsing heat between her legs, the heavy ache in her breasts, the hectic spin inside of her.

She didn't have to speak his language to know whatever he muttered then was a curse.

If she were smart, the way she'd tried to be for years now, she would pull her hand away and run. Just as he'd told her she should. Just as she'd promised herself she would. Everything about this was too extreme, too intense, as if he wasn't only a strange man in a club but the kind of drug that usually went with this kind of rolling, wildly out-of-control feeling. As if she was much too close to being high on *him*.

"Last chance," he said then, as if he could read her mind.

He was giving her a warning. Again.

In her head, she listened. She smiled politely and extricated herself. She marched herself to the nearest exit, hailed a taxi, then headed straight home to the comfort of her bloody laundry. Because she knew she couldn't be trusted outside the confines of the rules she'd made for herself. She'd been living the consequences of having no rules for a long, long time.

But here, now, in this loud place surrounded by so many people and all of that pounding music, she didn't feel like the person she'd been when she'd arrived. Everything she knew about herself had twisted inside out. Turned into something else entirely in that electric blue of his challenging gaze.

As if this really was a Shoreditch fairy tale, after all.

"What big eyes you have," she teased him.

His hard mouth curved then, and she felt it like a burst of heat, like sunlight. She couldn't do anything but smile back at him.

"So be it," he said, as if he despaired of them both.

Alicia laughed, then laughed again at the startled look in his eyes.

"The dourness is a lovely touch," she told him. "You must be beating them off with a stick. A very grim stick."

"No stick," he said, in an odd tone. "A look at me is usually sufficient."

"A wolf," she said, and grinned. "Just as I suspected."

He blinked, and again looked at her in that strange way of his, as if she was an apparition he couldn't quite believe was standing there before him.

Then he moved with the same decisiveness he'd used when he'd taken control of that kiss, tucking her into his side as he navigated his way through the dense crowd. She tried not to think about how well she fitted there, under his heavy arm, tight against the powerful length of his torso as he cut through the crowd. She tried not to drift away in the scent of him, the heat and the power, all of it surrounding her and pouring into that ache already inside of her, making it bloom and stretch and grow.

Until it took over everything.

Maybe she was under some kind of spell, Alicia thought with the small part of her that wasn't consumed with the feel of his tall, lean frame as he guided her so protectively through the crowd. It should have been impossible to move through the club so quickly, so confidently. Not in a place like this at the height of a Saturday night. But he did it.

And then they were outside, in the cold and the damp November night, and he was still moving in that same breathtaking way, like quicksilver. Like he knew exactly where they were headed—away from the club and the people still milling about in front of it. He led her down the dark street, deeper into the shadows, and it was then Alicia's sense of self-preservation finally kicked itself into gear.

Better late than never, she thought, annoyed with herself, but it actually *hurt* her to pull away from the magnificent shelter of his body, from all of that intense heat and strength. It felt like she'd ripped her skin off when she stepped away from him, as if they'd been fused together.

He regarded her calmly, making her want to trust him when she knew she shouldn't. She couldn't.

"I'm sorry, but…" She wrapped her arms around her own waist in an attempt to make up for the heat she'd lost when she'd stepped away from him. "I don't know a single thing about you."

"You know several things, I think."

He sounded even more delicious now that they were alone and she could hear him properly. *Russian,* she thought, as pleased as if she'd learned his deepest, darkest secrets.

"Yes," she agreed, thinking of the things she knew. Most of them to do with that insistent ache in her belly, and lower. His mouth. His clever hands. "All lovely things. But none of them worth risking my personal safety for, I'm sure you'll agree."

Something like a smile moved in his eyes, but didn't make it to his hard mouth. Still, it echoed in her, sweet and light, making her feel far more buoyant than she should have on a dark East London street with a strange man even she could see was dangerous, no matter how much she wanted him.

Had she ever wanted anything this much? Had anyone?

"A wolf is never without risk," he told her, that voice of his like whiskey, smooth and scratchy at once, heating her up from the inside out. "That's the point of wolves. Or you'd simply get a dog, pat it on the head." His eyes gleamed. "Teach it tricks."

Alicia wasn't sure she wanted to know the tricks this man had up his sleeve. Or, more to the point, she wasn't sure she'd survive them. She wasn't certain she'd survive this as it was.

"You could be very bad in bed," she said, conversationally, as if she picked up strange men all the time. She hardly recognized her own light, easy, flirtatious tone. She hadn't heard it since before that night in her parents' back garden. "That's a terrible risk to take with any stranger, and awkward besides."

That smile in his eyes intensified, got even bluer. "I'm not."

She believed him.

"You could be the sort who gets very, very drunk and weeps loudly about his broken heart until dawn." She gave a mock shudder. "So tedious, especially if poetry is involved. Or worse, *singing*."

"I don't drink," he countered at once. His dark brows arched over those eyes of his, challenging her. Daring her. "I never sing, I don't write poems and I certainly do not weep." He paused. "More to the point, I don't have a heart."

"Handy, that," she replied easily. She eyed him. "You could be a killer, of course. That would be unfortunate."

She smiled at that. He didn't.

"And if I am?"

"There you go," she said, and nodded sagely. Light, airy. Enchanted, despite herself. "I can't possibly go off into the night with you now, can I?"

But it was terrifying how much she *wanted* to go off with him, wherever he'd take her, and instead of reacting to that as she should, she couldn't stop smiling at him. As if she already knew him, this strange man dressed all in black, his blue eyes the only spot of color on the cold pavement as he stared at her as if she'd stunned him somehow.

"My name is Nikolai," he said, and she had the oddest impression he hadn't meant to speak at all. He shifted, then reached over and traced her lips with his thumb, his expression so fierce, so intent, it made her feel hollowed out inside, everything scraped away except that wild, wondrous heat he stirred in her. "Text someone my name and address. Have them ring every fifteen minutes if you like. Send the police. Whatever you want."

"All those safeguards are very thoughtful," she pointed out, but her eyes felt too wide and her voice sounded insubstantial. Wispy. "Though not exactly wolfish, it has to be said."

His mouth moved into his understated version of a smile

"I want you." His eyes were on fire. Every inch of him that wolf. "What will it take?"

She swayed back into him as if they were magnets and she'd simply succumbed to the pull. And then she had no choice but to put her hand to his abdomen, to feel all that blasting heat right there beneath her palm.

Even that didn't scare her the way it should.

"What big teeth you have," she whispered, too on edge to laugh, too filled with that pulsing ache inside of her to smile.

"The biting part comes later." His eyes gleamed again, with the kind of sheer male confidence that made it difficult to breathe. Alicia stopped trying. "If you ask nicely."

He picked up her hand and lifted it to his mouth, tracing a dark heat over the back of it. He didn't look away.

"If you're sure," she said piously, trying desperately to pretend she wasn't shaking, and that he couldn't feel it. That he didn't know exactly what he was doing to her when she could see full well that he did. "I was promised a wolf, not a dog."

"I eat dogs for breakfast."

She laughed then. "That's not particularly comforting."

"I can't be what I'm not, *solnyshka*." He turned her hand over, then kissed her palm in a way that made her hiss in a sharp breath. His eyes were smiling again, so bright and blue. "But I'm very good at what I am."

And she'd been lost since she'd set eyes on him, hadn't

she? What use was there in pretending otherwise? She wasn't drunk. It wasn't like that terrible night, because she knew what she was doing. Didn't she?

"Note to self," Alicia managed to say, breathless and dizzy and unable to remember why she'd tried to stop this in the first place, when surrendering to it—to him—felt so much like triumph. Like fate. "Never eat breakfast with a wolf. The sausages are likely the family dog."

He shrugged. "Not *your* family dog," he said with that fierce mouth of his, though she was sure his blue eyes laughed. "If that helps."

And this time, when she smiled at him, the negotiation was over.

The address he gave her in his clipped, direct way was in an extraordinarily posh part of town Alicia could hardly afford to visit, much less live in. She dutifully texted it to Rosie, hoping that her friend was far too busy to check it until morning. And then she tucked her phone away and forgot about Rosie altogether.

Because he still moved like magic, tucking her against him again as if there was a crowd he needed to part when there was only the late-night street and what surged between them like heat lightning. As if he liked the way she fitted there as much as she did. And her heart began to pound all over again, excitement and anticipation and a certain astonishment at her own behavior pouring through her with every hard thump.

At the corner, he lifted his free hand almost languidly toward the empty street, and for a second Alicia truly believed that he was so powerful that taxis simply materialized before him at his whim—until a nearby engine turned over and a powerful black SUV slid out of the shadows and pulled to a stop right there before them.

More magic, when she was enchanted already.

Nikolai, she whispered to herself as she climbed inside the SUV, as if the name was a song. Or a spell. *His name is Nikolai.*

He swung in behind her on the soft leather backseat, exchanged a few words in curt Russian with the driver and then pressed a button that raised a privacy shield, secluding them. Then he settled back against the seat, near her but not touching her, stretching out his long, lean body and making the spacious vehicle seem tight. Close.

And then he simply looked at her.

As if he was trying to puzzle her out. Or giving her one last chance to bolt.

But Alicia knew she wasn't going to do that.

"More talk of dogs?" he asked mildly, yet all she heard was the hunger beneath. She could see it in his eyes, his face. She could feel the echo of it in her, new and huge and almost more than she could bear. "More clever little character assessments couched as potential objections?"

"I got in your car," she pointed out, hardly recognizing her own voice. The thick heat in it. "I think I'm done."

He smiled. She was sure of it, though his mouth didn't move. But she could see the stamp of satisfaction on his hard face, the flare of a deep male approval.

"Not yet, *solnyshka,*" he murmured, his voice a low rasp. "Not quite yet."

And she melted. It was a shivery thing, hot and desperate, like she couldn't quite catch her breath against the heat of it.

"Come here," he said.

They were cocooned in the darkness, light spilling here and there as the car sped through the city, and still his blue gaze was brilliant. Compelling. And so knowing—so certain of himself, of her, of what was about to happen—it made her blood run hot in her veins.

Alicia didn't move fast enough and he made a low noise. *A growl*—like the wolf he so resembled. The rough sound made her shake apart and then melt down into nothing but need, alive with that crazy heat she couldn't seem to control any longer.

He simply picked her up and pulled her into his lap, his mouth finding hers and claiming her all over again with an impatience that delighted her. She met him with the same urgency. His hands marveled down the length of her back, explored the shape of her hips, and Alicia's mind blanked out into a red-hot burst of that consuming, impossible fire. Into pure and simple *need*.

It had been so long. *So long,* and yet her body knew exactly what to do, thrilling to the taste of him, the feel of his hard, capable hands first over and then underneath her bright red shirt. His hands on her stomach, her waist, her breasts. So perfect she wanted to die. And not nearly enough.

He leaned back to peel off his jacket and the tight black T-shirt beneath, and her eyes glazed over at the sight of all of that raw male beauty. She pressed herself against the hard planes of his perfect chest, tracing the large, colorful tattoos that stretched over his skin with trembling fingers, with her lips and her tongue, tasting art etched across art.

Intense. Hot. Intoxicating.

And that scent of his—of the darkest winter, smoke and ice—surrounded her. Licked into her. Claimed her as surely as he did.

One moment she was fully clothed, the next her shirt and the bra beneath it were swept away, while his hard mouth took hers again and again until she thought she might die if he stopped. Then he did stop, and she moaned out her distress, her desperation. That needy ache so deep in the core of her. But he only laughed softly, before he fastened his hot mouth to the tight peak of one breast and sucked on it, not quite gently, until she thought she really *had* died.

The noises she heard herself making were impossible. Nothing could really feel this good. This perfect. This wild or this *right*.

Nikolai shifted, lifting her, and Alicia helped him peel her trousers down from her hips, kicking one leg free and not caring what happened to the other. She felt outside herself and yet more fully *in* herself than she had been in as long as she could remember. She explored the expanse of his gorgeous shoulders, the distractingly tender spot behind his ear, the play of his stunning muscles, perfectly honed beneath her.

He twisted them both around, coming down over her on the seat and pulling her legs around his hips with an urgency that made her breath desert her. She hadn't even been aware that he'd undressed. It was more magic—and then he was finally naked against her, the steel length of him a hot brand against her belly.

Alicia shuddered and melted, then melted again, and he moved even closer, one of his hands moving to her bottom and lifting her against him with that devastating skill, that easy mastery, that made her belly tighten.

He was muttering in Russian, that same word he'd used before like a curse or a prayer or even both at once, and the sound of it made her moan again. It was harsh like him, and tender, too. It made her feel as if she might come out of her own skin. He teased her breasts, licking his way from one proud nipple to the other as if he might lose himself there, then moved to her neck, making her shiver against him before he took her mouth again in a hard, deep kiss.

As raw as she was. As undone.

He pulled back slightly to press something into her hand, and she blinked at it, taking much longer than she should have to recognize it was the condom she hadn't thought about for even an instant.

A trickle of unease snaked down the back of her neck, but she pushed it away, too far gone for shame. Not when his blue eyes glittered with sensual intent and his long fingers moved between them, feeling her damp heat and then stroking deep into her molten center, making her clench him hard.

"Hurry," he told her.

"I'm hurrying. You're distracting me."

He played his fingers in and out of her, slick and hot, then pressed the heel of his hand into her neediest part, laughing softly when she bucked against him.

"Concentrate, *solnyshka.*"

She ripped open the foil packet, then took her time rolling it down his velvety length, until he cursed beneath his breath.

Alicia liked the evidence of his own pressing need. She liked that she could make his breath catch, too. And then he stopped, braced over her, his face close to hers and the hardest part of him poised at her entrance but not *quite—*

He groaned. He sounded as tortured as she felt. She liked that, too.

"Your name."

She blinked at the short command, so gruff and harsh. His arms were hard around her, his big body pressed her back into the soft leather seat, and she felt delicate and powerful all at once.

"Tell me your name," he said, nipping at her jaw, making her head fall back to give him any access he desired, anything he wanted.

Alive, she thought again. *At last.*

"Alicia," she whispered.

He muttered it like a fierce prayer, and then he thrust

into her—hot and hard and so perfect, so beautiful, that tears spilled from her eyes even as she shattered around him.

"Again," he said.

It was another command, arrogant and darkly certain. Nikolai was hard and dangerous and between her legs, his eyes bright and hot and much too intense on hers. She turned her head away but he caught her mouth with his, taking her over, conquering her.

"I don't think I can—" she tried to say against his mouth, even while the flames still licked through her, even as she still shuddered helplessly around him, aware of the steel length of him inside her, filling her.

Waiting.

That hard smile like a burst of heat inside her. "You will."

And then he started to move.

It was perfect. More than perfect. It was sleek and hot, impossibly good. He simply claimed her, took her, and Alicia met him. She arched into him, lost in the slide and the heat, the glory of it. Of him.

Slick. Wild.

Perfect.

He moved in her, over her, his mouth at her neck and his hands roaming from her bottom to the center of her shuddering need as he set the wild, intense pace. She felt it rage inside her again, this mad fire she'd never felt before and worried would destroy her even as she hungered for more. And more. *And more.*

She met every deep thrust. She gloried in it.

"Say my name," he said, gruff against her ear, his voice washing through her and sending her higher, making her glow. "Now, Alicia. Say it."

When she obeyed he shuddered, then let out another low,

sexy growl that moved over her like a newer, better fire. He reached between them and pressed down hard against the heart of her hunger, hurtling her right over the edge again.

And smiled, she was sure of it, with his warrior's mouth as well as those winter-bright eyes, right before he followed her into bliss.

Nikolai came back to himself with a vicious, jarring thud.

He couldn't move. He wasn't sure he breathed. Alicia quivered sweetly beneath him, his mouth was pressed against the tender junction of her neck and shoulder, and he was still deep inside her lovely body.

What the hell was that?

He shifted her carefully into the seat beside him, ignoring the way her long, inky-black lashes looked against the creamy brown of her skin, the way her perfect, lush mouth was so soft now. He ignored the tiny noise she made in the back of her throat, as if distressed to lose contact with him, which made him grit his teeth. But she didn't open her eyes.

He dealt with the condom swiftly, then he found his trousers in the tangle of clothes on the floor of the car and jerked them on. He had no idea what had happened to his T-shirt, and decided it didn't matter. And then he simply sat there as if he was winded.

He, Nikolai Korovin, *winded*. By a woman.

By *this* woman.

What moved in him then was like a rush of too many colors, brilliant and wild, when he knew the only safety lay in gray. It surged in his veins, it pounded in his temples, it scraped along his sex. He told himself it was temper, but he knew better. It was everything he'd locked away for all these years, and he didn't want it. He wouldn't allow it. It made him feel like an animal again, wrong and violent and insane and drunk....

That was it.

It rang like a bell in him, low and urgent, swelling into everything. Echoing everywhere. No wonder he felt so off-kilter, so dangerously unbalanced. This woman made him feel *drunk*.

Nikolai forced a breath, then another.

Everything that had happened since she'd tripped in front of him flashed through his head, in the same random snatches of color and sound and scent he remembered from a thousand morning-afters. Her laughter, that sounded the way he thought joy must, though he'd no basis for comparison. The way she'd tripped and then fallen, straight into him, and hadn't had the sense to roll herself as he would have done, to break her fall. Her brilliant smile that cracked over her face so easily. Too easily.

No one had ever smiled at him like that. As if he was a real man. Even a good one.

But he knew what he was. He'd always known. His uncle's fists, worse after Ivan had left to fight their way to freedom one championship at a time. The things he'd done in the army. Veronika's calculated deception, even Ivan's more recent betrayal—these had only confirmed what Nikolai had always understood to be true about himself down deep into his core.

To think differently now, when he'd lost everything he had to lose and wanted nothing more than to shut himself off for good, was the worst kind of lie. Damaging. Dangerous. And he knew what happened when he allowed himself to become intoxicated. How many times would he have to prove that to himself? How many people would he hurt?

He was better off blank. Ice cold and gray, all the way through.

The day after Veronika left him, Nikolai had woken bruised and battered from another fight—or *fights*—he couldn't recall. He'd been shaky. Sick from the alcohol and sicker still with himself. Disgusted with the holes in his memory and worse, with all the things he *did* remember. The things that slid without context through his head, oily and barbed.

His fists against flesh. His bellow of rage. The crunch of wood beneath his foot, the shattering of pottery against the stone floor. Faces of strangers on the street, wary. Worried. Then angry. Alarmed.

Blood on a fist—and only some of it his. *Fear in those eyes*—never his. Nikolai was what grown men feared, what they crossed streets to avoid, but he hadn't felt fear himself in years. Not since he'd been a child.

Fear meant there was something left to lose.

That was the last time Nikolai had drunk a drop of alcohol and it was the last time he'd let himself lose control.

Until now.

He didn't understand this. He was not an impulsive man. He didn't pick up women, he *picked* them, carefully—and only when he was certain that whatever else they were, they were obedient and disposable.

When they posed no threat to him at all. Nikolai breathed in, out.

He'd survived wars. This was only a woman.

Nikolai looked at her then, memorizing her, like she was a code he needed to crack, instead of the bomb itself, poised to detonate.

She wore her dark black hair in a cloud of tight curls around her head, a tempting halo around her lovely, clever face, and he didn't want any part of this near-overpowering desire that surged in him, to bury his hands in the heavy thickness of it, to start the wild rush all over again. Her body was lithe and ripe with warm, mouthwatering curves that he'd already touched and tasted, so why did he feel as if it had all been rushed, as if it wasn't nearly enough?

He shouldn't have this longing to take his time, to really explore her. He shouldn't hunger for that lush, full mouth of hers again, or want to taste his way along that elegant neck for the simple pleasure of making her shiver. He shouldn't find it so impossible to look at her without imagining himself tracing lazy patterns across every square inch of the sweet brown perfection of her skin. With his mouth and then his hands, again and again until he *knew* her.

He'd asked her name, as if he'd needed it. He'd wanted her that much, and Nikolai knew better than to want. It could only bring him pain.

Vodka had been his one true love, and it had ruined him. It had let loose that monster in him, let it run amok. It had taken everything that his childhood and the army hadn't already divided between them and picked down to the bone. He'd known it in his sober moments, but he hadn't cared. Because vodka had warmed him, lent color and volume to the dark, silent prison of his life, made him imagine he could be something other than a six-foot-two column of glacial ice.

But he knew better than that now. He knew better than this.

Alicia's eyes fluttered open then, dark brown shot through with amber, almost too pretty to bear. He hated that he noticed, that he couldn't look away. She glanced around as if she'd forgotten where they were. Then she looked at him.

She didn't smile that outrageously beautiful smile of hers, and it made something hitch inside him, like a stitch in his side. As if he'd lost that, too.

She lifted one foot, shaking her head at the trousers that were still attached to her ankle, and the shoe she'd never removed. She reached down, picked up the tangle of her bright red shirt and lacy pink bra from the pile on the floor of the car, and sighed.

And Nikolai relaxed, because he was back on familiar ground.

Now came the demands, the negotiations, he thought cynically. The endless manipulations, which were the reason he'd started making any woman who wanted him agree to his rules before he touched her. Sign the appropriate documents, understand exactly how this would go before it started. Nikolai knew this particular dance well. It was why he normally didn't pick up women, let them into the sleek, muscular SUV that told them too much about his net worth, much less give them his address....

But instead of pouting prettily and pointedly, almost always the first transparent step in these situations, Alicia looked at him, let her head fall back and laughed.

CHAPTER THREE

THAT DAMNED LAUGH.

Nikolai would rather be shot again, he decided in that electric moment as her laughter filled the car. He would rather take another knife or two to the gut. He didn't know what on earth he was supposed to do with laughter like that, when it sparkled in the air all around him and fell indiscriminately here and there, like a thousand unwelcome caresses all over his skin and something worse—much worse—deep beneath it.

He scowled.

"Never let it be said this wasn't classy," Alicia said, her lovely voice wry. "I suppose we'll always have that going for us."

There was no we. There was no *us*. Neither of those words were *disposable*. Alarms shrieked like air raid sirens inside of him, mixing with the aftereffects of that laugh.

"I thought you understood," he said abruptly, at his coldest and most cutting. "I don't—"

"Relax, Tin Man." Laughter still lurked in her voice. She tugged her trousers back up over her hips, then pulled her bra free of her shirt, shooting him a breezy smile that felt not unlike a blade to the stomach as she clipped it back into place. "I heard you the first time. No heart."

And then she ignored him, as if he wasn't vibrating

beside her with all of that darkness and icy intent. As if he wasn't Nikolai Korovin, feared and respected in equal measure all across the planet, in a thousand corporate boardrooms as well as the grim theaters of too many violent conflicts. As if he was the kind of man someone could simply *pick up* in a London club and then dismiss…

Except, of course, he was. Because she had. She'd done exactly that.

He'd let her.

Alicia fussed with her shirt before pulling it over her head, her black curls springing out of the opening in a joyful froth that made him actually ache to touch them. *Her.* He glared down at his hands as if they'd betrayed him.

When she looked at him again, her dark eyes were soft, undoing him as surely as if she really had eviscerated him with a hunting knife. He would have preferred the latter. She made it incalculably worse by reaching over and smoothing her warm hand over his cheek, offering him… comfort?

"You look like you've swallowed broken glass," she said. *Kindly.*

Very much as if she cared.

Nikolai didn't want what he couldn't have. It had been beaten out of him long ago. It was a simple, unassailable fact, like gravity. Like air.

Like light.

But he couldn't seem to stop himself from lifting his hand, tracing that tempting mouth of hers once more, watching the heat bloom again in her eyes.

Just one night, he told himself then. He couldn't help it. That smile of hers made him realize he was so tired of the cold, the dark. That he felt haunted by the things he'd lost, the wars he'd won, the battles he'd been fighting all his life. Just once, he *wanted.*

One night to explore this light of hers she shone so indiscriminately, he thought. Just one night to pretend he was something more than ice. A wise man didn't step onto a land mine when he could see it lying there in front of him, waiting to blow. But Nikolai had been through more hells than he could count. He could handle anything for a night. Even this. Even her.

Just one night.

"You should hold on," he heard himself say. He slid his hand around to cup the nape of her neck, and exulted in the shiver that moved over her at even so small a touch. As if she was his. That could never happen, he knew. But he'd allowed himself the night. He had every intention of making it a long one. "I'm only getting started."

If only he really had been a wolf.

Alicia scowled down at the desk in her office on Monday and tried valiantly to think of something—*anything*—other than Nikolai. And failed, as she'd been doing with alarming regularity since she'd sneaked away from his palatial penthouse in South Kensington early on Sunday morning.

If he'd really been a wolf, she'd likely be in hospital right now, recovering from being bitten in a lovely quiet coma or restful medicated haze, which would mean she'd be enjoying a much-needed holiday from the self-recriminating clamor inside her head.

At least I wasn't drunk....

Though if she was honest, some part of her almost wished she had been. *Almost.* As if that would be some kind of excuse when she knew from bitter experience that it wasn't.

The real problem was, she'd been perfectly aware of what she was doing on Saturday. She'd gone ahead and done it precisely *because* she hadn't been drunk. For no other reason than that she'd wanted him.

From her parents' back garden to a stranger in a car. She hadn't learned much of anything in all these years, had she? Given the chance, she'd gleefully act the promiscuous whore—drunk *or* sober.

That turned inside of her like bile, acidic and thick at the back of her throat.

"I think you must be a witch," he'd said at some point in those long, sleepless hours of too much pleasure, too hot and too addicting. He'd been sprawled out next to her, his rough voice no more than a growl in the dark of his cavernous bedroom.

A girl could get lost in a room like that, she'd thought. In a bed so wide. In a man like Nikolai, who had taken her over and over with a skill and a thoroughness and a sheer masculine prowess that made her wonder how she'd ever recover from it. *If* she would. But she hadn't wanted to think those things, not then. Not while it was still dark outside and they were cocooned on those soft sheets together, the world held at bay. There'd be time enough to work on forgetting, she'd thought. When it was over.

When it was morning.

She'd propped herself up on an elbow and looked down at him, his bold, hard face in shadows but those eyes of his as intense as ever.

"I'm not the driving force in this fairy tale," she'd said quietly. Then she'd dropped her gaze lower, past that hard mouth of his she now knew was a terrible, electric torment when he chose, and down to that astonishing torso of his laid out before her like a feast. "Red Riding Hood is a hapless little fool, isn't she? Always in the wrong place at the wrong time."

Alicia had meant that to come out light and breezy, but

it hadn't. It had felt intimate instead, somehow. Darker and deeper, and a different kind of ache inside. Not at all what she'd intended.

She'd felt the blue of his gaze like a touch.

Instead of losing herself there, she'd traced a lazy finger over the steel plates of his harshly honed chest. Devastatingly perfect. She moved from this scar to that tattoo, tracing each pucker of flesh, each white strip of long-ago agony, then smoothing her fingertip over the bright colors and Cyrillic letters that flowed everywhere else. Two kinds of marks, stamped permanently into his flesh. She'd been uncertain if she was fascinated or something else, something that made her mourn for all his body had suffered.

But it wasn't her place to ask.

"Bullet," he'd said quietly, when her fingers moved over a slightly raised and shiny patch of skin below his shoulder, as if she had asked after all. "I was in the army."

"For how long?"

"Too long."

She'd flicked a look at him, but had kept going, finding a long, narrow white scar that slashed across his taut abdomen and following the length of it, back and forth. So much violence boiled down to a thin white line etched into his hard, smooth flesh. It had made her hurt for him, but she still hadn't asked.

"Kitchen knife. My uncle." His voice had been little more than a rasp against the dark. She'd gone still, her fingers splayed across the scar in question. "He took his role as our guardian seriously," Nikolai had said, and his gruff voice had sounded almost amused, as if what he'd said was something other than awful. Alicia had chanced a glance at him, and saw a different truth in that wintry gaze, more vulnerable in the clasp of the dark than she'd imagined he knew. "He didn't like how I'd washed the dishes."

"Nikolai—" she'd begun, not knowing what she could possibly say, but spurred on by that torn look in his eyes.

He'd blinked, then frowned. "It was nothing."

But she'd known he was lying. And the fact that she'd had no choice but to let it pass, that this man wasn't hers to care for no matter how it felt as if he should have been, had rippled through her like actual, physical pain.

Alicia had moved on then to the tattoo of a wild beast rendered in a shocking sweep of bold color and dark black lines that wrapped around the left side of his body, from his shoulder all the way down to an inch or so above his sex. It was fierce and furious, all ferocious teeth and wicked claws, poised there as if ready to devour him.

As if, she'd thought, it already had.

"All of my sins," he'd said then, his voice far darker and rougher than before.

There'd been an almost-guarded look in his winter gaze when she'd glanced up at him, but she'd thought that was that same vulnerability again. And then he'd sucked in a harsh breath when she'd leaned over and pressed a kiss to the fearsome head of this creature that claimed him, as if she could wash away the things that had hurt him—uncles who wielded kitchen knives, whatever battles he'd fought in the army that had got him shot, all those shadows that lay heavy on his hard face. One kiss, then another, and she'd felt the coiling tension in him, the heat.

"Your sins are pretty," she'd whispered.

He'd muttered something ferocious in Russian as he'd hauled her mouth to his, then he'd pulled her astride him and surged into her with a dark fury and a deep hunger that had thrilled her all the way through, and she'd been lost in him all over again.

She was still lost.

"For God's sake, Alicia," she bit out, tired of the endless

cycle of her own thoughts, and her own appalling weakness. Her voice sounded loud in her small office. "You have work to do."

She had to snap out of this. Her desk was piled high after her two weeks abroad, her in-box was overflowing and she had a towering stack of messages indicating calls she needed to return now that she was back in the country. To say nothing of the report on the Latin American offices she'd visited while away that she had yet to put together, that Charlotte, her supervisor, expected her to present to the team later this week.

But she couldn't sink into her work the way she wanted, the way she usually could. There was that deep current of shame that flared inside of her, bright like some kind of cramp, reminding her of the last night she'd abandoned herself so completely....

At least this time, she remembered every last second of what she'd done. What *they'd* done. Surely that counted for something.

Her body still prickled now, here, as if electrified, every time she thought of him—and she couldn't seem to stop. Her nipples went hard and between her legs, she ran so hot it almost hurt, and it was such a deep betrayal of who she'd thought she'd become that it made her feel shaky.

Her thighs were still tender from the scrape of his hard jaw. There was a mark on the underside of one breast that he'd left deliberately, reminding her in that harsh, beautiful voice that *wolves bite, solnyshka*, making her laugh and squirm in reckless delight beneath him on that wide, masculine bed where she'd obviously *lost her mind*. Even her hips held memories of what she'd done, reminding her of her overwhelming response to him every now and again with a low, almost-pleasant ache that made her hate herself more every time she felt it.

She'd been hung over before. Ashamed of herself come the dawn. Sometimes that feeling had lingered for days as she'd promised herself that she'd stop partying so hard, knowing deep down that she wouldn't, and hadn't, until that last night in the back garden. But this wasn't *that*. This was worse.

She felt out of control. Knocked flat. Changed, utterly. A stranger to herself.

Alicia had been so sure the new identity she'd built over these past eight years was a fortress, completely impenetrable, impervious to attack. Hadn't she held Rosie at bay for ages? But one night with Nikolai had showed her that she was nothing but a glass house, precarious and fragile, and a single stone could bring it all crashing down. A single touch.

Not to mention, she hadn't even *thought* about protection that first time. He'd had to *put it in her hand*. Of all her many betrayals of herself that night, she thought that one was by far the most appalling. It made the shame that lived in her that much worse.

The only bright spot in all of this recrimination and regret was that her text to Rosie hadn't gone through. There'd been a big X next to it when she'd looked at her mobile that next morning. And when she'd arrived back at their flat on Sunday morning, Rosie had still been out.

Which meant that no one had any idea what Alicia had done.

"I wish I'd gone home when you did," Rosie had said with a sigh while they sat in their usual Sunday-afternoon café, paging lazily through the Sunday paper and poking at their plates of a traditional full English breakfast. "That place turned *absolutely mental* after hours, and I have to stop getting off with bankers who talk about the flipping property ladder like it's the most thrilling thing on the planet." Then she'd grinned that big grin of hers that meant she didn't regret a single thing, no matter what she said. "Maybe someday I'll actually follow your example."

"What fun would that be?" Alicia had asked lightly, any guilt she'd felt at lying by giant, glaring omission to her best friend drowned out by the sheer relief pouring through her.

Because if Rosie didn't know what she'd done, Alicia could pretend it had never happened.

There would be no discussing Nikolai, that SUV of his or what had happened in it, or that astonishing penthouse that she'd been entirely too gauche not to gape at, openly, when he'd brought her home. There would be no play-by-play description of those things he could do with such ease, that Alicia hadn't known could feel like that. There would certainly be no conversations about all of these confusing and pointless things she felt sloshing around inside of her when she thought about those moments he'd showed her his vulnerable side, as if a man whose last name she didn't know and hadn't asked was something more than a one-night stand.

And if there was no one to talk about it with, all of this urgency, this driving sense of loss, would disappear. *It had to.* Alicia would remain, outwardly, as solid and reliable and predictably boring as she'd become in these past years. An example. The same old Saint Alicia, polishing her halo.

And maybe someday, if she was well-behaved and lucky, she'd believe it again herself.

"Are you ready for the big meeting?"

Her supervisor's dry voice from the open doorway made Alicia jump guiltily in her chair, and it was much harder than it should have been to smile at Charlotte the way she usually did. She was sure what she'd done over her weekend was plastered all over her face. That Charlotte could *see* how filthy she really was, the way her father had. All her sins at a single glance, like that furious creature that bristled on Nikolai's chest.

"Meeting?" she echoed weakly.

"The new celebrity partnership?" Charlotte prompted her. At Alicia's blank look, she laughed. "We all have to show our faces in the conference hall in exactly five minutes, and Daniel delivered a new version of his official presidential lecture on tardiness last week. I wouldn't be late."

"I'll be right along," Alicia promised, and this time, managed a bit of a better smile.

She sighed heavily when Charlotte withdrew, feeling much too fragile. Hollow and raw, as if she was still fighting off that hangover she hadn't had. But she knew it was him. Nikolai. That much fire, that much wild heat, had to have a backlash. She shouldn't be surprised.

This will fade, she told herself, and she should know, shouldn't she? She'd had other things to forget. *It always does, eventually.*

But the current of self-loathing that wound through her then suggested otherwise.

This was not the end of the world. This was no more than a bit of backsliding into shameful behavior, and she wasn't very happy with herself for doing it, but it wouldn't happen again.

No one had walked in on her doing it. No one even knew. Everything was going to be fine.

Alicia blew out a shaky breath, closed down her computer, then made her way toward the big conference hall on the second floor, surprised to find the office already deserted. That could only mean that the celebrity charity in question was a particularly thrilling one. She racked her brain as she climbed the stairs, but she couldn't remember what the last memo had said about it or even if she'd read it.

She hated these meetings, always compulsory and always

about standard-waving, a little bit of morale-building, and most of all, PR. They were a waste of her time. Her duties involved the financial planning and off-site management of the charity's regional offices scattered across Latin America. Partnering with much bigger, much more well-known celebrity charities was more of a fundraising and publicity endeavor, which always made Daniel, their president, ecstatic—but didn't do much for Alicia.

She was glad she was a bit late, she thought as she hurried down the gleaming hallway on the second level. She could slip in, stand at the back, applaud loudly at something to catch Daniel's eye and prove she'd attended, then slip back out again and return to all that work on her messy desk.

Alicia silently eased open the heavy door at the rear of the hall. Down at the front, a man was talking confidently to the quiet, rapt room as she slipped inside.

At first she thought she was imagining it, given where her head had been all day.

And then it hit her. Hard.

She wasn't hearing things.

She knew that voice.

She'd know it anywhere. Her body certainly did.

Rough velvet. Russian. That scratch of whiskey, dark and powerful, commanding and sure.

Nikolai.

Her whole body went numb, nerveless. The door handle slipped from her hand, she jerked her head up to confirm what couldn't possibly be true, couldn't possibly be happening—

The heavy door slammed shut behind her with a terrific crash.

Every single head in the room swiveled toward her, as if she'd made her entrance in the glare of a bright, hot spotlight and to the tune of a boisterous marching band, complete with clashing cymbals.

But she only saw him.

Him. Nikolai. *Here.*

Once again, everything disappeared. There was only the fearsome blue of his beautiful eyes as they nailed her to the door behind her, slamming into her so hard she didn't know how she withstood it, how she wasn't on her knees from the force of it.

He was even more devastating than she'd let herself remember.

Still dressed all in black, today he wore an understated, elegant suit that made his lethal frame look consummately powerful rather than raw and dangerous, a clever distinction. And one that could only be made by expert tailoring to the tune of thousands upon thousands of pounds. The brutal force of him filled the room, filled her, and her body reacted as if they were still naked, still sprawled across his bed in a tangle of sheets and limbs. She felt too hot, almost feverish. His mouth was a harsh line, but she knew how it tasted and what it could do, and there was something dark and predatory in his eyes that made her tremble deep inside.

And remember. Dear God, what she remembered. What he'd done, how she'd screamed, what he'd promised and how he'd delivered, again and again and again....

It took her much too long to recollect where she was *now*.

Not in a club in Shoreditch this time, filled with drunken idiots who wouldn't recall what they did, much less what she did, but *in her office*. Surrounded by every single person she worked with, all of whom were staring at her.

Nikolai's gaze was so blue. So relentlessly, impossibly, mercilessly blue.

"I'm so sorry to interrupt," Alicia managed to murmur, hoping she sounded appropriately embarrassed and apologetic, the way anyone would after slamming that door—and not as utterly rocked to the core, as lit up with shock and horror, as she felt.

It took a superhuman effort to wrench her gaze away from the man who stood there glaring at her—who wasn't a figment of her overheated imagination, who had the same terrifying power over her from across a crowded room as he'd had in his bed, whom she'd never thought she'd see again, *ever*—and slink to an empty seat in the back row.

She would never know how she did it.

Down in the front of the room, a phalanx of assistants behind him and the screen above him announcing who he was in no uncertain terms, NIKOLAI KOROVIN OF THE KOROVIN FOUNDATION, she saw Nikolai blink. Once.

And then he kept talking as if Alicia hadn't interrupted him. As if he hadn't recognized her—as if Saturday night was no more than the product of her feverish imagination.

As if she didn't exist.

She'd never wished so fervently that she didn't. That she could simply disappear into the ether as if she'd never been, or sink into the hole in the ground she was sure his icy glare had dug beneath her.

What had she been thinking, to touch this man? To give herself to him so completely? Had she been drunk after all? Because today, here and now, he looked like nothing so much as a sharpened blade. Gorgeous and mesmerizing, but terrifying. That dark, ruthless power came off him in waves the way it had in the club, even stronger without the commotion of the music and the crowd, and this time, Alicia understood it.

This was who he was.

She *knew* who he was.

He was Nikolai Korovin. His brother was one of the most famous actors on the planet, which made Nikolai famous by virtue of his surname alone. Alicia knew his name like every other person in her field, thanks to his brilliant, inspired management of the Korovin Foundation since its creation two years ago. People whispered he was a harsh and demanding boss, but always fair, and the amount of money he'd already raised for the good causes the Korovin Foundation supported was staggering.

He was *Nikolai Korovin*, and he'd explored every part of her body with that hard, fascinating mouth. He'd held her in his arms and made her feel impossibly beautiful, and then he'd driven into her so hard, so deep, filling her so perfectly and driving her so out of her mind with pleasure, she had to bear down now to keep from reacting to the memory. He'd made her feel so wild with lust, so deliciously addicted to him, that she'd sobbed the last time she'd shattered into pieces all around him. *She knew how he tasted*. His mouth, his neck, the length of his proud sex. That angry, tattooed monster crouched on his chest. She knew what made him groan, fist his hands into her hair.

More than all of that, she knew how those bright eyes looked when he told her things she had the sense he didn't normally speak of to anyone. She knew too much.

He was Nikolai Korovin, and she didn't have to look over at Daniel's beaming face to understand what it meant that he was here. For Daniel as president, for making this happen. For the charity itself. A partnership with the Korovin Foundation was more than a publicity opportunity—it was a coup. It would take their relatively small charity with global ambitions and slam it straight into the big time, once and for all. And it went without saying that Nikolai Korovin, the legendary CEO of the Korovin Foundation and the person responsible for all its business decisions, needed to be kept happy for that to happen.

That look on his face when he'd seen her had been anything but happy.

Alicia had to force herself to sit still as the implications of this washed through her. She had betrayed herself completely and had a tawdry one-night stand. That was bad enough. But it turned out she'd done it with a man who could end her career.

Eight years ago she'd lost her father's respect and her own self-respect in the blur of a long night she couldn't even recall. Now she could lose her job.

Today. At the end of this meeting. Whenever Nikolai liked.

When you decide to mess up your life, you really go for it, she told herself, fighting back the panic, the prick of tears. *No simple messes for Alicia Teller! Better to go with total devastation!*

Alicia sat through the meeting in agony, expecting something to happen the moment it ended—lightning to strike, the world to come crashing to a halt, Nikolai to summon her to the front of the room and demand her termination at once—but nothing did. Nikolai didn't glance in her direction again. He and his many assistants merely swept from the hall like a sleek black cloud, followed by the still-beaming Daniel and all the rest of the upper level directors and managers.

Alicia told herself she was relieved. This had to be relief, this sharp thing in the pit of her stomach that made it hard to breathe, because nothing else made sense. She'd known he was dangerous the moment she'd met him, not that it had stopped her.

Now she knew exactly *how* dangerous.

She was an idiot. A soon-to-be-sacked idiot.

Her colleagues all grimaced in sympathy as they trooped

back downstairs. They thought the fact she'd slammed that door was embarrassing enough. Little did they know.

"Can't imagine having a man like that look at me the way he did you," one said in an undertone. "I think I'd have nightmares!"

"I believe I will," Alicia agreed.

She spent the rest of the afternoon torn between panic and dread. She attacked all the work on her desk, like a drowning woman grasping for something to hold. Every time her phone rang, her heart leaped in her chest. Every time she heard a noise outside her office door, she tensed, thinking she was finished.

Any minute now, she'd be called up to Daniel's office. She could see it spool out before her like a horror film. Daniel's secretary would message the salacious news to half the office even as Alicia walked to her doom. So not only would Alicia be dismissed from her job because of a tawdry one-night stand with a man most people would have recognized and she certainly should have—but everyone she worked with and respected would know it.

It would be as it had been that morning her father had woken her up and told her what he'd seen, what she'd done—but this time, far more people would know what kind of trollop she was. People she'd impressed with her work ethic over the years would now sit about imagining her naked. *Having sex. With Nikolai.* She felt sick even thinking about it.

"I warned you!" Charlotte said as she stuck her head through the doorway, making Alicia jump again. A quick, terrified glance told her that her supervisor looked...sympathetic. Not horribly embarrassed. Not scandalized in the least. "I told Daniel you were on a call that ran a bit long, so no worries there."

"Thank you." Alicia's voice sounded strained, but Charlotte didn't seem to notice.

"Nikolai Korovin is very intense, isn't he?" Charlotte shook her head. "The man has eyes like a laser beam!"

"I expect he doesn't get interrupted very often," Alicia said, fighting for calm. "I don't think he cares for it."

"Clearly not," Charlotte agreed. And then laughed.

And that was it. No request that Alicia pack up her things or don a scarlet letter. No summons to present herself in Daniel's office to be summarily dismissed for her sexually permissive behavior with the fiercely all-business CEO of their new celebrity partner foundation. Not even the faintest hint of a judgmental look.

But Alicia knew it was coming. She'd not only seen the way Nikolai had looked at her, but now that she knew that he was Nikolai *Korovin,* she was afraid she knew exactly what it meant.

He was utterly ruthless. About everything. The entire internet agreed.

It was only a matter of time until all hell broke loose, so she simply put her head down, kept off the internet because it only served to panic her more, and worked. She stayed long after everyone else had left. She stayed until she'd cleared her desk, because that way, when they tittered behind their hands and talked about how they'd never imagined her acting *that way,* at least they wouldn't be able to say she hadn't done her job.

Small comfort, indeed.

It was almost nine o'clock when she finished, and Alicia was completely drained. She shrugged into her coat and wrapped her scarf around her neck, wishing there was a suit of armor she could put on instead, some way to ward off what she was certain was coming. Dread sat heavy in her stomach, leaden and full, and there was nothing she could do about it but wait to see what Nikolai did. Go home, hole up on the couch with a takeaway and Rosie's usual happy chatter, try to ease this terrible anxiety with bad American television and wait to see what he'd do to her. Because he was Nikolai Korovin, and he could do whatever he liked.

And would. Of that, she had no doubt.

Alicia made her way out of the building, deciding the moment she stepped out into the cold, clear night that she should walk home instead of catching the bus. It was only thirty-five minutes or so at a brisk pace, and it might sort out her head. Tire her out. Maybe even allow her to sleep.

She tucked her hands into her pockets and started off, but had only made it down the front stairs to the pavement when she realized that the big black SUV pulled up to the curb wasn't parked there, but was idling.

A whisper of premonition tingled through her as she drew closer, then turned into a tumult when the back door cracked open before her.

Nikolai Korovin appeared from within the way she should have known he would, tall and thunderous and broadcasting that dark, brooding intensity of his. He didn't have to block her path. He simply closed the door behind him and stood there, taking over the whole neighborhood, darker than the sky above, and Alicia was as unable to move as if he'd pinned her to the ground himself.

She was caught securely in his too-knowing, too-blue gaze all over again, as if he held her in his hands, and the shiver of hungry need that teased down the length of her spine only added insult to injury. She despaired of herself.

If she respected herself at all, Alicia knew with that same old kick of shame in her gut, she wouldn't feel even that tiny little spark of something far too much like satisfaction that he was here. That he'd come for her. As if maybe he was as thrown by what had happened between them as she was...

"Hello, Alicia," Nikolai said, a dark lash in that rough voice of his, velvet and warning and so very Russian, smooth power and all of that danger in every taut line of his beautiful body. He looked fierce. Cold and furious. "Obviously, we need to talk."

CHAPTER FOUR

FOR A MOMENT, Alicia wanted nothing more than to run.

To bolt down the dark street like some desperate animal of prey and hope that this particular predator had better things to do than follow.

Something passed between them then, a shimmer in the dark, and Alicia understood that he knew exactly what she was thinking. That he was picturing the same thing. The chase, the inevitable capture, and *then*...

Nikolai's eyes gleamed dangerously.

Alicia tilted up her chin, settled back on her heels and faced him, calling on every bit of courage and stamina at her disposal. She wasn't going to run. She might have done something she was ashamed of, but she hadn't done it alone. And this time she had to face it—she couldn't skulk off back to university and limit her time back home as she'd done for years until the Reddicks moved to the north.

"Well," she said briskly. "This is awkward."

His cold eyes blazed. He was so different tonight, she thought. A blade of a man gone near incandescent with that icy rage, a far cry from the man she'd thought she'd seen in those quieter moments—the one who had told her things that still lodged in her heart. The change should have terrified her. Instead, perversely, she felt that hunger shiver deeper into her, settling into a hard knot low in her belly, turning into a thick, sweet heat.

"This is not awkward," he replied, his voice deceptively mild. Alicia could see that ferocious look in his eyes, however, and wasn't fooled. "This is a quiet conversation on a deserted street."

"Perhaps the word loses something in translation?" she suggested, perhaps a shade too brightly, as if that was some defense against the chill of him.

"Awkward," he bit out, his accent more pronounced than before and a fascinating pulse of temper in the hinge of his tight jaw, "was looking up in the middle of a business meeting today to see a woman I last laid eyes upon while I was making her come stare right back at me."

Alicia didn't want to think about the last time he'd made her come. She'd thought they were finished after all those long, heated hours. He'd taken that as a challenge. And he'd held her hips between his hands and licked into her with lazy intent, making her writhe against him and sob....

She swallowed, and wished he wasn't watching her. He saw far too much.

"You're looking at me as if I engineered this. I didn't." She eyed him warily, her hands deep in the pockets of her coat and curled into fists, which he couldn't possibly see. Though she had the strangest notion he could. "I thought the point of a one-night stand with no surnames exchanged was that this would never happen."

"Have you had a great many of them, then?"

Alicia pretended that question didn't hit her precisely where she was the most raw, and with a ringing blow.

"If you mean as many as you've had, certainly not." She shrugged when his dark brows rose in a kind of affronted astonishment. "There are no secrets on the internet. Surely you, of all people, must know that. And it's a bit late to tally up our numbers and draw unflattering conclusions, don't you think? The damage is well and truly done."

"That damage," Nikolai said, that rough voice of his too tough, too cold, and that look on his hard face merciless, "is what I'm here to discuss."

Alicia didn't want to lose her job. She didn't want to know what kind of pressure Nikolai was prepared to put on her, what threats he was about to issue. She wanted this to go away again—to be the deep, dark secret that no one ever knew but her.

And it still could be, no matter how pitiless he looked in that moment.

"Why don't we simply blank each other?" she asked, once again a touch too brightly—which she could see didn't fool him at all. If anything, it called attention to her nervousness. "Isn't that the traditional method of handling situations like this?"

He shook his head, his eyes looking smoky in the dark, his mouth a resolute line.

"I do not mix business and pleasure," he said, with a finality that felt like a kick in the stomach. "I do not *mix* at all. The women I sleep with do not infiltrate my life. They appear in carefully orchestrated places of my choosing. They do not ambush me at work. Ever."

Alicia decided that later—much later, when she knew how this ended and could breathe without thinking she might burst into panicked, frustrated tears—she would think about the fact that a man like Nikolai had so many women that he'd developed *policies* to handle them all. *Later.* Right now, she had to fight back, or surrender here and now and lose everything.

"I assure you," she said, as if she had her own set of violated policies and was considering them as she met his gaze, "I feel the same way."

Nikolai shifted, and then suddenly there was no distance between them at all. His hands were on her neck, his thumbs at her jaw, tipping her head back to look up at him. Alicia should have felt attacked, threatened. She should have leaped for safety. Screamed. *Something*.

But instead, everything inside of her went still. And hot.

"I am not here to concern myself with your feelings," he told her in that rough velvet whisper. That fascinating mouth was grim again, but she could almost touch it with hers, if she dared. She didn't. "I am here to eliminate this problem as swiftly and as painlessly as possible."

But his hands were on her. Just as they'd been in the club when he'd told her to run. And she wondered if he was as conflicted as she was, and as deeply. What it would take to see that guarded look on his face again, that vulnerable cast to his beautiful mouth.

"You really are the gift that keeps on giving, Nikolai," she managed to say, retreating to a sarcastic tone, hoping the bite of it might protect her. She even smiled, thinly. "I've never felt happier about my reckless, irresponsible choices."

He let out a short laugh, and whatever expression that was on his hard face then—oddly taut and expectant, dark and hot—was like a flame inside of her. His hands were strong and like brands against her skin. His thumbs moved gently, lazily, as if stroking her jaw of their own accord.

"I don't like sharp women with smart mouths, Alicia," he told her, harsh and low, and every word was a caress against her skin, her sex, as if he was using those long fingers deep in her heat. "I like them sweet. Soft. Yielding and obedient and easily dismissed."

That same electricity crackled between them even here on the cold street, a bright coil that wound tight inside of her, making her feel mad with it. Too close to an explosion she knew she couldn't allow.

"What luck," she said, sharp and smart and nothing like soft at all. "I believe there's a sex shop in the next street, filled with exactly the kind of plastic dolls you prefer. Shall I point you in the right direction?"

He let go of her as if she'd burned him. And she recognized that dark heat in his gaze, the way it changed his expression, the things it did to that mouth.

"Get in the car, Alicia," he ordered her darkly. "I have an aversion to discussing my private life on a public street, deserted or not."

It was her turn to laugh, in disbelief.

"You have to be crazy if you think I'm getting back in that thing," she told him. "I'd rather get down on my hands and knees and crawl across a bed of nails, thank you."

She knew it was a mistake almost before the words left her mouth, and that sudden wolfish look on his face nearly undid her. It was impossible, then, not to picture herself down on her hands and knees, crawling toward that ravenous heat in his winter eyes she could remember too well, and could see right there before her now.

"I wasn't thinking about sex at present," he said coolly, and even though she could see from that fire in his gaze that he'd imagined much the same thing she had, she felt slapped. Shamed anew. "Why? Were you?"

It was time to go, Alicia realized then. It had been time to go the moment she'd seen that SUV idling at the curb. Before this thing got any worse—and she had no doubt at all that it would.

"It was lovely to finally meet you properly, Mr. Korovin," she said crisply. She put a faint emphasis on the word *properly,* and he blinked, looking almost...abashed? But that was impossible. "I'm sure your partnership with the charity will be a huge boost for us, and I'm as grateful as anyone else. And now I'm going home, where I will continue to actively pretend none of this ever happened. I can only hope you'll do the same."

"You didn't tell me you worked for a children's charity."

She didn't know what she'd expected him to say, but it wasn't that, with that sting of accusation. She eyed him warily. "Neither did you."

"Did you know who I was, Alicia?" Nikolai's face was so hard, his gaze so cold. She felt the chill suddenly, cutting into her. "You stumbled into my arms. Then you stumbled into that conference room today. Convenient." His eyes raked over her, as if looking for evidence that she'd planned this nightmare. "Your next stumble had best not involve any tabloid magazines or tell-all interviews. You won't like how I respond."

But she couldn't believe he truly thought that, she realized when the initial shock of it passed. She'd been in that bed with him. She knew better. Which meant he was lashing out, seeing what would hurt her. *Eliminating problems,* as he'd said he would.

"There's no need to draw out this torture," she told him, proud of how calm she sounded. "If you want me sacked, we both know you can do it easily. Daniel would have the entire staff turn cartwheels down the length of the Mall if he thought that would please you. Firing me will be a snap." She squared her shoulders as if she might have to sustain a blow. As if she already had. "If that's what you plan to do, I certainly can't stop you."

He stared at her for a long moment. A car raced past on the street beside them and in the distance she could hear the rush of traffic on the main road. Her breath was coming hard and fast, like she was fighting whole battles in her head while he only stood there, still and watchful.

"You're a distraction, Alicia," he told her then, something like regret in his voice. "I can't pretend otherwise."

"Of course you can," she retorted, fighting to keep calm. "All people do is pretend. I pretended to be the sort of woman—" She didn't want to announce exactly what she'd been pretending for eight years, not to him, so she frowned instead. "Just ignore me and I'll return the favor. It will be easy."

"I am not the actor in the family."

"I didn't ask you to play *King Lear*," she threw at him, panicked and exasperated in equal measure. "I only asked you to ignore me. How difficult can that possibly be? A man like you must have that down to a science."

"What an impression you have of me," Nikolai said after a moment, his voice silken, his eyes narrow. "I treated you very well, Alicia. Have you forgot so soon? You wept out your gratitude, when you weren't screaming my name."

She didn't need the reminder. She didn't need the heat of it, the wild pulse in her chest, between her legs.

"I was referring to your wealth and status," Alicia said, very distinctly. "Your position. The fact you have armies of assistants to make sure no one can approach you without your permission. Not your..."

"Particular talents?" His voice was mild enough as he finished the thought for her. The effect his words had on her, inside her, was not.

But then he leaned back against the side of his car, as if he was perfectly relaxed. Even his face changed, and she went still again, because there was something far more predatory about him in this moment than there had been before. It scraped the air thin.

"I have a better solution," he said, in the confident and commanding tone she recognized from the conference room. "I don't need to fire you, necessarily. It will serve my purposes far better to use this situation to my advantage."

Alicia could only shake her head, looking for clues on

that face of his that gave nothing away. "I don't know what that means."

"It means, Alicia," he said almost softly, a wolf's dangerous smile in those winter eyes if not on that hard mouth, "that I need a date."

He could use this, Nikolai thought, while Alicia stared up at him as if he'd said that last sentence in Russian instead of English. He could use her.

A problem well managed could become a tool. And every tool could be a weapon, in the right hands. Why not Alicia?

He'd expected her to want more than Saturday night—they always did. And the sex they'd had had been...troubling. He'd known it while it was happening. He'd known it in between, when he'd found himself talking of things he never, ever talked about. He'd known it when he'd opened his eyes to watch her tiptoe from his room on Sunday morning, and had discovered he wanted her to stay.

He knew it now, remembering her sweet, hot mouth against his tattoo as if she'd blessed that snarling representation of the monster in him. As if she'd made it sacred, somehow. The moment he'd seen her, he'd expected she would try to leverage that, take it from him somehow. He'd planned to make it clear to her she had to go—before she could try.

But she claimed she wanted to ignore him. He should have been thrilled.

He told himself he was.

"I'm sorry." Her voice was carefully blank when she finally spoke, to match the expression on her face. "Did you say you needed a *date?*"

"I did." It occurred to him that he was enjoying himself, for the first time since he'd looked up and seen her standing in that conference room, in clear violation of all his rules. "There is a Christmas ball in Prague that I must attend in a few weeks, and it will go much more smoothly with a woman on my arm."

These things were always better with a date, it was true. It didn't matter who it was. The presence of any date at his side would repel most of the vulturelike women who always circled him like he was fresh meat laid out in the hot sun, allowing Nikolai to concentrate on business. And in the case of this particular charity ball, on Veronika—who had only this morning confirmed that she and her lover would attend.

Because Nikolai had realized, as he looked at her in the light of the streetlamps and thought strategy instead of containment, that Alicia could very well turn out to be the best weapon yet in his dirty little war.

"I'm certain there are hordes of women who would love nothing more than to fill that opening for you," she said, with none of the deference or courtesy he was used to from his subordinates and dates alike. There was no reason on earth he should find that intriguing. "Perhaps one of your many assistants has a sign-up sheet? A call list? Maybe even an audition process to weed out the lucky winner from the multitudes?"

He'd told her he liked sweet and biddable, and he did. But he liked this, too. He liked the way she talked to him, as if it hadn't occurred to her that she should fear him like everyone else did. It made him want to lick her until all of that tartness melted all over him, and he didn't want to examine that particular urge any closer.

"Something like that," he said. "But it's all very tedious. All I want is a pretty dress, a polite smile. I don't have time for the games."

"Or the person, apparently," she said, her voice dry. "I'm

sure that's very rewarding for whichever pretty dress you choose. But what does this have to do with me?"

Nikolai smiled, adrenaline moving through him the way it always did before a tactical strike. Before another win.

"You want nothing to do with me." His voice was a silken threat in the cold night. "Or so you claim."

"You're right," she said, but her voice caught. "I don't."

"Then it's perfect," he said. "It's only a handful of weeks until the ball. We'll allow ourselves to be photographed on a few dates. The world will think I'm smitten, as I am very rarely seen with the same woman more than once. More specifically, my ex-wife will think the same. And as she has always greatly enjoyed her fantasy that she is the only woman to have any power over me, and has never been one to resist a confrontation, it will put her right where I want her."

She stared at him. "And where is that, exactly?"

"Veronika and I need to have a conversation," Nikolai said with cool dismissal. "Hopefully, our last. The idea that I might have moved on will expedite that, I think."

"How tempting," she said after a moment, her voice as arid as that look in her eyes. "I've always aspired to be cold-bloodedly used to make another woman jealous, of course. It's truly every girl's dream. But I think I'll pass."

"This has nothing to do with jealousy," he said impatiently. "The only thing left between Veronika and me is spite. If that. I'm sure you'll see it yourself at the ball."

"Even more appealing. But still—no."

"Your whole office saw me stare at you today." He shrugged when her eyes narrowed. "They could hardly miss it. How much of a leap will it be for them to imagine that was the beginning of an infatuation?"

"But they won't have to make that leap." Her eyes were

glittering again. "I've declined your lovely offer and we're going to ignore each other."

"I don't think so." He watched her take that in. Knew she didn't like it. Found he didn't much care if she was happy about it, so long as she did it. "I'm going to take an interest in you, Alicia. Didn't you know? Everybody loves a romance."

"They won't believe it." Her voice sounded thick, as if the idea of it horrified her, and he was perverse enough to take that as a challenge. "They won't believe someone like you could get infatuated at all, much less with me."

He smiled. "They will. And more to the point, so will Veronika."

And he could kill two birds with one stone. He could dig into this attraction, the unacceptable intoxication this woman made him feel, and in so doing, strip away its power over him. Make certain he never again felt the need to unburden himself in such a shockingly uncharacteristic manner to a total stranger. At the same time, he could use Veronika's smug certainty about her place in his life against her. It was perfect.

Alicia stared back at him, so hard he thought he could hear her mind racing.

"Why bring any of this into the office at all?" she asked, sounding frustrated. Panicked, even. "If you want me to go to this ball, fine. I'll do it, but I don't see why anyone needs to know about it but us. No unlikely romance necessary."

"And how will that work?" he asked mildly. "When pictures of us at that ball show up in all the papers, and they will, it will look as if we were keeping our relationship a secret. As if we were hiding something. Think of the gossip then."

"You said you're not an actor," she said. "Yet this seems like a very elaborate bit of theater."

"I told you, you're a distraction," he replied, almost gently. He wanted to show her what he meant. To bury his face in that crook of her neck. To make her quiver for him the way he knew he could. Only the fact he wanted it too much kept him from it. "I don't allow distractions, Alicia. I neutralize them or I use them for my own ends."

"I don't want to be in any papers." Her voice was low, her eyes intense on his. It took him a moment to realize she was panicked. A better man might not have enjoyed that. "I don't want *pictures* of me out there, and certainly not with you."

"There's a certain liberty in having no choices, Alicia," he told her, not sure why it bothered him that she was so opposed to a picture *with him*. It made his voice harsher. "It makes life very simple. Do what I tell you to do, or look for a new job."

Nikolai didn't think that was the first moment it had occurred to her that he held all the power here, but it was no doubt when she realized he had every intention of using it as he pleased. He saw it on her face. In her remarkable eyes.

And he couldn't help but touch her again then, sliding his hand over her cheek as he'd done before. He felt the sweet heat of her where his fingertips touched her hairline, the chill of her soft skin beneath his palm. And that wild heat that was only theirs, sparking wild, charging through him.

Making him almost wish he was a different man.

She wore a thick black coat against the cold, a bright red scarf looped around her elegant neck. Her ink-black curls were pulled back from her face with a scrap of brightly patterned fabric, and he knew that beneath it she was dressed in even more colors, bright colors. Emerald greens and chocolate browns. She was so bright it made his head spin, even here in the dark. It made him achingly hard.

She is nothing more than an instrument, he told himself.

Another weapon for your arsenal. And soon enough, this intoxication will fade into nothing.

"Please," she whispered, and he wished he were the kind of man who could care. Who could soothe her. But he wasn't, no matter what he told her in the dark. "You don't understand. I don't want to lose my job, but I can't do this."

"You can," Nikolai told her. "And you will." He felt more in control than he had since she'd slammed into him at the edge of that dance floor, and he refused to give that up again. He wouldn't. "I'll be the one infatuated, Alicia. You need only surrender."

She shook her head, but she didn't pull her face from his grasp, and he knew what that meant even if she didn't. He knew what surrender looked like, and he smiled.

"Feel free to refuse me at first," he told Alicia then, his voice the only soft thing about him, as if he was a sweet and gentle lover and these words were the poetry he'd told her he didn't write. As if he was someone else. Maybe it would help her to think so. "Resist me, if you can. That will only make it look better."

"I won't do it," Alicia told him, hearing how unsteady her voice was and hating that he heard it, too. Hating all of this. "I won't play along."

"You will," he said in that implacable way that made something inside her turn over and shiver, while that half smile played with the corner of his hard mouth as if he knew something she didn't. "Or I'll have you sacked so fast it will make your head spin. And don't mistake sexual attraction for mercy, Alicia. I don't have any."

"Of course not," she bit out, as afraid that she would burst into tears right there as she was that she would nestle further into his hand, both impulses terrible and overwhelming at once. "You're the big, bad wolf. Fangs and teeth. I get the picture. I still won't do it."

She wrenched herself away from the terrible beguilement of his touch then, and ran down the street the way she should have at the start, panic biting at her heels as if she thought he might chase her.

He didn't—but then, he didn't have to chase her personally. His words did that for him. They haunted her as she tossed and turned in her sleepless bed that night. They moved over her like an itch she couldn't scratch. Like a lash against her skin, leaving the kind of scars he wore in their wake. Kitchen knives and bullets.

Do what I tell you to do.

Alicia was appalled at herself. He could say terrible things, propose to use her in some sick battle with his ex-wife, and still, she wanted him. He was mean and surly and perfectly happy to threaten her—and she wanted him. She lay awake in her bed and shivered when she thought about that last, simple touch, his hand hot despite the chill of the night air, holding her face so gently, making everything inside her run together and turn into honey.

Because that fool inside of her wanted that touch to mean something more. Wanted this attraction between them to have more to do with that vulnerability he'd shown her than the sex they'd had.

Wanted Saturday night to be different from that terrible night eight years ago.

He wants to use you, nothing more, she reminded herself for the millionth time, punching at her pillow in exhausted despair. *It means nothing more than that.*

But Alicia couldn't have pictures of herself in the tabloids. Not at all, and certainly not in the company of a man who might have been called a playboy, had he been less formidable. Not that it mattered what they called him—her father would know exactly what he was. Too wealthy, too hard. Too obvious. A man like that wanted women for one thing only, and her father would know it.

He would think she was back to old tricks. She knew he would.

Alicia shuddered, her face pressed into her pillow. She could *see* that awful look on her father's face that hideous morning as if he stood in front of her the way he'd done then.

"He is a *married man*. You know his wife, his children," her father had whispered, looking as deeply horrified as Alicia had felt.

"Dad," she'd managed to say, though her head had pounded and her mouth had been like sand. "Dad, I don't know what happened.... It's all—I don't remember—"

"I know what happened," he'd retorted, disgust plain in his voice and all across his face. "I saw you, spread-eagled on the grass with a *married man,* our *neighbor*—"

"Dad—" she'd tried again, tears in her voice and her eyes, afraid she might be sick.

"The way you dress, the way you flaunt yourself." He'd shaken his head, condemnation and that deep disgust written all over him. "I knew you dressed like a common whore, Alicia, but I never thought you'd *act* like one."

She couldn't go through that again, she thought then, staring in mute despair at her ceiling. She wouldn't go through it again, no matter how *infatuated* Nikolai pretended he was. No matter what.

He was going to have to fire her, she decided. She would call his bluff.

"No," she said, very firmly, when a coworker ran up to her the following day as she fixed herself a midmorning cup of tea and breathlessly asked if she'd *heard*. "Heard what?"

But she had a terrible suspicion she could guess. Ruthless and efficient, that was Nikolai.

"Nikolai Korovin *expressly* asked after you at the meeting this morning!" the excitable Melanie from the PR team whispered in that way of hers that alerted the entire office and most of the surrounding neighborhood, her eyes wide and pale cheeks red with the thrill of it all. "He *grilled* the team about you! Do you think that means he…?"

She couldn't finish that sentence, Alicia noted darkly. It was too much for Melanie. The very idea of Nikolai Korovin's interest—his *infatuation*—made the girl practically crumple into a shivering heap at Alicia's feet.

"I imagine he's the kind of man who keeps an annotated enemies list within arm's reach and several elaborate revenge plots at the ready," Alicia said as calmly as possible, dumping as much cold water on this fire of his as she could, even though she suspected it wouldn't do any good. "He certainly doesn't *like* me, Melanie."

The other woman didn't looked particularly convinced, no doubt because Alicia's explanation flew in the face of the grand romance she'd already concocted in her head. Just as Nikolai had predicted.

"No, thank you," Alicia told the emissary from his army of assistants two days after that, who walked up to Alicia as she stood in the open plan part of the office with every eye trained on her and asked if she might want to join them all for a meal after work?

"Mr. Korovin wanted me to tell you that it's a restaurant in Soho he thinks you'd quite enjoy," the woman persisted, her smile never dropping from her lips. "One of his favorites in London. And his treat, of course."

Alicia's heart hammered in her chest so hard she wondered for a panicked moment if she was having some kind of heart attack. Then she remembered how many people were watching her, much too avidly, and forced a polite smile in return.

"I'm still catching up from my trip," she lied. "I'll have to work late again, I'm afraid. But please do thank Mr. Korovin for thinking of me."

Somehow, that last part didn't choke her.

By the end of that week, the fact that ruthless and somewhat terrifying billionaire Nikolai Korovin had *taken an interest* in Alicia was the only thing anyone in the office seemed able to talk about, and he'd accomplished it without lowering himself to speak to her directly. She felt hunted, trapped, and she hadn't even seen him since that night on the street.

He was diabolical.

"I believe Nikolai Korovin wants to *date* you, Alicia," Charlotte said as they sat in her office on Friday morning, going over the presentation for their team meeting later that afternoon. She grinned widely when Alicia looked at her. "I don't know whether to be excited or a bit overwhelmed at the idea of someone like him dating a normal person."

"This is so embarrassing," Alicia said weakly, which was perhaps the first honest thing she'd said on the topic all week. "I honestly don't know why he's doing this."

"Love works in mysterious ways," Charlotte singsonged, making Alicia groan.

Everybody loves a romance, he'd said in that cold, cynical voice of his. Damn him.

"This is a man who could date anyone in the world, and has done," Alicia said, trying to sound lighter, breezier, than she felt. "Why on earth should a man like that want to date *me?*"

"You didn't drop at his feet on command, obviously," Charlotte said with a shrug. Only because he hadn't issued that particular command that night, Alicia thought sourly, fighting to keep her expression neutral. "Men like Nikolai Korovin are used to having anything they desire the moment they desire it. Ergo, they desire most what they can't have."

Alicia hadn't been so happy to see the end of a work week in years. She hated him, she told herself that weekend, again and again and again, until she could almost pretend that she really did. That it was that simple.

"I hate him," she told Rosie, taking out her feelings on the sad little boil-in-the-bag chicken curry they'd made for Sunday dinner with a violent jab of her fork. It had been two blessed Nikolai-free days. She couldn't bear the thought of what tomorrow might bring. "He's incredibly unprofessional. He's made the whole office into a circus! Nothing but gossip about him and me, all day every day!"

Rosie eyed Alicia from her side of the sofa, her knees pulled up beneath her and her blond hair piled haphazardly on her head.

"Maybe he likes you."

"No. He does not. This is some kind of sick game he's playing for his own amusement. That's the kind of man he is."

"No kind of man goes to all that trouble," her friend said slowly. "Not for a game. He really could simply like you, Alicia. In his own terrifyingly wealthy sort of way, I mean."

"He doesn't like *me,* Rosie," Alicia retorted, with too much heat, but she couldn't stop it. "The women he likes come with their own *Vogue* covers."

But she could see that Rosie was conjuring up Cinderella stories in her head, like everyone else, as Nikolai had known they would. Alicia felt so furious, so desperate and so trapped, that she shook with it. She felt his manipulation like a touch, like he was sitting right there next to her, that big body of his deceptively lazy, running his amused fingers up and down her spine.

You wish you were anything as uncomplicated as furious, a little voice taunted her, deep inside.

"Maybe you should play along," Rosie said then, and she grinned wide. "It's not going to be a drink down at the pub on a date with the likes of him, is it? He's the sort who has *mistresses,* not *girlfriends.* He could fly you to Paris for dinner. He could whisk you off to some private island. Or one of those great hulking yachts they always have."

"He could ruin my reputation," Alicia countered, and yet despite herself, wondered what being Nikolai's *mistress* would entail—what sort of lover he would be, what kind of sensual demands he would make if he had more than one night to make them. All of that lethal heat and all the time in the world… How could anyone survive it? She shoved the treacherous thoughts aside. "He could make things very difficult for me at work."

"Only because they'll all be seething with jealousy," Rosie said with a dismissive sniff. "And your reputation could use a little ruining."

Because she couldn't imagine what it was like to *actually* be ruined, Alicia knew. To have gone and ruined herself so carelessly, so irrevocably. She couldn't know what it was like to see that disgust in her own father's eyes whenever he looked at her. To feel it in her own gut, like a cancer.

Rosie smiled again, wickedly. "And I think Nikolai Korovin sounds like the kind of man who knows his way around a ruining."

Alicia only stabbed her chicken again. Harder. And then scowled at the television as if she saw anything at all but Nikolai, wherever she looked.

CHAPTER FIVE

ALICIA WAS RUNNING a file up to Charlotte's office the following week when she finally ran into him, larger than life, sauntering down the stairs in the otherwise-empty stairwell as if he hadn't a care in the world.

The shock of it—the force and clamor that was Nikolai—hit her as hard as it had at the club. As it had outside the office building that night. Making her feel restless in her own skin. Electric.

Furious, she told herself sternly.

He saw her instantly and smiled, that tug in the corner of his hard mouth that made her insides turn to water no matter how much she wished it didn't. No matter how much she wanted to be immune to it. To him.

Because whatever she was, whatever this *thing* was that made her so aware of him, she certainly wasn't immune.

And Nikolai knew it.

He moved like water, smooth and inexorable. He seemed bigger than he actually was, as if he was so powerful he couldn't be contained and so expanded to fit—and to effortlessly dominate—any and all available space. Even an ordinary stairwell. Today he wore another absurdly well-fitting suit in his usual black, this one a rapturous love letter to his lean, muscled, dangerous form. He looked sinfully handsome, ruthless and cool, wealthy beyond imagining, and it infuriated her. So deeply it hurt.

Alicia told herself that was all it did.

"This is harassment," she informed him as she marched up the stairs, her heels clicking hard against each step, her tone as brisk as her spine was straight.

"No," he said, his gaze on hers. "It isn't."

Alicia stopped moving only when she'd reached the step above him, enjoying the fact it put her on eye level with him, for once. Even if those eyes were far too blue, bright and laughing at her, that winter cold moving in her, heating her from within.

She hated him.

God, how she wished she could hate him.

"It most certainly is," she corrected him with a bit of his own frostiness. "And I hate to break this to you when you've gone ahead and made your pretend infatuation so public, but it's actually quite easy to resist you."

"Is it?" He shouldn't sound so amused. So indulgent.

She would have scowled at him, but thought he would read that as weakness. Instead, she tilted up her chin and tried to project the kind of tough, cool competence she wished she felt as she called his bluff to his face.

"I'm not going to take part in your little bit of revenge theater no matter how much time you spend feeding the office gossip mill," she told him. Tough. Calm. Cool. "If you want to have me fired because you took me home from a club of your own free will, go right ahead." She let that sit there for a moment, then angled her head ever so slightly closer to his, for emphasis. "I didn't do anything wrong, I'm not afraid of you and I'd advise you try to communicate with your ex-wife through more traditional channels."

Nikolai simply…shifted position.

He moved with a primal grace that robbed her of speech,

pivoting without seeming to do so much as breathe. All Alicia knew was that she was facing him one moment and the next her back was up against the wall. As if he'd *willed* her to let him cage her there, his hands flat against the smooth wall on either side of her face.

He hadn't laid so much as a single finger upon her. He didn't now. He leaned in.

Much too close, and her body reacted as if he'd plugged her into the nearest socket. The white-hot light of this shocking heat between them pulsed through her, making her gasp. Her body betrayed her in a shivering flush, sensation scraping through her, making her skin pull taut, her breasts feel suddenly full and that wet, hot hunger punch its way into her belly before settling down between her legs. Where it stayed, a wild and greedy need, and all of it his. *His.*

As if she was, too.

"What the hell are you doing?" But it was no more than a whisper, and it gave her away as surely as that treacherous ache inside of her that Alicia was sure he could sense, somehow.

"I am a man possessed," Nikolai murmured, his mouth so close to hers she felt the pull of it, the ache, roll through her like a flash of pain, despite the hint of laughter she could hear in his voice. "Infatuated. Just as I promised you."

"I can see why your brother is the famous actor while you storm about, growling at other rich men and demanding their money." But her voice was little more than a breath, completely insubstantial, and she had to dig her fingers into the folder she carried to keep from touching that glorious chest that was right there in front of her, taunting her. "Because you're not terribly convincing, and by the way, I'm fairly certain this counts as stalking."

"Those are very strong words, Alicia." He didn't sound

concerned. Nikolai rested his considerable, sleek weight on his hands and surrounded her. Hemmed her in. Let his body remind her of all those things she wanted to forget. *Needed* to forget. "Harassment. Stalking."

"Strong, yes." She could feel her pulse in her throat, a frantic staccato. "And also accurate."

Alicia felt more than heard his small laugh against the tender skin of her neck, and she knew he saw the goose bumps that prickled there when he lifted that knowing gaze to hers.

"This is the first time I've seen you inside this office since you walked into the conference hall." Nikolai didn't move back. He gave her no room to breathe. If she tried to twist away, to escape him the way she wanted to do, she would have to brush up against him—and she didn't dare do that. She couldn't trust herself. Not when he smelled like winter. Not when she had the alarming urge to bury her face in his chest. "I haven't followed you around making suggestive comments. I extended a single invitation to you, Alicia. I didn't even do it myself. And you declined it without any repercussions at all."

"Says the man who has me pinned up against a wall."

"I'm not touching you," Nikolai pointed out, that dangerously lazy gleam in his bright gaze. "I'm not restraining you in any way. I could, of course." That gleam grew hotter, making her toes curl inside her shoes, making that need inside her rage into a wildfire. Making her despair of herself. "All you have to do is ask."

"I want you to stop this," she managed to get out, desperate to fight off the maelstrom he'd unleashed in her, the images carnal and tempting that chased through her head and made her much too aware of how weak she was.

How perilously close to compounding the error she'd already made with this man, right here in her office. In the *stairwell*. Every inch of her the whore her father had called her.

"Which *this?*" He sounded impossibly male, then. Insufferably smug, as if he knew exactly how close she was to capitulation. "Be specific."

She shifted then, and it was agonizing. He was *right there,* and she knew she couldn't allow herself to touch him, not even by accident—but she was terribly afraid she wasn't going to be able to help herself. How could she fight herself *and* him?

"I'd rather be sacked right now than have to put up with this," she whispered fiercely.

He laughed again then, and she wished that sound didn't get to her. She wished she could simply ignore it and him along with it. But it made him that much more beautiful, like a perfect sunset over a rugged mountain, and it made something inside of her ignite no matter how much she wished it didn't.

"You and I both know I could prove you a liar." He dropped his head slightly, and inhaled, as if pulling the scent of her skin deep into his lungs, and that fire in her began to pulse, greedy and insistent. Her nipples pressed against the soft fabric of her dress, and she was terrified he'd see it. Terrified he'd *know.* "How long do you think it would take, *solnyshka?* One second? Two? How long before you wrap yourself around me and beg?"

Of course he knew. Hadn't that long night with him taught her anything?

Alicia stiffened, panic like a drumbeat inside of her, but it only seemed to make that fire in her burn hotter. Nikolai moved even closer, somehow, though that shouldn't have been possible, and he was so big, so powerful, that it was as if nothing existed except the breadth of his shoulders. He surrounded her, and there was a part of her way down deep that wasn't at all conflicted. That simply exulted in it. In him.

But that was the part that had started all this. The part that had looked up into his face in that dark club and surrendered, there and then. She couldn't succumb to his version of dark magic again. She had too much to lose.

"You don't understand," she said hurriedly, almost desperately. "This is—you are—" She pulled in a breath. "I'm afraid—"

But she couldn't tell Nikolai Korovin the things she feared. She couldn't say them out loud, and anyway, this was only a bitter little game to him. The ways she hated herself, the ways she'd let herself down, the way she'd destroyed her relationship with her father—he didn't need to know about any of that.

She couldn't understand why she had the strange urge to tell him anyway, when she'd never told a soul.

It seemed to take him a very long time to pull his head back far enough to look her in the eyes, to study her too-hot face. Even through her agitation, she could see him grow somber as he watched her. Darker. He pushed back from the wall, letting his hands drop to his sides, and Alicia told herself that was exactly what she'd wanted.

"Good," he said quietly, an expression she couldn't read on his hard face. "You should be afraid of me. You should have been afraid that night."

She scowled at him, not caring anymore what he read into it.

"For God's sake," she snapped, not liking that look on his face and not at all sure why it bothered her so much and so deeply. "I'm not afraid of *you*."

That sat there between them, telling him things she should have kept to herself, and the expression on his face made her think of that moment in his bed, suddenly. When he'd talked of kitchen knives and sins and she'd kissed his tattoo, as if she could kiss it all away. As if he was wounded.

"I thought you liked the fact that I *don't* want you," she said after a moment, when all he did was stare at her, in a manner she might have called haunted if it was someone other than Nikolai. "Why are you so determined to prove otherwise?"

"You mistake me." His voice was silky then, but there was a dark kick beneath it, and it shivered over her skin like a caress. "I know you want me. I still want you. I told you this was a distraction." He stuck his hands in his pockets, shifting back on his heels, and his expression grew cooler. More distant. Assessing her. "It's your disinterest in having any kind of connection to me, your horror at the very idea, that makes the rest of this possible."

"And by that do you mean keeping my job?" she asked, ignoring his talk of who wanted who, because she didn't dare let herself think about it. She couldn't go there, or who knew what would become of her? "Or the twisted game you feel you need to play with your ex-wife?"

Nikolai only stared back at her, his face a study in ice. Impassive and cool.

"Let me guess," she said tightly. "You only want what you can't have."

"But you don't qualify, Alicia," he said, in that dangerously soft way of his that was like a seismic event inside of her, and she had to fight to hide the aftershocks. "I've already had you."

"That was a mistake," she retorted, and she wanted to play it down. Laugh, smile. But his eyes flashed and she knew she'd sounded too dark. Too close to *hurt.* "There won't be a repeat."

"You don't want to challenge me to prove you wrong."

His winter eyes probed hers, moved over her face, saw things she didn't want to share. "Or perhaps you do."

That last was a low growl. Wolf again, not man, and she wasn't sure she could survive it without imploding. Without betraying herself all over again, and there was no *wild night* to lose herself in, not here in this chilly stairwell. No pounding music, no shouting crowd. She felt the danger in him, the profound sensual threat, like heat all around her, seducing her without a single word or touch. She could smell that scent that was only his, the faint smoke and crisp slap of winter. She felt the strength of him, that lethal power, and her fingers ached to explore it again, every last lean muscle, until he groaned beneath her hands.

And she *wanted*.

Suddenly, and with every last cell in her body, Alicia wanted to be someone else. Someone free of her past, free to throw herself heedlessly into all of this wondrous fire and not care if it swallowed her whole. Someone who could do what she liked with this man without bringing her whole world down around her all over again.

Someone very much like the person she'd seemed to think she was the night she'd met him.

But she couldn't. And Nikolai still didn't touch her, which almost made it worse.

"It's time to move into the public phase of this arrangement," he told her in that distant way again, as if this was a planned meeting in the stairwell to calmly discuss the calendar of events that would lead to her downfall. "We'll start with dinner tomorrow night. There are things we need to discuss."

"What a lovely invitation—"

"It's not a request."

She studied him for a moment, all that ice and steel. "I'm otherwise engaged."

"Cancel."

"And if I refuse?"

Nikolai's smile turned dangerous. Her stomach contracted hard at the sight, and the ache of it sank low, turning molten and making her despair of herself anew.

It was that easy. *She* was that easy.

"You can try to run from me if you like." He looked intrigued at the prospect, and something dark and sensual twisted through her, leaving marks. "But I should give you fair warning—I'll find you. And you might not like the mood I'm in when I do."

"Fine," she made herself say, because she couldn't think of an alternate plan, certainly not while he stood there in front of her with a look on his face that told her he'd love to spend more time convincing her. She couldn't have that. And she certainly didn't want him to pursue her through the streets of London, to run her to ground like some mutinous fox, which she had no doubt he would do.... Did she? "Tomorrow night we'll suffer through the date from hell. That sounds delightful. Where do you want me to meet you?"

He reached out then and she braced herself, but he only wrapped a sprig of her curls around his finger, gave them a tug that was very nearly gentle, then let his hand drop, an odd cast to his fierce, proud mouth as he did it.

There was no reason at all that should pierce her heart.

"Don't try to top from the bottom, Alicia," he said, laughter in his brilliant gaze for a moment before it chilled into something much harder. More ruthless. "I'll let you know what I want tomorrow. And you'll do it. Because I really will have you fired if you don't, and despite this entertaining display of bravado, I think you know it."

And there it was.

She didn't want to lose her job—which meant she'd have to figure out how to survive losing her father all over again, once there were pictures to prove once more that she was nothing but a whore. And if there was a tiny spark inside of her, because some foolish part of her wished this wasn't all a game, that it wasn't all for show, that she was the kind of person men didn't use, she did her best to ignore it.

"I don't want to do this." Her voice was small, but still firm, and she thought she'd be proud, later, that she kept her head high. Even in defeat. "Any of it."

"I know you don't," Nikolai said, whole winters in his voice, in his beautiful eyes, so blue she wanted to cry. And there was a flash of something there, bright for a moment and then gone, as if this was more of a struggle for him than it seemed. It scared her, how much she wanted to believe that. "But you will."

Alicia sat where Nikolai had put her, at the corner of the dark wood table that stretched across a significant length of the great two-story room that was the center of his apartment, all low-slung modern couches and soaring windows. Nikolai could read her stiff tension in the way she sat, the way she held her lips too tight, the precise, angry movements of her hands.

His staff had served a five-star dinner that she'd barely touched. Nikolai hadn't spoken a word, and she hadn't broken the silence. Now she was pushing her dessert around on her plate, and he was well aware that her agitation level had skyrocketed even higher than before.

Bastard that he was, that amused him. He lounged in his seat, at the head of the table with her at his right, and studied her. He would figure her out. He would solve the mystery of this woman and when he did, lose interest in her. It was inevitable.

But he hadn't anticipated he would enjoy the process quite this much.

"You're a terrible date," he told her, and her dark eyes flashed when they met his. Then, after a moment, she rolled them. *At* him.

No one else would dare.

"Thank you," she said in that dry way that made him want her beneath him, right there on the table. He had to yank himself back under control, and it was significantly harder than it should have been. *Focus,* he ordered himself. "I can see why you're considered such a catch."

"This is an excellent opportunity to discuss my expectations," Nikolai said, as if her fearless defiance didn't make him want to lick his way into the heat of her, to make her writhe and sob in his hands. And he would, he promised himself, as soon as they came to an understanding. "Dating me comes with a number of requirements, Alicia. Making appropriate dinner conversation is only one of them."

"You're perfectly capable of making conversation," she pointed out in the same dry tone. "In fact, you're doing it right now, though I don't know if it qualifies as 'appropriate.'" She considered him for a moment, a small smile that he didn't like, yet found he wanted to taste, flirting with her full lips. "I suspected there must be some kind of application process and I'm delighted I'm right, but I'm not dating you. This isn't real." Her gaze turned hard on his. "This is blackmail."

"Call it whatever you like," he said, with a careless shrug. "The result is the same."

"Blackmail," she repeated, very distinctly. "I think you'll find that's what it's called when you force someone into doing something they don't want to do by holding something else over their head."

Nikolai could see all of that temper in her dark gaze, the flash of it when she couldn't hide her feelings. She wore a sleeveless wool top tonight in a deep aubergine shade, with

a neck that drooped down low and left her smooth, toned
arms on display, looking soft and sweet in the candlelight.
But most important, he could see every time she tensed,
every time she forced herself to relax, written up and down
the lean, elegant shape of those arms and all across her slender frame. Like now, when she forced her shoulders back
and down, then smiled at him as if she wasn't agitated at all.

She didn't know, yet, that he could read her body the
way others read words on a page. But she would learn, and
he would greatly enjoy teaching her. First, though, they
had business to take care of. If it alarmed him that he had
to remind himself of business before pleasure for the first
time in living memory, he ignored it.

"There is a confidentiality agreement that you'll need to
sign," he told her, dismissing her talk of blackmail, which
he could see she didn't like. "Beyond that, I have only
standard expectations. Don't venture out into public unless
you're prepared to be photographed, as terrible pictures of
you could lead to negative coverage of me, which is unacceptable. I'll let you know what pleases me—"

"If you mention a single thing about altering my appear-
ance to suit your tastes, whatever those might be," she said
almost conversationally, though there was murder in her
eyes, "I will stab you with this fork. I'm not dating you,
Nikolai. I'm acquiescing to your bizarre demands because
I want to keep my job, but we're not reenacting some sick
little version *My Fair Lady*. I don't care about pleasing you."

Nikolai was definitely enjoying himself. Especially
when he saw that little shiver move through her, and knew
they were both thinking about all the ways she could please
him. All the ways she had. He smiled slightly.

"Is that a passive-aggressive demand that I compliment
your looks?" he asked silkily. "I had no idea you were so in-
secure, Alicia. I'd have thought the fact that I had my mouth

on every inch of that gorgeous body of yours would have told you my feelings on that topic in no uncertain terms. Though I'm happy to repeat myself."

"I may stab you with this fork anyway." She met his gaze then and smiled. But he could see that her breathing had quickened. He knew arousal when he saw it. When he'd already tasted it. All of that heat and need, sweet against her dark skin. "Fair warning."

"You can always try."

She considered that for a moment, then sat back against her chair, inclining her head slightly as if she held the power here and was granting him permission to carry on.

"Don't ever keep me waiting," Nikolai said, continuing as if she hadn't interrupted him. "Anywhere. For any reason. My time is more valuable than yours."

Her eyes narrowed at that, but she didn't speak. Perhaps she was learning, he thought—but he hoped not. He really hoped not. He wanted her conquered, not coerced. He wanted to do it himself, step by delectable step.

"Don't challenge my authority. In your case, I'll allow some leeway because I find that smart mouth of yours amusing, but only a little leeway, Alicia, and never in public. Your role is as an ornament. I won't tolerate disrespect or disobedience. And I will tell you what you are to me, explicitly—never imagine yourself anything else. I can't stress that enough."

The silence between them then felt tighter. Hotter. Breathless, as if the great room had shrunk down until there was nothing but the two of them and the gently flickering candles. And her eyes were big and dark and he realized he could no longer read the way she looked at him.

"You're aware that this is a conversation about dating you *for show,* not working for you as one of your many interchangeable subordinates at the Korovin Foundation," she said after a moment. "Aren't you?"

"The roles aren't dissimilar."

He stretched his legs out in front of him and lounged even lower in the chair.

"Is this your usual first date checklist, then?"

Her gaze swept over him, and he had no idea what she saw. It surprised him how much he wanted to know.

He nodded, never taking his gaze from hers. "More or less."

"You actually ask a woman to dinner and then present her with this list." She sounded dubious, and something else he wasn't sure he recognized. "Before or after you order starters? And what if she says no? Do you stand up and walk out? Leave her with the bill for her temerity?"

"No one has ever said no." He felt that fire between them reach higher, pull tighter. He could see it on her face. "And I don't take women to dinner without a signed confidentiality agreement. Or anywhere else."

Alicia tapped a finger against her lips for a moment, and he wanted to suck that finger into his own mouth almost more than he wanted his next breath. Need raked through him, raw and hungry.

"You brought me here that night," she pointed out, her tone light, as if there was no tension between them at all. "I certainly didn't sign anything."

Nikolai almost smiled. "You are an anomaly."

"Lucky me," she murmured, faint and dry, and there was no reason that should have worked through him like a match against flint. He didn't like anomalies. He shouldn't have to keep telling himself that.

"If you've absorbed the initial requirements," he said, watching her intently now, "we can move on."

"There are more? The mind boggles."

She was mocking him, he was sure of it. He could see the light of it bright in her eyes and in that wicked twist of her lips, and for some reason, he didn't mind it.

"Sex," he said, and liked the way she froze, for the slightest instant, before concealing her reaction. He had to shift in his seat to hide his.

"You don't really have rules for sex with your girlfriends, Nikolai," she said softly. Imploring him. "Please tell me you're joking."

"I think of this as setting clear boundaries," he told her, leaning forward and smiling when she shivered and sat back. "It prevents undue confusion down the line."

"Undue confusion is what relationships are all about," Alicia said, shaking her head. Her dark eyes searched his, then dropped to her lap. "I rather think that might be the whole point."

"I don't have relationships." He waited until her eyes were on him again, until that tension between them pulled taut and that electric charge was on high, humming through them both. "I have sex. A lot of it. I'll make you come so many times your head will spin, which you already know is no idle boast, but in return, I require two things."

Nikolai watched her swallow almost convulsively, but she didn't look away. She didn't even blink. And he didn't quite know why he felt that like a victory.

"Access and obedience," he said, very distinctly, and was rewarded with the faintest tremor across those lips, down that slender frame. "When I want you, I want you—I don't want a negotiation. Just do what I tell you to do."

He could hear every shift in her breathing. The catch, the slow release. It took every bit of self-control he possessed to wait. To keep his distance. To let her look away for a moment and collect herself, then turn that dark gaze back on him.

"I want to be very clear." She leaned forward, putting her elbows on the table and keeping her eyes trained on him. "What you're telling me, Nikolai, is that every woman pictured on your arm in every single photograph of you online has agreed to all of these *requirements*. All of them."

He wanted to taste her, a violent cut of need, but he didn't. He waited.

"Of course," he said.

And Alicia laughed.

Silvery and musical, just as he remembered. It poured out of her and deep into him, and for a moment he was stunned by it. As if everything disappeared into the sound of it, the way she tipped back her head and let it light up the room. As if she'd hit him from behind and taken him down to the ground without his feeling a single blow.

That laughter rolled into places frozen so solid he'd forgotten they existed at all. It pierced him straight through to a core he hadn't known he had. And it was worse now than it had been that first night. It cut deeper. He was terribly afraid it had made him bleed.

"Laugh as much as you like," he said stiffly when she subsided, and was sitting back in her chair, wiping at her too-bright eyes. "But none of this is negotiable."

"Nikolai," she said, and that clutched at him too, because he'd never heard anyone speak his name like that. So warm, with all of that laughter still moving through her voice. It was almost as if she spoke to someone else entirely, as if it wasn't his name at all—but she looked directly at him, those dark eyes dancing, and he felt as if she'd shot him. He wished she had. He knew how to handle a bullet wound. "I'll play this game of yours. But I'm not going to do any of that."

He was so tense he thought he might simply snap into pieces, but he couldn't seem to move. Her laughter sneaked inside him, messing him up and making even his breathing feel impossibly changed. He hated it.

So he couldn't imagine why he wanted to hear it again, with an intensity that very nearly hurt.

"That's not one of your options," he told her, his voice the roughest he'd ever heard it.

But she was smiling at him, gently, and looked wholly uncowed by his tone.

"If I were you, Nikolai," she said, "I'd start asking myself why I'm so incapable of interacting with other people that I come up with ridiculous rules and regulations to govern things that are supposed to come naturally. That are *better* when they do."

"Because I am a monster," he said. He didn't plan it. It simply came out of his mouth and he did nothing to prevent it. She stopped smiling. Even the brightness in her eyes dimmed. "I've never been anything else. These rules and regulations aren't ridiculous, Alicia. They're necessary."

"Do they make you feel safe?" she asked with a certain quiet kindness he found deeply alarming, as if she knew things she couldn't possibly guess at, much less *know.*

But this was familiar ground even so. He'd had this same conversation with his brother, time and again. He recognized the happy, delusional world she'd come from that let her ask a question like that, and he knew the real world, cynical and bleak. He recognized himself again.

It was a relief, cold and sharp.

"Safety is a delusion," he told her curtly, "and not one I've ever shared. Some of us live our whole lives without succumbing to that particular opiate."

She frowned at him. "Surely when you were a child—"

"I was never a child." He pushed back from the table and rose to his feet. "Not in the way you mean."

She only watched him, still frowning, as he crossed his

arms over his chest, and she didn't move so much as a muscle when he glared down at her. She didn't shrink back the way she should. She looked at him as if he didn't scare her at all, and it ate at him. It made him want to show her how bad he really was—but he couldn't start down that road. He had no idea where it would lead.

"Why do you think my uncle tried to keep me in line with a kitchen knife? It wasn't an accident. He knew what I was."

"Your parents—"

"Died in a fire with seventy others when I was barely five years old," he told her coldly. "I don't remember them. But I doubt they would have liked what I've become. This isn't a bid for sympathy." He shrugged. "It's a truth I accepted a long time ago. Even my own brother believes it, and this after years of being the only one alive who thought I could be any different. I can't." He couldn't look away from her dark eyes, that frown, from the odd and wholly novel notion that she wanted to fight *for* him that opened up a hollow in his chest. "I won't."

"Your brother is an idiot." Her voice was fierce, as if she was prepared to defend him against Ivan—and even against himself, and he had no idea what to do with that. "Because while families always have some kind of tension, Nikolai, monsters do not exist. No matter what an uncle who holds a knife on a child tells you. No matter what we like to tell ourselves."

"I'm glad you think so." Nikolai wasn't sure he could handle the way she looked at him then, as if she hurt for him. He wasn't sure he knew how. "Soft, breakable creatures like you *should* believe there's nothing terrible out there in the dark. But I know better."

CHAPTER SIX

THAT WAS *PAIN* on his face.

In those searing eyes of his. In the rough scrape of his voice. It was like a dark stain that spilled out from deep inside of him, as if he was torn apart far beneath his strong, icy surface. *Ravaged*, it dawned on her, as surely as if that ferocious thing on his chest rent him to pieces where he stood.

Alicia felt it claw at her, too.

"I'm neither soft nor breakable, Nikolai." She kept her voice steady and her gaze on his, because she thought he needed to see that he hadn't rocked her with that heartbreakingly stark confession, even if he had. "Or as naive as you seem to believe."

"There are four or five ways I could kill you from here." His voice was like gravel. "With my thumb."

Alicia believed him, the way she'd believed he'd be good in bed when he'd told her he was, with a very similar matter-of-fact certainty. It occurred to her that there were any number of ways a man could be talented with his body—with his clever hands for pleasure, with his thumb for something more violent—and Nikolai Korovin clearly knew every one of them. She thought she ought to be frightened by that.

What was wrong with her that she wasn't?

"Please don't," she said briskly, as if she couldn't feel the sting of those claws, as if she didn't see that thick blackness all around him.

Nikolai stared at her. He stood so still, as if he expected he might need to bolt in any direction, and he held himself as if he expected an attack at any moment. As if he expected *she* might be the attacker.

Alicia thought of his coldness tonight, that bone-deep chill that should have hurt, so much harsher than the gruff, darkly amusing man she'd taken by surprise in that club. Who'd surprised her in return. She thought about what little he'd told her of his uncle meant for the boy he must have been—what he must have had to live through. She thought about a man who believed his own brother thought so little of him, and who accepted it as his due. She thought of his lists of rules that he obviously took very seriously indeed, designed to keep even the most intimate people in his life at bay.

I am a monster, he'd said, and she could see that he believed it.

But she didn't. She couldn't.

She ached for him. In a way she was very much afraid—with that little thrill of dark foreboding that prodded at her no matter how she tried to ignore it—would be the end of her. But she couldn't seem to make it stop.

"Nikolai," she said when she couldn't stand it any longer—when she wanted to reach over and touch him, soothe him, and knew she couldn't let herself do that, that *he* wouldn't let her do that anyway, "if you were truly a monster, you would simply *be* one. You wouldn't announce it. You wouldn't know how."

A different expression moved across his face then, the way it had once before in the dark, and tonight it broke her heart. That flash of a vulnerability so deep, so intense. And then she watched him pack it away, cover it in ice, turn it hard and cold.

"There are other things I could do with my thumb," he said, his voice the rough velvet she knew best. Seductive. Demanding. "That wouldn't kill you, necessarily, though you might beg for it before I was done."

But she knew what he was doing. She understood it, and it made her chest hurt.

"Sex is easier to accept than comfort," she said quietly, watching his face as she said it. He looked glacial. Remote. And yet that heat inside of him burned, she could feel it. "You can pretend it's not comfort at all. Just sex."

"I like sex, Alicia." His voice was a harsh lash through the room, so vicious she almost flinched. "I thought I made that clear our first night together. Over and over again."

He wanted to prove he was the monster he said he was. He wanted to prove that he was exactly as bad, as terrifying, as he claimed he was. Capable of killing with nothing more than his thumb. She looked at that cold, set face of his and she could see that he believed it. More—that he simply accepted that this was who he was.

And she found that so terribly sad it almost crippled her.

She got up and went to him without consciously deciding to move. He didn't appear to react, and yet she had the impression he steeled himself at her approach, as if she was as dangerous to him as he was to her. But she couldn't let herself think about that stunning possibility.

Nikolai watched her draw near, his expression even colder. Harder. Alicia tilted her head back and looked into his extraordinary eyes, darker now than usual as he stared back at her with a kind of defiance, as if he was prepared to fight her until she saw him as he saw himself.

Until she called him a monster, too.

"Do you want to know what I think?" she asked.

"I'm certain I don't."

It was a rough scrape of sound, grim and low, but she thought she saw a kind of hunger in his eyes that had nothing to do with his sexual prowess and everything to do with that flash of vulnerability she almost thought she'd imagined, and she kept going.

"I think you hide behind all these rules and boundaries, Nikolai." She felt the air in the room go electric, but she couldn't seem to stop herself. "If you tell yourself you're a monster, if you insist upon it and act upon it, you make it true. It's a self-fulfilling prophecy."

And she would know all about that, wouldn't she? Hadn't she spent eight long years doing exactly that herself? That unexpected insight was like a kick in the stomach, but she ignored it, pushing it aside to look at later.

"Believe me," she said then, more fiercely than she'd intended. "I know."

His hands shot out and took her by the shoulders, then pulled her toward him, toward his hard face that was even more lethal, even more fierce than usual. His touch against her bare arms burned, and made her want nothing more than to melt into him. It was too hot. Too dark.

And he was close then, so powerful and furious. *So close.* Winter and need, fire and longing. The air was thick with it. It made her lungs ache.

"Why don't you have the good sense to be afraid of me?" he said in an undertone, as if the words were torn from that deep, black part of him. "What is the matter with you? Why do you *laugh* when anyone else would cry?"

"I don't see any monsters when I look at you, Nikolai," she replied, winning the fight to keep her tone light, her gaze on his, no matter how ravaged he looked. How undone. Or how churned up she felt inside. "I only see a man. I see you."

His hands tightened around her shoulders for a brief

instant, and then he let her go. Abruptly, as if he'd wanted to do the opposite.

As if he couldn't trust himself any more than she could.

"You don't want to play with this particular fire," he warned her, his expression fierce and dark, his gaze drilling holes into her. "It won't simply burn you—it will swallow you whole. That's not a self-fulfilling prophecy. It's an inevitability."

Alicia didn't know what seared through her then, shocking and dark, thrilling to the idea of it. Of truly losing herself in him, in that fire neither one of them could control, despite the fact there was still that panicked part of her—that part of her that wished she'd gone home and done her laundry that night and never met him—that wanted anything but that. And he saw it. All of it.

She had no idea what was happening to her, or how to stop it, or why she had the breathless sense that it was already much too late.

"Get your coat," he growled at her. "I'll take you home."

Alicia blinked, surprised to find that she was unsteady on her own feet. And Nikolai was dark and menacing, watching her as if no detail was too small to escape his notice. As if he could see all those things inside of her, the fire and the need. That dark urge to demand he throw whatever he had at her, that she could take it, that she understood him—

Of course you don't understand him, she chided herself. *How could you?*

"That's unnecessary," she said into the tense silence, stiffly, and had to clear the roughness from her voice with a cough.

She straightened her top, smoothed her hands down the sides of her trousers, then stopped when she realized she was fidgeting and he'd no doubt read the anxiety that betrayed the way he did everything else.

"You don't have to take me home," she said when he didn't respond. When he only watched her, his expression brooding and his blue eyes cold. She frowned at him. "This night has been intense enough, I think. I'll get a taxi."

The ride across London—in the backseat of Nikolai's SUV with him taking up too much of the seat beside her because he'd informed her a taxi was not an option—was much like sitting on simmering coals, waiting for the fire to burst free.

Not exactly comfortable, Alicia thought crossly. And as the fever of what had happened between them in his penthouse faded with every mile they traveled, she realized he'd been right to warn her.

She felt scorched through. Blackened around the edges and much too close to simply going up in flames herself, until she very much feared there'd be nothing left of her. A few ashes, scattered here and there.

Had she really stood there thinking she wanted more of this? Anything he had to give, in fact? What *was* the matter with her?

But then she thought of that bleak look in his beautiful eyes, that terrible certainty in his voice when he'd told her what a monster he was, and she was afraid she knew all too well what was wrong with her.

"You can go," she told him, not bothering to hide the tension in her voice as they stood outside the door that led into her building in a narrow alcove stuck between two darkened shops.

Nikolai had walked her to the door without a word, that winter fire roaring all around them both, and now stood close beside her in the chilly December night. Too close beside her. Alicia needed to get inside, lock her doors, take a very long soak in the bath—*something* to sort her head out before she lost whatever remained of her sanity, if not something far worse than that. *She needed him to go.* She dug for her keys in her bag without looking at him, not trusting herself to look away again if she did.

"I'm fine from here. I don't need an escort."

He didn't respond. He plucked the keys from her hand when she pulled them out, and then opened the door with no hesitation whatsoever, waving her inside with a hint of edgy impatience.

It would not be wise to let him in. That was perfectly clear to her.

"Nikolai," she began, and his gaze slammed into her, making her gulp down whatever she might have said.

"I understand that you need to fight me on everything," he said, his accent thicker than usual. "If I wanted to psychoanalyze you the way you did me, I'd say I suspect it makes you feel powerful to poke at me. But I wouldn't get too comfortable with that if I were you."

"I wasn't psychoanalyzing you!" she cried, but he brushed it off as if she hadn't spoken.

"But you should ask yourself something." He put his hand on her arm and hauled her into the building, sent the door slamming shut with the back of his shoulder and then held her there in the narrow hall. "Exactly what do you think might happen if you get what you seem to want and I lose control?"

"I don't want—"

"There are reasons men control themselves," he told her, his face in hers, and she should have been intimidated. She should have been terrified. And instead, all she felt was that greedy pulse of need roll through her. That impossible kick of this jagged-edged joy he brought out in her no matter what she thought she *ought* to feel. "Especially men like me, who stand like wolves in the dark corners of more than just London clubs. You should think about what those reasons are. There are far worse things than a list of demands."

"Like your attempts to intimidate me?" she countered, trying to find her footing when she was so off balance she suspected she might have toppled over without him there to hold her up.

"Why don't you laugh it off?" he asked softly, more a taunt than a question, and she had the wild thought that this might be Nikolai at his most dangerous. Soft and deadly and much too close. His gaze brushed over her face, leaving ice and fire wherever it touched. "No? Is this not funny anymore?"

"Nikolai." His name felt unwieldy against her tongue, or perhaps that was the look in his eyes, spelling out her sure doom in all of that ferocious blue. "I'm not trying to make you lose control."

"Oh, I think you are." He smiled, though it was almost feral and it scraped over her, through her. "But you should make very, very sure that you're prepared to handle the consequences if you succeed. Do you think you are? Right here in this hallway, with a draft under the door and the street a step away? Do you think you're ready for that?"

"Stop threatening me," she bit out at him, but it was a ragged whisper, and he could see into her too easily.

"I don't make threats, Alicia." He leaned in closer and nipped at her neck, shocking her. Making her go up in flames. And flinch—or was that simply an electric charge? "You should think of that, too."

And then he stepped away and jerked his head in an unspoken demand that she lead him up the stairs. And Alicia was so unsteady, so chaotic inside, so unable to process all the things that had happened tonight—what he'd said, what she'd felt, that deep ache inside of her, that fire that never did anything but burn hotter—that she simply marched up the stairs to the flat she shared with Rosie on the top floor without a word of protest.

He didn't ask if she wanted him inside when they reached her door, he simply strode in behind her as if he owned the place, and the insanity of it—of *Nikolai Korovin* standing there *in her home*—was so excruciating it was like pain.

"I don't want you here," she told him as he shut her door behind him, the sound of the latch engaging and locking him inside with her too loud in her ears. "I didn't invite you in."

"I didn't ask."

He was still dressed in black, and that very darkness made him seem bigger and more lethal as he walked inside, his cold gaze moving over the cheerful clutter that was everywhere. Bright paperbacks shoved haphazardly onto groaning shelves, photographs in colorful frames littering every surface, walls painted happy colors and filled with framed prints of famous art from around the world. Alicia tensed, expecting Rosie to pad into view at any moment, but the continuing stretch of silence suggested she was out. *Thank God.*

"It's messy," she said, aware she sounded defensive. "We never quite get around to cleaning it as we should. Of course, we also don't have a household staff."

"It looks like real people live here," he replied, frowning at one of Rosie's abandoned knitting projects, and it took her a moment to understand that this, too, was a terribly sad thing to say.

That ache in her deepened. Expanded. Hurt.

Alicia tossed her keys on the table in the hall, her coat over the chair, and then followed Nikolai warily as he melted in and out of the rooms of the flat like a shadow.

"What are you looking for?" she asked after a few minutes of this.

"There must be a reason you're suicidally incapable of recognizing your own peril when you see it," he said, his eyes moving from place to place, object to object, taking everything in. Cataloging it, she thought. Examining every photograph the way he did every dish left in the sink, every pair of shoes kicked aside in the hall, and the spine of every book piled on the overstuffed bookshelves. "Perhaps there are environmental factors at play."

He moved past the kitchen off to the right and stood at the far end of the hall that cut down the middle of the flat, where the bedrooms were.

"And what would those be, do you think?" she asked, her voice tart—which felt like a vast improvement. Or was perhaps a response to what had sounded like the faintest hint of that dark humor of his. It was absurd how much she craved more of it. "Fearlessness tucked away in the walls like asbestos?"

Nikolai didn't answer her, he only sent one of those simmering looks arrowing her way down the hallway, as effective from a few feet away as it was up close. And almost as devastating.

Alicia blew out a breath when he opened the door to her bedroom, the aftershocks of that winter-blue look shifting into something else again. A kind of nervous anticipation. He looked inside for a long moment, and her heart raced. She wished, suddenly, that she'd had the presence of mind to prevent this. She didn't like the fact that he knew, now, that she favored all those silly, self-indulgent throw pillows, piled so high on her bed, shouting out how soft and breakable she really was. They felt like proof, somehow—and when he looked back at her it was hard to stand still. To keep from offering some kind of explanation.

"A four-poster bed." It could have been an innocent comment. An observation. But the way he looked at her made her knees feel weak. "Intriguing."

Alicia thought she understood then, and somehow, that eased the relentless pulse of panic inside.

"Let me guess." She leaned her hip against the wall and watched him. "The faster you puzzle me out, the less you think you'll have to worry about losing this control of yours."

"I don't like mysteries."

"Will it make you feel safe to solve whatever mystery you think I am, Nikolai? Is that what this is?"

The look he gave her then did more than simply *hurt*. It ripped straight down into the center of her, tearing everything she was in two, and there was nothing she could do but stand there and take it.

"I'm not the one who believes in safety, Alicia," he said softly. "It's nothing more than a fairy tale to me. I never had it. I wouldn't recognize it." His expression was hard and bleak. Almost challenging. "The next time you tally up my scars, keep a special count of those I got when I was under the age of twelve. That knife was only one among many that drew my blood. My uncle used the back of his hand if I was lucky." His beautiful mouth twisted, and her heart dropped to her feet. "But I was never very lucky."

He stood taller then. Almost defiant. And it tore at her. She felt her eyes heat in a way that spelled imminent tears and knew she couldn't let herself cry for this hard, damaged man. Not where he could see it. She knew somehow that he would never forgive her.

"Don't waste your pity on me." His voice was cold, telling her she'd been right. No sympathy allowed. No compassion. He sounded almost insulted when he continued, as if whatever he saw on her face was a slap. "Eventually,

I learned how to fight back, and I became more of a monster than my uncle ever could have been."

"We're all monsters," she told him, her voice harsh because she knew he wouldn't accept anything softer. Hoping against hope he'd never know about that great tear inside of her that she could feel with every breath she took, rending her further and further apart. "Some of us actually behave like monsters, in fact, rather than suffer through the monstrous actions of others. No one escapes their past unscathed."

"What would you know about it, Alicia?" His gaze was cold, his tone a stinging lash. "What past misdeeds could possibly haunt you while you're tucked up in your virginal little bedroom, laughing your way through your cheery, happy life? What blood do you imagine is on your hands?"

And so she told him.

Alicia had never told a soul before, and yet she told Nikolai as easily as if she'd shared the story a thousand times. Every detail she could remember and all the ones she couldn't, that her father had filled in for her that awful morning. All of her shame, her despicable actions, her unforgivable behavior, without garnishment or pretense. As if that tear in her turned her inside out, splayed there before him.

And when she was finished, she was so light-headed she thought she might sag straight down to the floor, or double over where she stood.

"Everyone has ghosts," she managed to say, crossing her arms over her chest to keep herself upright.

Nikolai turned away from her bedroom door and moved toward her, thrusting his hands into the pockets of his trousers as he did. It made him look more dangerous, not less. It drew her attention to the wide strength of his shoulders, the long, lethal lines of his powerful frame. It made her wonder how anyone could have hurt him so badly when he'd been small that he'd felt he needed to transform himself into so sharp, so deadly a weapon. It made her feel bruised to the core that he'd no doubt look at her now the way her father had....

His eyes burned as they bored into hers, and he let out one of those low laughs that made her stomach tense.

"That doesn't sound like any ghost," he said, his voice dark and sure. "It sounds like an older man who took advantage of a young girl too drunk to fight him off."

Alicia jolted cold, then flashed hot, as he turned her entire life on end that easily. She swayed where she stood.

"No," she said, feeling desperate, as some great wave of terror or emotion or *something* rolled toward her. "My father said—"

"Your father should have known better than to speak to you like that." Nikolai scowled at her. "News flash, Alicia. Men who aren't predators prefer to have sex with women who are capable of participating."

Her head was spinning. Her stomach twisted, and for a panicked moment she thought she might be sick. She felt his words—so matter-of-fact, as if there could be no other interpretation of that night, much less the one that she'd held so close all these years—wash through her, like a quiet and devastating tsunami right there in her own hallway.

"What's his name?" Nikolai asked, in that soft, lethal way of his that lifted the hairs at the back of her neck. "The man who did these things to you? Does he still live next door to your parents?"

He was the first person she'd told. And the only one to defend her.

Alicia couldn't understand how she was still standing upright.

"That doesn't sound like a question a monster would ask," she whispered.

"You don't know what I'd do to him," he replied, that dark gleam in his gaze.

And he looked at her like she was important, not filthy. Not a whore. Like what had happened had been done to *her,* and hadn't been something *she'd* done.

Like it wasn't her fault after all.

She couldn't breathe.

His gaze shifted from hers to a spot down at the other end of the flat behind her, and she heard the jingling of keys in the hall outside. She felt as if she moved through sticky syrup, as if her body didn't understand what to do any longer, and turned around just as Rosie pushed her way inside.

Rosie sang out her usual hello, slinging her bags to the floor. Nikolai stepped closer to Alicia's back, then reached around to flatten his hand against the waistband of her trousers before pulling her into his bold heat. Holding her to his chest as if they were lovers. Claiming her.

"What...?" Alicia whispered, the sizzle of that unexpected touch combining with the hard punch of the revolution he'd caused inside of her, making her knees feel weak.

"I told you we were taking this public," he replied, his voice a low rumble pitched only to her that made her shiver helplessly against him. "Now we have."

Rosie's head snapped up at the sound of his voice. Her mouth made a perfect, round O as if the devil himself stood there behind Alicia in the hall, no doubt staring her down with those cold winter eyes of his. And then she dropped the bottle of wine she'd been holding in her free hand, smashing it into a thousand pieces all over the hall floor.

Which was precisely how Alicia felt.

Nikolai stared out at the wet and blustery London night on the other side of his penthouse's windows while he waited for the video conference with Los Angeles to begin. His office was reflected in the glass, done in imposing blacks and burgundies, every part of it carefully calculated to trumpet his wealth and power without him having to say a word to whoever walked in. The expensive view out of all the windows said it for him. The modern masterpieces on the walls repeated it, even louder.

It was the sort of thing he'd used to take such pleasure in. The application of his wealth and power to the most innocuous of interactions, the leverage it always afforded him. War games without a body count. It had been his favorite sport for years.

But now he thought only of the one person who seemed as unimpressed with these trappings of wealth and fame as she did with the danger he was well aware he represented. Hell, *exuded*. And instead of regaining his equilibrium the more time he spent with Alicia, instead of losing this intense and distracting interest in her the more he learned about her, he was getting worse.

Much worse. Incomprehensibly worse. And Nikolai knew too well what it felt like to spiral. He knew what obsession tasted like. *He knew.*

She was a latter-day version of his favorite drink, sharp and deadly. And he was still nothing but a drunk where she was concerned.

He'd ordered himself not to hunt down the man who had violated her, though he knew it would be easy. Too easy. The work of a single phone call, an internet search.

You are not her protector, he told himself over and over. *This is not your vengeance to take.*

He'd sparred for hours with his security team in his private gym, throwing them to the floor one after the next, punching and kicking and flipping. He'd swum endless laps in his pool. He'd run through the streets of London in the darkest hours of the night, the slap of the December weather harsh against his face, until his lungs burned and his legs shook.

Nothing made the slightest bit of difference. Nothing helped.

She'd all but pushed him out her front door that night, past her gaping flatmate and the wine soaking into her floorboards, her eyes stormy and dark, and he'd let her.

"Rosie calls me *Saint Alicia* and I *like* it," she'd whispered fiercely to him, shoving him into the narrow hall outside her flat. She'd been scolding him, he'd realized. He wasn't sure he'd ever experienced it before. His uncle had preferred to use his belt. "It's better than some other things I've been called. But you looming around the flat will be the end of that."

"Why?" he'd asked lazily, those broken, jagged things moving around inside of him, making him want things he couldn't name. Making him want to hurt anyone who'd dared hurt her, like she was his. "I like saints. I'm Russian."

"Please," she'd scoffed. "You have 'corruptor of innocents' written all over you."

"Then we are both lucky, are we not, that neither one of us is innocent," he'd said, and had enjoyed the heat that had flashed through her eyes, chasing out the dark.

But by the next morning, she'd built her walls back up, and higher than before. He hadn't liked that at all, though he'd told himself it didn't matter. It shouldn't matter. He told himself that again, now.

It was the end result he needed to focus on: Veronika. The truth about Stefan at long last, and the loose thread she represented snipped off for good. Whatever he suffered on the way to that goal would be worth it, and in any case, Alicia would soon be nothing but a memory. One more instrument he'd use as he needed, then set aside.

He needed to remember that. There was only a week left

before the ball. Nikolai could handle anything for one last week, surely. He'd certainly handled worse.

But she was under his skin, he knew, no matter how many times he told himself otherwise. No matter how fervently he pretended she wasn't.

And she kept clawing her way deeper, like a wound that wouldn't scar over and become one more thing he'd survived.

He'd picked her up to take her to the Tate Modern on the opening night of some desperately chic exhibit, which he'd known would be teeming with London's snooty art world devotees and their assorted parasites and photographers. It wasn't the kind of place a man took a woman he kept around only for sex. Taking a woman to a highly intellectual and conceptual art exhibit suggested he might actually have an interest in her thoughts.

It was a perfect place for them to be "accidentally spotted," in other words. Nikolai hadn't wanted to dig too deeply into his actual level of interest in what went on inside her head. He hadn't wanted to confront himself.

Alicia had swung open the door to her flat and taken his breath that easily. She'd worn a skimpy red dress that showed off her perfect breasts and clung to her curves in mouthwatering ways he would have enjoyed on any woman, and deeply appreciated on her—and yet he'd had the foreign urge to demand she hide all of her lush beauty away from the undeserving public. That she keep it for him alone. He'd been so startled—and appalled—at his line of thought that he'd merely stood there, silent and grim, and stared at her as if she'd gone for his jugular with one of her wickedly high shoes.

Alicia had taken in the black sweater with the high collar he wore over dark trousers that, he'd been aware, made him look more like a commando than an appropriately urbane date to a highly anticipated London art exhibit.

Not that commandos wore cashmere, in his experience.

"Have you become some kind of spy?" she'd asked him, in that dry way that might as well have been her hands on his sex. His body hadn't been at all conflicted about how he should figure her out. It had known exactly what it wanted.

When it came to Alicia, he'd realized, it always did.

"You must be confusing me for the character my brother plays in movies," he'd told her dismissively, and had fought to keep himself from simply leaning forward and pressing his mouth to that tempting hollow between her breasts, then licking his way over each creamy brown swell until he'd made them both delirious and hot. He'd almost been able to taste her from where he stood in the doorway.

Alicia had pulled on her coat from the nearby chair and swept her bag into her hand. She hadn't even been looking at him as she stepped out into the hall and turned to lock her door behind her.

"Your brother plays you in his Jonas Dark films," she'd replied in that crisp way of hers that made his skin feel tight against his bones. "A disaffected kind of James Bond character, stretched too thin on the edge of what's left of his humanity, yet called to act the hero despite himself."

Nikolai had stared at her when she'd turned to face him, and she'd stared back, that awareness and a wary need moving across her expressive face, no doubt reflecting his own. Making him wish—

But he'd known he had to stop. He'd known better from the first with her, hadn't he? He should have let her fall to the floor in that club. He'd known it even as he'd caught her.

"I'm no hero, Alicia," he'd said, sounding like sandpaper and furious that she'd pushed him off balance again. Hadn't he warned her what would happen? Was that what she wanted? She didn't know what she was asking—but he did. "Surely you know this better than anyone."

She'd looked at him for a long moment, her dark gaze shrewd, seeing things he'd always wanted nothing more than to hide.

"Maybe not," she'd said. "But what do you think would happen if you found out you were wrong?"

And then she'd turned and started down the stairs toward the street, as if she hadn't left the shell of him behind her, hollow and unsettled.

Again.

Nikolai saw his own reflection in his office windows now, and it was like he was someone else. He was losing control and he couldn't seem to stop it. He was as edgy and paranoid and dark as he'd been in those brutal days after he'd quit drinking. Worse, perhaps.

Because these things that raged in him, massive and uncontrollable and hot like acid, were symptoms of a great thaw he knew he couldn't allow. A thaw she was making hotter by the day, risking everything. Oceans rose when glaciers melted; mountains fell.

He'd destroy her, he knew. It was only a matter of time.

If he was the man she seemed to think he was, the man he sometimes wished he was when she looked at him with all of those things he couldn't name in her lovely dark eyes, he'd leave her alone. Play the hero she'd suggested he could be and put her out of harm's way.

But Nikolai knew he'd never been any kind of hero. Not even by mistake.

CHAPTER SEVEN

NIKOLAI HADN'T HEARD his family nickname in such a long time that when he did, he assumed he'd imagined it.

He frowned at the sleek and oversize computer display in front of him, realizing that he'd barely paid attention to the video conference, which was unlike him. Stranger still, no one remained on his screen but his brother.

Nikolai wasn't sure which was more troubling, his inattention during a business meeting or the fact he'd imagined he'd heard Ivan speak his—

"Kolya?"

That time there was no mistaking it. Ivan was the only person alive who had ever used that name, very rarely at that, and Nikolai was looking right at him as he said it from the comfort of his Malibu house a world away.

It was the first time he'd spoken directly to Nikolai in more than two years.

Nikolai stared. Ivan was still Ivan. Dark eyes narrowed beneath the dark hair they shared, the battered face he'd earned in all of those mixed martial arts rings, clothes that quietly proclaimed him Hollywood royalty, every inch of him the action hero at his ease.

Nikolai would have preferred it if Ivan had fallen into obvious disrepair after turning his back on his only brother so cavalierly. Instead, it appeared that betrayal and delusion suited him.

That, Nikolai reflected darkly, and the woman who'd caused this rift between them in the first place, no doubt.

"What's the matter with you?" Ivan asked in Russian, frowning into his camera. "You've been staring off into space for the past fifteen minutes."

Nikolai chose not to investigate the things that churned in him, dark and heavy, at the way Ivan managed to convey the worry, the disappointment and that particular wariness that had always characterized the way he looked at Nikolai, talked to him, in two simple sentences after so much silence. And yet there was a part of him that wanted nothing more than to simply take this as a gift, take his brother back in whatever way Ivan was offering himself....

But he couldn't let himself go there. Ivan's silence had been a favor to him, surely. He knew where it led, and he wanted nothing to do with that particular prison any longer.

"I'm reeling from shock," he said. "The mighty Ivan Korovin has condescended to address me directly. I imagine I ought to feel festive on such a momentous occasion." He eyed Ivan coolly, and without the faintest hint of *festive*. "I appreciate the show of concern, of course."

Nikolai could have modified his tone, the sardonic slap of it. Instead, he kept his face expressionless, his gaze trained on his brother through the screen. *Your brother is an idiot,* Alicia had said, so emphatically. It felt like encouragement, like her kind hand against his cheek even when she wasn't in the room.

But he didn't want to think about Alicia. She didn't know what he'd done to deserve the things his brother thought of him. And unlike her confession of the sins of others, Nikolai really had done each and every thing Ivan thought he had.

Ivan's mouth flattened and his dark eyes flashed with his familiar temper.

"Two years," he said in that gruff way of his, his long-suffering older brother voice, "and that's what you have to say to me, Nikolai? Why am I not surprised that you've learned nothing in all this time?"

"That's an excellent question," Nikolai replied, his voice so cold he could feel the chill of it in his own chest. "If you wanted me to learn something you should have provided some kind of lesson plan. Picked out the appropriate hair shirts for me to wear, outlined the confessions you expected me to make and at what intervals. But you chose instead to disappear, the way you always do." He shrugged, only spurred on by the flash of guilt and fury he knew too well on his brother's face. "Forgive me if I am not weeping with joy that you've remembered I exist, with as much warning as when you decided to forget it." He paused, then if possible, got icier. *"Brother."*

"Nikolai—"

"You come and you go, Vanya," he said then, giving that darkness in him free rein. Letting it take him over. Not caring that it wasn't fair—what was *fair?* What had ever been *fair?* "You make a thousand promises and you break them all. I stopped depending on you when I was a child. Talk to me or don't talk to me. What is it to me?"

Ivan's face was dark with that same complicated fury—his guilt that he'd left Nikolai years before to fight, his frustrated anger that Nikolai had turned out so relentlessly feral despite the fact he'd rescued him, eventually; even his sadness that this was who they were, these two hard and dangerous men—and Nikolai was still enough his younger brother to read every nuance of that. And to take a kind of pleasure in the fact that despite the passage of all this time, Ivan was not indifferent.

Which, he was aware, meant he wasn't, either.

"One of these days, little brother, we're going to fight this out," Ivan warned him, shoving his hands through his dark hair the way he'd no doubt like to shove them around Nikolai's neck and would have, had this conversation taken place in person. Nikolai felt himself shift into high alert, readying for battle automatically. "No holds barred, the way we should have done two years ago. And when I crush you into the ground, and I will, this conversation will be one of the many things you'll apologize for."

"Is that another promise?" Nikolai asked pointedly, and was rewarded when Ivan winced. "I understand this is your pet fantasy and always has been. And you could no doubt win a fight in any ring, to entertain a crowd. But outside the ring? In real life with real stakes?" Nikolai shook his head. "You'd be lucky to stay alive long enough to beg for mercy."

"Why don't you fly to California and test that theory?" Ivan suggested, his expression turning thunderous. "Or is it easier to say these things when there are computer screens and whole continents to hide behind?"

"You would follow the rules, Vanya," Nikolai said with a certain grim impatience. "You would fight fair, show mercy. This is who you are." He shrugged, everything inside of him feeling too sharp, too jagged. "It will be your downfall."

"Mercy isn't weakness," Ivan growled.

"Only good men, decent men, have the luxury of dispensing it," Nikolai retorted, ignoring the way his brother stared at him. "I wouldn't make that kind of mistake. You might put me on the ground, but I'd sink a knife in you on my way back up. You should remember that while you're issuing threats. I don't fight fair. I fight to survive."

They stared at each other for an uncomfortable moment. Ivan settled back in his chair, crossing his strong arms over his massive chest, and Nikolai sat still and watchful, like the sentry he'd once been.

"Is this about your new woman?" Ivan asked. Nikolai didn't betray his surprise by so much as a twitch of his eyelid, much less a reply. Ivan sighed. "I've seen the papers."

"So I gather."

Ivan studied him for another moment. "She's not your usual type."

"By which you mean vapid and/or mercenary, I presume," Nikolai said coldly. He almost laughed. "No, she's not. But you of all people should know better than to believe the things you read."

Ivan's gaze on his became curiously intent.

"Tabloid games don't always lead where you think they will, brother. You know that."

It was Nikolai's turn to sigh. "And how is your favorite tabloid game gone wrong?" he asked. "Your wife now, if I'm not mistaken. Or so I read in the company newsletter."

"Miranda is fine," Ivan said shortly, and then looked uncomfortable, that guilty look flashing through his dark eyes again. "It was a very private ceremony. No one but the man who married us."

"I understand completely," Nikolai murmured smoothly. "It might have been awkward to have to explain why your only living family member, the acting CEO of your foundation, was not invited to a larger wedding. It might have tarnished your image, which, of course, would cost us all money. Can't have that."

"She's my family, Kolya." Ivan's voice was a hard rumble, his jaw set in that belligerent way of his that meant he was ready to fight. Here and now.

And that really shouldn't have felt like one of his brother's trademark punches, a sledgehammer to the side of the head. It shouldn't have surprised him that Ivan considered that woman his family when he'd so easily turned his back on his only actual blood relation. Or that he was prepared to fight Nikolai—again—to defend her.

And yet he felt leveled. Laid out flat, no air in his lungs.

"Congratulations," he ground out. Dark and bitter. Painful. "I hope your new family proves less disappointing than the original version you were so happy to discard."

Ivan wasn't the only one who could land a blow.

Nikolai watched him look away from the screen, and rub one of his big hands over his hard face. He even heard the breath that Ivan took, then blew out, and knew his brother was struggling to remain calm. That should have felt like a victory.

"I know you feel that I abandoned you," Ivan said after a moment, in his own, painful way. "That everyone did, but in my case, over and over, when you were the most vulnerable. I will always wish I could change that."

Nikolai couldn't take any more of this. Ice floes were cracking apart inside of him, turning into so much water and flooding him, drowning him—and he couldn't allow this to happen. He didn't know where it was heading, or what would be left of him when he melted completely. He only knew it wouldn't be pretty. For anyone. He'd always known that. The closest he'd ever been to *melted* was drunk, and that had only ever ended in blood and regret.

"It's only been two years, Ivan." He tried to pull himself back together, to remember who he was, or at least pretend well enough to end this conversation. "I haven't suddenly developed a host of tender emotions you need to concern yourself with trampling."

"You have emotions, Nikolai. You just can't handle them," Ivan corrected him curtly, a knife sliding in neat and hard. Deep enough to hit bone. His eyes were black and intense, and they slammed into Nikolai from across the globe with all of his considerable power. "You never learned how to have them, much less process them, so your first response when you feel something is to attack. Always."

"Apparently things *have* changed," Nikolai shot back with icy fury. "I wasn't aware you'd followed your wife's example and become no better than a tabloid reporter, making up little fantasies and selling them as fact. I hope the tips of the trade you get in bed are worth the loss of self-respect."

"Yes, Nikolai," Ivan bit out, short and hard. "Exactly like that."

Nikolai muttered dark things under his breath, fighting to keep that flood inside of him under control. Not wanting to think about what his brother had said, or why it seemed to echo in him, louder and louder. Why he had Alicia's voice in his head again, talking about sex and comfort in that maddeningly intuitive way of hers, as if she knew, too, the ways he reacted when he didn't know how to feel.

Did he ever know how to feel?

And Ivan only settled back in his chair, crossing his arms over his chest, and watched Nikolai fall apart.

"I'm the thing that goes bump in the night," Nikolai said through his teeth after a moment or two. "You know this. I've never pretended to be anything else."

"Because our uncle told you so?" Ivan scoffed. "Surely you must realize by now that he was in love with our mother in his own sick way. He hated us both for representing the choice she made, but you—" He shook his head. "Your only sin was in resembling her more than I did."

Nikolai couldn't let that in. He couldn't let it land. Because it was nothing but misdirection and psychological inference when he knew the truth. He'd learned it the hard way, hadn't he?

"I know what I am," he gritted out.

"You like it." Ivan's gaze was hard. No traces of any guilt now. "I think it comforts you to imagine you're an irredeemable monster, unfit for any kind of decent life."

You make it true, Alicia had told him, her dark eyes filled with soft, clear things he hadn't known how to define. *It's a self-fulfilling prophecy.*

"You think it yourself," Nikolai reminded Ivan tightly. "Or did I misunderstand your parting words two years ago?"

"If I thought that," Ivan rumbled at him, "I wouldn't think you could do better than this, would I? But you don't want to accept that, Nikolai, because if you did, you'd have to take responsibility for your actions." He held Nikolai's gaze. "Like a man."

I only see a man, Alicia had told him, her dark gaze serious. *I see you.*

But that wasn't what Nikolai saw. Not in the mirror, not in Alicia's pretty eyes, not in his brother's face now. He saw the past.

He saw the truth.

He'd been nine years old. Ivan had been off winning martial arts tournaments already, and Nikolai had borne the brunt of one of his uncle's drunken rages, as usual.

He'd been lucky the teeth he'd lost were only the last of his milk teeth.

"I can see it in you," his uncle had shouted at him, over and over again, fists flying. "It looks out of your eyes."

He'd towered over Nikolai's bed, Nikolai's blood on his hands and splattered across his graying white shirt. That was the part Nikolai always remembered so vividly, even now—that spray of red that air and time had turned brown, set deep in the grungy shirt that his uncle had never bothered to throw out. That he'd worn for years afterward, like a promise.

His uncle had always kept his promises. Every last one, every time, until his nephews grew big enough to make a few of their own.

"Soon there'll be nothing left," his uncle had warned him, his blue eyes, so much like Nikolai's, glittering. "That thing in you will be all you are."

Ivan hadn't come home for days. Nikolai had thought that his uncle had finally succeeded in killing him, that he'd been dying. By the time Ivan returned and had quietly, furiously, cleaned him up, Nikolai had changed.

He'd understood.

There was nothing good in him. If there had been, his uncle wouldn't have had to beat him so viciously, so consistently, the way he had since Nikolai had come to live with him at five years old.

It was his fault his uncle had no choice but to beat the bad things out.

It was his fault, or someone would have rescued him.

It was his fault, or it would stop. But it wouldn't stop, because that thing inside of him was a monster and eventually, he'd understood then, it would take him over. Wholly and completely.

And it had.

"Nikolai."

Maybe Ivan had been right to sever this connection, he thought now. What did they have between them besides terrible memories of those dark, bloody years? Of course Ivan hadn't protected him, no matter how Nikolai had prayed he might—he'd barely managed to protect himself.

And now he'd made himself a real family, without these shadows. Without all of that blood between them.

"Kolya—"

"I can't tell you how much I appreciate this brotherly talk," Nikolai said, his tone arctic. Because it was the only way he knew to protect Ivan. And if Nikolai could give that to him, he would, for every bruise and cut and broken bone that Ivan had stoically tended to across the years. "I've missed this. Truly."

And then he reached out and cut off the video connection before his brother could say another word. But not before he saw that same, familiar sadness in Ivan's eyes. He'd seen it all his life.

He knew it hurt Ivan that this was who Nikolai was. That nothing had changed, and nothing ever would.

Ivan was wrong. Nikolai *was* changing, and it wasn't for the better. It was a terrible thing, that flood inside him swelling and rising by the second, making all of that ice he'd wrapped himself in melt down much too quickly.

He was changing far more than he should.

Far more than was safe for anyone.

He knew he needed to stop it, he knew how, and yet he couldn't bring himself to do it. At his core, he was nothing but that twisted, evil thing who had earned his uncle's fists.

Because he wasn't ready to give her up. He had a week left, a week of that marvelous smile and the way she frowned at him without a scrap of fear, a week of that wild heat he needed to sample one more time before he went without it forever. He wanted every last second of it.

Even if it damned them both.

Alicia stood in a stunning hotel suite high above the city of Prague, watching it glow in the last of the late-December afternoon, a storybook kingdom brought to life before her. Snow covered the picturesque red rooftops and clung to the spires atop churches and castles, while the ancient River Vltava curved like a sweet silver ribbon through the heart of it. She listened as bells tolled out joyful melodies from every side, and reminded herself—again—that she wasn't the princess in this particular fairy tale, despite appearances to the contrary.

That Nikolai had told her the night he'd met her that it would end in teeth. And tears.

The charity Christmas ball was the following night, where he would have that conversation with his ex-wife at last, and after that it wouldn't matter how perfect Prague looked, how achingly lovely its cobbled streets or its famous bridges bristling with Gothic saints. It didn't matter how golden it seemed in the winter sunset, how fanciful, as if it belonged on a gilded page in an ancient manuscript. She would leave this city as she'd found it, and this agonizing charade would end. Nikolai would get what he wanted and she would get her life back.

She should want that, she knew. She should be thrilled.

If she stuck her head out her door she could hear the low rumble of Nikolai's voice from somewhere else in the great, ornate hotel suite he'd chosen, all golds and reds and plush Bohemian extravagance. He was on a call, taking care of business in that ruthless way of his. Because he didn't allow distractions—he'd told her so himself.

Not foreign cities that looked too enchanted to be real. Certainly not her.

And Alicia was in a room that was twice the size of her flat and a hundred times more lush, one deep breath away from losing herself completely to the things she was still afraid to let herself feel lest she simply explode across the floor like that bottle of wine, practicing her prettiest smile against the coming dark.

None of this was real, she reminded herself, tracing her finger across the cold glass of the window. None of this was hers.

In the end, none of it would matter.

The only thing that would remain of these strange

weeks were the pictures in the tabloids, stuck on the internet forever like her very own scarlet letter. There would be no record of the way she ached for him. There would be no evidence that she'd ever felt her heart tear open, or that long after he'd left that night, she'd cried into her mountain of frilly pillows for a scared little boy with bright blue eyes who'd never been lucky or safe. And for the girl she'd been eight years ago, who only Nikolai had ever tried to defend from an attack she couldn't even remember. No one would know if she healed or not, because no one would know she'd been hurt.

There would only be those pictures and the nonexistent relationship Nikolai had made sure they showed to the world, that she'd decided she no longer cared if her father knew about.

Let him think what he likes, she'd thought.

Alicia had taken the train out for his birthday dinner the previous week, and had sat with her sisters around the table in his favorite local restaurant, pretending everything was all right. The way she always pretended it was.

But not because she'd still been racked with shame, as she'd been for all those years. Instead, she'd realized as she'd watched her father *not* look at her and *not* acknowledge her and she understood at last what had actually happened to her, she'd been a great deal closer to furious.

"Will you have another drink, love?" her mother had asked her innocuously enough, but Alicia had been watching her father. She'd seen him wince at the very idea, as if another glass of wine would have Alicia doffing her clothes in the middle of the King's Arms. And all of that fury and pain and all of those terrible years fused inside of her. She'd been as unable to keep quiet as she'd been when she'd told Nikolai about this mess in the first place.

"No need to worry, Dad," she'd said brusquely. "I haven't

been anywhere close to drunk in years. Eight years to be precise. And would you like to know why?"

He'd stared at her, then looked around at the rest of the family, all of them gaping from him to Alicia and back.

"No need," he'd said sharply. "I'm already aware."

"I was so drunk I couldn't walk," she'd told him, finally. "I take full responsibility for that. My friends poured me into a taxi and it took me ages to make it up to the house from the lane. I didn't want to wake anyone, so I went into the garden and lay down to sleep beneath the stars."

"For God's sake, Alicia!" her father had rumbled. "This isn't the time or place to bring up this kind of—"

"I passed out," she'd retorted, and she'd been perfectly calm. Focused. "I can't remember a single thing about it because I was *unconscious*. And yet when you saw Mr. Reddick helping himself to your comatose daughter, the conclusion you reached was that I was a whore."

There'd been a long, highly charged silence.

"He tried it on with me, too," her older sister had declared at last, thumping her drink down on the tabletop. "Vile pervert."

"I always thought he wasn't right," her other sister had chimed in at almost the same moment. "Always staring up at our windows, peering through the hedge."

"I had no idea," her mother had said urgently then, reaching over and taking hold of Alicia's hand, squeezing it tightly in hers. Then she'd frowned at her husband. "Bernard, you should be ashamed of yourself! Douglas Reddick was a menace to every woman in the village!"

And much later, after they'd all talked themselves blue and teary while her father had sat there quietly, and Douglas Reddick's sins had been thoroughly documented, her father had hugged her goodbye for the first time in nearly a decade. His form of an apology, she supposed.

And much as she'd wanted to rail at him further, she hadn't. Alicia had felt that great big knot she'd carried around inside of her begin to loosen, and she'd let it, because she'd wanted her father back more than she'd wanted to be angry.

She'd have that to carry with her out of her fake relationship. And surely that was something. Only she would know who had helped her stand up for herself eight years later. Only she would remember the things he'd changed in her when this was over. When the smoke cleared.

That was, if the smoke didn't choke her first.

"It's not even real," Alicia had blurted out one night, after a quarter hour of listening to Rosie rhapsodize about what a wedding to a man like Nikolai Korovin might entail, all while sitting on the couch surrounded by her favorite romance novels and the remains of a box of chocolates.

"What do you mean?"

"I mean, it's not real, Rosie. It's for show."

Alicia had regretted that she'd said anything the instant she'd said it. There'd been an odd, twisting thing inside of her that wanted to keep the sordid facts to herself. That hadn't wanted anyone else to know that when it came down to it, Nikolai Korovin needed an ulterior motive and a list of requirements to consider taking her out on a fake date.

Not that she was bitter.

"You're so cynical," Rosie had said with a sigh. "But I'll have you know I'm optimistic enough for the both of us." She'd handed Alicia a particularly well-worn romance novel, with a pointed look. "I know you sneak this off my shelf all the time. I also know that this tough, skeptical little shell of yours is an act."

"It's not an act," Alicia had retorted.

But she'd also taken the book.

If she'd stayed up too late some nights, crouched over

her laptop with her door locked tight, looking through all the photos of the two of them together online, she'd never admit it. If she'd paused to marvel over the way the tabloids managed to find pictures that told outright lies—that showed Nikolai gazing down at her with something that looked like his own, rusty version of affection, for example, or showed him scowling with what looked like bristling protectiveness at a photographer who ventured too close, she'd kept that to herself, too. Because if she'd dared speak of it, she might betray herself—she might show how very much she preferred the tabloid romance she read about to what she knew to be the reality.

And then there was Nikolai.

"Kiss me," he'd ordered her a few days before they'd had to leave for Prague, in that commanding tone better suited to tense corporate negotiations than a bright little café in his posh neighborhood on a Tuesday morning. She'd frowned at him and he'd stared back at her, ruthless and severe. "It will set the scene."

He'd been different these past few days, she'd thought as she'd looked at him over their coffees. Less approachable than he'd been before, which beggared belief, given his usual level of aloofness. He'd been much tenser. Darker. The fact that she'd been capable of discerning the differences between the various gradations of his glacial cold might have worried her, if she'd had any further to fall where this man was concerned.

"What scene?" she'd asked calmly, as if the idea of kissing him hadn't made her whole body tremble with that ever-present longing, that thrill of heat and flame. "There's a wall between us and the street. No one can see us, much less photograph us."

"We live in a digital age, Alicia," he'd said icily. "There are mobile phones everywhere."

Alicia had looked very pointedly at the people at the two other tables in their hidden nook, neither of whom had been wielding a mobile. Then she'd returned her attention to her steaming latte and sipped at it, pretending not to notice that Nikolai had continued to stare at her in that brooding, almost-fierce way.

"They took pictures of us walking here," she'd pointed out when the silence stretched too thin, his gaze was burning into her like hot coals and she'd worried she might break, into too many pieces to repair. "Mission accomplished."

Because nothing screamed *contented domesticity* like an early-morning stroll to a coffee place from Nikolai's penthouse, presumably after another long and intimate night. That was the story the tabloids would run with, he'd informed her in his clipped, matter-of-fact way, and it was guaranteed to drive his ex-wife crazy. Most of Nikolai's women, it went without saying—though her coworkers lined up to say the like daily—were there to pose silently beside him at events and disappear afterward, not stroll anywhere with him as if he *liked* them.

She'd been surprised to discover she was scowling. And then again when he'd stood up abruptly, smoothing down his suit jacket despite the fact it was far too well made to require smoothing of any kind. He'd stared at her, hard, then jerked his head toward the front of the café in a clear and peremptory command before storming that way himself.

Alicia had hated herself for it, but she'd smiled sheepishly at the other patrons in the tiny alcove, who'd eyed Nikolai's little display askance, and then she'd followed him.

He stood in the biting cold outside, muttering darkly into his mobile. Alicia had walked to stand next to him, wondering if she'd lost her spine when she'd felt that giant ripping thing move through her in her flat that night, as if she'd traded it for some clarity about what had happened to her eight years ago. Because she certainly hadn't used it since. She hadn't been using it that morning, certainly. The old, spined Alicia would have let Nikolai storm off as he chose, while she'd sat and merrily finished her latte.

Or so she'd wanted to believe.

Nikolai had slid his phone into a pocket and then turned that winter gaze on her, and Alicia had done her best to show him the effortlessly polite—if tough and slightly cynical—mask she'd tried so hard to wear during what he'd called *the public phase of this arrangement*. Yet something in the way he'd stared down at her that gray morning, that grim mouth of his a flat line, had made it impossible.

"Nikolai…" But she hadn't known what she'd meant to say.

He'd reached over to take her chin in his leather-gloved hand, and she'd shivered though she wasn't cold at all.

"There are paparazzi halfway down the block," he'd muttered. "We must bait the trap, *solnyshka*."

And then he'd leaned down and pressed a very hard, very serious, shockingly swift kiss against her lips.

Bold and hot. As devastating as it was a clear and deliberate brand of his ownership. His possession.

It had blown her up. Made a mockery of any attempts she'd thought she'd been making toward politeness, because that kiss had been anything but, surging through her like lightning. Burning her into nothing but smoldering need, right there on the street in the cold.

She'd have fallen down, had he not had those hard fingers on her chin. He'd looked at her for a long moment that had felt far too intimate for a public street so early in the morning, and then he'd released her.

And she'd had the sinking feeling that he knew exactly

what he'd done to her. Exactly how she felt. That this was all a part of his game. His plan.

"Let me guess what that word means," she'd said after a moment, trying to sound tough but failing, miserably. She'd been stripped down to nothing, achingly vulnerable, and she'd heard it clear as day in her voice. There'd been every reason to suppose he'd read it as easily on her face. "Is it Russian for gullible little fool, quick to leap into bed with a convenient stranger and happy to sell out her principles and her self-respect for any old photo opportunity—"

"Little sun," he'd bit out, his own gaze haunted. Tormented. He'd stared at her so hard she'd been afraid she'd bear the marks of it. She'd only been distantly aware that she trembled, that it had nothing to do with the temperature. He'd raised his hand again, brushed his fingers across her lips, and she'd had to bite back something she'd been terribly afraid was a sob. "Your smile could light up this city like a nuclear reactor. It's a weapon. And yet you throw it around as if it's nothing more dangerous than candy."

Here, now, staring out at the loveliest city she'd ever seen, as night fell and the lights blazed golden against the dark, Alicia could still feel those words as if he'd seared them into her skin.

And she knew it would be one more thing that she'd carry with her on the other side of this. One more thing only she would ever know had happened. Had been real. Had mattered, it seemed, if only for a moment.

She blinked back that prickly heat behind her eyes, and when they cleared, saw Nikolai in the entrance to her room. No more than a dark shape behind her in the window's reflection. As if he, too, was already disappearing, turning into another memory right before her eyes.

She didn't turn. She didn't dare. She didn't know what she'd do.

"We leave in an hour," he said.

Alicia didn't trust herself to speak, and so merely nodded.

And she could feel that harshly beautiful kiss against her mouth again, like all the things she couldn't allow herself to say, all the things she knew she'd never forget as long as she lived.

Nikolai hesitated in the doorway, and she held her breath, but then he simply turned and melted away, gone as silently as he'd come.

She dressed efficiently and quickly in a sleek sheath made of a shimmery green that made her feel like a mermaid. It was strapless with a V between her breasts, slicked down to her waist, then ended in a breezy swell at her knees. It had been hanging in her room when she'd arrived, next to a floor-length sweep of sequined royal blue that was clearly for the more formal ball tomorrow night. And accessories for both laid out on a nearby bureau. She slid her feet into the appropriate shoes, each one a delicate, sensual triumph. Then she picked up the cunning little evening bag, the green of the dress with blues mixed in.

He's bought and paid for you, hasn't he? she asked herself as she walked down the long hall toward the suite's main room, trying to summon her temper. Her sense of outrage. Any of that motivating almost-hate she'd tried to feel for him back in the beginning. *There are words to describe arrangements like this, aren't there? Especially if you're foolish enough to sleep with him....*

But she knew that the sad truth was that she was going to do this, whether she managed to work herself into a state or not. She was going to wear the fine clothes he'd bought her and dance to his tune, quite literally, because she no longer had the strength to fight it. To fight him.

To fight her own traitorous heart.

And time was running out. By Monday it would be as if she'd dreamed all of this. She imagined that in two months' time or so, when she was living her normal life and was done sorting out whatever Nikolai fallout there might be, she'd feel as if she had.

A thought that should have made her happy and instead was like a huge, black hole inside of her, yawning and deep. She ignored it, because she didn't know what else to do as she walked into the lounge. Nikolai stood in front of the flat-screen television, frowning at the financial report, but turned almost before she cleared the entryway, as if he'd sensed her.

She told herself she hardly noticed anymore how beautiful he was. How gorgeously lethal in another fine suit.

Nikolai roamed toward her, his long strides eating up the luxurious carpet beneath his feet, the tall, dark, brooding perfection of him bold and elegant in the middle of so much overstated opulence. Columns wrapped in gold. Frescoed ceilings. And his gaze was as bright as the winter sky, as if he made it daylight again when he looked at her.

There was no possibility that she would survive this in anything like one piece. None at all.

You can fall to pieces next week, she told herself firmly. It would be Christmas. She'd hole up in her parents' house as planned, stuff herself with holiday treats and too much mulled wine, and pretend none of this had ever happened. That *he* hadn't happened to her.

That she hadn't done this to herself.

"Are you ready?" he asked.

"Define ready." She tried to keep her voice light. Amused. Because anything else would lead them to places she didn't want to go, because she doubted she'd come back from them intact. "Ready to attend your exciting whirl of corporate events? Certainly. Ready to be used in my capacity as weapon of choice, aimed directly at your ex-wife's face?" She even smiled then, and it felt almost like the real thing. "I find I'm as ready for *that* as I ever was."

"Then I suppose we should both be grateful that there will be no need for weaponry tonight," he said, in that way of his that insinuated itself down the length of her back, like a sliver of ice. The rest of her body heated at once, inside and out, his brand of winter like a fire in her, still. "This is only a tedious dinner. An opportunity to make the donors feel especially appreciated before we ask them for more money tomorrow."

When he drew close, he reached over to a nearby incidental table and picked up a long, flat box. He held it out to her without a word, his expression serious. She stared at it until he grew impatient, and then he simply cracked open the box himself and pulled out a shimmering necklace. It was asymmetrical and bold, featuring unusually shaped clusters of blue and green gems set in a thick rope that nonetheless managed to appear light. Fun. As fanciful, in its way, as this golden city they stood in.

The very things this man was not.

"I would have taken you for the black diamond sort," Alicia said, her eyes on the necklace instead of him, because it was the prettiest thing she'd seen and yet she knew it would pale next to his stark beauty. "Or other very, very dark jewels. Heavy chunks of hematite. Brooding rubies the color of burgundy wine."

"That would be predictable," he said, a reproving note in his low voice, the hint of that dark humor mixed in with it, making her wish. *Want.*

He slid the necklace into place, cool against her heated skin, his fingers like naked flame. She couldn't help the sigh that escaped her lips, and her eyes flew to his, finally, to find him watching her with that lazy, knowing intensity in his gaze that had been her undoing from the start.

He reached around to the nape of her neck, taking his time fastening the necklace, letting his fingertips dance and tease her skin beneath the cloud of her curls, then smoothing over her collarbone. He adjusted it on her neck, making sure it fell as he wanted it, one end stretched down toward the upper swell of one breast.

Alicia didn't know if he was teasing her or tearing her apart. She could no longer tell the difference.

When he caught her gaze again, neither one of them was breathing normally, and the room around them felt hot and close.

"Come," he said, and she could hear it in his voice. That fire. That need. That tornado that spiraled between them, more and more out of control the longer this went on, and more likely to wreck them both with every second.

And it would, she thought. *Soon.*

Just as he'd warned her.

CHAPTER EIGHT

A GOLD-MIRRORED LIFT delivered them with hushed and elegant efficiency into the brightly lit foyer of the presidential suite in one of Prague's finest hotels, filled with the kind of people who were not required to announce their wealth and consequence because everything they did, said and wore did it for them. Emphatically.

These were Nikolai's people. Alicia kept her polite smile at the ready as Nikolai steered her through the crowd. This was his world, no matter how he looked at her when they were in private. No matter what stories she'd told herself, she was no more than a tourist, due to turn straight back into a pumpkin the moment the weekend was over. And then stay that way, this strange interlude nothing more than a gilt-edged memory.

She could almost feel the heavy stalk beginning to form, like a brand-new knot in her stomach.

Nikolai pulled her aside after they'd made a slow circuit through the monied clusters of guests, into a small seating area near the farthest windows. Outside, in the dark, she could see the magnificence of Prague Castle, thrusting bright and proud against the night. And inside, Nikolai looked down at her, unsmiling, in that way of his that made everything inside of her squeeze tight, then melt.

"I told you this would be remarkably boring, did I not?"

"Perhaps for you," she replied, smiling. "I keep wondering if the American cattle baron is going to break into song at the piano, and if so, if that very angry-looking German banker will haul off and hit him."

His blue eyes gleamed, and she felt the warmth of it all over, even deep inside where that knot curled tight in her gut, a warning she couldn't seem to heed.

"These are not the sort of people who fight with their hands," Nikolai said, the suggestion of laughter in his gaze, on his mouth, lurking in that rough velvet voice of his. "They prefer to go to war with their checkbooks."

"That sounds a bit dry." She pressed her wineglass to her lips and sipped, but was aware of nothing but Nikolai. "Surely throwing a few punches is more exciting than writing checks?"

"Not at all." His lips tugged in one corner. "A fistfight can only be so satisfying. Bruises heal. Fight with money, and whole companies can be leveled, thousands of lives ruined, entire fortunes destroyed in the course of an afternoon." That smile deepened, became slightly mocking. "This also requires a much longer recovery period than a couple of bruises."

Alicia searched his face, wondering if she was seeing what she wanted to see—or if there really was a softening there, a kind of warmth, that made that wide rip in her feel like a vast canyon and her heart beat hard like a drum.

He reached over and traced one of the clever shapes that made up the necklace he'd given her, almost lazily, but Alicia felt the burn of it as if he was touching her directly. His gaze found hers, and she knew they both wished he was.

It swelled between them, bright and hot and more complicated now, that electric connection that had shocked her in that club. It was so much deeper tonight. It poured into every part of her, changing her as it went, making her realize she didn't care what the consequences were any longer. They'd be worth it. Anything would be worth it if it meant she could touch him again.

She couldn't find the words to tell him that, so she smiled instead, letting it all flow out of her. Like a weapon, he'd said. Like candy.

Like love.

Nikolai jerked almost imperceptibly, as if he saw what she thought, what she felt, written all over her. As if she'd said it out loud when she hardly dared think it.

"Alicia—" he began, his tone deeper than usual, urgent and thick, and all of her confusion and wariness rolled into the place where she'd torn in two, then swelled into that ache, making it bloom, making her realize she finally knew what it was....

But then the energy in the suite all around them shifted. Dramatically. There was a moment of shocked silence, then an excited buzz of whispering.

Nikolai's gaze left hers and cut to the entryway, and then, without seeming to move at all, he froze solid. She watched him do it, saw him turn from flesh and blood to ice in a single breath.

It was the first time he'd scared her.

Alicia turned to see the crowd parting before a graceful woman in a deceptively simple black dress, flanked by two security guards. She was cool and aristocratic as she walked into the room, smiling and exchanging greetings with the people she passed. Her dark red hair was swept back into an elegant chignon, she wore no adornment besides a hint of diamonds at her ears and the sparkle of the ring on her hand, and still, she captivated the room.

And had turned Nikolai to stone.

Alicia recognized her at once, of course.

"Isn't that...?"

"My brother's wife. Yes."

Nikolai's tone was brutal. Alicia flicked a worried glance at him, then looked back to the party.

Miranda Sweet, wife of the legendary Ivan Korovin and easily identifiable to anyone with access to Rosie's unapologetic subscription to celebrity magazines, swept through the assembled collection of donors with ease. She said a word or two here, laughed there and only faltered when her gaze fell on Nikolai. But she recovered almost instantly, squaring her shoulders and waving off her security detail, and made her way toward him.

She stopped when she was a few feet away. Keeping a safe distance, Alicia thought, her eyes narrowing. Miranda Sweet was prettier in person, and taller, and the way she looked at Nikolai was painful.

While Nikolai might as well have been a glacier.

Alicia could have choked on the thick, black tension that rose between the two of them, so harsh it made her ears ring. So intense she glanced around to see if anyone else had noticed, but Miranda's security guards had blocked them off from prying eyes.

When she looked back, Nikolai and his brother's wife were still locked in their silent battle. Alicia moved closer to Nikolai's side, battling the urge to step in front of him and protect him from this threat, however unlikely the source.

Then, very deliberately, Nikolai dropped his gaze. Alicia followed it to the small swell of Miranda's belly, almost entirely concealed by her dress. Alicia never would have seen it. She doubted anyone was supposed to see it.

When Nikolai raised his gaze to his sister-in-law's again, his eyes were raw and cold. Alicia saw Miranda swallow. Hard. Nervously, even.

Another terrible moment passed.

Then Miranda inclined her head slightly. "Nikolai."

"Miranda," he replied, in the same tone, so crisp and hard and civil it hurt.

Miranda glanced at Alicia, then back at Nikolai, and something moved across her face.

Fear, Alicia thought, confused. *She's* afraid *of him.*

Miranda hid it almost immediately, though her hand moved to brush against her belly, her ring catching the light. She dropped her hand when she saw Nikolai glance at it.

"He misses you," she said after a moment, obvious conflict and a deep sadness Alicia didn't understand in her voice. "You broke his heart."

"Are you his emissary?"

"Hardly." Miranda looked at Nikolai as if she expected a reply, but he was nothing but ice. "He would never admit that. He'd hate that I said anything."

"Then why did you?" Cold and hard, and Alicia thought it must hurt him to sound like that. To be that terribly frigid.

Miranda nodded again, a sharp jerk of her head. Her gaze moved to Alicia for a moment, as if she wanted to say something, but thought better of it. And then she turned and walked away without another word, her smile in place as if it had never left her.

While Alicia stood next to Nikolai and hurt for him, hard and deep, and all the things he didn't—couldn't—say.

"I take it you weren't expecting her," she said after a while, still watching Miranda Sweet work the party, marveling at how carefree she looked when she'd left a wind chill and subzero temperatures in her wake.

"I should have." Nikolai's gaze was trained on the crowd, dark and stormy. "She often makes appearances at high-level donor events when Ivan is held up somewhere else. It helps bring that little bit of Hollywood sparkle."

He sounded as if he was reporting on something he'd read a long time ago, distant and emotionless, but Alicia knew better. She felt the waves of that bitter chill coming off him, like arctic winds. This was Nikolai in pain. She could feel it inside her own chest, like a vise.

"A bit of a chilly reunion, I couldn't help but notice."

Nikolai shifted. "She believes I tried to ruin her relationship with Ivan."

Alicia frowned up at him. "Why would she think that?"

It took Nikolai a breath to look down, to meet her eyes. When he did, his gaze was the coldest she'd ever seen it, and her heart lurched in her chest.

"Because I did."

She blinked, but didn't otherwise move. "Why?"

A great black shadow fell over him then, leaving him hollow at the eyes and that hard mouth of his too grim. *Grief,* she thought. And something very much like shame, only sharper. Colder.

"Why do I do anything?" he asked softly. Terribly. "Because happiness looks like the enemy to me. When I see it I try to kill it."

Alicia only stared at him, stricken. Nikolai's mouth tugged in one corner, a self-deprecating almost smile that this time was nothing but dark and painful. Total devastation in that one small curve.

"You should be afraid of me, Alicia," he said, and the bleak finality in his voice broke her in two. "I keep warning you."

He turned back to the crowd.

And Alicia followed an instinct she didn't fully understand, that had something to do with that deep ache, that wide-open canyon in her chest she didn't think would ever go away, and the proud, still way he stood next to her, ruthlessly rigid and straight, as if bracing himself for another blow.

Like that brave boy he must have been a lifetime ago, who was never safe. Or lucky. Who had given up all hope.

She couldn't bear it.

Alicia reached over and slid her hand into his, as if it belonged there. As if they fitted together like a puzzle, and she was clicking the last piece into place.

She felt him flinch, but then, slowly—almost cautiously—his long fingers closed over hers.

And then she held on to him with all of her might.

Nikolai hadn't expected Alicia to be quite so good at this, to fill her role so seamlessly tonight, as if she'd been born to play the part of his hostess. As if she belonged right there at his side, the limb he hadn't realized he'd been missing all along, instead of merely the tool he'd planned to use and then discard.

He stood across the room, watching from a distance as she charmed the two men she'd thought might break into a fight earlier. She was like a brilliant sunbeam in the middle of this dark and cold winter's night, outshining his wealthiest donors in all their finery even here, in a luxurious hotel suite in a city renowned for its gleaming, golden, incomparable light.

Nikolai had never seen her equal. He never would again.

She'd held on to his hand. *To him.* Almost ferociously, as if she'd sensed how close he'd been to disappearing right where he stood and had been determined to stand as his anchor. And so she had.

Nikolai couldn't concentrate on his duties tonight the way he usually did, with that single-minded focus that was his trademark. He couldn't think too much about the fact that Ivan had a child on the way, no matter the vows they'd made as angry young men that they would never inflict the uncertain Korovin temper on more innocent children.

He couldn't think of anything but that press of Alicia's palm against his, the tangling of their fingers as if they belonged fused together like that, the surprising strength of her grip.

As if they were a united front no matter the approaching threat—Miranda, the pregnancy Ivan had failed to mention, the donors who wanted to be celebrated and catered to no matter what quiet heartbreaks might occur in their midst, even the ravaged wastes of his own frigid remains of a soul.

She'd held his hand as if she was ready to fight at his side however she could and that simple gesture had humbled him so profoundly that he didn't know how he'd remained upright. How he hadn't sunk to his knees and promised her anything she wanted, anything at all, if she would only do that again.

If she would choose him, support him. Defend him. Protect him.

If she would treat him like a man, not a wild animal in need of a cage. If she would keep treating him like that. Like he really could be redeemed.

As if she hadn't the smallest doubt.

Because if he wasn't the irredeemable monster he'd always believed—if both she and Ivan had been right all along—then he could choose. He could choose the press of her slender fingers against his, a shining bright light to cut through a lifetime of dark. Warmth instead of cold. Sun instead of ice. *He could choose.*

Nikolai had never imagined that was possible. He'd stopped wanting what he couldn't have. He'd stopped *wanting*.

Alicia made him believe he could be the man he might have been, if only for a moment. She made him regret, more deeply than he ever had before, that he was so empty. That he couldn't give her anything in return.

Except, a voice inside him whispered, *her freedom from this.*

From him. From this dirty little war he'd forced her to fight.

Nikolai nearly shuddered where he stood. He kept his eyes trained on Alicia, who looked over her shoulder as if she felt the weight of his stare and then smiled at him as if he really was that man.

As if she'd never seen anything else.

That swift taste of her on a gray and frigid London street had led only to cold showers and a gnawing need inside of him these past few days, much too close to pain. Nikolai didn't care anymore that he hardly recognized himself. That he was drowning in this flood she'd let loose in him. That he was almost thawed through and beyond control, the very thing he'd feared the most for the whole of his life.

He wanted Alicia more. There was only this one last weekend before everything went back to normal. Before he had his answer from Veronika. And then there was absolutely no rational reason he should ever spend another moment in her company.

He'd intended to have her here, in every way he could. To glut himself on her as if that could take the place of all her mysteries he'd failed to solve, the sweet intoxication that was Alicia that he'd never quite sobered up from. He'd intended to make this weekend count.

But she'd let him imagine that he was a better man, or could be. He'd glimpsed himself as she saw him for a brief, brilliant moment, and that changed everything.

You have to let her go, that voice told him, more forcefully. *Now, before it's too late.*

He imagined that was his conscience talking. No wonder he didn't recognize it.

Nikolai took her back to their hotel when the dinner

finally ground to a halt not long after midnight. They stood outside her bedroom and he studied her lovely face, committing it to memory.

Letting her go.

"Nikolai?" Even her voice was pretty. Husky and sweet. "What's the matter?"

He kissed her softly, once, on that very hand that had held his with such surprising strength and incapacitating kindness. It wasn't what he wanted. It wasn't enough. But it would be something to take with him, like a single match against the night.

"You don't need to be here," he said quietly, quickly, because he wasn't sure he'd do it at all if he didn't do it fast. "Veronika will seek me out whether you're with me or not. I'll have the plane ready for you in the morning."

"What are you talking about?" Her voice was small. It shook. "I thought we had a very specific plan. Didn't we?"

"You're free, Alicia." He ground out the words. "Of this game, this blackmail. Of me."

"But—" She reached out to him, but he caught her hand before she could touch him, because he couldn't trust himself. Not with her. "What if I don't particularly want to be free?"

Under any other circumstances, he wouldn't have hesitated. But this was Alicia. She'd comforted him, protected him, when anyone else would have walked away.

When everyone else had.

It wasn't a small gesture to him, the way she'd held his hand like that. It was everything. He had to honor that, if nothing else.

"I know you don't," Nikolai said. He released her hand, and she curled it into a fist. Fierce and fearless until the end. That was his Alicia. "But you deserve it. You deserve better."

And then he'd left her there outside her room without another word, because a good man never would have put her in this position in the first place, blackmailed her and threatened her, forced her into this charade for his own sordid ends.

Because he knew it was the right thing to do, and for her, he'd make himself do it, no matter how little he liked it.

"But I love you," Alicia whispered, knowing he was already gone.

That he'd already melted into the shadows, disappeared down the hall, and that chances were, he wouldn't want to hear that anyway.

She stood there in that hall for a long time, outside the door to her bedroom in a mermaid dress and lovely, precarious heels he'd chosen for her, and told herself she wasn't falling apart.

She was fine.

She was in love with a man who had walked away from her, leaving her with nothing but a teasing hint of heat on the back of her hand and that awful finality in his rough, dark voice, but Alicia told herself she was absolutely, perfectly *fine*.

Eventually, she moved inside her room and dutifully shut the door. She pulled off the dress he'd chosen for her and the necklace he'd put around her neck himself, taking extra care with both of them as she put them back with the rest of the things she'd leave behind her here.

And maybe her heart along with them.

She tried not to think about that stunned, almost-shattered look in his beautiful eyes when she'd grabbed his hand. The way his strong fingers had wrapped around hers, then held her tight, as if he'd never wanted to let her go. She tried not to torture herself with the way he'd looked at her across the dinner table afterward, over the sounds of merriment and too much wine, that faint smile in the corner of his austere mouth.

But she couldn't think of anything else.

Alicia changed into the old T-shirt she wore to sleep in, washed soft and cozy over the years, and then she methodically washed her face and cleaned her teeth. She climbed into the palatial bed set high on a dais that made her feel she was perched on a stage, and then she glared fiercely at that book Rosie had given her without seeing a single well-loved sentence.

The truth was, she'd fallen in love when she'd fallen into him at that club.

It had been that sudden, that irrevocable. That deeply, utterly mad. The long, hot, darkly exciting and surprisingly emotional night that had followed had only cemented it. And when he'd let her see those glimpses of his vulnerable side, even hidden away in all that ice and bitter snow, she'd felt it like a deep tear inside of her because she hadn't wanted to accept what she already knew somewhere inside.

Alicia let out a sigh and tossed the paperback aside, sinking back against the soft feather pillows and scowling at the billowing canopy far above her.

She wasn't the too-drunk girl she'd been at twenty-one any longer—and in fact, she'd never been the shameful creature she'd thought she was. Had she tripped and fallen into any other man on that dance floor that night, she would have offered him her embarrassed apologies and then gone straight home to sort out her laundry and carry on living her quiet little life.

But it had been Nikolai.

The fact was, she'd kicked and screamed and moaned about the way he'd forced her into this—but he hadn't. She could have complained. Daniel was a CEO with grand plans for the charity, but he wasn't an ogre. He wouldn't have simply let her go without a discussion; he might not have let her go at all. And when it came down to it, she hadn't even fought too hard against this mad little plan of Nikolai's, had she?

On some level, she'd wanted all of those tabloid pictures with their suggestive captions, because her fascination with him outweighed her shame. And more, because they proved it was real. That the night no one knew about, that she'd tried so hard to make disappear, had really, truly happened.

She'd tasted him in that shiny black SUV, and she'd loved every moment of his bold possession. She'd explored every inch of his beautiful body in that wide bed of his. She'd kissed his scars and even the monster he wore on his chest like a warning. And he'd made her sob and moan and surge against him as if she'd never get enough of him, and then they'd collapsed against each other to sleep in a great tangle, as if they weren't two separate people at all.

All of that had happened. All of it was real.

All of this is real, she thought.

Alicia picked up the paperback romance again, flipping through the well-worn pages to her favorite scene, which she'd read so many times before she was sure she could quote it. She scanned it again now.

Love can't hinge on an outcome. If it does, it isn't love at all, the heroine said directly to the man she loved when all was lost. When he had already given up, and she loved him too much to let him. When she was willing to fight for him in the only way she could, even if that meant she had to fight every last demon in his head herself. *Love is risk and hope and a terrible vulnerability. And it's worth it. I promise.*

"You either love him or you don't, Alicia," she told herself then, a hushed whisper in her quiet room.

And she did.

Then she took a deep breath to gather her courage, swung out of the high bed and went to prove it.

Nikolai sat by the fire in the crimson master bedroom that dominated the far corner of the hotel suite, staring at the flames as they crackled and danced along the grate.

He wished this wasn't the longest night of the year, with all of that extra darkness to lead him into temptation, like one more cosmic joke at his expense. He wished he could take some kind of pride in the uncharacteristic decision he'd made instead of sitting here like he needed to act as his own guard, as if a single moment of inattention would have him clawing at her door like an animal.

He wished most of all that this terrible thaw inside of him wasn't an open invitation for his demons to crawl out and fill every extra, elongated hour with their same old familiar poison.

He shifted in the plush velvet armchair and let the heat of the fire play over his skin, wishing it could warm him inside, where too many dark things lurked tonight, with their sharp teeth and too many scenes from his past.

He hated Prague, happy little jewel of a city that it was, filled to the top of every last spire with all the joyful promises of a better life even the Iron Curtain had failed to stamp out. Anywhere east of Zurich he began to feel the bitter chill of Mother Russia breathing down his neck, her snow-covered nails digging into his back as if she might drag him back home at any moment.

It was far too easy to imagine himself there, struggling to make it through another vicious winter with no end, dreamless and broken and half-mad. Feral to the bone. In his uncle's bleak home in Nizhny Novgorod. In corrupt, polluted, snowbound Moscow with the equally corrupt and polluted Veronika, when he'd been in the military and had thought, for a time, it might save him from himself.

Or, even sadder in retrospect, that Veronika might.

Being in Prague was too much like being back there. Nikolai was too close to the raw and out-of-control creature he'd been then, careening between the intense extremes that were all he'd ever known. Either losing himself in violence or numbing himself however he could. One or the other, since the age of five.

He could feel that old version of him right beneath his skin, making him restless. On edge.

Then again, perhaps it wasn't Prague at all. Perhaps it was the woman on the other side of this hotel suite even now, with her dark eyes that saw more of him than anyone else ever had and that carnal distraction of a mouth.

He was in trouble. He knew it.

This was the kind of night that called for a bottle of something deliberately incapacitating, but he couldn't allow himself the escape. He couldn't numb this away. He couldn't slam it into oblivion. He had to sit in it and wait for morning.

Nikolai scowled at the fire while his demons danced on, bold and sickening and much too close, tugging him back into his dirty past as if he'd never left it behind.

As if he never would.

A scant second before Alicia appeared in his door, he sensed her approach, his gaze snapping to meet hers as she paused on the threshold.

He almost thought she was another one of his demons, but even as it crossed his mind, he knew better. Alicia was too alive, that light of hers beaming into his room as if she'd switched on the lamps, sending all of those things that tortured him in the dark diving for the shadows.

She'd changed out of her formal attire and was standing

there in nothing but an oversized wide-necked T-shirt—a pink color, of course—that slid down her arm to bare her shoulder and the upper slope of one breast. Her curls stood around her head in abandon, and her feet were bare.

Nikolai's throat went dry. The rest of him went hard.

"It's below zero tonight," he barked at her, rude and belligerent. *Desperate*. "You shouldn't be walking around like that unless you've decided to court your own death, in which case, I can tell you that there are far quicker ways to go."

The last time he'd used a tone like that on a woman, she'd turned and run from him, sobbing. But this was Alicia. His strong, fearless Alicia, and she only laughed that laugh of hers that made him want to believe in magic.

When he looked at her, he thought he might.

"I've come to your room wearing almost nothing and your first reaction is to talk about the weather and death," she said in that dry way of hers, and God help him, this woman was worse than all his demons put together. More powerful by far. "Very romantic, indeed. My heart is aglow."

Nikolai stood up then, as if that would ward her off. He didn't know which was worse. That she was standing there with so much of her lush brown skin on display, her lithe and supple legs, that shoulder, even the hint of her thighs—naked and smooth and far too tempting. Or that teasing tone she used, so dry and amused, that set off brushfires inside him.

His body felt as if it was someone else's, unwieldy and strange. He wished he hadn't stripped down to no more than his exercise trousers, low on his hips, the better to while away a sleepless night at war with himself.

There was too much bare flesh in the room now. Too many possibilities. He could only deny himself so much....

He scowled at her, and she laughed again.

"Relax," she said, in that calm, easy way that simultaneously soothed and inflamed him. "*I'm* seducing *you,* Nikolai. You don't have to do anything but surrender."

"You are not seducing me," he told her, all cold command, and she ignored it completely and started toward him as if he hadn't spoken. As if he hadn't said something similar to her what seemed like a lifetime ago. "And I am certainly not surrendering."

"Not yet, no," she agreed, smiling. "But the night is young."

"Alicia." He didn't back away when she roamed even closer, not even when he could see her nipples poking against the thin material of her shirt and had to fight to keep himself from leaning down and sucking them into his mouth, right then and there. "This is the first time in my life I've ever done the right thing deliberately. Some respect, I beg you."

Her smile changed, making his chest feel tight though he didn't know what it meant.

"Tell me what the right thing is," she said softly, not teasing him any longer, and she was within arm's reach now. Warm and soft. *Right there.* "Because I think you and I are using different definitions."

"It's leaving you alone," he said, feeling the stirrings of a kind of panic he thought he'd excised from himself when he was still a child. "The way I should have done from the start."

She eased closer, her scent teasing his nose, cocoa butter and a hint of sugar, sweet and rich and *Alicia.* He was so hard it bordered on agony, and the way she looked up at him made his heart begin to hit at him, erratic and intense, like it wanted to knock him down. Like it wouldn't take much to succeed.

"You vowed you didn't want to sleep with me again," he reminded her, almost savagely. "Repeatedly."

"I'm a woman possessed," she told him, her voice husky and low, washing over him and into him. "Infatuated, even."

He remembered when he'd said those same words to her in that far-off stairwell, when her scent had had much the same effect on him. Her dark eyes had been so wide and anxious, and yet all of that heat had been there behind it, electric and captivating. Impossible to ignore. Just as she was.

Tonight, there was only heat, so much of it he burned at the sight. And he wanted her so badly he was afraid he shook with it. So badly he cared less and less with every passing second if he did.

"I've never had the slightest inclination to behave the way a good man might," he began, throwing the words at her.

"That simply isn't true."

"Of course it is. I keep telling you, I—"

"You've dedicated your life to doing good, Nikolai," she said, cutting him off, her voice firm. "You run a foundation that funds a tremendous amount of charity work. Specifically, children's charities."

"I'm certain bands of activists would occupy me personally if they could pin me down to a single residence or office." He glared at her, his voice so derisive it almost hurt, but he knew he wasn't talking to her so much as the demons in all the corners of the room, dancing there in his peripheral vision. "I take money from the rich and make it into more money. I am the problem."

"Like Robin Hood, then? Who was, as everyone knows, a great villain. Evil to the very core."

"If Robin Hood were a soulless venture capitalist, perhaps," Nikolai retorted, but there was that brilliant heat inside of him, that terrible thaw, and he was on the verge of something he didn't want to face. He wasn't sure he could.

Alicia shook her head, frowning at him as if he was hurting her. He didn't understand that—this was him *not* hurting her. This was him *trying*. Why was he not surprised that he couldn't do that right, either?

"You help people," she said in that same firm, deliberate way, her gaze holding his. "The things you do and the choices you make *help people*. Nikolai, you do the right thing *every single day*."

He didn't know what that iron band was that crushed his chest, holding him tight, making everything seem to contract around him.

"You say that," he growled at her, or possibly it was even a howl, torn from that heart he'd abandoned years ago, "but there is blood on my hands, Alicia. More blood than you can possibly imagine."

She stepped even closer, then picked up his much larger hands in hers. He felt a kind of rumbling, a far-off quake, and even though he knew there was nothing but disaster heading toward him, even though he suspected it would destroy him and her and possibly the whole of the city they stood in, the world, the stars above, he let her.

And he watched, fascinated beyond measure and something like terrified, that tight, hard circle around him pulling tighter and tighter, as she turned each hand over, one by one, and pressed a kiss into the center of each.

The way she'd done for the creature on his chest, that she'd called *pretty*.

She looked up at him again, and her dark eyes were different. Warm in a way he'd never seen before. Sweet and something like admiring. Filled with that light that made him feel simultaneously scraped hollow and carved new.

Shining as if whatever she saw was beautiful.

"I don't see any blood," she said, distinct and direct, her gaze fast to his. "I only see you. I've never seen anything but you."

And everything simply...ended.

Nikolai shattered. He broke. All of that ice, every last glacier, swept away in the flood, the heat, the roaring inferno stretching high into the night, until he was nothing but raw and wild and *that look* she gave him took up the world.

And replaced it with fire. Fire and heat and all of the things he'd locked away for all those bleak and terrible reasons. Color and light, flesh and blood. Rage and need and all of that hunger, all of that pain, all of that sorrow and grief, loss and tragedy. His parents, taken so young. His brother, who should never have had to fight so hard. The uncle who should have cared for them. The army that had broken him down and then built him into his own worst nightmare. Veronika's lies and Stefan's sweet, infant body cradled in his arms, like hope. Every emotion he'd vowed he didn't have, roaring back into him, filling him up, tearing him into something new and unrecognizable.

"You have to stop this," he said, but when it left his mouth it was near to a shout, furious and loud and she didn't even flinch. "You can't be *kind* to a man like me! You don't know what you've done!"

"Nikolai," she said, without looking away from him, without hiding from the catastrophic storm that was happening right there in front of her, without letting go of his hands for an instant or dropping her warm gaze, "I can't be anything else. That's what *you* deserve."

And he surrendered.

For the first time in his life, Nikolai Korovin stopped fighting.

CHAPTER NINE

NIKOLAI DROPPED TO his knees, right there in front of her

For a moment he looked ravaged. Untethered and lost, and then he slid his arms around her hips, making Alicia's heart fall out of her chest, her breath deserting her in a rush. She could feel the storm all around them, pouring out of him, enveloping them both. His hard face became stark, sensual. Fierce.

It all led here. Now. To that look in his beautiful eyes that made her own fill with tears. A fledging kind of joy, pale and fragile.

Hope.

And she loved him. She thought she understood him. So when that light in his eyes turned to need, she was with him. It roared in her too, setting them both alight.

He pulled up the hem of her T-shirt with a strong, urgent hand that shook slightly, baring her to his view, making her quiver in return. And that fire that was always in her, always his, turned molten and rolled through her, making her heavy and needy and almost scared by the intensity of this. Of him. Of these things she felt, storming inside of her.

Her legs shook, and he kissed her once, high on her thigh. She could feel the curve of his lips, that rare smile, and it went through her like a lightning bolt, burning her straight down to the soles of her feet where they pressed into the thick carpet.

And then slowly, so slowly, he peeled her panties down her legs, then tossed them aside.

Alicia heard a harsh sort of panting, and realized it was her.

"Solnyshka," he said, in that marvelous voice of his, darker and harsher than ever, and it thrilled her, making her feel like the sun he thought she was, too bright and hot to bear. "I think you'd better hold on."

He wrapped one strong arm around her bottom and the back of her thighs, and then, using his shoulder to knock her leg up and out of his way, he leaned forward and pressed his mouth against her heat.

And then he licked into her.

It was white-hot ecstasy. Carnal lightning. It seared through her, almost like pain, making her shudder against him and cry out his name. She fisted her hands in his hair, his arms were tight around her to keep her from falling, and she simply went limp against his mouth.

His wicked, fascinating, demanding mouth.

She detonated. Her licked her straight over the edge, and she thought she screamed, lost in a searingly hot, shuddering place where there was nothing left but him and these things he did to her, this wild magic that was only his. *Theirs.*

"Too fast," he rumbled, from far away, but everything was dizzy, confused, and it took her a long breath, then another, to remember who she was. And where.

And then another to understand that he'd flipped them around to spread her out on the deep rug in front of the fire.

"Nikolai," she said, or thought she did, but she lost whatever half-formed thought that might have been, because he was taking up where he'd left off.

He used his mouth again, and his hands. He stroked deep into her core, throwing her straight back into that inferno as if she'd never found release. Soon she was writhing against him, exulting in how he held her so easily, with such confident mastery, and used his tongue, his teeth, even that smile again, like sensual weapons.

Alicia arched up against him, into him. Her hands dug at the carpet below her, and his mouth was an impossible fire, driving her wild all over again, driving her higher and higher, until he sucked hard on the very center of her heat and she exploded all around him once again.

When she came back to herself this time, he was helping her up, letting her stumble against him and laughing as he pulled her T-shirt over her head, then muttering something as he took her breasts in his hands. He tested their weight, groaned out his approval, and then pulled each hard, dark nipple into his mouth.

Lighting the fire in her all over again. Making her burn.

He picked her up and carried her to the bed, following her down and stretching out beside her, sleek and powerful, tattooed and dangerous. He'd rid himself of his trousers at some point and there was nothing between them then.

Only skin and heat. Only the two of them, at last.

For a while, it was enough. They explored each other as if this was the first time, this taut delight, this delicious heat. Alicia traced the bright-colored shapes and lines that made up his monster with her tongue, pressed kisses over his heart, hearing it thunder beneath her. Nikolai stroked his big hands down the length of her back, testing each and every one of her curves as he worshipped every part of her equally.

He didn't speak. And Alicia kissed him, again and again, as if that could say it for her, the word she dared not say, but could show him. With her mouth, her hands. Her kiss, her smile.

They teased the flames, built them slowly, making up for all those lost weeks since the last time they'd touched like this. Until suddenly, it was too much. They were both out of breath and the fire had turned into something darker, more desperate. Hotter by far.

Nikolai reached for the table near his bed and then rolled a condom down his hard length, his eyes glittering on hers, and Alicia almost felt as if he was stroking her that way, so determined and sure. She could feel his touch inside of her, stoking those flames. Making her wild with smoke and heat and need.

Alicia couldn't wait, as desperate to have him inside her again as if she hadn't already found her own pleasure, twice. As if this was new.

Because it felt that way, she thought. It felt completely different from what had gone before, and she knew why. She might have fallen hard for him the night she met him, but she loved the man she knew. The man who had saved her from a prison of shame. This man, who looked at her as if she was a miracle. This man, who she believed might be one himself.

"Kiss me," she ordered him, straddling his lap, pressing herself against his delicious hardness, torturing them both.

He took her face in his hands and then her mouth with a dark, thrilling kiss, making her moan against him. He tasted like the winter night and a little bit like her, and the kick of it rocketed through her, sensations building and burning and boiling her down until she was nothing but his.

His.

The world was his powerful body, his masterful kiss, his strong arms around her that anchored her to him. And she loved him. She loved him with every kiss, every taste. She couldn't get close enough. She knew she never would.

He lifted her higher, up on her knees so she knelt astride him, then held her there. He took her nipple into his mouth again, the sharp pull of it like an electric charge directly into her sex, while his wicked fingers played with the other. Alicia shuddered uncontrollably in his arms, but he held her still, taking his time.

And all the while the hardest part of him was just beneath her, just out of reach.

"Please..." she whispered frantically. "Nikolai, *please*..."

"Unlike you," he said in a voice she hardly recognized, it was so thick with desire, with need, with this mighty storm that had taken hold of them both, "I occasionally obey."

He shifted then, taking her hips in his hands, and then he thrust up into her in a single deep stroke, possessive and sure.

At last.

And for a moment, they simply stared at each other. Marveling in that slick, sweet, perfect fit. Nikolai smiled, and she'd never seen his blue eyes so clear. So warm.

Alicia moved her hips, and his breath hissed out into a curse. And then she simply pleased them both.

She moved on him sinuously, sweetly. She bent forward to taste the strong line of his neck, salt and fire. She made love to him with every part of her, worshipping him with everything she had. She couldn't say the words, not to a man like Nikolai, not yet, but she could show him.

And she did.

Until they were both shuddering and desperate.

Until he'd stopped speaking English.

Until he rolled her over and drove into her with all of his dark intensity, all of that battle-charged skill and precision. She exulted beneath him, meeting every thrust, filled with that ache, that wide-open rift he'd torn into her, that only this—only he—could ever soothe.

And when he sent her spinning off into that wild magic for the third time, he came with her, holding her as if he loved her too, that miraculous smile all over his beautiful face.

At last, she thought.

"You're in love with him, aren't you?"

Alicia had been so lost in her own head, in Nikolai, that she hadn't heard the door to the women's lounge open. It took her a moment to realize that the woman standing next to her at the long counter was speaking to her.

And another moment for what she'd said to penetrate.

Veronika.

The moment stretched out, silent and tense.

Alicia could hear the sounds of the ball, muffled through the lounge's walls. The music from the band and the dull roar of all those well-dressed, elegant people, dancing and eating and making merry in their polite way. She'd almost forgotten that *this* was the reason she was here at all. This woman watching her with that calculating gleam in her eyes, as if she knew things about Alicia that Alicia did not.

There was nothing hard or evil-looking about Veronika, as Alicia had half expected from what little Nikolai had said of her. Her hair cascaded down her back in a tumble of platinum waves. She wore a copper gown that made her slender figure look lithe and supple. Aside from the way she looked at Alicia, she was the picture of a certain kind of smooth, curated, very nearly ageless beauty. The kind that, amongst other things, cost a tremendous amount to maintain and was therefore an advertising campaign in itself.

Alicia told herself there was no need for anxiety. She was wearing that bold, gorgeous blue dress, alive with sequins, that had been waiting for her in her room. It clung to her from the top of one shoulder to the floor, highlighting all of her curves, sparkling with every breath, and until this moment she'd felt beautiful in it. Nikolai had smiled that sexy wolf's smile when he saw her in it, and they'd been late coming here tonight. Very late.

Standing with him in this castle-turned-hotel, dressed for a ball in a gorgeous gown with the man she loved, she'd felt as if she might be the princess in their odd little fairy tale after all.

She'd let herself forget.

"Tell me that you're not so foolish," Veronika said then, breaking the uncomfortable silence. She sounded almost... sympathetic? It put Alicia's teeth on edge. "Tell me you're smart enough to see his little games for what they are."

It was amazing how closely this woman's voice resembled the ones in her head, Alicia thought then. It was almost funny, though she was terribly afraid that if she tried to laugh, she'd sob instead. She was still too raw from last night's intensity. A bit too fragile from a day spent in the aftermath of such a great storm.

She wasn't ready for this—whatever this was.

"If you want to speak to Nikolai," she said when she was certain her tone would be perfectly even, almost blandly polite, "he's in the ballroom. Would you like me to show you?"

"You must have asked yourself why he chose you," Veronika said conversationally, as if this was a chat between friends. She leaned closer to the mirror to inspect her lipstick, then turned to face Alicia. "Look at you. So wholesome. So *real*. A charity worker, of all things. Not his usual type, are you?"

She didn't actually *tell* Alicia to compare the two of them. She didn't have to, as Alicia was well aware that all of Nikolai's previous women had been some version of the one who stood in front of her now. Slender like whippets, ruthlessly so. Immaculately and almost uniformly manicured in precisely the same way, from their perfect hair to their tiny bodies and their extremely expensive clothes. The kind of women rich men always had on their arms, like interchangeable trophies, which was precisely how Nikolai treated them.

Hadn't Alicia told him no one would believe he was interested in her after that kind of parade?

"I can't say I have the slightest idea what his 'type' is," she lied to Veronika. "I've never paid it as much attention as you've seemed to do."

Veronika sighed, as if Alicia made her sad. "He's using you to tell a very specific story in the tabloids. You must know this."

Alicia told herself she didn't feel a chill trickle down her spine, that something raw didn't bloom deep within at that neat little synopsis of the past few weeks of her life. She told herself that while Veronika was partly right, she couldn't know about the rest of it. She couldn't have any idea about the things that truly mattered. The things that were only theirs.

"Or," she said, trying desperately not to sound defensive, not to give any of herself away, "Nikolai is a famous man, and the tabloids take pictures of him wherever he goes. No great conspiracy, no 'story.' I'm sorry to disappoint you."

But she was lying, of course, and Veronika shook her head.

"Who do you think was the mastermind behind Ivan Korovin's numerous career changes—from fighter to Hollywood leading man to philanthropist?" she asked, a razor's edge beneath her seemingly casual tone, the trace of Russian in her voice not nearly as appealing as Nikolai's. "What about Nikolai himself? A soldier, then a security specialist, now a CEO—how do you think he manages to sell these new versions of himself, one after the next?"

"I don't see—"

"Nikolai is a very talented manipulator," Veronika said, with that sympathetic note in her voice that grated more each time Alicia heard it. "He can make you believe anything he wants you to believe." Her gaze moved over Alicia, and then she smiled. Sadly. "He can make you fall in love, if that's what he needs from you."

Alicia stared back at her, at this woman who *smiled* as she listed off all of Alicia's worst fears, and knew that she should have walked away from this conversation the moment it started. The moment she'd realized who Veronika was. Nothing good could come of this. She could already feel that dark hopelessness curling inside of her, ready to suck her in....

But her pride wouldn't let her leave without putting up some kind of fight—without making it clear, somehow, that Veronika hadn't got to her. Even if she had.

"You'll forgive me," she said, holding the other woman's gaze, "if I don't rush to take your advice to heart. I'm afraid the spiteful ex makes for a bit of a questionable source, don't you think?"

She was congratulating herself as she turned for the door. What mattered was that she loved Nikolai, and what she'd seen in him last night and today. What she knew to be true. Not the doubts and fears and possible outright lies this woman—

"Do you even know what this is about?"

Alicia told herself not to turn back around. Not to cede her tiny little bit of higher ground—

But her feet wouldn't listen. They stopped moving of their own accord. She stood there, her hand on the door, and ordered herself to walk through it.

Instead, like a fool, she turned around.

"I try not to involve myself in other people's relationships, past or present," she said pointedly, as if the fact she hadn't left wasn't evidence of surrender. As if the other woman wasn't aware of it. "As it's none of my affair."

"He didn't tell you."

Veronika was enjoying herself now, clearly. She'd dropped the sympathy routine and was now watching Alicia the way a cobra might, when it was poised to strike.

Leave, Alicia ordered herself desperately. *Now.*

Because she knew that whatever Veronika was about to say, she didn't want to hear it.

"Of course he didn't tell you." Veronika picked up her jeweled clutch and sauntered toward Alicia. "I told you, he's very manipulative. This is how he operates."

Alicia felt much too hot, her pulse was so frantic it was almost distracting, and there was a weight in her stomach that felt like concrete, pinning her to the ground where she stood. Making it impossible to move, to run, to escape whatever blow she could feel coming.

She could only stare at Veronika, and wait.

The other woman drew close, never taking her intent gaze from Alicia's.

"Nikolai wants to know if my son is his," she said.

It was like the ground had been taken out from under her, Alicia thought. Like she'd been dropped into a deep, black hole. She almost couldn't grasp all the things that swirled in her then, each more painful than the next.

Not here, she thought, fighting to keep her reaction to herself, and failing, if that malicious gleam in Veronika's eyes was any indication. *You can't deal with this here!*

She would have given anything not to ask the next question, not to give this woman that satisfaction, but she couldn't help herself. She couldn't stop. None of this had ever been real, and she needed to accept that, once and for all. None of this had ever been—nor ever would be—hers.

No matter how badly she wished otherwise. No matter how deeply, how terribly, how irrevocably she loved him.

"Is he?" she asked, hating herself. Betraying herself. "Is your son Nikolai's?"

And Veronika smiled.

Nikolai saw Alicia from the other side of the ballroom, a flash of shimmering blue and that particular walk of hers that he would know across whole cities.

He felt it like a touch. Like she could reach him simply by entering the same room.

Mine, he thought, and that band around his chest clutched hard, but he was almost used to it now. It meant this woman and her smile were his. It meant that odd sensation, almost a dizziness, that he found he didn't mind at all when he looked at her.

It meant this strange new springtime inside of him, this odd thaw.

At some point last night, it had occurred to him that he might survive this, after all.

Nikolai had lost track of how many times they'd come together in the night, the storm in him howling itself out with each touch, each taste of her impossible sweetness. All of her light, his. To bathe in as he pleased.

And in the morning, she'd still been there. He couldn't remember the last time any woman had slept in his bed, and he remembered too well that the first time, Alicia had sneaked away with the dawn.

Daylight was a different animal. Hushed, he thought. Something like sacred. He'd washed every inch of her delectable body in the steamy shower, learning her with his eyes as well as his greedy hands. Then he'd slowly lost his mind when she'd knelt before him on the thick rug outside the glass enclosure, taking him into her mouth until he'd groaned out his pleasure to the fogged-up mirrors.

He didn't think he'd ever get enough of her.

She curled her feet beneath her when she sat on the sofa beside him. Her favorite television program was so embarrassing, she'd claimed, that she refused to name it. She was addicted to cinnamon and licked up every last bit of it from the pastries they'd had at breakfast, surreptitiously wetting her fingertip and pressing it against the crumbs until they were gone. She read a great many books, preferred tea first thing in the morning but coffee later, and could talk, at length, about architecture and why she thought that if she had it to do over again, she might study it at university.

And that was only today. One day of learning her, and he'd barely scratched the surface. Nikolai thought that maybe, this time, he wouldn't have to settle for what he could get. This time, he might let himself want…everything. Especially the things he'd thought for so long he couldn't have, that she handed him so sweetly, so unreservedly, as if they were already his.

Mine, he thought again, in a kind of astonishment that it might be true. That it was even possible. *She's mine.*

Alicia disappeared in the jostling crowd, and when she reappeared she'd almost reached him. Nikolai frowned. She was holding herself strangely, and there was a certain fullness in her eyes, as if she were about—

But then he saw the woman who walked behind her, that vicious little smile on her cold lips and victory in her gaze, and his blood ran cold.

Like ice in his veins and this time, it hurt. It burned as he froze.

"*Privyet,* Nikolai," Veronika purred triumphantly when the two of them finally reached him. As sure of herself as she'd ever been. And as callous. "Look who I discovered. Such a coincidence, no?"

This, he thought, was why he had no business anywhere near a bright creature like Alicia. He'd destroy her without even meaning to do it. He'd already started.

This is who you are, he reminded himself bitterly, and it was worse because he'd let himself believe otherwise. He'd fallen for the lie that he could ever be anything but the monster he was. It only took a glance at Veronika, that emblem of the bad choices he'd made and with whom, to make him see that painful truth.

"Alicia. Look at me."

And when she did, when she finally raised her gaze to his, he understood. It went off inside him like a grenade, shredding him into strips, and that was only the tiniest fraction of the pain, the torment, he saw in Alicia's lovely brown eyes.

Dulled with the pain of whatever Veronika had said to her.

He'd done this. He'd put her in harm's way. He was responsible.

Nikolai had been tested last night. He'd had the opportunity to do the right thing, to imagine himself a good man and then act like one, and he'd failed. Utterly.

All of his demons were right.

Nikolai moved swiftly then, a cold clarity sweeping through him like a wind. He ordered Veronika to make herself scarce, told her he'd come find her later and that she'd better have the answer he wanted, and he did it in Russian so Alicia wouldn't hear the particularly descriptive words he used to get his point across.

"No need," Veronika said, also in Russian, looking satisfied and cruel. He wanted to wring her neck. "I had the test done long ago. You're not the father. Do you want to know who is?" She'd smiled at Nikolai's frigid glare. "I'll have the paperwork sent to your attorney."

"Do that," Nikolai growled, and if there was a flash of pain at another small hope snuffed out, he ignored it. He'd see to it that Stefan was taken care of no matter what, and right now, he had other things to worry about.

He forgot Veronika the moment he looked away. He took Alicia's arm and he led her toward the door, amazed that she let him touch her. When they got to the great foyer, he let her go so he could pull his mobile from his tuxedo jacket and send a quick, terse text to his personal assistant.

"Whatever you're about to say, don't," he told her when she started to speak, not sure he could keep the riot of self-hatred at bay just then. She pressed her lips together and scowled fiercely at the floor, and his self-loathing turned black.

Your first response when you feel something is to attack, Ivan had said. But Nikolai had no idea how to stop. And for the first time since he was a boy, he realized that that sinking feeling in him was fear.

He slipped his mobile back in his pocket, and guided her toward the front of the hotel, not stopping until they'd reached the glass doors that led out through the colonnaded entrance into the December night. Above them, the palatial stairs soared toward the former palace's grand facade, but this entranceway was more private. And it was where his people would meet them and take her away from him. Take her somewhere—anywhere she was safe.

Finally, he let himself look at her again.

She was hugging herself, her arms bare and tight over her body. There was misery in her dark eyes, her full lips trembled, and he'd done this. He'd hurt her. Veronika had hurt *him,* and he'd been well nigh indestructible. Why had he imagined she wouldn't do her damage to something as bright and clean as Alicia, simply to prove she could? She'd probably been sharpening her talons since the first picture hit the tabloids.

This was entirely his fault.

"Your ex-wife is an interesting woman," Alicia said.

"She's malicious and cruel, and those are her better qualities," Nikolai bit out. "What did she say to you?"

"It doesn't matter what she said." There was a torn, thick sound in her voice, and she tilted back her chin as if she was trying to be brave. He hated himself. "Everyone has secrets. God knows, I kept mine for long enough."

"Alicia—"

"I know what it's like to disappoint people, Nikolai," she said fiercely. "I know what it's like to become someone the people you love won't look at anymore, whether you've earned it or not."

He almost laughed. "You can't possibly understand the kind of life I've led. I dreamed about a father who would care about me at all, even one who shunned me for imagined sins."

"Congratulations," she threw at him. "Your pain wins. But a secret is still a—"

"Secrets?" He frowned at her, but then he understood, and the sound he let out then was far too painful to be a laugh. "She told you about Stefan."

And it killed him that Alicia smiled then, for all it was a pale shadow of her usual brightness. That she gave him that kind of gift when he could see how much she hurt.

"Is that his name?"

"He's not mine," he said harshly. "That's what she told me back there. And it's not a surprise. I wanted to be sure."

"But you wanted him to be yours," Alicia said, reading him as she always did, and he felt that band around his chest pull so tight it hurt to breathe, nearly cutting him in half.

"You want to make me a better man than I am," he told her then, losing his grip on that darkness inside of him. "And I want to believe it more than you can imagine. But it's a lie."

"Nikolai—"

"The truth is, even if Stefan was my son, he'd be better off without me." It was almost as if he was angry—as if this was his temper. But he knew it was worse than that. It was that twisted, charred, leftover thing she'd coaxed out of its cave. It was what remained of his heart, and she had to *see*. She had to *know*. "I was drunk most of the five years I thought I was his father. And now I'm—" He shook his head. *"This."*

"You're what?" Her dark eyes were glassy. "Sober?"

He felt that hard and low, like a kick to the gut. He didn't know what was happening to him, what she'd done. He only knew he had to remove her from this—get her to a minimum safe distance where he could never hurt her again, not even by mistake.

"Seeing Veronika made things perfectly clear to me," he told her. "All I will ever do is drag you down until I've stolen everything. Until I've ruined you. I can promise you that." He wanted to touch her, but he wouldn't. He couldn't risk it. "I would rather be without you than subject you to this—this sick, twisted horror show."

He was too close to her, so close he could hear that quick, indrawn breath, so close he could smell that scent of hers that drove him wild, even now.

He was no better than an animal.

Alicia looked at him for a long moment. "Are you still in love with her?" she asked.

"Do I *love* her?" Nikolai echoed in disbelief. "What the hell is *love,* Alicia?"

His voice was too loud. He heard it bouncing back at

him from the polished marble floors, saw Alicia straighten her back as if she needed to stand tall against it. He hated public scenes and yet he couldn't stop. He rubbed his hands over his face to keep himself from punching the hard stone wall. It would only be pain, and it would fade. And he would still be right here. He would still be him.

"Veronika made me feel numb," he said instead, not realizing the truth of it until he said it out loud. Something seemed to break open in him then, some kind of painful knotted box he'd been holding on to for much too long. "She was an anesthetic. And I thought that was better than being alone." He glared at her. "And she didn't love me either, if that's your next question. I was her way out of a dead-end life, and she took it."

"I think that however she's capable of it, she does love you," Alicia argued softly. "Or she wouldn't want so badly to hurt you."

"Yes," he said, his voice grim. "Exactly. That is the kind of love I inspire. A vile loathing that time only exacerbates. A hatred so great she needed to hunt you down and take it out on you. Such are my gifts." He prowled toward Alicia then, not even knowing what he did until she'd backed up against one of the marble columns.

But he didn't stop. He couldn't stop.

"I was told I loved my parents," he said, the words flooding from him, as dark and harsh as the place they'd lived inside him all this time. "But I can't remember them, so how would I know? And I love my brother, if that's what it's called." He looked around, but he didn't see anything but the past. And the demons who jeered at him from all of those old, familiar shadows. "Ivan feels a sense of guilt and obligation to me because he got out first, and I let him feel it because I envy him for escaping so quickly while

I stayed there and rotted. And then I made it my singular goal to ruin the only happiness he'd ever known."

He'd thought he was empty before, but now he knew. This was even worse. This was unbearable, and yet he had no choice but to bear it.

"That's a great brotherly love, isn't it?"

"Nikolai," she said thickly, and she'd lost the battle with her tears. They streaked down her pretty face, each one an accusation, each one another knife in his side. "You aren't responsible for what happened to you as a child. With all the work you do, you can't truly believe otherwise. You *survived*, Nikolai. That's what matters."

And once again, he wanted to believe her. He wanted to be that man she was called to defend. He wanted to be anything other than *this*.

"I've never felt anything like these things I feel for you," he told her then, raw and harsh, so harsh it hurt him, too, and then she started to shake, and that hurt him even more. "That light of yours. The way you look at me—the way you *see* me." He reached out as if to touch her face, but dropped his hand back to his side. "I knew it that first night. I was *happy* when you walked into that conference room, and it terrified me, because do you know what I do with *happy?*"

"You do not kill it," she told him fiercely. "You try, and you fail. Happiness isn't an enemy, Nikolai. You can't beat it up. It won't fight back, and eventually, if you let it, it wins."

"I will suck you dry, tear you down, take everything until nothing remains." He moved closer, so outside himself that he was almost glad that he was so loud, that he was acting like this so she could see with her own eyes what kind of man he was. "Do I love you, Alicia? Is that what this is? This charred and twisted thing that will only bring you pain?"

"I love you," she said quietly. Clearly and distinctly, her

eyes on his. Without a single quaver in her voice. Without so much as a blink. Then she shifted, moved closer. "I love you, Nikolai."

Nikolai stilled. Inside and out. And those words hung in him like stained glass, that light of hers making them glow and shine in a cascade of colors he'd never known existed before.

He thought he almost hated her for that. He told himself he'd rather not know.

He leaned in until her mouth was close enough to kiss, and his voice dropped low. Savage. "Why would you do something so appallingly self-destructive?"

"Because, you idiot," she said calmly, not backing away from him, not looking even slightly intimidated. "*I love you.* There's always a risk when you give someone your heart. They might crush it. But that's no reason not to do it."

He felt as if he was falling, though he wasn't. He only wished he was. He leaned toward her, propping his hands on either side of her head as he had once before, then lowering his forehead until he rested it against hers.

And for a moment he simply breathed her in, letting his eyes fall shut, letting her scent and her warmth surround him.

He felt her hands come up to hold on to him, digging in at his hips with that strong grip that had already undone him once before, and he felt a long shudder work through him.

"This is the part where you run for cover, Alicia," he whispered fiercely. "I told you why I couldn't lose control. Now you know."

He heard her sigh. She tipped back her head, then lifted her hands up to take his face between them. When he opened his eyes, what he saw in her gaze made him shake.

"This is where you save yourself," he ground out at her.

She smiled at him, though more tears spilled from her eyes. She held him as if she had no intention of letting him go. She looked at him as if he was precious. Even now. "And then who saves you?"

CHAPTER TEN

NIKOLAI'S HANDS SLIPPED from the marble column behind her, his arms came around her, and he held her so tightly, so closely, that Alicia wasn't sure she could breathe.

And she didn't care.

He held her like that for a long time.

A member of the hotel staff came over to quietly inquire if all was well, and she waved him away. A trio of black-suited people who could only be part of Nikolai's pack of assistants appeared, and she frowned at them until they backed off.

And outside, in the courtyard of the former palace, it began to snow.

Nikolai let out a long, shaky breath and lifted his head. He kissed her, so soft and so sweet it made her smile.

"If I had a heart, I would give it to you," he said then, very seriously. "But I don't."

She shook her head at him, and kissed him back, losing herself in that for a long time. His eyes were haunted, and she loved him so much she didn't know if she wanted to laugh or cry or scream—it seemed too big to contain.

And he loved her, too. He'd as much as said so. He just didn't know what that meant.

So Alicia would have to show him. Step by step, smile by smile, laugh by laugh, until he got it. Starting now.

"You have a heart, Nikolai," she told him gently, smiling up at that beautifully hard face, that perfectly austere mouth, her would-be Tin Man. "It's just been broken into so many pieces, and so long ago, you never learned how to use it properly."

"You're the only one who thinks so," he said softly.

She reached out and laid her hand on his chest, never looking away from him.

"I can feel it. It's right here. I promise."

"And I suppose you happen to know how one goes about putting back together a critically underused heart, no doubt fallen into disrepair after all these years," he muttered, but his hands were moving slow and sweet up her back and then down her arms to take her hands in his.

"I have a few ideas," she agreed. "And your heart is not a junked-out car left by the side of a road somewhere, Nikolai. It's real and it's beating and you've been using it all along."

He looked over his shoulder then, as if he'd only then remembered where they were. One of his assistants appeared from around the corner as if she'd been watching all along, and he nodded at her, but didn't move. Then he looked out the glass doors, at the snow falling into the golden-lit courtyard and starting to gather on the ground.

"I hate snow," he said.

"Merry Christmas to you, too, Ebenezer Scrooge," Alicia said dryly. She slid an arm around his waist and looked outside. "It's beautiful. A fairy tale," she said, smiling at him, "just as you promised me in the beginning."

"I think you're confused." But she saw that smile of his.

It started in his eyes, made them gleam. "I promised you fangs. And tears. Both of which I've delivered, in spades."

"There are no wolves in a story involving ball gowns, Nikolai. I believe that's a rule."

"Which fairy tale is this again? The ones I remember involved very few ball gowns, and far more darkness." His mouth moved into that crooked curve she adored, but his eyes were serious when they met hers. "I don't know how to be a normal man, Alicia. Much less a good one." His smile faded. "And I certainly don't know how to be anything like good for you."

Alicia smiled at him again, wondering how she'd never known that the point of a heart was to break. Because only then could it grow. And swell big enough to hold the things she felt for Nikolai.

"Let's start with normal and work from there," she managed to say. "Come to Christmas at my parents' house. Sit down. Eat a huge Christmas dinner. Make small talk with my family." She grinned. "I think you'll do fine."

He looked at her, that fine mouth of his close again to grim.

"I don't know if I can be what you want," he said. "I don't know—"

"I want you," she said. She shook her head when he started to speak. "And all you have to do is love me. As best you can, Nikolai. For as long as you're able. And I'll promise to do the same."

It was like a vow. It hung there between them, hushed and huge, with only the falling snow and the dark Prague night as witness.

He looked at her for a long time, and then he leaned down and kissed her the way he had on that London street. Hard and demanding, hot and sure, making her his.

"I can do that," he said, when he lifted his head, a thousand brand-new promises in his eyes, and she believed every one. "I can try."

Nikolai stood facing his brother on a deep blue July afternoon. The California sky arched above them, cloudless and clear, while out beyond them the Pacific Ocean rolled smooth and gleaming all the way to the horizon.

"Are you ready?" Ivan barked in gruff Russian. He wore his game face, the one he'd used in the ring, fierce and focused and meant to be terrifying.

Nikolai only smiled.

"Is this the intimidating trash talk portion of the afternoon?" he asked coolly. "Because I didn't sign up to be bored to death, Vanya. I thought this was a fight."

Ivan eyed him.

"You insist on writing checks you can't cash, little brother," he said. "And sadly for you, I am the bank."

They both crouched down into position, studying each other, looking for tells—

Until a sharp wail cut through the air, and Ivan broke his stance to look back toward his Malibu house and the figures who'd walked out from the great glass doors and were heading their way.

Nikolai did a leg sweep without pausing to think about it, and had the great satisfaction of taking Ivan down to the ground.

"You must never break your concentration, brother," he drawled, patronizingly, while Ivan lay sprawled out before him. "Surely, as an undefeated world champion, you should know this."

Ivan's dark eyes promised retribution even as he jackknifed up and onto his feet.

"Enjoy that, Kolya. It will be your last and only victory."

And then he grinned and slapped Nikolai on the back, throwing an arm over his shoulders as they started toward the house and the two women who walked to meet them.

Nikolai watched Alicia, that smile of hers brighter even than a California summer and her lovely voice on the wind, that kick of laughter and cleverness audible even when he couldn't hear the words.

"You owe him an apology," she'd told him. It had been January, and they'd been tucked up in that frilly pink bedroom of hers that he found equal parts absurd and endearing. Though he did enjoy her four-poster bed. "He's your brother. Miranda is afraid of you, and she still risked telling you how hurt he was."

He'd taken her advice, stilted and uncertain.

And now, Nikolai thought as he drew close to her with his brother at his side, he was learning how to build things, not destroy them. He was learning how to trust.

The baby in Miranda's arm wailed again, and both women immediately made a cooing sort of sound that Nikolai had never heard Alicia make before his plane had landed in Los Angeles. Beside him, Ivan shook his head. And then reached over to pluck the baby from his wife's arms.

"Naturally, Ivan has the magic touch," Miranda said to Alicia with a roll of her eyes, as the crying miraculously stopped.

"How annoying," Alicia replied, her lips twitching.

Nikolai stared down at the tiny pink thing that looked even smaller and more delicate in Ivan's big grip.

"Another generation of Korovins," he said. He caught Miranda looking at him as he spoke, and thought her smile was slightly warmer than the last time. Progress. He returned his attention to Ivan and the baby. "I don't think you thought this through, brother."

"It's terrible, I know," Ivan agreed. He leaned close and

kissed his daughter's soft forehead, contentment radiating from him. "A disaster waiting to happen."

Nikolai smiled. "Only if she fights like you."

Later, after he and Ivan spent a happy few hours throwing each other around and each claiming victory, he found Alicia out on the balcony that wrapped around their suite of rooms. He walked up behind her silently, watching the breeze dance through the cloud of her black curls, admiring the short and flirty dress she wore in a bright shade of canary yellow, showing off all of those toned brown limbs he wanted wrapped around him.

Now. Always.

She gasped when he picked her up, but she was already smiling when he turned her in his arms. As if she could read his mind—and he often believed she could—she hooked her legs around his waist and let him hold her there, both of them smiling at the immediate burst of heat. The fire that only grew higher and hotter between them.

"Move in with me," he said, and her smile widened. "Live with me."

"Here in Malibu in this stunning house?" she asked, teasing him. "I accept. I've always wanted to be a Hollywood star. Or at least adjacent to one."

"The offer is for rain and cold, London and me," he said. He shifted her higher, held her closer.

"This is a very difficult decision," she said, but her eyes were dancing. "Are you sure you don't want to come live with me and Rosie instead? She's stopped shrieking and dropping things when you walk in rooms. And she did predict that the night we met would be momentous. She's a prophet, really."

"Move in with me," he said again, and nipped at her neck, her perfect mouth. He thought of that look on his brother's face, that deep pleasure, that peace. "Marry me, someday. When it's right. Make babies with me. I want to live this life of yours, where everything is multicolored and happiness wins."

And then he said the words, because he finally knew what they meant. She'd promised him he had a heart, and she'd taught it how to beat. He could feel it now, pounding hard.

"I love you, Alicia."

She smiled at him then as if he'd given her the world, when Nikolai knew it was the other way around. She'd lit him up, set him free. She'd given him back his brother, broke him out of that cold, dark prison that had been his life. She was so bright she'd nearly blinded him, all those beautiful colors and all of them his to share, if he liked. If he let her.

"Is that a yes?" He pulled back to look at her. "It's okay if you don't—"

"Yes," she said through her smile. "Yes to everything. Always yes."

She'd loved him when he was nothing more than a monster, and she'd made him a man.

Love hardly covered it. But it was a start.

"Look at you," she whispered, her dark eyes shining. She smoothed her hands over his shoulder, plucking at the T-shirt she'd bought him and made him wear. He'd enjoyed the negotiation. "Put the man in a blue shirt and he changes his whole life."

She laughed, and as ever, it stopped the world.

"No, *solnyshka*," Nikolai murmured, his mouth against hers so he could feel that smile, taste the magic of her laughter, the miracle of the heart she'd made beat again in him, hot and alive and real. "That was you."

* * * * *

BRIDESMAID SAYS, 'I DO!'

BARBARA HANNAY

I wish to remember those who suffered
the devastation of the Queensland floods in
January, 2011. Many homes and lives were lost in
the very places where this story is set.

CHAPTER ONE

IT BEGAN on an everyday, average Monday morning. Zoe arrived at the office punctually at eight forty-five, clutching her takeaway coffee, a necessary comfort when facing the start of the working week. To her surprise, her best friend Bella was already at work.

Bella was usually a bit late, and as she'd just spent another weekend away visiting her father in the country Zoe had expected her to be later than ever. This Monday morning, however, Bella was not only at her desk *early*, but she had a huge grin on her face. *And* she was surrounded by a semicircle of excited workmates.

She was holding out her hand as if she was showing off a new manicure. No big surprise. Bella had a thing for manicures and she often chose very out-there nail polish with an interesting assortment of decorative additions.

But as Zoe drew closer, curious to check out her friend's latest fashion statement, she saw that Bella's nails were painted a subdued and tasteful taupe. And they were *not* the focus of everyone's attention.

The grins and squeals were for a sparkling ring.

On Bella's left hand.

Zoe's cardboard coffee cup almost slipped from her

suddenly weak grasp. She managed to catch it just in time.

She was stunned.

And a bit stung, too.

Struggling to hang on to her smile, she hastily dumped the coffee and her handbag on her desk and hurried over to Bella.

She told herself she was misreading this. Bella couldn't be engaged. Her best friend would most definitely have told her if wedding bells were in the air. Zoe knew for a fact that Bella wasn't even dating anyone at the moment. Together, they'd been commiserating about their date drought, and they'd talked about trying for a double date online.

They'd even considered going on an overseas holiday together—a reconnaissance tour, checking out guys in other countries. Deepening the gene pool, Bella had called it during one of their regular Friday nights together.

Admittedly, for the past three weekends in a row Bella had travelled to her country home on the Darling Downs, and Zoe had been beginning to wonder what the attraction was. Bella had said she was worried about her widowed father, which was totally understandable, as her dad had been in a miserable slump for the past eighteen months ever since her mum died.

Bella had also mentioned her close and supportive neighbours, the Rigbys, and their son, Kent—literally, the boy next door, whom she'd known all her life.

Was something going on with this guy? Had he given Bella this ring?

Bella hadn't breathed a *hint* about a romance with anyone, but it was abundantly clear that the sparkle on her friend's finger was most definitely a diamond. And the name on her lips was…

'Kent Rigby.'

Bella was grinning directly at Zoe now, an expectant light shining in her pretty green eyes.

'Wow!' Zoe managed, squeezing her cheek muscles to make sure she was smiling and not still looking like a stunned mullet. 'You're engaged!'

Bella dipped her head ever so slightly, as if she was trying to read Zoe's reaction, and Zoe cranked her smile another notch while she hunted for the right things to say. 'So—does this mean you and the boy next door have taken the plunge after all?'

She was trying not to sound too surprised, and she *hoped* she looked happy. She certainly didn't want the entire office to realise she was totally clueless about her best friend's romance.

Just in time, she remembered to give Bella a hug, and then she paid due homage to her ring—a solitaire diamond, very tasteful, in a platinum setting, and appropriately delicate for Bella's slim, pale hands.

'It's gorgeous,' Zoe told Bella with genuine honesty. 'It's perfect.'

'Must have cost a bomb,' commented one of the girls behind her in an awed voice.

Eric Bodwin, their boss, arrived then and an awkward hush fell over the office until someone piped up with Bella's happy news.

Eric frowned, dragging his bushy eyebrows low, as if an employee's impending marriage was a huge inconvenience. But then he managed to say 'Congratulations,' with a grunting nod in Bella's direction, before he disappeared into his private den.

He'd never been the type of boss who chatted with

his staff, so everyone was used to his gruffness. Nevertheless, his dampening presence put an end to the morning's excitement.

The semicircle of onlookers melted away. Only Zoe remained, her head so brimming with a thousand questions she was reluctant to go back to her desk. And she couldn't help feeling a tad put out that Bella had never confided in her.

'Are you all right, Zoe?' Bella asked cautiously.

'Of course, I'm fine.' Zoe touched Bella's ring finger. 'I'm stoked about this.'

'But you didn't reply to my text.'

'What text?'

'The one I sent you last night. Just before I left Willara Downs, I texted you with my good news.'

'Oh?' Zoe pulled a sheepish face. 'Sorry, Bell. I took myself to the movies last night, and I turned my phone off. Then I forgot to switch it back on.'

'Must have been a good movie,' Bella said dryly, but she was smiling again.

'It was. A lovely, mushy romance.'

Bella rolled her eyes, but they grinned at each other and Zoe was ridiculously pleased that she hadn't been left out after all.

'Meet me at The Hot Spot at lunchtime?' Bella asked next.

'Absolutely.' The busy little café on the corner was their favourite, and a meeting today was top priority.

Back at her desk, however, Zoe's spirits took another dive as she came to grips with the reality of Bella's startling news. She was losing her best friend. Bella would move back to the country to live with Kent Rigby and that would be the end of her close friendship—their mutual support over office grumbles, their lunchtime chats, their Friday night cocktails and joint shopping sprees.

It was definitely the end of their overseas holiday plans. And it was very puzzling that Bella had never confided in her about Kent. What did that say about their supposedly close friendship?

Glumly, Zoe retrieved her phone from her handbag and flicked it on to find two unread messages—both from Bella.

At 6.35 p.m. last night:

The most amazing thing! Kent and I are engaged. So much to tell you. B xx

And then at 9.00 p.m.:

Where r u? Gotta talk. x

Zoe winced. If she'd been available for a heart-to-heart chat last night, she'd know everything now and perhaps she'd understand how this engagement had happened so quickly.

Instead, she had to get through an entire morning's work before she received a single answer to her thousand and one questions.

'You're getting *married*?'

'Sure.' Kent pitchforked fresh hay into the horse stall, then angled a meaningful glance to his mate Steve who leaned on the rails, watching. 'Why else would I be asking you to be my best man?'

Steve's eyes widened. 'So you're dead-set serious?'

'I'm serious.' Kent grinned. 'Getting married isn't something to joke about.'

'I guess it isn't. It's just that we all thought—' Steve stopped and grimaced.

'You all thought I'd carry on playing the field for ever,' Kent supplied.

'Maybe not for ever.' Steve's grin was sly. 'But heck man, you never gave the impression you were planning to settle down just yet, even though plenty of girls have tried their hardest.'

Kent's jaw tightened as he thrust the pitchfork back into the hay bale. He'd anticipated Steve's surprise— and yeah, maybe his disbelief—but his friend's reaction still rankled. It was true that he'd dated plenty of girls without getting serious. In the past. But those days were over now. He had responsibilities to shoulder.

Steve's ruddy face twisted into a baffled smile, and he scratched at the side of his sunburned neck. 'Crikey.'

'You're supposed to say congratulations.'

'Of course, mate. Goes without saying.' Balancing a booted foot on the rail, Steve leaned into the stall, holding out his hand. His eyes blazed with goodwill. 'Congratulations, Kent. I mean it. Bella's an ace girl. She's terrific. The two of you will be a great team.'

He shook Kent's hand.

'Thanks.'

'I shouldn't have been so surprised,' Steve added, accompanying the words with a shrug. 'It makes sense. You and Bella have always been like—' He held up a hand, displaying his index finger and forefinger entwined.

Kent acknowledged this truth with a nod and a smile. He and Bella Shaw had been born six months apart to families on neighbouring properties. As infants they'd shared a playpen. As youngsters they had joint swimming and riding lessons. They'd gone to school together, travelling into Willara each day on the rattling school bus, swapping the contents of their lunch boxes and sharing the answers to their homework.

From as far back as Kent could remember, their two families had gathered on the banks of Willara Creek for regular barbecues. Their fathers had helped each other with shearing or mustering. Their mothers had swapped recipes, knitting patterns and old wives' tales.

When Kent was just six years old, Bella's dad had saved his life...

And now, with luck, Kent was returning the favour.

He felt OK about it. Honestly, he was happy with the future he and Bella had planned.

Just the same, Kent would have been relieved to get a few things off his chest to Steve. In the past few years his load had mounted steadily.

When his dad had hankered for an early retirement, Kent had taken on the bulk of the farm work. Then Bella's mother had died, and her father, the very man who'd saved his life when he was a kid, had started drinking himself to death. Desperately worried, Kent had helped out there as well, putting in long hours ploughing fields and mending neglected fences.

Bella, of course, had been distraught. She'd lost her mother and now she was likely to lose her father, and if these weren't enough troubles to bear, her family's property was rapidly going down the drain.

A host of heavy emotions was tied up in their decision to marry, but although Kent was tempted to confide in Steve he wouldn't off-load his baggage, not even to his best friend.

'I hear Bella's dad's in a bad way,' Steve said. 'He's been keeping very much to himself and he needs to slow down on his drinking.'

Kent's head shot up. Had Steve guessed things were worse than most people realised?

'Tom has the beginnings of heart failure,' he said slowly.

'That's a worry.'

'It is, but if he looks after himself, he should be OK.'

Steve nodded. 'And once you're his son-in-law, you'll be able to keep a closer eye on him.'

Clearly, Steve thought their decision was reasonable, but then his eyes flashed as he sent Kent a cheeky smirk. 'You and Bella are a sly pair though, keeping this under wraps in a gossipy town like Willara.' He snapped a piece of straw between his fingers and raised his eyebrows. 'So, when's the happy day? I suppose I'll have to wear a penguin suit.'

When Zoe burst into The Hot Spot, Bella was already there, waiting in their favourite corner booth with salad sandwiches and two chai lattes.

'That was the longest morning of my life,' Zoe moaned as she hurled herself into a seat. 'Thanks for getting lunch.'

'It was my turn.'

Reaching across the table, Zoe touched the diamond on Bella's left hand. 'This is real, isn't it? You're properly engaged. I'm not dreaming.'

'It's totally real.' Bella gave a crooked little grin. 'But I must admit I still have to pinch myself.'

'You, too?' Drawing a deep breath to calm her racing thoughts, Zoe asked carefully, 'So...you weren't expecting this engagement?'

'Not really,' Bella said, blushing. 'But it wasn't exactly a surprise either.'

Zoe blinked and gave a helpless flap of her hands.

'I'm sorry, I'm lost already. You're going to have to explain this.' She took a sip of her chai latte, but she was too intent on Bella's response to register the sweet and spicy flavour she usually loved.

'There's not a lot to explain.' Bella tucked a shiny strand of smooth blond hair behind one ear. 'The thing is…even when we were kids there was a lingering suggestion from Kent's and my parents that we might eventually—you know—end up together some day. They teased us when we were little, then toned it down later, but all the time we were growing up it was there in the background as a possibility.'

This was news to Zoe and she couldn't help asking, 'How come you've never mentioned it?'

Bella looked contrite. 'You must think I'm crazy, talking so much about guys without ever really mentioning Kent.'

'You spoke about him, but you said he was just a friend.'

'He was. For ages. We were just…neighbours…and good mates…' Her shoulders lifted in a casual shrug. 'To be honest, I'd never seriously thought about marrying him. But then—'

Zoe leaned closer. 'Is Kent the reason you've headed for home every weekend lately?'

Pink crept into Bella's cheeks and her green eyes took on a touching mistiness as she held out her left hand and admired her ring again. 'It sort of crept up on us. Kent's been so sweet.'

'Oh-h-h…' Watching the dewy smile on Bella's lips, Zoe was overcome by the romantic possibilities of her friend's situation. Her skin turned to goose bumps and she could picture it all: a wonderful, long-term friendship where a couple felt really comfortable with each other, and knew each other inside out—all the good bits and the bad. Then, suddenly, they were hit by a blinding and beautiful truth.

So different from Zoe's soul-destroying experience with Rodney the Rat.

'Out of the blue you just realised you were in love and meant for each other,' she said.

Bella nodded.

'And you definitely know Kent's Mr Right?'

Another nod.

Zoe couldn't believe the way her throat was choking up. 'I thought those blinding flashes of insight only happened in movies, but look at you. This is a real life friends-to-lovers romance!' To her embarrassment, a tear spilled down her cheek.

'So you understand?' Bella's smile was a mixture of sympathy and relief.

'My head's still trying to catch up, but I guess I understand here.' Not caring how melodramatic she looked, Zoe pressed a hand over her heart. 'I'm happy for you, Bell. Truly.'

'Thanks.' In a blink, Bella was out of her chair and the girls were hugging. 'I knew you'd understand.'

'Your dad must be thrilled,' Zoe said when Bella had sat down again.

To her surprise, a flood of colour rushed into Bella's face and then she paled and looked down at the sandwich in front of her. She pulled at a piece of lettuce poking out from the bread. 'Yes, he's very happy,' she said quietly.

Puzzled, and just a little worried by the reaction, Zoe wasn't sure what to say next. Something wasn't right here.

Or was she imagining Bella's tension?

She wondered if Bella's dad had expressed mixed feelings. It would be bittersweet for Mr Shaw to watch his daughter's engagement blossom so soon after his wife's death. He'd miss having her there to share the joy with him.

Zoe thought about her own parents, settled at last, running their little music shop in Sugar Bay and raising her little brother, Toby. After Toby's unexpected arrival when Zoe was fourteen, her mum and dad had undergone a dramatic transformation. By the time she'd started work and Toby was ready for school, they'd given up their nomadic existence, travelling round the country in a second-rate rock band.

But becoming conventional parents hadn't dimmed their love for one another. They'd remained fixed in a crazy love-struck-teenager groove and, although their relationship had always left Zoe feeling on the outside, she couldn't imagine either of them having to manage alone. Not for ages, at any rate.

Poor Mr Shaw...

'Earth to Zoe. Are you there?'

Zoe blinked, and realised Bella had been talking, and by the look of frustration on her face she'd been saying something important. 'Sorry. I—ah—missed what you said.'

Bella sighed and gave a little, heaven-help-me eye roll. 'I said I was hoping you'd be my bridesmaid.'

Zap!

Zoe's heart gave a jolt, like a soldier jumping to attention. She'd been so busy getting her head around Bella's new status as fiancée, she'd given no thought to her actual wedding. But bridesmaid?

Wow!

She had a sudden vision of Bella looking lovely in

white, with a misty veil…and herself in a beautiful bridesmaid's gown…

There'd be bouquets…and handsome guys in formal suits…

She'd never been a bridesmaid.

Warmth flooded her and she felt quite dizzy with excitement. 'I'd love to be your bridesmaid. I'd be totally honoured.'

This was no exaggeration. In fact, Zoe was quite sure Bella could never guess how over-the-top excited she was about this.

She'd heard other girls groan about being bridesmaids. They seemed to look on the honour as a boring chore and they told war stories about having to wear horrible satin gowns in the worst possible colours and styles.

Talk about ungrateful! For Zoe, being a bridesmaid was a wonderful privilege. She would wear anything Bella chose—puce coloured lace or slime-toned velvet—she wouldn't care. Being Bella's bridesmaid was clear, indisputable evidence that she was someone's really close friend.

Finally.

Oh, cringe. Anyone would think she was a total loser.

Well…truth was…she'd actually felt like a loser for much of her childhood. She'd had so few chances to make close friends, because her parents had dragged her all around the country, living—honest to God—in the back of a bus. There'd never been time for her friendships to get off the ground.

Her best effort had been in the fifth grade when the band broke up for a bit and her parents had stayed in Shepparton for almost twelve months. Zoe had become really good friends with Melanie Trotter. But then the band had regrouped and her parents had moved on, and the girls' letter exchange had lasted six months before slowing to a trickle, then, inevitably, dried up.

It wasn't until Zoe started work at Bodwin & North and met Bella that she'd finally had the chance to form the kind of ongoing friendship she'd always longed for. And now, here was the proof—an invitation to be Bella's bridesmaid.

Zoe beamed at Bella. 'Will it be a country wedding?'

'Yes—on the Rigbys' property—Willara Downs.'

'Wow. That sounds utterly perfect.' Ever since her childhood, travelling through endless country towns, Zoe had known a secret yearning to drive through a farm gateway instead of whizzing past. Now, she wouldn't merely be driving through the farm gate, she'd be totally involved in the proceedings.

Wow, again. She could picture Bella's big day so easily—white-covered trestle tables on a homestead veranda. A ceremony beneath an archway of pale pink roses. Male guests with broad shoulders and suntans. Women in pearls.

'So...how many bridesmaids are you planning' She tried to sound casual, which wasn't easy when she was holding her breath. Would she be sharing this honour with six bridesmaids? Hadn't she read somewhere that a celebrity had eighteen attendants—all of them in purple silk?

'Only one,' Bella said calmly as she spooned fragrant froth from the inside of her glass. 'It won't be a big flashy wedding. Just family and close friends. I've never wanted a swarm of bridesmaids.' She smiled. 'I just want you, Zoes. You'll be perfect.'

Perfect. What a wonderful word.

'I'll do everything I can to make the day perfect for *you*,' Zoe said.

There was no question—she would try her utmost to be the *perfect* bridesmaid. She would research her duties and carry them out conscientiously. No bride had ever had a more dedicated wedding attendant. 'So, do we have a date? Is there a time line?'

'Actually, we were thinking about October twenty-first.'

'Gosh, that's only a few weeks away.'

'I know, but Kent and I didn't want to wait.'

How romantic.

Zoe supposed she'd hear the phrase *Kent and I* rather a lot in the next few weeks. She wondered, as she had many times, what it was like to be so deeply in love.

But then another thought struck. Leaning closer, she whispered, 'Bell, you're not pregnant, are you?'

'No, of course not.'

'Just checking, seeing you're in such a rush, in case my bridesmaid's duties involved knitting bootees.'

Bright red in the face, Bella slapped her wrist. 'Shut up, idiot.'

'Sorry.' Zoe smiled. 'Well, a tight deadline can focus the mind wonderfully.'

'It shouldn't be too hard to organise. Everything will happen at the homestead, so we won't need to book a church, or cars or a reception venue, and the local rector is a good friend of the Rigbys.'

'So you only have to buy a wedding dress and order a cake.'

'Yes. Too easy,' Bella said with a laugh, and then as they started on their sandwiches her face grew more serious. 'I've made an appointment with Eric Bodwin. I'll have to resign, because I'll be living at Willara, but

I was also hoping we might be able to arrange time off for you as well, so you can come out and help with all the last minute organising. I don't want to burden Kent with too much of the legwork. But I know the time off would eat into your holiday allowance—'

'That's fine,' Zoe said quickly. 'I'd love a week or so in the country.' She was feeling a bit down at the thought of Bella resigning, but then she grinned. 'As a bonus, I might have a chance to wangle a nice country romance of my own.'

Bella's eyes danced. 'Now that's a thought.'

It wasn't just an idle thought for Zoe. As a young girl, experiencing constant brief tastes of country towns before moving on, she'd developed something of a penchant for the jeans-clad sons of farmers with their muscular shoulders and rolling, loose-hipped strides.

'Mind you,' Bella said, 'I've grown away from country life since I moved to Brisbane.'

'But you're looking forward to going back and settling down as a farmer's wife, aren't you?'

Bella gave her lower lip a slightly troubled chew. 'It will certainly be an adjustment.'

'I think it sounds idyllic,' Zoe said honestly. 'But then I probably have a romanticised idea of life on a farm. I've never actually been on one.'

'Why don't you come home with me next weekend?' Bella suggested with a sudden beaming smile. 'We could go together after work on Friday. It only takes a little over an hour. You can meet Kent and I can show you where we're planning to have the wedding, and you can help me to nut out the details.'

'Wow. That sounds wonderful.'

'Actually, you know how hopeless I am at organis-

ing. I'll probably hand you pen and paper and a list of
phone numbers for caterers.'

'That's OK.' No doubt it was pathetic, but Zoe loved
to feel needed. 'I'd love to come. Are you sure there's
room for me to stay?'

'Of course I'm sure. We won't stay with my dad.
He hasn't been well and he'd get in a stew about clean
sheets and things. We can stay at Willara Downs. The
homestead is huge and Kent's a wonderful host. His parents live in town these days, but they'll probably come
out and you can meet them, too. They'll welcome you
with open arms.'

Again Zoe thought of all the times her parents had
whizzed in and out of country towns when she'd longed
to stay. She'd been constantly looking in from the outside, never really getting to know the locals.

Now, for a short time, for the *first* time, she would
be an insider.

'I'd love that. We can take my car,' she offered, eager
to help any way she could. 'It's so much easier than getting the bus.'

Already, in her head, she was compiling a list of her
bridesmaid's responsibilities. Number one—she would
support Bella and help her to stay calm through the next
nerve-wrangling weeks. Perhaps she would also help
her to address the wedding invitations, and then there
would be a hen night to arrange…and a bridal shower…

It was going to be fabulous. She was determined to
carry out every task to the very best of her ability. Her
aim was nothing less than perfection.

CHAPTER TWO

THE next weekend, fifteen kilometres from Willara Downs, Zoe heard an unmistakable flap, flap, flap coming from her car's rear tyre. Her stomach took a dive. *Not now. Please, no!*

But it was useless to hope. She'd heard that flapping sound too many times in her childhood—her dad had always been changing flat tyres on their bus. Now she knew with sickening certainty that she had no choice but to pull over onto the grassy verge and try to remember what to do.

It wasn't fun to be alone, though, on the edge of an unknown country road at dusk on a Friday evening. Zoe wished she hadn't been so convincing when she'd assured Bella she'd be fine to drive on to Willara Downs by herself, while Bella visited her dad.

Two days ago, Bella's father had been admitted to hospital. Apparently, Kent Rigby had found Mr Shaw in a very bad state and insisted on rushing him in to Willara.

Understandably, Bella had been beside herself with anxiety and Zoe had dropped her in town.

'Kent's not answering his phone, so he's probably out on the farm, but he'll understand if you turn up alone,' Bella had assured her.

'And one of us will come back to pick you up in an hour or so,' Zoe suggested.

'Yes, that will be great.'

And so…after expressing the wish that Mr Shaw was much improved, Zoe had set off happily enough—at least she was driving her own car and she felt at ease behind the wheel. And apart from concern about Mr Shaw's illness, she was dead excited about this weekend away and getting to meet Bella's fiancé… seeing the wedding venue…being part of the planning.

The very last thing she needed was a flat tyre.

Damn.

Briefly, Zoe toyed with the idea of trying the Willara Downs number to see if Kent Rigby could help. But it was such a bad way to start the weekend, to be seen as a useless city chick who wouldn't even *try* to fix a simple problem by herself.

Resigned, she climbed out. The tyre was as flat as a burst balloon, and she went to her boot to hunt for the jack and the thingamabob that loosened the wheel nuts.

Mosquitoes buzzed as she hunted. The jack was, of course, buried under all the luggage—two overnight bags, two make-up bags, two sets of hot rollers.

'You never know, there *might* be a party,' Bella had said.

Now, with their belongings scattered haphazardly on the side of the road, Zoe squatted beside the wheel, positioned the jack and got on with turning its handle.

So far so good…except she didn't really know how high she was supposed to raise the car. And once that was done…she wasn't certain she was strong enough to loosen the wheel nuts. They looked mighty tight. And even if she did get them off, would she be able to tighten them up again?

Zoe's unhelpfully vivid imagination threw up a picture of her car driving off with the back wheel spinning free and bouncing into the bush, while she struggled with an out-of-control steering wheel.

Maybe she *should* try to ring for help.

Standing again, she reached into the car for her handbag. As usual, because she really needed it, her phone had slipped from its handy side pouch to the very bottom of her bag, so she had to feel around among movie tickets, keys, lipsticks, pens, old shopping lists, tissues...

She was still fumbling when she heard the sound of a vehicle approaching. Her spirits lifted. This *might* be nice, friendly country folk only too happy to stop and help her.

The thought was barely formed, however, before Zoe felt a shaft of hot panic. If only she hadn't watched all those horror movies. Here she was—totally alone in the silent, empty bush wondering if the driver was an axe murderer, an escaped prisoner, a rapist.

She made a final, frantic fumble in the bottom of her bag, and her fingers closed around her phone just as a white utility vehicle shot around the curve.

There was only one person in the ute and all she could see was a black silhouette, distinctly masculine. He was slowing down.

Zoe's nervous heart gave a sickening thud as his ute came to a complete stop and he leaned out, one strong, suntanned forearm resting casually on the window's rim.

In panic, she depressed the call button on her phone and glanced quickly at the screen.

No signal. She was out of the network. *Oh, terrific.* There was no hope of a rescue.

'Need a hand?' the driver called.

At least he had a friendly voice—mellow and warm with a hint of good humour.

Zoe gulped, and forced herself to look at him properly. She saw dark, neatly trimmed hair and dark eyes. Not threatening eyes, but genial, friendly, and framed by a handsome face. Nicely proportioned nose, strong jaw and a generous mouth.

Already his door was swinging open, and he stepped out.

He was wearing a crisp blue shirt with long sleeves rolled back from his wrists and pale cream moleskin trousers. His elastic sided riding boots were tan and well polished. Zoe had always fancied that look—clean cut with a hint of cowboy. Surely, an axe murderer wouldn't go to so much trouble?

'I see you've got a flat,' he said, coming towards her with the easy loose gait of a man of the land. 'That's rotten luck.'

He smiled and his eyes were deep, coffee-brown—friendly eyes, with a spark of fun, and with laughter lines fanning from the corners.

In spite of her fears, Zoe couldn't help smiling back at him. 'I've just about got the car jacked up, but I wasn't sure how far I should take it.'

'I'd say you have it just right. The perfect height.'

Perfect. It was fast becoming one of her favourite words.

Suddenly, she couldn't remember why she'd been scared of this fellow. There was something about his smile and about his face that was incredibly, importantly *right*.

In fact…Zoe felt as if a gong had been struck deep inside her, and it took a magnificent effort to force her attention away from this stranger to her problem. 'I was—um—about to tackle the wheel nuts.'

'Would you like a hand with them?' He was smiling again and her skin tingled deliciously. 'If that doesn't offend you.'

'Why would I be offended by an offer of help?' *From a gorgeous man*, she added silently.

He shrugged. 'Thought you might be like my little sister—the independent type. She hates it when guys assume she needs help when she doesn't.'

'Oh, I see.' The mention of his sister relaxed Zoe even further. Actually, she was so relaxed she was practically floating, and she offered him a radiant smile. 'I'd love to say I could manage this tyre on my own, but, to be honest, I'm really not sure I *can* manage. I was just about to phone for help.'

'No need. It won't take long.'

'That's awfully kind of you.' Holding out the wheel thingamajig, she hoped her saviour didn't get grease on his clothes.

Clearly not sharing her concern for his pristine trousers, he hunkered down beside the wheel and began working smoothly and efficiently.

Nice hands, Zoe noticed. He was nice all over, actually. Tall and muscular. Not too lean, not too beefy. She suppressed a little sigh, and told herself she was a fool to feel fluttery over the first country fellow she met. Before this wedding was over she'd meet tons of cute rural guys.

But there was something special about this man, something totally entrancing about the warmth in his brown eyes and the quirk of his smile, a subtle *something* that made her heart dance and her insides shimmy.

Strange she could feel so much when all his attention was focused on her car's rear wheel.

'Now for the spare.' Having loosened the wheel, he was standing up again, and he glanced Zoe's way.

Their gazes linked and…

He went very still. And a new kind of intensity came into his eyes. He stared at Zoe…as if he'd had a shock, a pleasant, yet deeply disturbing shock.

Trapped in his gaze, she could feel her face glowing hot as a bonfire, and she was struck by the weirdest sense that she and this helpful stranger were both experiencing the same awesome rush. Deep tremors—happy and scary at once—as if they had been connected on an invisible wavelength.

This can't be what I think it is.

Back to earth, Zoe.

She realised that the stranger was frowning now and looking upset. Or was he angry? It was hard to tell. His brow was deeply furrowed and he dropped his gaze to the ground and his throat worked as he stared at a dried mud puddle.

Zoe held her breath, unable to speak or even think, and yet incredibly aware that something beyond the ordinary had happened.

Then her rescuer blinked and shook his head, as if he was ridding himself of an unwanted thought. He cleared his throat. 'Ah—the spare tyre. I guess it's in the boot?'

Turning away from Zoe, he made his way to the back of the car, skilfully stepping between the scattered pieces of luggage.

'I'm sorry,' Zoe spluttered, struggling to shake off the unsettling spell that seemed to have gripped her. 'I should have fetched the spare tyre and had it ready for you.'

'No worries.' He spoke casually enough, but when he looked back at her he still seemed upset, as if she'd done something wrong. But then, without warning, he smiled.

His smile was warm and friendly again, and once more Zoe was electrified. Instantly. Ridiculously. She found herself conjuring a picture of him in a farmhouse kitchen, smiling that same yummy smile across the breakfast table at her, after a night of delicious love-making.

Good grief. Next minute she'd be imagining him naked.

Could he guess?

'Excuse me.'

His voice roused her. Blushing, she stepped out of his way as he carried the new wheel and hefted it into position. But, heaven help her, she was mesmerised by the strength of his shoulders and the sureness of his hands as he lined up the wheel as if it weighed no more than a cardboard button, and fitted it into place.

'You've done this before,' she said.

'So many times, I could do it in my sleep.'

Zoe wasn't sure it was wise to let her mind wander in the direction of this man's sleep. Better to keep the talk flowing.

She said, 'I've watched my dad change tyres on country roads enough times. I should have picked up a few more clues.'

He looked up at her, clearly surprised. 'Which country roads? You're not from around here, are you?'

'No. My parents were in a band and they toured all around the various country shows.' She hoped any resentment she felt for those nomadic gypsy years hadn't crept into her voice.

'Which band?' he asked, pausing in the middle of tightening a nut.

'Lead the Way.'

'You're joking.'

Laughing, Zoe shook her head. 'No, I'm afraid I'm serious.'

'Were both your parents in Lead the Way?'

'Yep. My dad was the lead singer and my mum was on drums.'

'So you're Mick Weston's daughter?'

'His one and only.' It wasn't an admission Zoe needed to make very often. Since she'd started work in the city she'd hardly met anyone who'd heard of her parents or their band.

'Amazing.' To her surprise, he threw his head back and laughed. 'Wait till I tell my old man. He's a huge fan of Mick Weston. Never missed a Lead the Way performance in Willara.'

Fancy that. Zoe beamed at him. It was heartening to be reminded that her dad had been very popular out here.

But, heavens, now she and this stranger had something in common and she found herself liking him more than was sensible. Perhaps encouraging conversation wasn't such a bright idea.

She busied herself with securing the punctured tyre in the boot and restowing all the bits and pieces of luggage.

By the time she'd finished, her good Samaritan was removing the jack. 'That's done,' he said, straightening and dusting off his hands.

'Thank you so much. It's incredibly kind of you. I

really am very grateful.' *And just a little sad that we'll have to say goodbye now...*

He stood with his feet apart, hands resting lightly on his hips, watching her with an enigmatic smile. 'What about you?' he asked. 'Do you sing or play the guitar?'

''Fraid not.' Zoe returned his smile—seemed her face was permanently set in smile mode. 'The musical genes totally bypassed me.'

'But you inherited your dad's talent for flat tyres on country roads.'

'Yes...unfortunately.'

Wow. Instead of rushing off, he was making conversation with her. And Zoe loved it. She was no longer bothered that he was a stranger. She was too busy enjoying this amazing experience—the most awesome sensation of being swept high and pumped full of excitement, as if she were riding a magnificent, shining wave.

Were her feet still touching the ground?

She'd never felt like this before. Not with a complete stranger. Not with this bursting-from-a-geyser intensity. Rodney the Rat didn't count. He'd been a work colleague and she'd known him for twelve months before he asked her out.

Truth was—Zoe usually lacked confidence around guys. She guessed it was part of an overall lack of confidence, a problem that stemmed from her childhood when she'd always been the new girl in town, always arriving late in the term when all the friendship groups were firmly established. She'd grown up knowing she'd never quite fitted in.

But this man's gorgeous smile made her feel fabulously confident and suddenly her biggest fear was that he would simply drive away—out of her life.

'I'll tell my dad I met the son of one of his fans,' she told him.

'Do you have far to go?' her helper asked.

'I don't think it's much farther. I'm heading for Willara Downs.'

He stiffened. 'Willara Downs?'

'It's a property near here—a farm.'

'Yes, I know.' Now, he was frowning again. 'It's my property.'

His property?

Really?

A sudden chill swept over Zoe. He wasn't...

He couldn't be...

'You're—you're not—a Rigby, are you?'

'I certainly am.' He smiled, but it was a shade too late, and with only a fraction of its former warmth. 'The name's Kent Rigby.' His smile wavered as he asked uncertainly, 'Should I know you?'

Oh, God, he was Bella's Kent...Bella's boy next door.

Kent's been so sweet, Bella had said.

No wonder he was nice. He was the man her best friend was about to marry.

A cool breeze made icy goose bumps on Zoe's skin. The purple tinged dusk crowded in and she felt suddenly, terribly weary. And wary.

'We haven't met,' she said quietly, hoping she didn't sound as ridiculously disappointed as she felt. 'But we'll soon have a lot to do with each other. I'm Zoe. Bella's bridesmaid.'

Kent Rigby's eyes darkened and his features were momentarily distorted, as if he tried to smile but couldn't quite manage it.

But if he'd been caught out, he was very good at covering it up. 'Sorry, I should have guessed,' he said,

speaking smoothly once more, with no hint of distur-
bance. 'But I expected you to be with Bella.'

Calmly, he held out his hand.

Unhappily, she felt the warmth and strength of his
hand enclose hers in a firm clasp. 'Hello, Kent.'

'Hi, Zoe.'

'I dropped Bella off at the hospital. She tried to call
you to explain that I'd be arriving on my own.'

Kent had forgotten to let go of her hand. 'I'm actually on my way back from seeing Tom myself,' he said.

'How—how is he?'

'Slightly improved, thank God.'

Suddenly he realised he was still holding her hand.
Letting go, he cracked a slightly embarrassed grin, then
thrust his hands into his jeans pockets. He straightened
his shoulders, then looked to the sky in the east where
a huge full moon was already poking its golden head
above a dark, newly ploughed field. 'I guess Bella will
ring when she's ready to be picked up.'

'Yes.'

'We'd better get going, then. Would you like to follow me? I'll keep you in my rear vision, so I'll know
you're OK.'

'Thanks.'

As Zoe followed Kent Rigby's ute she tried to laugh
at herself. What a fool she'd been, getting all hot and
bothered about a stranger she'd met on a road side.

Shouldn't she have guessed that a hot-looking guy
like Kent would have already been taken? Hadn't she
learned anything from her experience with Rodney?

OK, so she was feeling ridiculously disappointed
right now, but she'd get over it. She'd been looking forward to this weekend too much to let anything spoil
it. She'd been so excited about Bella's wedding and

being her bridesmaid. She'd wanted to be the *perfect* bridesmaid.

That was still her goal. Having a fan-girly moment over the bridegroom had been a minor hiccup, but she'd recover in no time.

In the fading light of dusk, which just happened to be Zoe's favourite time of day, the track she and Kent were driving along emerged out of a purple-shadowed tunnel of trees onto sweeping lawns, dusky and magical in the twilight.

Zoe saw an archway of rambler roses and a weeping willow…an elegant, Federation-style house, long and low, with lights already glowing on the veranda.

The car's wheels crunched on white gravel as she pulled up behind Kent's ute in front of smooth sandstone steps flanked by garden beds filled with agapanthus and lilies. When Kent got out, she saw him silhouetted against the backdrop of his home. Damn. It was such an attractive image—but she had to stop thinking like that.

She had no choice. This gorgeous man was Bella's future husband and there was no way she would let her silly imagination give into any more reckless fantasies.

'I'll show you to your room,' Kent said with the gracious charm of a perfect host, which showed that he at least knew exactly what *his* role was.

Zoe followed him down a hallway past an elegant lounge room with deep squishy sofas and rich Oriental rugs to a pretty bedroom that was the epitome of comfort and tasteful country-style décor.

With her things stowed, she was taken out to a wisteria-scented back veranda, and soon found herself sitting in a deep cushion-lined cane chair, sipping chilled white wine while she and Kent looked out in the fading light to the most beautiful view of fields and distant hills.

She suppressed an urge to sigh. Everything about Kent Rigby's home was as gorgeous as he was. And it was all so beautifully presented she supposed he must have a housekeeper and a gardener. Lucky Bella wouldn't be a slave to housework.

As a child, looking out of the bus window, Zoe had dreamed of living in a lovely farmhouse like the Rigbys', but she'd never been the jealous type and she wasn't about to start now.

Very soon Bella would return from the hospital and take her rightful place at Kent Rigby's side. And Zoe's silly road side mistake would be a thing of the past.

Clutching an icy glass of beer as if his life depended on it, Kent struggled to ignore the girl sitting beside him. Not an easy task when he was her host and hospitable manners had been ingrained in him from birth.

Problem was, he was badly rattled and he couldn't really understand how he'd got this way. Anyone would think he wasn't used to meeting new girls—when the truth was quite the opposite.

He could only assume the problem arose because he hadn't adjusted to his newly engaged status. No doubt that would explain the crazy chemistry that had gripped him from the moment he set eyes on Bella's bridesmaid.

Why the hell hadn't he introduced himself to Zoe Weston as soon as he stepped up to help her? If he'd known who she was, he could have avoided those telling moments—those shocking spellbinding seconds when he'd felt drawn to her, as if a bizarre spell had been cast over him.

Chances were, he'd never have noticed her inexplicable appeal, that special *something* in her eyes, and in the sheen of her hair or the tilt of her smile—a quality that rocked his easy-going nature to its very foundations.

How crazy was that? He'd exchanged nothing more than a few glances with her.

Kent knew it was nothing more than an illusion. A mistake. It was more than likely that every man experienced a similar difficulty in his pre-wedding weeks. Commitment to one girl didn't automatically stop a guy from noticing other girls. Learning to ignore their appeal was part of the adjustment to being engaged or married.

In Kent's case, his commitment was binding on all kinds of levels, and there was no going back. No regrets. He was a man of his word.

Besides, if he was rational about this, there wasn't even anything particularly special about Zoe Weston. Her brown hair and blue eyes and slim build were nice enough, but her looks were average. Surely?

The imagined attraction was merely a blip, and now he could put it behind him.

That settled, Kent took a deep, reassuring draft of beer, pleased to realise he'd been overreacting.

It wasn't as easy as Zoe had hoped to relax while sitting beside Kent on his veranda. She found herself crossing and uncrossing her legs, fiddling with the stem of her wine glass, or sneaking sideways glances at her host's stare-worthy profile. Hardly the behaviour of a perfect bridesmaid.

Desperate to stop this nonsense, she jumped to her feet and leaned on the veranda railing, looking out at the parklike sweep of gardens that stretched to a timber fence, and fields of golden crops and grazing animals.

Concentrate on the wedding—not the groom.

Casually, she asked, 'Are you planning a garden wedding, Kent?'

He looked surprised, as if the question had caught him out, but he responded readily enough. 'An outdoor ceremony would be great and the weather forecast is promising. What do you think?'

Rising from his chair, he joined her at the veranda's edge, and once again Zoe was struggling to ignore his proximity. Now there was the tantalising whiff of his cologne to deal with as well.

She concentrated on the lawns and banks of shrubbery. 'A garden wedding would be perfect. Would you hire a caterer?'

'That's one of the things we need to discuss this weekend. But Bella's a bit...distracted.'

'Yes, her dad's health is a big worry for her.'

Kent nodded, then let out a heavy sigh.

'You're worried, too,' Zoe said, seeing the sudden tension in his face.

'I have to be careful what I say around Bella, but I'm angry with her dad.' Kent sighed again. 'Don't get me wrong. Tom Shaw's a wonderful guy. In many ways he's been my hero. But his wife died eighteen months ago and he dropped his bundle. He started drinking heavily, and now he has the beginnings of heart failure.'

'From drinking?'

'From drinking and generally not looking after himself.' Kent's hand fisted against the railing. 'Bella's beside herself, of course.'

'I hadn't realised his health was so bad,' Zoe said with concern. 'Poor Bell.'

'Don't worry.' Kent spoke quietly, but with unmistakable determination. 'I'll look after her. And I'm damned if I'll let Tom kill himself.'

Wow, Zoe thought. Kent had sounded so—so *noble*; he really was Bella's knight in shining armour.

And clearly he was happy in that role. He was turning to Zoe now with a smile. 'Bella said you're going to be a great help with the wedding.'

'I—I'm certainly happy to do all I can to help.'

'She claims you're a fabulous organiser and list-maker.'

'I suppose I can be. I've never organised a wedding, but I quite like planning our office Christmas party. A smallish wedding won't be too different.' To Zoe's dismay, her cheeks had grown very hot. She shot a quick glance out to the expanse of lawn. 'I imagine you'd need to hire tables and chairs.'

'Yes, definitely.'

'And table cloths, crockery, glassware et cetera.'

'I dare say.' Kent flashed a gorgeous crooked smile. 'If you keep talking like that you'll land yourself a job, Zoe.'

And if he kept smiling at her like that she wouldn't be able to refuse.

CHAPTER THREE

IT WAS late on Sunday night before the girls arrived back in Brisbane. As Zoe drove they discussed practical matters—the style of wedding gowns and invitations, and the things they needed to hire for the garden reception. They were both tired, however, and, to Zoe's relief, they spent much of the journey in reflective silence.

She dropped Bella off at her flat in Red Hill, declining her invitation to come in for a drink with the excuse that they both had another Monday morning to face in less than ten hours.

'Thanks for spending the weekend with me,' Bella said as she kissed Zoe's cheek. 'And thanks for offering to help Kent with organising the reception. Well, you didn't actually offer, but thanks for agreeing when I pleaded. We all know I can't organise my way out of a paper bag.'

'That's OK,' Zoe responded glibly, hoping that she sounded much calmer than she felt about ongoing communication with Bella's fiancé—even if it was only via email or telephone.

'And thanks for taking your car, Zoe. So much better than bumping along in the old bus.'

'My pleasure.' However, Zoe couldn't possibly share Bella's opinion on this matter. If she hadn't taken her car, she wouldn't have had a flat tyre and she wouldn't have had a private meeting with Kent. And her week-end would have been a darned sight easier.

'Thanks for inviting me, Bell. It was—wonderful. You're going to have the most gorgeous wedding ever.'

'I know. I'm so lucky.' Bella's green eyes took on a wistful shimmer. 'You do like Kent, don't you?'

Zoe's heart took a dive, but she forced a bright smile. 'Of course. What's not to like? He's lovely. Perfect hus-band material. You should have snapped him up years ago.'

Bella smiled, looking genuinely happy now, as if she'd needed this reassurance. Then she grabbed the straps of her overnight bag, slammed the door and called, 'See you in the morning.'

Zoe watched as Bella hurried up her front steps, pale hair shining in the glow cast by a streetlight, then she drove on, feeling the last of her strength ebb away.

All weekend she'd held herself together—remaining upbeat and excited for Bella's sake, while keeping a lid on her own private turmoil. Dropping any interest in Kent had proved much harder than she'd expected, and now the ordeal was over she was totally drained. She just wanted to crawl into her own little space and let go.

Finally, she reached her flat in Newmarket, let her-self into the kitchen, dumped her bag in the corner.

She loved her little home. For the first time in her life she had a proper place to call home that had four walls instead of four wheels.

First she checked her goldfish—Brian, Ezekiel and Orange Juice. They'd survived beautifully without her. Then she dashed out onto her balcony to make sure her pot plants were still alive.

Zoe had always kept pot plants, even when they

were in the bus. Her mum said she'd inherited Granny Weston's green thumb, and Zoe saw it as a sign that she was meant to have her own plot of land.

One day.

Back in the kitchen, she reached for the kettle. First priority was a comforting mug of tea, accompanied by a long soak in a warm bath. She could sort out her laundry tomorrow night after work. For now, she was going to be totally self-indulgent.

Five minutes later, warm, rose-scented water enveloped her, and at last she could set her thoughts free.

Unfortunately, her thoughts zeroed straight to Kent Rigby.

She let out the loud groan she'd been holding in for two whole days, ever since the road-side revelation on Friday evening. All weekend, honest to God, she'd tried unbelievably hard to stop liking Kent.

It should have been easy. He was her best friend's fiancé, and Zoe had already dated a previously engaged man. She'd been burned. Horribly. After she'd dated Rodney for several months and helped him to get over his break-up, he'd moved in with her and she'd been deeply in love with him. Then she'd come home unexpectedly early one evening and found him in bed with Naomi, his former fiancée.

Rodney the Rat.

Never again would Zoe set herself up for that kind of heartache.

So why hadn't she found the 'off' switch for her attraction to Bella's fiancé?

It was ridiculous, as if she'd contracted a mutant strain of a virus that was resistant to all known treatments.

The truth was that deep down she was genuinely

thrilled for Bella. Willara Downs was the lifestyle her friend had been born into. Bella's parents had always lived in the district. Her father would soon be out of hospital and home on his farm, and her grandfather still lived in an aged care facility in Willara township. On top of that, the Shaw and Rigby properties were adjoining and so Bella and Kent had the whole dynasty thing happening.

Beyond all these practical considerations, Bella and Kent were so sweet together, and so very at ease. Maybe they weren't all touchy-feely, but that was to be expected when others were around. Just the same, it was clear as daylight that they belonged together.

Without question, Bella fitted in. She'd found where she belonged, while once again, as always, Zoe was the outsider.

Oh, God.

Zoe dunked her face under the water to wash away her stupid tears. She had to get a grip. Had to stop this nonsense now.

Curse that flat tyre.

This problem would never have arisen if she and Bella had driven to the homestead together. If Bella had been there, from the moment Zoe met Kent she would have known who he was, and the first thing she would have seen was Kent embracing his bride-to-be. She would have been excited for Bella, and her heart would have stayed safely immune to Kent's charms.

Instead, cruel fate had delivered her a punctured tyre and twenty minutes alone with a wonderful man who'd arrived like a gift from heaven.

She kept reliving that thrilling moment—only a few seconds admittedly—when their gazes had connected. She could have sworn something huge and earth-shattering had passed between them.

Had it all been in her stupid head?

She hated to admit that she'd deluded herself, but there was no other explanation. Thank heavens Kent hadn't noticed.

His behaviour had been beyond reproach. He'd been unfailingly polite and friendly to Zoe, and he'd been wonderful about her damaged tyre, organising a replacement to be sent out from a garage in Willara and then fitting it for her.

Appropriately, he'd devoted the bulk of his attention to Bella. There'd been no sign that he was remembering the moment when he and Zoe had looked into each other's eyes and the world had stopped.

And she was going to be just as sensible.

It was time for self-discipline and maturity. Time to get a grip on reality.

Kent-slash-man-of-her-dreams-Rigby was going to marry her best friend in less than two months and she, Zoe Weston, was going to be their happy, loyal, non-jealous, and perfect-in-every-way bridesmaid.

Kent couldn't breathe. Pinned at the bottom of a dark muddy pool, he could feel his lungs bursting, his legs thrashing. He couldn't see a thing. Couldn't hear anything either, just a dull roaring in his head.

Fear, blacker than the night, pressed down with a weighty and smothering hand.

He fought, struggling, gasping…shooting awake out of a tangle of sheets.

He dragged in air. His heart raced, but he wasn't panicking. He knew it would slow down soon. He was used to this dream. He knew its familiar pattern, even though he had no real memories of almost drowning in Willara Creek.

The dreams were based on what his family had told him—that he'd been pinned under a rock and Tom Shaw had saved him, and that little Bella had been there, white-faced and sobbing.

Don't let Kent die. Please, please don't let him die...

It was years later, in his teens, that the dreams had begun. By then it had finally sunk in that all life was tenuous and that Kent's own life had nearly ended when he was six years old.

A kid showing off. All over red rover. Then a man with good instincts diving down and dragging him free.

Tom Shaw had given Kent a second chance at life, and with that gift had come responsibility.

The dreams never let Kent forget. He owed. Big time.

To: Kent Rigby<willaraKR@hismail.com>
From: Zoe Weston<zoe.weston@flowermail.com>
Subject: Caterers etc.
Dear Kent,

Thanks for your kind hospitality on the weekend. It was great meeting you and having the chance to see where the wedding will take place.

I'm sure you'll be pleased to hear that my spare car tyre held up splendidly, so thanks for your help with that as well.

As you know, I had a good chat with your mother about the best caterers to approach for the wedding and I've rung them all and am sending you their quotes as an attachment for your perusal.

I showed the quotes to Bella, but she has enough to think about with finding her dress and worrying about her dad and she's more than happy to leave the planning details to us.

I thought the menu supplied by Greenslades sounded delicious and it also provides a range of dishes to suit most tastes, but they're a little more expensive than the others.

I'm also sending a link to a website with the table settings that Bella and I think will be perfect. If you like them, I'll go ahead and place an order.

Oh, and are you still happy to use the homestead verandas if there's a threat of rain, or would you like me to look into hiring a marquee?

If there's anything else I can do to help, please let me know.

Kind regards,

Zoe Weston

To: Zoe Weston<zoe.weston@flowermail.com>
From: Kent Rigby<willaraKR@hismail.com>
Subject: Re: Caterers etc.

Hi Zoe,

Thanks for your email with the quotes and the link. Has it occurred to you that you may have missed your calling as a wedding planner?

I agree that the Greenslades menu is a standout, so let's go with them, especially as they're based in Toowoomba and they can send out a mobile kitchen. Great find.

The table settings look terrific—I'm happy to go with whatever you girls choose.

Zoe, you might be Bella's best friend, but I think

you've just become mine, too. Such a load off my mind to have this sorted so quickly and easily.
Cheers
Kent
P.S. I was wondering—do you have a favourite colour?

To: Kent Rigby<willaraKR@hismail.com>
From: Zoe Weston<zoe.weston@flowermail.com>
Subject: Re: Caterers etc.
Dear Kent,
All the bookings are made and both Greenslades and the Perfect Day hire company will be sending you their invoices with details about deposits etc.

Ouch. I hope you don't get too much of a shock.

I'm leaving the ordering of drinks to you. Bella and I will look after the flower arrangements and decorations. So now the major details are planned, but I'd also like to have a bridal shower and a hens' party for Bella, so there's a bit more to be sorted. I guess you and your best man will be having a bucks' night?

As Bella has probably told you, she's found a dress she loves, so it looks as if everything is coming together.

I can't imagine why you want to know my favourite colour. I'm not even sure I can answer that question. It depends if you're talking about a colour to wear, or a colour to look at. It can make quite a difference, you know.
Regards,
Zoe

To: Zoe Weston<zoe.weston@flowermail.com>
From: Kent Rigby<willaraKR@hismail.com>
Subject: Re: Caterers etc.
Hi Zoe,
Once again, thanks for all your help. I can't imagine how this wedding could have happened without you.

As for the question about your favourite colour, I'm afraid I can't really explain. It's a small but pleasant task Bella has assigned to me.

That's a fascinating observation you've made about colours. For now, could you give me both your favourite colour to wear and your favourite colour to look at?
Cheers
Kent

On the following Saturday morning, Bella bought her wedding dress. Zoe had been with her when she'd first seen the dress on the previous Saturday, and they'd loved it. Twice during the week Bella had been back to the shop to look at it again, and now she'd dragged Zoe along with her to approve her final decision.

'Each time I see it, I love it more,' Bella had confided, and as Zoe watched her parade across the store's plush carpet she totally understood why. The floor-length gown was very simple, but its elegant lack of fussiness totally suited Bella's blond, country-girl beauty. Its style, with beautifully embroidered straps and Grecian draping, was perfect for an outdoor country wedding.

'Kent will adore you in this,' Zoe said as she pictured Bella coming across the lawn to her waiting bridegroom. 'You'll stop him in his tracks.'

She was proud that she said this with a genuine smile, although putting the Kent nonsense out of her thoughts hadn't been as easy as she'd expected. Emails in which he asked about her favourite colour hadn't helped.

She still hadn't answered that one. It was silly of her, but it felt too...personal.

'This is definitely the dress for me,' Bella said, giving a final twirl to admire her reflection in the full-length mirror.

She paid for her dress with her credit card, then linked her arm through Zoe's. 'OK, it's your turn now. We have to find something really lovely for you.'

Abruptly, in the middle of the salon, Bella stopped. 'Have I told you how incredibly grateful I am for everything you're doing to help? Kent told me how brilliant you've been.'

'I've enjoyed it,' Zoe said honestly. 'So far, it hasn't been a huge job. Really.'

'But it's such a relief to know it's all in hand,' Bella said. 'Since my dad got sick, I've been rather distracted.'

'That's why I was happy to help.'

'You're one in a million. You know that, don't you?'

It was hard not to bask in the warmth of Bella's smile. Zoe found it incredibly reassuring to be appreciated, to feel needed and important.

Businesslike once more, Bella turned to a rack of dresses. 'I thought if we chose something that didn't scream bridesmaid, you'd be able to wear it afterwards. Colour-wise, I was wondering about—'

Bella paused, looking at a row of dresses, and Zoe waited. Even though she hadn't answered Kent's question about colours, she rather liked pink. She knew lots of girls avoided pink like the plague, but she'd always thought the colour brought out the rosy tones in her skin and went rather well with her dark hair. So, she was thinking of a pretty shade of pink when Bella said, 'Green.'

'Green?'

Bella nodded emphatically. 'I can really see you in green, Zoe. It suits you beautifully. And it's so fresh, just right for a country wedding.'

Yes, green was fresh, no doubt about that. But it was also the colour of grass and trees, and there were rather a lot of both in the country. In the outdoors, green would work like camouflage, wouldn't it?

Worse, wasn't green the colour of jealousy? *Oh, cringe.* Zoe had worked extremely hard to rid herself of any jealousy. Even so, *green* was the last colour she wanted to wear to *this* particular wedding.

Bella was frowning at her. 'Don't you like green? I thought you loved it. That long green scarf of yours looks stunning with your black winter coat.'

But I won't be wearing my black winter coat, Zoe wanted to remind her. *We're supposed to be choosing a dress for a spring garden wedding. If not something with a hint of pink, why not a pretty pale primrose?*

Not that Zoe would actually say any of this out loud, not when she was still, in spite of her minor problem re the groom, trying to be the perfect, considerate bridesmaid.

With a pang of guilt, she remembered the Monday morning, almost two weeks ago now, when Bella had asked her to be her bridesmaid. She'd been ready to wear anything then, even a black plastic garbage bag.

Somewhat ashamed, she said, 'I'm sure a pale apple green could be very nice.'

'Hmm.' Bella was looking less certain now. 'I must admit I hardly wear green myself.' Already, she was heading over to a rack of pretty pastels. 'Our high-school uniform was green, so I had an overdose of it in my teenage years.'

'Oh,' Zoe gasped and smacked the side of her fore-head. 'I'd almost forgotten until you mentioned your high school. I had a message on Facebook from one of your old school friends.'

'Really?' Bella was already at a rack, reaching for a coat hanger with a rather pretty pink dress.

'I posted a message on Facebook, you see, about how excited I was to be a bridesmaid at a country wedding near Willara. I didn't actually mention Willara Downs and I didn't give full names, but I said the bride was my best friend, Bella. I hope you don't mind, Bell.'

'No, of course I don't mind. So who was it?'

'A guy. I think he's been living somewhere overseas, but he said he used to know a girl called Bella Shaw at Willara High and he wondered if she was my friend getting married.'

Bella was suddenly very still and she shot Zoe a strangely nervous glance.

'I haven't replied to him,' Zoe said, cautiously.

'What's his name?' Bella's voice was barely above a whisper now.

'I'm trying to remember. I think it might have been David. No, that's not right. Maybe Damon? Yes, I'm pretty sure it was Damon.'

'Damon Cavello?'

'Yes, that's it. I—' Zoe stopped, shocked into silence by the sight of Bella's deathly pale face and the coat hanger slipping from her hands, landing on the bridal salon's white carpet in a sea of frothy pink chiffon.

'Bell?' With a pang of dismay, Zoe bent down to pick up the fallen gown before any of the store's assistants noticed. 'Bella?' she repeated as she slipped the gown's straps onto the hanger and returned it to its rightful place on the rack. 'What's the matter?'

Bella gave a convulsive little shudder, then the colour rushed back into her face. 'Nothing. Nothing's the matter,' she said quickly. 'I just got a surprise. It's so long since I've heard from D-Damon.'

As she stammered his name her cheeks turned deep pink.

'Who is he?' Zoe had to ask. 'A high-school sweetheart?'

With a startled laugh, Bella whipped her gaze back to the rack, and began, rather distractedly, to check out the dresses. 'God, no. We were just friends.'

'Right.' Zoe frowned as she watched Bella's hands, with their smart navy-blue nail polish and sparkling diamond engagement ring, swish along the coat hangers.

Bella turned to her, eyes extra bright. 'When did you say Damon wrote to you?'

'I found his message when I got home from work last night.'

'But you haven't written back to him?'

'Not yet. I thought I'd better check with you first. I wasn't sure he was someone you wanted to know.'

'Of course you can answer him. There's no problem. Damon's—fine.'

Bella sounded calm enough on the surface, but something wasn't right. Zoe could sense her inner tension.

'Damon was always a bit of a daredevil.' Bella spoke a little too casually, as if she needed to prove she was mega cool about this subject. 'He moved back to Brisbane in the middle of his final year, and he went on to study journalism. He's been overseas for years—as a foreign correspondent, specialising in all the worst trouble spots.'

'He sounds like an adventurer.'

Softly, Bella said, 'I hate to think of the things he must have seen.'

Zoe nodded, still puzzled by the tension Bella couldn't quite disguise. 'I think he might be heading back to Australia,' she said. 'Or he could even be on his way already. So is it OK to pass on your email address?'

'Of course.' This time Bella gave an offhand shrug, as if Zoe had been trying to make Mount Everest out of a molehill.

Lifting a very pretty coffee-and-cream floral dress from the rack, she said, 'If Damon's back in Australia, he's bound to come out to Willara. His father doesn't live there any more, but his grandmother's in the same old folks' home as my grandad, and I'm sure he'll want to visit her. They've always been close. His gran shows me all the postcards he sends her.'

'That's nice.'

Bella bit her lip and gave an uncertain smile.

'Would you invite him to the wedding?' Zoe asked.

'Heavens, no.' A strange snorting laugh broke from Bella. 'He wouldn't be interested in my marriage.' Then her eyes met Zoe's and she frowned. 'Don't look at me like that, Zoe. Damon's not the type to enjoy a romantic country wedding.'

'OK. Just asking. I thought he might have been an old friend of Kent's, that's all.'

She heard the hiss of her friend's sharply indrawn breath.

'Well, yes,' Bella admitted, almost reluctantly. 'Kent and Damon were mates at one time, so I suppose I should tell Kent.' She sighed. 'Actually, he'll probably want to include Damon.'

Then, as if deliberately changing the subject, she held out the coffee-toned dress. 'Now, why don't you try this one on? I can see you in it already.'

It was pretty obvious that Bella wanted to drop the subject. 'All right.'

In the changing cubicle, however, Zoe took one look at herself in the pretty bridesmaid's dress, and she forgot about Bella and the old school friend.

The colour was perfect—tawny flowers on a creamy white background that totally flattered her complexion. But her first thought was not to wonder how she looked.

But— *Would Kent like me in this?*

This was getting tedious.

On Tuesday evening, Zoe was in the middle of important, toenail-painting research when the phone rang. She and Bella were wearing toe peepers to the wedding, and each night, following Bella's instructions, Zoe was trying out a different colour. Serious comparisons were made the next day in their lunch hour.

This evening, when the phone rang, Zoe had toe separators in place and three nails painted with rosy minx, so she was grumbling as she screwed the lid on the bottle and hobbled over to the phone. 'Hello?'

'Hi, Zoe.'

The caller was male with a smooth as molasses country drawl that she instantly recognised. Her heart tried to leap clear out of her chest.

He said, 'Kent Rigby here.'

Why was he ringing? Several scenarios flashed before Zoe. All of them impossible. *Good grief. Calm down.* He'd be ringing about another planning detail.

But when she tried to speak, she sounded distinctly breathless.

'Zoe, are you OK?' Kent sounded genuinely concerned.

'I'm perfectly fine,' she managed to insist, although it came out in a choked whisper. 'Just a bit puffed. I had to—' *quick breath* '—come running in from outside.'

Great. Now she could add dishonesty to her list of sins. Grimacing, Zoe willed herself to calm down. Developing high blood pressure before the wedding was not on the bridesmaids' list of duties.

She took another breath, deeper and slower, aiming for a tone that was friendly, but as businesslike as possible. 'What can I do for you, Kent?'

'I wondered if you've made a decision about the hens' night. I hear you're in charge of that, too.'

'Oh, right, do you want an invitation?' she teased.

Kent chuckled at her weak joke. 'My best man, Steve, has been pressuring me about a bucks' night, and I didn't want it to clash with your arrangements.'

'Actually, I sent you an email about it earlier this evening.'

'Sorry. I haven't checked my emails. I've been out on the tractor since the early hours and I just got back. Thought I'd give you a quick call while my dinner's heating up.'

Zoe pictured Kent up before dawn, out ploughing the fields as the sun rose. Farmers worked such long hours. She wondered if Bella would be the sort of wife who took her farmer husband a Thermos of coffee and a snack. Maybe they'd share a quick cuddle behind the machinery shed?

Oh, God. Stop it!

Assuming her briskest, most businesslike voice, she said, 'We'd like to have the hens' night in Willara, on the weekend before the wedding—that's the same weekend as the bridal shower. Bella's friends from Brisbane don't mind trekking off to the wilds of the country for two weekends in a row, but I think three would be expecting too much.'

'Fair enough.'

'So the girls are planning to book into the Willara pub—that is, unless you want to have your bucks' night there.'

'No, you stay with that arrangement. We'll have the bucks' party on the same night, but we'll go over to Mullinjim. It's not far out of town.'

'Great. That sounds like a plan.' Zoe let out a nervous, huffing laugh. 'So it looks like the wedding's all coming together?'

'Like clockwork. Piece of cake, thanks to you, Zoe.'

A small silence fell and Zoe was shocked to hear her heartbeats, still galloping away like a cattle stampede. She would rather keep talking than risk Kent hearing them, so she asked the question that had been on her mind for days.

'Has Bella mentioned Damon Cavello, the old school friend who made contact?'

'No,' Kent said slowly. 'She hasn't.'

There was no mistaking the surprise in his voice. A beat later, he asked, 'So…what's the wild boy up to these days?'

Zoe could quite believe why Kent had called Damon a wild boy. She'd checked out photos of him on the internet and he had the dark, scruffy, bad-boy looks of a rock-and-roll star. It wasn't a look that appealed to her—

she'd seen enough of guys like that hanging around her parents' band while she was growing up—but she knew bad boys were considered very sexy by girls confident enough to attract them.

'Damon's on his way back to Australia,' she told Kent. 'Coming from Afghanistan, I think.'

Another small silence.

'Is he OK?' Kent asked.

'As far as I know, he's fine.'

'That's a miracle.' Kent spoke with uncharacteristic cynicism, but then he quickly corrected himself. 'Don't get me wrong. I'm relieved to hear that he's in one piece. But with Damon, there's always a risk of—' He left the sentence dangling. 'Do you know if he's likely to be around for the wedding?'

'I think there's a good chance.' Zoe hoped she wasn't breaching Bella's confidence. But then, because she was curious, she couldn't help adding, 'He sounds rather mysterious.'

'Yeah.' There was a barely concealed sigh on the other end of the phone line. 'He's always been a bit of a puzzle, but Bella knew what drove him better than any of us. What did she tell you?'

'Not much at all—just that he left Willara High in Year Twelve and ended up becoming a foreign correspondent. I got the impression he's attracted to danger.'

'No doubt about that,' he muttered.

She could hear definite tension in Kent's voice now, the same tight caution she'd sensed in Bella. What was it about this Damon guy that put everyone on high alert?

'How did Bella react to the news?' Kent asked carefully.

This last question was a curly one. Zoe sensed she was on dangerous ground, and, no matter what she thought of Kent, her loyalty lay with Bella. She certainly wouldn't tell him that Bella had been rather edgy and strange when she'd heard about Damon Cavello.

'Bella said—ah—that she'd talk to you to see if you wanted to invite him to the wedding.'

'But she didn't invite him straight out?'

'No. I'm sure she wants to talk to you first. Does Damon—um—pose a problem, Kent?'

'No, not at all. I didn't mean to give that impression.' He spoke almost too smoothly. 'Bella's right. He's just an old school friend, and it'll be great to catch up with him. Actually, I'd like his email address if that's OK. I presume Bella's already made contact with him?'

Kent sounded relaxed enough, but as they said goodnight and Zoe hung up she couldn't help wondering. And worrying.

She wished she'd left it to Bella to tell him about this Damon guy. A bridesmaid was supposed to be tactful and diplomatic. Instead, she'd opened her big mouth and she had the awful feeling she'd stirred up unnecessary trouble.

CHAPTER FOUR

GRABBING a beer from the fridge, Kent snapped the top off, then went out to the back veranda.

The night was hot and still and silent. Low clouds hid the moon and the stars, and the air was heavy and stifling, as if a thunderstorm was brewing.

Tipping back his head, he downed the icy liquid, hoping to wash away the sense of foreboding that hunkered inside him.

Foreboding wasn't an emotion Kent Rigby enjoyed, and it wasn't something that normally troubled him. Most times he was too busy working hard or playing hard. Besides, he liked to keep his life on an even keel and he left the rocking of boats to others. Like Damon Cavello.

Hell.

Kent downed another icy slug, and leaned his shoulder against a timber post, staring out into the black, fathomless night. Talk about lousy timing. Why the blue blazes had Cavello come back now, just when he and Bella had everything sorted and settled?

They hadn't heard from him in years.

Sure, they'd seen his news reports on television, delivered on battlefields while he was dodging explosions and bullets, or emerging from the rubble of an earthquake, covered in dust and grime.

Damon had made no personal contact with either of them for years. And now Kent and Bella had planned a future together, and they were doing it for all the right reasons.

Everything was working out so well. Tom Shaw was out of hospital and if he continued to follow his doctor's instructions, he'd be OK. He was looking forward to the wedding and walking his daughter down the aisle.

The rosy future Kent had planned was falling into place.

But now this Cavello bombshell had exploded.

Why now?

Zoe sat for ages after she hung up the phone. Curled in an armchair, she almost fell into her old habit of nibbling at her thumbnail. Actually, she did chew on the corner before she remembered that she had to keep her nails pristine for the wedding. So she chewed on the inside of her lip instead. And pondered.

The vibes for this wedding weren't as upbeat as she would have liked. There were so many undercurrents, not just her own silly crush on the groom—which she *so* hoped no one had guessed—but now, with the arrival of Damon on the scene, there were Bella's and Kent's subtle but unmistakable tensions.

Zoe wished they could all snap out of it. She wanted everything to be rosy and wonderful on planet Bella-and-Kent.

Guiltily, she felt an urge to run away for a bit, but, apart from the fact that she was needed at Willara next weekend, she didn't really have anywhere to go. It was a pity her parents didn't live closer. She would have loved to see her little brother, Toby—to go and watch him play soccer on Saturday afternoon perhaps, or to go surfing with her dad, help her mum make her habitual Friday night curry.

She wondered if Toby knew how lucky he was to live in a cosy house with parents who stayed in one place with a steady job now their dad ran a music store.

One thing was certain. If she ever found the right man, she definitely wanted to settle down and to stay in one place. She wanted her children to go to school with friends they'd known since kindergarten, and she wanted them to play sports together, to make memories together...

Just as Bella and Kent had, and as their children would, too...

Zoe sighed as jealousy coiled unpleasantly inside her. Immediately she felt ashamed of herself. It wasn't as if poor Bella enjoyed a perfect family life. She'd lost her mother. She had no brothers or sisters, and her only family consisted of her ill and grieving father, and a grandparent in an old people's home.

Was it any wonder Bella had turned to gorgeous, steady Kent Rigby and his happy, well-balanced family?

Zoe launched to her feet before she had a chance to feel the lurch of pain that followed any thoughts about Kent. Tonight she was more determined than ever to get over that nonsense. This wedding would be fantastic and she would be the best possible bridesmaid.

Her job for this weekend and over the next few weeks was clear. She had to steer Bella through any muddy waters that surfaced—including old flames—until she arrived safely beside Kent at the altar.

Yes, Zoe felt better now that plan was reaffirmed.

But as she reached for the kettle she saw her hand. Damn! She'd chewed her thumbnail to a nub.

Stripped to the waist, Kent was bending under an outside water tap, cleaning up the worst of the day's grime, when he heard the squeaky hinges of the backyard gate. He looked up, blinked water from his eyes, and saw Zoe Weston poised uncertainly just inside the gate.

She was dressed in city clothes, as if she'd come straight from the office, and her crisp white blouse and charcoal pencil skirt looked totally out of place against a backdrop of gumtrees and grazing land. Kent, however, found himself helplessly captivated.

Stunned might be a better word. He couldn't stop staring.

Zoe's office clothes emphasised her neat, slim curves, and her legs, in sheer stockings and shiny high heels, were—there was only one word—*sensational*. Her dark hair was pulled back beneath a narrow velvet band into some kind of knot, and she looked sophisticated and serious and—heaven help him—astonishingly sexy.

His reaction was as bad as last time. No, worse.

When he'd met her by the road side she'd been wearing a T-shirt and blue jeans. Ever since then he'd worked hard to stop thinking about her unique qualities—not just her sensible calm manner, but the cute tilt of her head, and the blue of her eyes, and the softness of her mouth.

Now, there was something else—something about the sight of her in her smart city clothes that grabbed him by the throat and sent a jolt arrowing south.

Hell.

Why was she here? Alone?

Where was Bella? Weren't Zoe and Bella supposed to be staying at Blue Gums this weekend with Tom Shaw? Tom was so much better now and he'd started going into Toowoomba to the AA meetings.

What had happened?

Shaking off his unwanted reaction, Kent called to her, 'Hello there.'

Zoe still hadn't moved. In fact, she seemed to be as transfixed as he was—watching him with a worried, staring gaze and with a hand pressed to the open V of her snowy-white blouse.

Hastily, Kent snapped off the water and reached for his discarded shirt, using it to dry his bare shoulders and chest as he hurried over to her.

'I wasn't expecting you,' he said, stating the obvious as he thrust his arms into the sleeves of the damp and crumpled shirt. 'Is everything OK?'

'I—' Zoe began, gulping and looking uncomfortable. 'Bella asked me to come here. We were supposed to stay at her father's place, but he's—' She grimaced, and looked embarrassed.

'Oh, no. Tom isn't drunk, is he?'

Zoe nodded. 'He's in a pretty bad way, I'm afraid.'

Kent swore and slammed a balled fist against his thigh. 'Tom was doing so well. He seemed to be on the mend.' He let out a heavy sigh. 'I'm sure Bella's upset.'

'Yes. She begged me to come over to your place, while she stayed with her dad.' Zoe's eyes were round with worry. 'I hope she's OK.'

'She won't come to any harm. Tom's never violent, and he'll certainly never hurt his daughter. Not physically.' Kent pulled the limp fronts of his shirt together, and started to fumble with the lower buttons. 'Just the same, I'll phone her straight away.'

Zoe glanced at his chest and then looked away, her colour deepening.

'Come inside,' he said, doing up another button, then nodding towards the house. 'You look like you could use a cuppa, or maybe something stronger.'

'Thanks. I'd love a cuppa.'

As they walked across the lawn to the screen door at the back of the house Kent's thoughts were for Bella and her devastation over Tom's lapse. He forced himself to ignore the slim, sophisticated woman walking beside him. He paid her no attention. He couldn't afford to think about her curve-hugging skirt and her long legs sheathed in filmy stockings, or her high city heels sinking into the grass.

Sitting at the granite island bench in the Rigbys' farmhouse kitchen, Zoe wrapped her hands around a mug of hot, sweet tea, closed her eyes and drew a deep breath.

From outside came the creamy vanilla scent of wisteria mixed with the danker scent of hay and a faint whiff of animals. But the pleasant country aromas did little to calm her. She was still shaken by the scene she'd witnessed at Blue Gums.

The sight of Bella's father, staggering and incoherent, had been beyond awful, and poor Bella had been so embarrassed and upset. She'd shooed Zoe out of there as quickly as she could.

But Zoe's arrival at Willara Downs had brought an equally disturbing close encounter with Kent's naked, *wet* torso.

OK, a man without his shirt should *not* have been a big deal. Zoe had seen plenty of bare male chests. Of course she had, but this was the first time she'd had a close encounter with Kent Rigby's smooth, bulky muscles, and tapering, hard-packed abs. Not to mention the enticing trail of dark hair heading downwards beneath his belt buckle.

It was an experience destined to rattle any girl senseless. What hope had Zoe?

For pity's sake, she'd gone into mourning over the closure of his shirt buttons...

In fact, Kent had been doing up his buttons crookedly and she'd *almost* offered to help him get them straight. How sad was that? Thank heavens she'd stopped herself just in time.

Now she cringed as she imagined the surprise and disapproval in his eyes if she'd actually reached out and touched him.

It's OK. I didn't do anything stupid. I'm calming down. I'm fine. I'm back in control.

Zoe took another sip of tea and then a bite of the scrumptious shortbread that Kent's mother had thoughtfully left in his pantry. Yes, she was definitely feeling calmer now. And sanity certainly returned as she heard the deep rumble of Kent's voice down the hall. He was talking to Bella on the telephone, and she could imagine him making sure Bella was OK and that her dad was fine, too. He would be reassuring Bella and telling her he loved her.

While their conversation continued, Zoe flicked through a country life magazine with articles about kitchen gardens and new breeds of chickens, and fabulous recipes using all kinds of cheese.

Zoe tried to imagine Bella reading one of these country magazines, and being inspired by the articles. Somehow, she couldn't quite picture her friend getting her beautifully manicured hands dirty in a veggie garden, or rolling pastry, or saving her kitchen scraps to feed to the chooks.

Bella had never actually talked about her future as a farmer's wife. In fact she seemed very much a city girl these days with a fondness for beauty salons and coffee shops rather than hay bales and farmhouse cooking. But then Bella was a bit of a dark horse. She'd never talked about her father's problems with alcohol either.

Clearly there were many strands to Bella's life, and the city office girl who loved high fashion and fancy nail polish was quite possibly a brave front. Now, more than ever, Zoe could understand why her friend had chosen a steadfast and reliable partner like Kent. A good, rock-solid husband. A loving man who knew all about her, a guy who would help to shoulder her worries about her father.

There was no doubt about it. Kent was Bella's perfect match in every way.

Right. OK.

Fortunately, Zoe locked in that thought scant seconds before she heard Kent's footsteps returning down the passage to the kitchen. She had her smile fixed in place before he entered.

Even so, she felt a zap of reaction the instant she saw him. There was something impossibly appealing about Kent Rigby, something about his tanned profile, about his dark, friendly eyes and the flash of his smile that made Zoe feel as bright and shimmering as a sunrise.

Which proved how very foolish she was. Apart from the very important fact that the man was taken—by her best friend, no less—she should have enough bad memories of Rodney the Rat to douse any sparks of unwanted libido.

'How's Bella?' she asked Kent.

'She's upset, of course, and mad as hell with her dad. He'd started going to AA and we thought he was going to be fine now.'

'Perhaps he's just had one slip and he'll be back on the wagon tomorrow.'

'Let's hope so.' Kent let out a sigh. 'Tom had problems with grog when he was young, but he was dry the whole time he and Mary were married. Since her death, he's been on a downhill slide.'

'Poor man. And poor Bella. She must feel so helpless.'

Kent nodded. 'It must have been a shock for you, too, coming across him like that.'

'Well, yes, it was, but only because it was so unexpected. And Bella was so upset.' Zoe lifted her now empty mug. 'Thanks for the tea. It was just what I needed.' She stood. 'I guess you'll want to get over to Bella's place straight away.'

'Later. Tom's asleep right now and Bella wants a bit of time to sort the place out.' Kent went to the fridge, opened it and stood staring at its contents. 'I'll fix a meal for us first.'

'For us?'

'Yep—we're on our own tonight.'

'B-but you don't have to feed me.' Zoe was stammering, rattled by the possibility of a meal alone with this man. 'I can go into town. I'll stay at the pub and grab a meal there.'

'Zoe, relax.' Shutting the fridge once more, Kent grinned at her. 'You're president and secretary of our wedding planning committee. Of course, you're very welcome here. You can stay the night, and you can have the same room as last time.'

She was about to protest again, when she realised it

might come across as rude. Kent was keeping up his reputation for country hospitality. He might be upset if she refused.

'Thanks,' she said. Then, to cover any giveaway signs of attraction, she surveyed the kitchen with her most businesslike glance. 'So what can I do to help you?'

'If we dig out the sheets now, you can make up your bed while I throw a couple of steaks in a pan.'

Already Kent was heading out of the kitchen and Zoe hurried after him. The linen cupboard was in a hallway, and he flipped the louvred doors open, releasing a faint scent of lavender.

'This is where I run into trouble.' A small smile made attractive creases around his dark eyes. 'I haven't a clue which sheets I'm supposed to give you.'

Zoe gulped. Discussing bed sheets with Kent was her wickedest fantasy rolled into her worst nightmare. 'I think I used those pink striped sheets last time.'

'Terrific.' He was already lifting them from the shelf. 'I'm sure they'll do.'

His wrists brushed against her as he handed her the sheets. It was a relief to disappear into the guest room and get busy making the bed.

Once this was done, she freshened up in the bathroom, brushed her hair and changed into shorts and a T-shirt. If only she could switch off her hormones as easily as she changed her clothes.

The scent of frying steak and onions greeted her when she came back into the kitchen. And the rather fetching sight of Kent standing at the stove, changed into a clean white, correctly buttoned shirt.

He sent her another of his flashing smiles, but then

his smile went super still, and he continued to stare at Zoe, a slight frown now warring with his grin.

'What's wrong?'

'You've let your hair down.'

Zap! A bushfire scorched her skin. She fingered her hair, dark and straight like her mum's, and now skimming her shoulders. 'I didn't know it was a crime for a girl to let her hair down on a Friday evening.'

'Course it isn't.' Kent shrugged and turned back to the steaks, flipping them over. Without looking at her, he said, 'It looks great either way. In your bridesmaid's outfit you're going to knock the local yokels for six.'

The comment warranted another very stern lecture to herself. His compliment would go to her head. It should be possible to have a normal conversation with him without overreacting to every second sentence.

Desperate to appear cool and unaffected, she said glibly, 'That's reassuring to know. I'm on the lookout for a spare farmer.'

'Are you?'

It wasn't the flippant or teasing response she'd expected from Kent. His head had jerked around and his dark eyes were surprisingly intense.

Now she was more flustered than ever. 'Of course I'm not serious,' she said tightly. 'That was my poor attempt at a joke.'

Time to put an end to this subject. She looked around her. 'What can I do to help? Why don't I make a salad to go with the steak?'

Kent's thoughts were apparently elsewhere and he took a moment to answer her.

'Sure,' he said at last, and then, after a beat, his usual

smile was back in place. 'Trust a girl to want to spoil a good steak with rabbit food.'

They ate on the back veranda, looking out at the idyllic view of the soft, velvety hills and fields as they were slowly enveloped by the shadowy night.

Zoe wondered what she and Kent would talk about now. Given her recent gaffes, she wasn't sure she could cope with a conversation about Bella and the wedding. She wanted to ask Kent about the property. That was safe, and she was genuinely curious about the crops and grazing herds. Details of farm life had always fascinated her.

But it seemed Kent had other ideas. As he speared a tomato cube and a chunk of cucumber he said, 'So, tell me about yourself, Zoe.'

'Me?'

'Why not?' His smile was relaxed and easy once more and when she hesitated, he said, 'You're Bella's best friend and your friendship's not going to come to an end when we're married. I expect you'll be an important part of our lives for a very long time.'

Would she? Zoe had been hoping that her life beyond the wedding would be Kent-free. How else could she get back to normal? How could she stand the strain of an ongoing friendship with Bella and Kent if they remained close friends way into the future? Good grief, surely she wouldn't still be a jangling wreck when she was eighty?

It was an alarming prospect. Added to that, Zoe didn't really enjoy talking about herself. As a child she'd been forever arriving at new schools and answering the same old questions over and over. 'I've already told you about my parents and how I spent most of my childhood on the road.'

'But your parents have stopped touring now, haven't they?'

She nodded, then took a sip of the chilled white wine Kent had poured for her. And as she put the glass down she found herself telling him about the music shop in Sugar Bay and her little brother, Toby. And then, because he smiled so encouragingly, she told him about Toby's soccer ambitions and his endless experiments and their family's Saturday night barbecues when her parents had jam sessions with old mates.

'Sounds like they're a lot of fun,' Kent said sincerely. 'Would you like to live at the bay?'

'I—I'm not sure.' Zoe pulled a face. 'If I'm honest I feel a bit resentful that Mum and Dad waited till Toby came along before they settled down. He's having a very different childhood from mine.'

She shrugged. 'The bay's a great place to visit, but I like Brisbane, too.' *And the country.* But she wouldn't tell Kent that. 'I have to make my own life, don't I?'

'Of course.' He was watching her carefully again. 'And the world's your oyster,' he said quietly.

'Well, yes… Actually, I'm thinking about heading overseas.'

'You'll love it,' he said, but now his smile was tinged with a bewildering hint of sadness and for the first time Zoe wondered if he felt trapped at Willara Downs.

Curiosity prompted her to say, 'I've often wondered what it's like to grow up in one place and know you'll spend your whole life there.'

'Do you think it sounds boring?'

'No, not at all. Quite the opposite, actually.'

A frown furrowed Kent's brow and his dark eyes registered something very close to dismay.

Fearing she'd said too much, Zoe took a quick sip of her wine.

But whatever had bothered Kent passed and he was soon relaxed again. 'I love living here,' he said. 'It's not just the land and the lifestyle. For me, it's the strong feeling of continuity. My family's been here from the start. My great-great-great-grandfather looked after the horses on one of the earliest explorations and he fell in love with this district and settled here more than a hundred and fifty years ago.'

'Wow.' Zoe looked out at the view that had almost disappeared. 'All that history.'

Kent nodded. 'My grandfather and my great-grandfather both went away to the wars, and while they were gone the women and children ran the farms for them.' Across the table Kent's eyes met Zoe's. 'The responsibility of continuing those traditions means a great deal to me.'

'I'm sure it does. I feel goose bumps just thinking about it.' Zoe loved the idea of such permanence and such a deeply rooted sense of belonging.

'But that doesn't mean I don't love travelling as well,' Kent added with a twinkling smile.

'Have you travelled very far?'

'When I was nineteen I had a year off—backpacking with Steve, my best man, around Europe.'

'What was your favourite place?'

'Prague,' he answered without hesitation.

'That's interesting. Most people choose Paris or London or Rome. Even Barcelona.'

'Or Venice.'

'Yes.' She smiled, pleased that Kent was relaxed

again. When he looked at her with his serious expression, the world seemed to tilt ever so slightly, but everything felt in the right balance again now. 'So what did you love about Prague?'

Kent laughed. 'If Steve was here, he'd rave about the Czech beer. But for me it was the old city at Christmas time. It was snowing and unbelievably beautiful—the buildings, the pavements, the cafés, the restaurants. Everything in Prague is so old and dripping with history. Not a plastic Christmas tree in sight.'

'That sounds lovely. I must remember to try to be in Prague at Christmas.'

'Yes, do that.' For a moment there was a flicker of something in Kent's eyes. It might have been regret, but then he cracked a grin. 'And send me a postcard.'

'I will. I promise.'

'By the way,' he said, 'you still haven't told me your favourite colour.'

'And you haven't told me why you want to know.'

'Patience, Zoe. All in good time.'

'What if said I don't have a favourite?'

He laughed. 'I'd believe you. Neither do I.'

They laughed together then, and for a heady few seconds their gazes reached across the table and locked. For Zoe, it was like the moment beside the road when her entire being had felt connected to Kent's.

Then Kent broke the spell by looking away and deliberately reaching for his beer. And Zoe thudded back to earth. To reality.

She was such an idiot.

After that, they both turned their attention to their meals, but, although Zoe's steak was tender and the salad crisp, she seemed to have lost her appetite. She took another sip of wine and vowed to keep her thoughts firmly fixed on the painful truth.

How could she be so hopeless, when poor Bella was stuck at Blue Gums, caring for her dad? It was Bella who should be here, alone with Kent, and having this nice romantic dinner.

Zoe felt a little better when she and Kent left the veranda and returned to the kitchen to rinse their cutlery and plates and stack them in the dishwasher.

'I hope Mr Shaw will be OK in the morning,' she said.

'Don't worry about Tom.' Kent gave an offhand shrug. 'I'm sure he'll be fine in the morning. He'll be full of remorse and Bella will give him an earful about following doctor's orders.'

Zoe nodded. 'There was a fellow in Lead the Way with a drinking problem. He wanted everyone to turn a blind eye.'

Kent's eyes widened with interest, then abruptly he let out a sigh. 'Got to admit, it's really hard to watch Tom sink into such a state. He used to be such a fine man. He was my hero for many years. He saved my life when I was a nipper.'

'Really?' Zoe couldn't resist asking, 'What happened?'

'I was acting the fool down at the local waterhole, dived in at the wrong spot and hit my head on a rock.' With a sheepish smile Kent leaned closer and pointed to a faint thin scar on his forehead.

Zoe caught the clean, male scent of his skin, mere inches from her. She could see the scar, but his proximity also gave her the chance for a close-up study of the rest of his face, the length of his eyelashes, the graininess of his jaw, the sexy curve of his lips.

Oh, man.

Perhaps Kent sensed her indecent interest. His expression took on a strange frowning tension, and the air around them seemed to pulse. It seemed like ages before he pulled back, and he let out a strangled laugh. 'Lucky I didn't break my flaming neck. I certainly would have drowned if Tom hadn't been there. He got me off the bottom, dragged me out and revived me.'

'Thank God he did.' Oh, heavens, that sounded far too fervent. Quickly, Zoe asked, 'Was Bella there, too?'

'Yes, she witnessed the whole thing. We've both looked on her dad as a hero ever since.'

Kent's voice was so rough and solemn as he said this that Zoe knew deep emotions were tied to the statement.

'I'm sure he'll get over this road bump,' she said gently.

She was also sure it was time for Kent to leave. Regrettably, their time together had been way too pleasant.

She made a shooing motion towards the door. 'Now, thanks for a lovely dinner, but you should get going over to Bella's.'

'Yes, I'll head off now. You know where the tea and coffee are, don't you? And the TV remote.'

'Yes, thanks. I'll be fine. Don't worry about me. I'm used to living on my own. Now, go, Kent. Get out of here.'

He went.

I'm used to living on my own...

Standing at the kitchen window, Zoe watched the twin red eyes of Kent's tail lights disappearing into the black night, and she discovered a huge difference between being alone and being consumed by horrible loneliness.

Dismayed, she went through to the lovely lounge room. Like the rest of the house it was elegant yet relaxing, with deep comfy sofas, brightly coloured throw pillows. With a feminine touch, there'd be cut-glass vases filled with flowers from the garden.

For a brief, unwise moment, she indulged a childhood fantasy and imagined being the mistress of a beautiful country homestead like this one—cutting and arranging flowers from her garden, baking hearty meals for her drop-dead gorgeous, farmer husband and their children, attending meetings of the local growers' association, waking each morning to fresh air and open spaces...

And waking to the drop-dead gorgeous, farmer husband in bed beside her.

OK. Fantasy over. Back to reality. Fast.

Zoe flicked on the TV, made herself comfortable, and settled to watch one of her favourite comedies. A good dose of on-screen hilarity would soon cure her of any lingering self-pity.

But unfortunately the usually lively script was dull and unfunny this evening, and Zoe couldn't raise a chuckle. Her thoughts kept drifting...

She was picturing Kent's arrival at Blue Gums...and Bella's happy, open-arm welcome.

Stop it. Stop it. Stop it.

The couple on the TV screen were embracing, and again Zoe thought about Kent and Bella. Right about now, Bella would probably be undoing the buttons on Kent's shirt, running her hands over his lovely, hard muscles...

Oh, good grief. Enough!

Snapping off the TV, Zoe jumped to her feet. She was *not* going to succumb to this nonsense. She needed to keep busy, to keep her mind occupied with something constructive. But what could she do in a stranger's house?

Heading for the kitchen, she prayed for an answer.

CHAPTER FIVE

KENT was in a black mood. His experience at Blue Gums this evening had been depressing to say the least. Disturbing, too, as he hadn't been able to offer Bella much comfort. She'd been distracted, not her usual self and troubled by more than her father's illness. And yet she wouldn't confide in Kent, wouldn't let him help.

After the pleasant dinner conversation he'd enjoyed with Zoe, his fiancée's reception had been like a bucket of icy water. He was sure it had been a relief for both of them when he left early.

Now, home again, he approached the kitchen and saw...

Candles.

Everywhere.

On every bench top and flat surface in the state-of-the-art kitchen his mother had so faithfully designed, small candles sat, glowing warmly. And in the middle of the dancing candlelight stood Zoe, looking lovely, yet wide-eyed and cautious, rather like a naughty angel caught playing with the devil.

'I'm going to shift all this,' she announced hurriedly as soon as she saw him. 'I was planning to tidy everything before you got back.'

Black mood gone, Kent suppressed a smile as he stepped through the doorway into his kitchen.

'I—I know I've been a little carried away,' she hastened to add. 'I wanted to see how these candles looked, but I wasn't expecting you so soon, Kent. You're early, aren't you?'

'Bella's…worn out,' he said quietly.

'Oh.' Zoe frowned. 'Well, I know you weren't expecting to come home to forty-eight candles, but they're for the wedding. What do you think?'

'They're beautiful.' He gave in to the smile tugging at his mouth. *And you're beautiful, too…*

The thought sprang unbidden, and the words trembled on his lips, but thank goodness he resisted the impulse to voice them aloud.

'I wanted to get the full impact,' Zoe was explaining earnestly. 'I thought the candles would be lovely for the wedding reception. I'd like to put them in little paper bags filled with sand and they should look lovely outside in the garden. But don't worry—they're battery powered, so they're not going to burn your house down.'

'That's a relief.' Stepping closer, Kent lifted a little candle. 'And they can't blow out either.'

'No. They're called smart candles.'

'Good name.' He smiled at her, and he couldn't help adding, 'Smart candles for a smart girl.' Too late, he realised how softly he'd spoken, almost seductively, as if a weird kind of spell had taken hold of him.

In response, Zoe's blue eyes grew wider, clearly surprised. Her lips parted in a small moue.

Kent found himself staring at her soft pink lips… gazing into her lovely, expressive blue eyes…until he was lost in those eyes…

He was in free fall…

And all he could think was how badly he wanted to kiss Zoe. Now. In the middle of his kitchen. Surrounded by the glow of her candles.

He would start by sweeping her into his arms and kissing her sweet, pouty lips, and then he would sample the pale, fine skin at the base of her throat.

But perhaps Zoe could read his mind. She dropped her gaze and a deep stain spread over her cheeks. Her hand shook as she pressed it to her forehead, pushing back a strand of hair with a small sound of dismay.

Kent blinked. What the hell had come over him? Why couldn't he shake off this strange feeling of enchantment?

Zoe was the bridesmaid, for crying out loud. He had to forget about kissing her. *Say something about the candles.*

With a supreme effort, he dragged his attention away from her. What had she said? Something about putting these candles in little bags of sand?

'Do you have the sand you need?' he asked.

Zoe shook her head. 'I—I'm really mad with myself. I meant to call in at a craft shop and I forgot.'

'A craft shop? For sand?'

'In Brisbane the craft shops sell lovely, fine white sand.'

At that, he couldn't help laughing.

'What's so funny?'

'You don't need to buy sand at a craft shop, Zoe. Willara Creek is full of it.'

She shook her head, clearly unimpressed. 'But creek sand is damp and dirty and full of little twiggy bits.'

'Not all creek sand. Why don't I take you down there tomorrow and you can see what you think?' When she hesitated, he said, 'If it's not up to scratch, no harm done.'

'Bella and your mother are both coming over tomorrow. We're going to be busy with all the preparations.'

'We'll go first thing in the morning, then. If you don't mind an early start. How about a quick trip down to the creek before breakfast?'

There was more than a slight hesitation this time, but then Zoe nodded. 'Thank you,' she said, although she didn't smile. Instead she became businesslike. 'I'll shift everything out of here now.' Already she was turning off the candles.

Sitting in bed, Zoe stared into the darkness, unable to sleep.

Hugging her knees, she rocked slightly, something she only did when she was worried.

Or puzzled.

And confused.

The foreboding she'd felt about this wedding was deepening. Something *really* wasn't right—and she was pretty sure it wasn't just her feelings about the bridegroom getting in the way.

She knew Bella wasn't happy and the unhappiness wasn't only related to her father's health problems. Now Zoe was beginning to suspect that Kent wasn't happy either.

This possibility shocked her.

How could such a gorgeous, successful man, who could no doubt have his pick of any girl in the district, allow himself to walk, with his eyes wide open, into a marriage that wasn't gloriously happy?

It was the kind of question that would keep a conscientious bridesmaid awake all night. Pity she'd agreed to be up at the crack of dawn.

When Zoe woke to Kent's knock the next morning she felt more like a sleep deprived bridesmaid than a conscientious one. The thought of leaving her nice comfy bed to look at sand in a creek bed held no appeal.

But Kent had brought her a mug of tea and a slice of hot toast with strawberry jam, and Zoe couldn't help being impressed by this, so she soon found herself in his ute, bumping down a rough dirt track to Willara Creek.

To discover the creek was stunningly beautiful.

Majestic twisted and knotted paperbarks and tall river gums stood guard above water that was quiet and still and cool, and edged by boulders entwined with grevillea roots. Wind whispered gently in the she-oaks.

Charmed, Zoe watched a flight of wild ducks take off from the water. 'It's so beautiful and peaceful,' she said in an awed whisper.

Kent smiled at her. 'I thought you might like it.'

As she climbed out of the ute she heard birds calling to each other as they hunted for honey in the bright red grevillea flowers.

'And here's the sand,' she said, almost straight away seeing a small beach of nice white quartz-like grains.

'There's even better sand over here.' Kent was pointing farther along the bank.

Sure enough, he was right. Trapped among rocks, the sand was so white it glistened. Kneeling, Zoe studied it more closely and saw flickers of gold—pale golden specks, shining brightly. 'Kent, that can't be real gold?'

'No, I'm afraid it's only fool's gold. Its technical name is pyrite. But it's pretty enough for what you want, isn't it?'

'It's perfect. Absolutely gorgeous for a wedding.'

With impressive efficiency, Kent filled a couple of good-sized buckets and stowed them in the back of his ute.

Zoe took a deep breath of the fresh morning air as she looked about her at the deep pool of cool, inviting water, the smooth boulders and magnificent trees. 'I guess we'll have to go back already, but what a pity. It's so beautiful here. It almost looks as if it's been land-scaped.'

'We don't have to rush away.' Kent left the ute and squatted on the bank, looking out across the still water. 'This place has always been special. We've always kept the cattle out of here and we pump water up to troughs for them.'

'It must be amazing to have a place like this that you actually own. You'd feel a very close affinity to it.'

To Zoe's surprise, Kent didn't respond straight away. Picking up a handful of polished river stones, he skipped them out over the water, watching them bounce. As the last stone plopped he said, without looking at her, 'This is where I nearly ended my young life.'

Oh, God.

A pang of horror arrowed through Zoe, and she had a sudden picture of a little boy with dark hair and dark eyes recklessly diving and hitting his head…

This lovely man had nearly died.

Here. In this idyllic setting.

Her throat stung and she might have cried, if Kent hadn't been watching.

He sent her a grin.

She blinked away the tears. 'So this is where Bella's dad saved you?'

He nodded. 'It was nearly a year before I got back in the water.'

'I'm not surprised.' And then, she *had* to ask, 'What was it like, Kent? Can you remember? Did you know you'd nearly died?'

As soon as the questions were out she felt embarrassed by her nosiness, but Kent, to her relief, didn't seem to mind.

'I have no recollection at all of diving in, but I have a very vivid memory of opening my eyes from a deep and terrible, dark dream where I was choking. I looked straight up into Tom Shaw's face, and beyond him I could see the vivid blue sky and the tops of the river gums.'

'Did you know what had happened?'

Kent nodded slowly. 'It's weird, but I seemed to understand that I'd been given a second chance at life.'

He'd only been six—so young to be confronted with something so profound.

'I'm surprised you're still happy to come down here,' she said.

'I love it here,' Kent replied quietly. 'This place always makes me think about survival. And fate.'

'And Tom Shaw.'

His dark eyes studied Zoe's face intently, and again she felt an unwilling connection, a silent *something* zinging between them. Quicksilver shivers turned her arms to goose bumps.

'And Tom Shaw,' Kent said quietly. 'I'll never forget that debt.'

* * *

Shortly after they got back to the homestead, Bella rang.

'How are things at your place this morning?' Kent asked her.

'Dad's fine, thank heavens. He slept in late, but he's just eaten a huge recovery breakfast. And he seems really well. No coughing or shortness of breath. And of course, he's full of remorse and promises.'

'Good. So you'll be coming over here soon?'

'Actually...' An awkward note crept into Bella's voice. 'That's what I'm ringing about. I've been thinking I really should scoot into town to see Paddy.'

'Your grandfather?' Surprise buzzed a low warning inside Kent. 'But Zoe's here. Don't you two have all kinds of jobs lined up for this weekend?'

'Well...yes...but I thought I could squeeze in a *very* quick trip to town. It's just that I haven't seen Paddy for ages and you know how dreary it can be in the old people's home.' Almost as an afterthought, Bella asked, 'Is Zoe at a loose end?'

Kent glanced through the open doorway across the veranda to the garden. His mother had driven out from town to discuss wedding plans and she and Zoe were deep in conversation. They were pacing out sections of lawn and, judging by their arm-waving movements and general nodding and jotting-down of notes, they were discussing the table and seating arrangements.

They'd started over coffee this morning, chatting about the bridal shower—something about making a wedding dress from wrapping paper. Then they'd moved on to the flowers for table centrepieces at the wedding, and the kinds of pot plants that looked best in the gazebo. Zoe had wondered if there should be little lights entwined with the greenery.

The two of them were getting on like a bushfire.

But Kent knew damn well that it should be Bella who was out there in the garden with his mother. Surely, the bride should be involved in all this planning.

Renewed uneasiness stirred in him. He did his best to suppress it. Bella had always been upfront with him. She would tell him if there was a problem.

'Zoe's certainly not at a loose end,' he told her now. 'She and my mother are pretty busy, actually. If you're not careful they'll have the whole wedding planned before you get here.'

'Wonderful,' Bella said with a laugh.

'Wonderful?' Kent tried not to sound too concerned, but he couldn't shake off the troubling sense that something was definitely off kilter. Last night when he'd gone over to the Shaws' place, Bella had been moody and despondent, but that was excusable. He'd understood how upset she was about Tom.

But this morning was different. Tom was on the mend again, and Bella seemed to be leaving all the arrangements for the wedding to Zoe. Surely she should be here?

'You know me, Kent,' Bella said smoothly. 'I've never been much of a planner. Remember how I always used to leave my assignments until the last minute.'

'Yeah, I remember. But I think *you* should remember that Zoe *is* a planner, and hosting a wedding with dozens of guests is hardly the same as a school assignment. Zoe's your only bridesmaid, for heaven's sake, and she's doing an incredible job, but you can't leave it all on her shoulders.'

'Kent, you're right. I'm sorry.' Bella's lowered voice was suddenly contrite. 'I mustn't leave everything to Zoe just because she's so capable. Look, I promise to be out there very, very soon. I'll just race into town, say a quick hello to Paddy, and I'll come straight over. I'll bring a cherry pie and some of that lovely stuffed bread from the Willara bakery for lunch.'

Still worried, Kent hung up and stood with his hand resting on the receiver. He frowned as he looked through the doorway to his mother and Zoe out in the garden.

They were examining a bed of roses now, heads together—one a shower of silver curls and the other a silky, dark brown fall. The two of them were talking animatedly and doing rather a lot of smiling and nodding.

Zoe leaned forward to smell a lush pink rose bloom, and her hair swung forward with the movement. She was wearing knee-length khaki shorts and sandals, and a soft floral top with a little frill that skimmed her collarbones—so different from yesterday afternoon's pencil-slim skirt, stockings and high heels, and yet every bit as appealing.

The women moved on, and his mother became busy with her secateurs, tidying, trimming, and apparently explaining something to Zoe. Every so often, a tinkle of feminine laughter floated over the lawn.

Watching them, Kent thought that any stranger, coming upon the idyllic scene, could be forgiven for assuming that Zoe was his mother's future daughter-in-law.

His bride.

Hell. A dangerous flame leapt in his chest. Hell no. Not Zoe. It was ridiculous. Impossible. Never going to happen.

Bella should be here. Now.

* * *

As it turned out, Zoe also made a trip into Willara that morning. Having settled on their plans for the bridal shower, she and Kent's mother needed several items from the newsagent, so Zoe volunteered to collect them.

'Perhaps Kent could go with you for company,' Stephanie Rigby suggested.

Out of the corner of her eye, Zoe saw Kent tense, and felt an answering whip-crack reaction. *No.* No way could she risk spending any more time alone with her best friend's bridegroom.

Without chancing another glance in Kent's direction, she said, 'Thanks, but I know Kent's busy, and I'll be fine on my own.'

To her relief, there was no argument.

'You never know your luck,' Stephanie said serenely. 'You might run into Bella and you could double check her preferences before you buy the ribbons and the paper daisies.'

'That's a good idea. I'll keep an eye out for her. I guess Willara's so small, it's quite possible to run into people on the main street.'

Stephanie laughed. 'It happens all the time.'

'Your best chance of catching Bella will be at the Greenacres home or the bakery,' Kent suggested in a dry, unreadable tone that made Zoe wonder if he was in a bad mood.

'OK, I'll try the home, then the bakery.'

Zoe had never visited a home for the aged. Her grandparents were still quite fit and healthy and lived in their own homes, so she was already a bit nervous when she pulled up at Greenacres on Willara's outskirts. Then she walked through sliding doors into the large, tiled foyer, and came to a frozen, heart-thudding halt.

Bella was standing on the far side of the reception

area, deep in conversation—an animated, intense conversation—with a young man.

Zoe took one at Bella's companion and immediately recognised the wild, dark hair and strong stubbled jaw from the photos she'd seen on the internet. Damon Cavello.

She felt a punch of shock in the centre of her chest, but she told herself she was overreacting. Damon was an old friend of Bella's and Kent's from their school days—and a chance meeting with him in an aged care home was perfectly harmless. It wasn't as if she'd caught Bella indulging in a sly assignation. This was no big deal.

So maybe they were leaning subtly towards each other and gazing intently into each other's eyes. And maybe their body language suggested a deep, mutual interest that locked out the rest of the world...

Or maybe Zoe was totally misreading the whole situation.

Unable to contain her curiosity a moment longer, she stepped forward. 'Bella!'

Her friend jumped and turned, and when she saw Zoe she blushed like litmus paper.

'Zoe, f-fancy seeing you here.' Bella shot a hasty glance to the man at her side, then back to her friend. 'Are you looking for me? Nothing's happened at home, has it?'

'There's no problem,' Zoe reassured her. 'I came into town to buy a few things from the newsagent, and I ducked in here first. We knew you were here and we'd like to have your approval on—'

Zoe hesitated, uncomfortably aware of Damon Cavello's steely and not particularly friendly gaze. 'We wanted to check on one or two—matters—for the wedding.'

'Oh, right.' Bella was her normal colour again, and she straightened her shoulders and lifted her chin, drawing dignity around her like armour. She smiled carefully as she turned to the man beside her. 'Damon, this is my bridesmaid, my wonderful friend, Zoe Weston.'

Despite the tension zinging in the air, Zoe was aware of a warm swelling of pride when she heard herself described in such glowing terms.

'Zoe, this is Damon Cavello, an old school friend.'

'Of course.' Zoe held out her hand and favoured him with her warmest smile. 'You contacted me on Facebook. Hi, Damon, nice to meet you.'

'How do you do, Zoe?' Damon shook her hand firmly, but his smile didn't quite reach his eyes. 'And thank you for engineering this chance to hook up with the old gang.'

He nodded towards Bella and his silver-grey eyes seemed to smoulder, but his voice was relaxed enough, so it shouldn't have been an awkward moment. Zoe, however, could feel unmistakable vibes of tension. And yikes, she could practically see the electricity sparking between this pair.

'Damon has been visiting his grandmother,' Bella said.

'And you ran into him while you were visiting your grandfather. What a lucky coincidence.'

'Yes.'

An elderly woman, shuffling past with a walking frame, beamed a radiant smile on the three of them.

'Well…as I said, I was on the way to the newsagents,' Zoe continued. 'So if you two have more catching up to do, I can wait for you there, Bella.'

'It's OK. I'll come with you now. Damon and I have said our hellos.'

Damon frowned and Zoe sent him another friendly smile. 'Will we see you at the wedding?'

'Sure.' He swallowed uncomfortably as if there was a painful constriction in his throat. 'Kent kindly emailed an invitation. Asked me to the bucks' party as well.'

'Great. We should run into you again, then, either some time next weekend, or on the big day.'

'Absolutely.'

The girls had driven into town in separate vehicles, so there was no chance for an in-depth conversation during their shopping jaunt or on their separate journeys back to Willara Downs. And for the rest of the weekend they were so busy, making decorations, or party favours, or cooking sweets and canapés to be stored or frozen that they didn't have time for an in-depth talk.

It was Sunday afternoon when they were heading back down the highway to Brisbane before they were alone and the subject of Damon could be properly aired.

Not that Bella was in a talkative mood. From the moment they left Willara, she seemed to slip lower and lower in the passenger seat, slumped in despondent silence.

'Missing Kent already?' Zoe asked tentatively.

Bella gave a guilty start and she frowned like a sleeper waking from a dream. 'Sorry...what did you say?'

'I asked if you were already missing Kent.'

'Oh...yes...of course.'

'At least you'll only have to wait two more weeks and then you can be with him all the time.'

'Yes,' Bella said softly.

Zoe had used every ounce of her inner strength to remain upbeat and supportive about Bella's good fortune, despite all the worrying niggles. Surely her friend could try a bit harder to act happy. Instead of rallying, however, Bella seemed to sink into even deeper misery.

By now, they were heading down the steep Too-woomba Range, and Zoe couldn't take her eyes off the road, but she had the horrible feeling that Bella was on the verge of crying. Then she heard a definite sob.

Casting a frantic sideways glance, Zoe saw tears streaming down her friend's face. Her heart gave a sickening lurch.

'Bell,' she cried, keeping her gaze fixed on the steep, winding road. 'What's the matter?'

'I'm OK,' Bella sobbed. 'I'm just being an idiot.'

Zoe couldn't help wondering if Damon was somehow the cause of these tears, but she had no idea how to ask such a probing question. Besides, it was her duty to keep Bella focused on Kent.

'It must be awful to have to say goodbye to Kent every weekend.'

'Oh, Zoe, don't,' Bella wailed.

Don't? Don't talk about Kent?

Thoroughly alarmed, Zoe held her tongue as she negotiated a particularly sharp hairpin bend. Out of the corner of her eye, she was aware of Bella pulling tissues from the bag at her feet and wiping her eyes and blowing her nose.

It wasn't till they reached the bottom of the range and the road levelled out once more that Zoe stole another glance Bella's way. Her friend was no longer crying, but her face was pale and blotchy and she still looked exceedingly unhappy.

'I really don't want to pry, Bell, but is there any way I can help?'

Bella released a drawn-out sigh. 'I don't think so, thanks.'

'I mean—tell me to shut up, but if you want to talk—about—*anything*—it's the bridesmaid's job to listen.'

This was greeted by a shaky little laugh. 'Oh, Zoe, you're such a sweetheart.'

A nice compliment, but not exactly true. A sweetheart did not fall for her best friend's fiancé.

A few minutes later, Zoe tried again. 'So…I suppose it's just tension. You have so much on your plate just now—worrying about your dad, and so many jobs crowding in with the wedding so close.'

Bella turned away to look out of the window at rows and rows of bright sunflowers standing with their heads high like soldiers in formation.

Clearly, she wasn't looking for a chance to talk about her problem, so Zoe drove on in silence…wondering… worrying…

Then out of the blue, as they approached Gatton, Bella sat up straighter. 'Zoe, I think I do need to talk. I can't deal with this on my own. Can we pull over?'

CHAPTER SIX

ZOE took the next ramp leading off the highway and parked beneath a jacaranda tree in an almost empty picnic area. At a distant table, a family were gathering up their tea things and packing them into a basket. The mother was calling to her little girl who was scooping up fallen jacaranda blossoms.

Suddenly needing air, Zoe lowered her window and dragged in deep breaths, catching the dank scent of newly turned earth from nearby fields and the sweeter scent of the flowering trees.

Her stomach churned uncomfortably and she unbuckled her seat belt. She was dead-set nervous now that Bella was about to confide her problem. Her friend's tears pointed to a serious dilemma, and Zoe wasn't confident she had the wisdom or the strength to advise her.

Honestly, could she trust herself to put her own silly, unwanted emotions aside?

Praying she would get this right, she said gently, 'I'm ready whenever you are, Bells.'

Bella pulled another tissue from her bag and blew her nose noisily, then, after only a moment's hesitation, she took the leap. 'There's no point in beating about the bush. I'm in a mess about this wedding.'

'Ah-h-h.'

Bella shot Zoe a sharp glance. 'So you're not surprised?'

'Not entirely. I must admit I've been waiting for you and Kent to show more—er—emotion about—well—everything. And right from the first time Damon made contact, it was pretty clear he made you edgy.'

Bella nodded. 'I know. Seeing Damon again has been a kind of wake-up call.'

'You mean you really care about him?'

'Oh, I don't really know, Zoes. He sends me kind of crazy. It's like I'm still in high school. Up and down and all over the place.'

'I'm sorry. I should never have posted that rave about your wedding on Facebook. It's my fault Damon found you.'

'Gosh, don't blame yourself. I think he heard about the wedding from other people as well.' Bella was pulling the tissue in her lap to shreds.

'Damon's not trying to stop you getting married, is he?'

Zoe had a sudden vision of Damon Cavello calling out in the middle of the wedding—at that moment when the minister asked the congregation to speak up or for ever hold their peace.

Bella shook her head, then, with another heavy sigh, she kicked off her shoes and drew her feet up onto the seat, hugging her knees. 'The thing is, when Damon rang me on Saturday morning, I had to see him. I thought if I saw him just once in the flesh—if I spoke to him, I'd get the old memories out of my system. But as soon as we met—'

Hairs stood on the back of Zoe's neck as she watched the flush spread across Bella's face. She tried to make light of it. 'So your heart took off like a racehorse? Your knees gave way?'

Bella nodded, then covered her face with her hands. 'What am I going to do?'

It was a question Zoe didn't want to answer. But poor Bella hadn't a mother to turn to and she was her best friend. Praying for wisdom, Zoe took a deep breath before she spoke. 'I—I guess it all depends on how you feel about Kent.'

At first Bella didn't answer. When she did, her voice was soft, wistful... 'That's my problem. I'm so worried that Kent and I are marrying for all the wrong reasons.'

'But he's stop-and-stare gorgeous,' Zoe suggested miserably.

Bella shot her a sharp, surprised glance.

'Just stating the obvious.' Zoe's shoulders lifted in a defensive shrug, and a dull ache curled around her heart.

'Well, I'm not going to argue with your good taste,' Bella said with a watery smile. 'But I just wish Kent and I had been in some sort of long-term relationship, or had at least been dating. The truth is, we haven't really seen very much of each other since I moved to Brisbane. We only caught up again properly when I started coming home, because Dad was so sick. We were both so worried about Dad and the farm, and Kent's gone out of his way to help.'

And he feels he owes your dad big-time for saving his life, Zoe wanted to say, but she kept the thought to herself.

Instead she said, 'I never totally understood how your engagement came about. It seemed a bit out of the blue to me. What made you say yes in the first place?'

Bella looked down at her diamond engagement ring

and her stunning, dark berry fingernails—enviably dramatic and gorgeous. 'It was a bit of an emotional whirlwind. It's not all that long since I lost my mum, and then it looked like I was losing my dad as well. The farm was going to rack and ruin. I felt like I was going under, too.'

'And yet you never mentioned anything about it to me.'

'Well…to be honest, I was a bit ashamed about my dad's drinking.'

Zoe gave a guilty sigh. If she'd been a better friend, the *right* kind of friend, Bella might have felt more comfortable about sharing her worries.

'I was coming home every weekend,' Bella went on. 'And I started seeing more and more of Kent, and he was so sweet, so supportive. He's been running our property as well as his own. And of course we have a deep bond that goes way back. Then one weekend, he just looked at me and said "Why don't we just do it? Why don't we get married?"'

Bella was smiling at the memory. 'In a flash, it all seemed to make wonderful sense. It was the perfect solution, and you should have seen the smile on Dad's face when we told him. He was *so* relieved I was being taken care of.'

To Zoe it was now blindingly obvious why Bella and Kent were marrying. Kent felt a huge debt to Tom Shaw. Bella was in danger of losing her family, her farm— losing everything, in other words. Bella and Kent had a long history, a shared background that made them suited to each other in every way. Duty and friendship had won, and Kent had saved the day.

Everything might have been fine if Damon hadn't arrived on the scene, no doubt reawakening Bella's school-girl fantasies of passion and romance...

Oh, man... Zoe's thought winged back to Friday night when Kent arrived home to find his kitchen filled with candles. Her skin flamed at the memory of the way he'd looked at her...

The flash of fire in his eyes had shocked her. Thrilled her. As had the roughness of emotion in his voice.

And next morning, there'd been another moment of connection down on the creek bank...

No, she mustn't think about that now. She mustn't let her own longings confuse Bella's situation.

In fact, Zoe knew she mustn't do or say anything to influence Bella right now. She had no similar experience to draw on, no wisdom to offer. Her role was to listen...

But surely Bella must see all the benefits of this marriage? Her life could be fabulous if she went ahead with it. Kent was perfect husband material. Gorgeous looks aside, if you factored in his easy manner, his beautiful home and garden, his prosperous farm and country lifestyle in a friendly, close-knit community, Willara Downs was like the closest thing to heaven.

Then again, Zoe knew that her nomadic childhood had given her a longing for security and a love of being settled that Bella might not share.

And yet, for Bella there was the added advantage that, with Kent as her husband, her father would almost certainly recover and grow stronger. Every day he would see his daughter happily married and living close by. It was such a strong incentive for Tom to throw off his bad habits and take care of his health.

Surely these were weighty plusses.

Bella, however, was sighing. 'I was so emotional at

the time Kent came up with the wedding proposal. But I know he only made the offer because he was worried about Dad, and he felt he owed something to my family. He's always had a highly developed sense of doing the right thing.'

'So he was being heroic instead of romantic?'

'Yes,' Bella admitted in a small voice.

A marriage of convenience. The thought suffocated Zoe.

Again, she forced her own longings aside. She had no doubt that Kent possessed the necessary strength of character to make a success of anything he set his mind to. Even if his marriage wasn't based on passion, he would be a loving and loyal husband.

'But the marriage could still work,' she said softly.

Bella turned to her, her eyes wide with dawning hope. 'That's true, Zoe. Even arranged marriages can work out happily.'

'So I've heard,' Zoe agreed, trying not to sound deeply miserable. Perhaps it was melodramatic of her, but she felt as if she were saying goodbye to her own last chance for happiness.

Bella was looking down at her sparkling engagement ring. 'So…you think I should go ahead and marry Kent?'

An agonising pain burst in Zoe's throat and she swallowed it down. She opened her mouth to speak, but changed her mind, afraid she might say something she'd regret.

Bella sat up straight. 'It *is* the right thing to do,' she said with sudden conviction. 'Kent's no fool. He wouldn't have offered to marry me if he wasn't happy about it.' She shot Zoe a pleading glance. 'Would he?'

Tension made Zoe tremble. She could feel the sharpened claws of her jealousy digging deep, but she forced a shaky smile. 'From where I'm looking, you'll have a wonderful life with Kent.'

She held her breath as Bella sat, staring through the windscreen, her eyes bright and thoughtful. Outside the car, the light was fading. A gust of wind sent jacaranda bells fluttering onto the windscreen.

'But you're the only one who can make the final decision,' Zoe said at last.

'You're right. I shouldn't be putting pressure on you like this.' Nevertheless, a smile dawned on Bella's face, as pretty as a sunrise. She took Zoe's hands and squeezed them tightly. 'I know what I must do. Damon threw me off track. He's always been dangerous like that. But Kent and I made our decision for all the right reasons and we should stick to our original instincts.'

Leaning forward, Bella kissed Zoe's cheek. 'Thank you for helping me to sort this out.'

Tears stung the backs of Zoe's eyes and she blinked madly to hold them back. 'No problem. Point thirty-nine in the bridesmaid's handbook. Lots of brides have second thoughts as the big day approaches.'

'I'm quite normal, then. That's a relief.'

Zoe tried to crack another smile, but couldn't quite manage it.

It didn't matter. Bella's arms were around her, hugging her tight. 'I'm so lucky,' she whispered. 'I have the best bridesmaid in the world.'

CHAPTER SEVEN

To KENT'S relief, his bucks' night wasn't too extreme. He'd heard of bridegrooms being tied naked to a pole in the main street, or bundled into a crop-dusting plane and transported to a remote outpost.

Fortunately, his best man, Steve, wangled just the right tempo. He'd done a great job of rounding up Kent's mates and the party was a blast. Not a city-style bash with strippers and pranks—just blokes enjoying themselves in a quiet country pub. Actually, the quiet country pub was growing rowdier by the minute, but the revelry was harmless enough.

There were the usual games with drinking penalties. Right now, anyone who raised taboo topics—cricket or football, the bride or her bridesmaid, the share market or politics—had to down his drink in one go. Merriment by the bucketful.

Later they'd sleep it off in the Mullinjim pub, and there'd be a few sore heads in the morning, but at least there was still a full week before the wedding.

Of course there were all kinds of comments flying about Kent's last chance for freedom.

It was a phrase that made him distinctly uneasy— but he wasn't prepared to dwell on that. He imagined most guys felt the cold snap of an iron noose about their throats whenever they thought too hard about the doors closing behind them when they stepped up to the altar.

One week to go…

He'd be glad when the tension was behind him, when he and Bella were safely settled…

Tonight, however, he had to put up with the good-natured ribbing from his mates, had to laugh as he agreed that his days as a carefree bachelor were numbered. But he wondered what the others would think if they knew how often his thoughts trailed back to earlier this evening when he'd driven through Willara and caught a glimpse of the girls at the pub.

Already in party mode after the bridal shower, Bella's friends had all been there, in shiny strapless dresses in a rainbow of colours. Looking like gaudy beetles, they'd wolf-whistled and waved glasses of pink champagne at Kent as he drove past.

He hadn't seen Bella, but she would have been in the mob somewhere, no doubt sporting a mock bridal headdress concocted from a piece of mosquito netting and a plastic tiara.

The girl he *had* seen and noted was Zoe.

She'd been standing in a doorway, chatting with a friend, and she was wearing a dress of striking tangerine silk, an exotic colour that highlighted her dark hair and slim elegance.

For a split second as Kent flashed past her eyes had met his. Startled, she'd half raised her glass.

He'd only caught that fleeting glimpse of her in the bright dress with one shoulder bared, but the image had shot a scorching flame through him. He'd remembered her in his kitchen, surrounded by four dozen smart candles and he'd felt that same thrust of longing he'd felt then.

Now, Kent consoled himself that this was the doppelgänger that haunted most men about to be married—the alter ego taking a final backward glance at freedom before diving into monogamy.

Get over it, man.

But even now, as he chatted and joked with his mates, his brain flashed to the memory.

Of Zoe. Not Bella.

Damn it, if he'd seen Bella at the pub he wouldn't be plagued by these memories now. He'd be thinking only of Bella, not Zoe with her shiny dark hair and soft smile. But now, instead of focusing on his bride, a treacherous part of his brain kept pressing rewind, kept replaying a picture of Zoe's slender curves encased in a sunburst of silk.

Why the hell now? Why tonight?

'Kent, old mate. Need to have a word.'

The voice behind Kent brought him swinging round.

Damon Cavello, glass in hand—a double shot of neat whisky by the look of it—greeted him with a morose smile.

They'd talked earlier, fighting to be heard above the hubbub, but it had been a superficial catch-up, skimming over the past decade in half a dozen carefully edited sentences. Now Damon held out his hand.

'I've overlooked congratulating the lucky bridegroom.'

'I'm sure you said something earlier.' Kent accepted the handshake uneasily, wondering if he'd detected a hint of stiffness in Damon's manner.

'You know you're a very lucky man,' Damon said.

'I do indeed.'

'You deserve her, of course.'

'Thank you.'

Why did he have the feeling that Bella's old flame was testing him? Rattling his antlers, so to speak.

Damon offered a mirthless grin. 'Bella's a—'

'Hold it!' Kent laughed as he raised his hand. 'There's a penalty tonight if you mention the bride's name.'

'Damn, I forgot.'

Before Kent could let him off the hook, Damon tossed down the contents of his glass.

Kent inhaled sharply, imagining the fire lacing the other man's veins.

'So, where was I?' Damon asked as he set the empty glass on the bar. 'Ah, yes.' Folding his arms across his chest, he sized Kent up with a knowing smile. 'I was agreeing that you've made an excellent choice of bride. You and your future wife will be the toast of Willara.'

Kent accepted this with a faint nod.

Damon's gaze shifted to a point in the distance beyond Kent's shoulder. His chest rose and fell as he drew in a deep breath, then exhaled slowly.

To Kent's dismay, the other man's eyes betrayed a terrible pain. 'I was a fool,' he said, his voice quiet yet rough with self loathing. 'I was the world's biggest fool to head off overseas, leaving her behind.'

A nightmare weight pressed down on Kent, crushing the air from his lungs and stilling his blood. He pulled himself together. 'That may be true, mate,' he said slowly. 'You were famous for doing crazy things back then. You were legend.'

'I was, but I regret it now.'

What was Damon implying? Was this some kind of mind-game strategy?

'Are you trying to tell me something?' Kent challenged in a deliberately exaggerated country drawl. 'Are you saying that you would have married young and settled down with a mob of kids in quiet old Willara?'

'Who knows? We can't turn back time.' Damon squared his shoulders, looked about him at the happy crowd, then whipped back to Kent. 'Promise me one thing.'

Kent eyed the other man levelly, refusing to be intimidated. 'What's that?'

Temporarily, Damon lost momentum. Dropping his gaze, he tapped a short drumbeat on the smooth timber-topped bar. When he looked up again, his grey eyes were blazing ice. 'Just make sure you don't have any doubts, my friend, not the slightest shadow.'

The words struck hammer blows, but Kent refused to flinch. 'Thanks for your advice,' he said coolly. 'It's heartening to know there's another man in town who understands how lucky I am to be marrying Bella Shaw.'

Looking Damon in the eye, Kent downed his drink.

It was well past midnight when Zoe heard the tap on her door. She hadn't been asleep, although her body was worn out from the huge effort of running both the bridal shower and then the hen night. The functions had been proclaimed a great success, but now her brain couldn't stop buzzing.

When the soft knock sounded, she slipped quickly from the bed, went to the door and opened it a crack. Bella was outside in the dark passageway, wild eyed and wrapped in a pink-and-blue kimono.

'Can I come in for a sec?' she whispered.

'Sure.' Zoe readily opened the door, but threads of fear were coiling in her chest. All night she'd been watching Bella with mounting alarm.

While the bride had laughed and chatted and joined
in the silly, light-hearted party games, Zoe had been
aware of the underlying pulse, a ticking time bomb of
tension. Plainly, things still weren't right for Bella. The
strain showed in her eyes, in her smile.

Luckily, all the other party girls had been too busy
drinking and having a good time to notice. But Zoe,
who'd taken her hen night responsibilities seriously, had
mostly drunk tonic water.

Clear-headed, she'd noticed plenty and she'd worried plenty. Most especially, she'd worried that Bella
still wasn't happy with the decision she'd reached last
week.

Now, her friend collapsed into the only chair in the
room. 'I've just had a text from Kent,' she said. 'He
wants to see me. To talk.'

'Tonight?'

'Yes, but I said it was too late. I rang back and talked
him into leaving it till first thing in the morning.'

'Do you know what he wants to talk about?'

'He wants to make sure I'm totally happy about—'
Bella let out a soft groan. 'He wants to discuss the wedding.'

Zoe's heart thudded. 'I assume this isn't just a planning meeting.'

'No. I'm pretty sure he wants to double check that
we're both still on the same page.'

'About getting married?'

Closing her eyes, Bella nodded.

'What are you going to tell him?'

A sob broke from Bella. 'I have to be totally honest,
Zoe. I don't think I can do it.'

CHAPTER EIGHT

FOR ages after Bella went back to her room, Zoe tossed and turned, her sheets damp with sweat, her thoughts rioting. Eventually, she got up and shut the window and switched on the air conditioning, but, although the system was efficient and the room cooled quickly, she couldn't settle down.

Everything was spinning round and round in her head. Bella's distress, Kent's ultimatum, the mystery surrounding Damon—and, of course, the beautiful wedding reception she'd planned....

Time crawled. It took for ever for dawn to finally arrive as a creamy glow around the edges of the curtains. Giving up any pretence of sleep, Zoe rolled out of bed and opened the curtains to a view down Willara's main street. At this early hour the little town was empty and silent, and it looked a little faded, too, like a ghost town in an old black-and-white movie.

Was Kent already on his way?

She showered and shampooed her hair, then blow-dried it and packed her bags, shoving all the leftover party glitter, shredded cellophane, cardboard and felt pens into an outside pocket. She had no idea why she was saving this stuff, couldn't imagine ever using it again.

There'd been no special arrangements made for breakfast—all the hen-night girls wanted to sleep off the party after-effects. But Zoe's room had started to feel like a jail cell. She knew Bella wouldn't eat until after she'd spoken to Kent, so she decided to go downstairs to dine alone.

As she went past Bella's door she thought she heard the soft murmur of voices. Perhaps, even now, Bella and Kent were making a decision. Just thinking about it made Zoe's eyes and throat sting with hot tears.

The hotel's dining room was old-fashioned with dark panelled walls and vases of bright flowers on the tables. It was still very early, and the room was empty, but a girl was there, ready to take orders.

Zoe glanced at the menu. It offered a full country breakfast with bacon, scrambled eggs, mushrooms and fried tomatoes, but, while she'd been ravenous an hour ago, her anxious stomach rebelled now.

She ordered tea and toast and sat in a sunny corner near a window. She was drinking her second cup of tea and eating hot buttered toast spread with local orange marmalade when a tall, broad-shouldered figure appeared at the dining-room doorway.

Kent.

Zoe's knife clattered to her plate.

Had he already spoken to Bella? If he hadn't, what was she supposed to say?

Kent came across the room, weaving past the empty tables covered by clean white cloths. He sent her a cautious smile, but it was impossible to gauge his mood.

He didn't look utterly heartbroken, but perhaps he was very good at masking his feelings. He was definitely paler than usual and there were shadows under his eyes, as if his night had been as restless and as tormented hers.

'I was hoping I'd find you,' he said when he reached her.

'Have you seen Bella?'

'Yes. We've been talking in her room for the past hour.'

A chill skittered over Zoe's arms. She was still unsure how to handle this.

'Can I join you?' Kent asked.

Zoe nodded, and once he was seated she realised she'd been holding her breath. The tension was unbearable. What had they decided?

Kent placed his hands squarely on the table. 'I wanted you to be the first to know. Bella and I are calling off the wedding.'

Zoe's heart gave a painful thud. Even though this wasn't totally unexpected, she felt as if she'd stepped from solid ground into thin air. 'I'm so sorry.' Tears stung her eyes and her throat. 'I can't begin to imagine how you must be feeling right now, Kent.'

'It had to be done,' he said with a shaky smile.

Zoe didn't know how to respond to that. She was dazed—and shell-shocked.

No wedding.

After all the excitement and planning and busyness of the past few weeks—now, nothing. *Nada.*

'How's Bella?'

'She's worn out from over-thinking this whole deal, but she's OK, I guess, or at least she will be after a good night's sleep.'

'I should go upstairs to see her. She might want some friendly support.'

'Actually, she's not here.' Kent lifted his hands in a

don't-ask-me gesture. 'She had to rush off to Green-acres. There's been some sort of problem there.'

'No…not her grandfather?'

'I think so.'

'Oh, God. Poor Bella. As if she hasn't had enough to worry about.'

'I offered to go with her, but she said she wanted to handle it herself, which was understandable, I guess.'

'Maybe there's something I can do?' Zoe was already rising from her chair.

'I told Bella to ring if we can help.'

As Zoe sat once more she let out a sigh. Her mind flashed to her excitement when Bella first asked her to be a bridesmaid. Who would have thought it would come to this?

The waitress appeared at Kent's side. 'Would you like to order breakfast, sir?'

'Ah, no…but perhaps some tea. Zoe, shall we order a fresh pot?'

Considering the awkwardness of their situation, Zoe found his politeness and self-control impressive. As soon as the girl had left she reached across the table and squeezed Kent's hand. It was meant to be a comforting gesture, but for her the brief contact still sparked the usual silly electricity.

'Thanks for being such a good friend to Bella,' he said.

Zoe gave a rueful shake of her head. 'My big chance to be a bridesmaid. Gone down the tube.'

'You would have been perfect,' he said warmly.

'Well, for that matter, I thought you and Bella would have been the perfect couple.'

'Did you really?'

Tension shadowed his lovely dark eyes as he waited for her answer.

Zoe found herself suddenly flustered. 'You had so much in common.'

'Maybe that was the problem.'

The waitress returned with the tea and a fresh cup and saucer for Kent, so they became busy with pouring and helping themselves to milk and sugar.

When they were alone again, Kent said, 'Zoe, the decision to call the wedding off was mutual.'

She was almost giddy with relief. 'Gosh, I'm—I'm—'

'Mad with us both for messing you around?'

'No, I'm not mad. If I'm honest, Kent, I've been worried for ages. The vibes weren't right between you.'

Kent grimaced and rubbed at his jaw in a way that was intensely masculine.

'But for what it's worth,' Zoe added, 'I think your motives for proposing were honourable.'

'What do you know about my motives?'

'I don't want to say anything out of place, but I'm guessing you wanted to look after Bella, and you wanted to put Tom's mind at ease.'

Kent's mouth tilted in a lopsided smile. 'You're not just a pretty bridesmaid, are you?'

Despite everything, Zoe drank in the sight of him sitting opposite her in his moleskin trousers threaded with a crocodile leather belt.

'The truth is,' he said, after a bit, 'I had a revealing chat with Damon last night. We started off toe to toe like two duelling bucks, all bluster and bravado. But then I started really listening to the guy. He was talking about Bella, and I watched his face, his body language. I heard the depth of emotion in his voice…'

Kent paused and his impressive chest expanded as he drew a deep breath. 'I don't know if he's the right man for Bella, or if she even wants him, but last night I found myself questioning—everything. I realised that I was denying Bella—denying both of us the chance to have a marriage based on something *more* than friendship.'

He was looking directly at Zoe and she felt heat spreading over her skin. She told herself to stop it. Just because Kent was no longer marrying Bella, she couldn't start imagining he was going to dive into a new relationship. And even if he did, why would he choose her?

Suddenly, with her role as bridesmaid swept away, her old insecurities were rushing back.

She was relieved when Kent returned to practicalities.

'I've told Bella I'll take the heat as far as the wedding's concerned. I'll talk to our families and friends.'

What a task. Zoe pictured the girls upstairs. They'd be getting up soon and would have to be told the news, and there were so many others who would need to know. It was all going to be awkward and embarrassing, and Kent was shouldering the load. She felt a rush of sympathy for him, another layer to add to the emotional storm inside her.

'Perhaps I could help with ringing the caterers and the hire people?'

Kent considered this. 'I'd like to say don't worry. You've done more than enough, and I'll take care of it. But with all these other calls to make, I'd really appreciate your help, Zoe. As it is, I think I'll be spending all day on the phone.'

On cue, Kent's mobile phone rang and he quickly retrieved it from his pocket. 'It's Bella,' he said as he checked the caller ID.

Zoe watched the concern in his eyes as he listened. She tried not to eavesdrop, but she couldn't help catching his rather alarming responses.

'Do you think that's wise, Bella?... What about the police?... Yes, I've spoken to Zoe. I'm with her now. Yes, sure.'

To Zoe's surprise, he handed her the phone. 'Bella wants to speak to you.'

'What's happening?' she whispered.

He rolled his eyes. 'Big drama. Bella will explain.'

Heavens, what else could go wrong? Zoe lifted the phone. 'Hi, Bella.'

'Zoe, I'm so sorry I dashed off, but you won't believe what's happened. My grandfather and Damon's grandmother have taken off.'

'Taken off?' Zoe almost shrieked. 'You mean they've run away from Greenacres? Together?'

'Yes. They've taken Damon's grandmother's car.' Bella's sudden laugh was almost hysterical. 'It's ridiculous, I know. It might only be a prank, and they're not senile or anything, but we can't let them drive off together without knowing what they plan to do. We have a lead, so Damon and I are going after them.'

'Far out. That's—that's incredible.'

'I know. I can't believe it either. But, Zoe, I'm really, really sorry to be abandoning you. I wanted to talk to you this morning, to explain everything.'

'Don't worry about me.' Lowering her voice, she said, 'Kent's explained about the wedding.'

'Is he OK?'

Zoe sent a glance Kent's way. Catching her eye, he gave her another crooked smile and she felt a flash of useless longing. 'He seems to be bearing up.'

'Zoe, can you look after Kent? Keep an eye on him?'

'I—I—' Zoe was so thrown by the thought of ongoing contact with Kent that she wasn't quite sure what to say. And yet, she couldn't overlook the pleading in Bella's voice. 'Yes, yes, of course I will.'

'Thank you. Thanks for everything, Zoes. I'm so sorry you're not going to be my bridesmaid after all, but at least we can be thankful we chose a dress you can wear to a nice party.'

Zoe rolled her eyes. The last thing on her mind was her dress.

'I'll stay in touch,' Bella said. 'But I've got to dash now. Talk soon. Bye.'

'Bye. And, Bella—'

'Yes?'

'Be careful, won't you?'

'Um…yeah, thanks for the warning.' Bella spoke softly, as if she knew very well that the warning was mostly about Damon Cavello.

Dazed, Zoe handed the phone back to Kent. 'I'm beginning to think I must be dreaming. Runaway grandparents, for crying out loud! None of this is happening, is it?' She held out her arm. 'If someone pinched me now, I'm sure I'd wake up.'

Laughing, Kent took her arm, and his warm fingers encircled her, creating a bracelet of heat. Instead of pinching her, however, he stroked a feather-light caress on the fine, pale skin of her inner wrist.

A tremor vibrated through her, and she gasped. Had he felt it?

His dark eyes flashed a message—inchoate and thrilling—unmistakable.

Her heart thundered. *Don't be an idiot.*

He was still watching her as he released her. He smiled. 'I'm quite sure you're wide awake.'

Then, as if to correct himself, he became business-like once more. 'Now,' he said. 'It's time to get cracking. We have a wedding to cancel.'

Rusty hinges squeaked as Kent pushed open the old timber gate that led to the tangle of shrubbery and weeds surrounding the Shaw family's homestead. Even on a pleasant spring afternoon, the unkempt jungle looked depressing—a far cry from the beautiful, prize-winning garden that had been Bella's mother's pride and joy. Mary Shaw would roll in her grave if she could see this mess now.

Kent called out, partly in greeting, partly as a warning. 'Tom, are you home?'

Tom's faithful border collie appeared, eyes eager and bright and tail wagging happily. Mounting the front steps, Kent greeted him. 'Where's your boss, Skip?'

'I'm in here,' called a deep male voice. 'In the kitchen.'

Relieved, Kent made his way down the hall, but his gut clenched as he thought of the task ahead of him.

He'd already broken the news about the wedding to his parents and they'd coped surprisingly well. His mother had made a gentle complaint about all the money she'd spent on her outfit.

'Where am I going to wear a brocade two-piece in Willara?' she'd demanded, with a rueful smile, but she hadn't really looked unhappy.

His father had given his shoulder a sympathetic thump and muttered that he was proud of Kent's courage.

And Bella had spoken to Tom, of course, so Kent wasn't about to drop a bombshell.

Just the same, as he entered the big, airy kitchen at the back of the old timber Queenslander it was hard to shake off the feeling that he'd let Tom Shaw down.

Kent looked about the kitchen filled with windows and painted sunshiny yellow. It had always been his favourite room in this homestead. In his primary school days, he'd regularly dropped in here for afternoon tea.

There'd always be home-made macadamia or ginger cookies and milk, and he and Bella had eaten them at the scrubbed pine table, or sometimes they'd taken their snack outside to sit in their cubbyhouse beneath an old weeping willow.

Now, Kent found Bella's father standing at the greasy stove, thin, unshaven and pale, with heavy shadows under his eyes. At least he appeared to be sober, which was something, and he was stirring the contents of a pot with a wooden spoon.

This Tom Shaw was such a different figure from the man Kent had known and admired for most of his life. It had been a rude shock to watch this man slide downhill so quickly and completely after his wife's death. He'd hated to stand by and witness his hero's self-destruction.

So, yeah…the wedding plan had been all about propping Tom up again. Now, Kent squared his shoulders.

'Evening,' Tom greeted him morosely.

'Evening, Tom.' Kent stood with two hands resting on the back of a kitchen chair, bracing himself.

'Bella rang and she explained about the wedding.'

'Yeah.' Kent swallowed. 'I'm sorry it hasn't worked out.'

'Well…actually—' Tom smiled wryly '—I'm relieved, son.'

'Relieved?'

Tom nodded. 'I know I was excited at first. It's true I was thrilled with the notion of you taking care of my Bella and Blue Gums. I could die happy. But it wasn't long before I realised something was missing. Something really important.'

Turning the flame down beneath his cooking pot, Tom folded his arms and leaned back against a cupboard. 'I've been in love, Kent. I had a great marriage, full of spark.' He fixed Kent with knowing eyes. 'That's the thing. There has to be a spark—something beyond friendship. Something to set your soul on fire.'

Kent knew he was right. This lack of a spark was exactly what he and Bella had finally acknowledged. They were very fond of each other. They were great mates. But deep down they knew the passion they both yearned for was never going to materialise.

'I'm ashamed that you were both prepared to take that huge step for my sake,' Tom said. 'Heck, Kent, marriage is a gigantic step.' His eyes took on a little of their old fire. 'I couldn't bear to think you were tying the knot to repay me for yanking you out of the flaming creek all those years ago.'

'But I owe you my life.'

'I happened to be on the spot, and I just did what anyone would have done.' Tom shook his head. 'Thank heavens you and Bella have come to your senses.'

Kent took a moment to digest this. He had a sneaking suspicion that his parents were as relieved as Tom was, although they hadn't expressed their views quite so strongly.

'I'm glad you understand,' he said quietly. 'But while we're being honest, there's something else I need to get off my chest.'

'What's that?' The other man's eyes narrowed.

Kent's grip on the chair tightened. 'It's your turn to wake up, Tom. I know it's been hard for you these past eighteen months, but you need to accept that no one else can take responsibility for your health. I can plough your fields and mend your fences, and I can even offer to marry your daughter, but none of that will help you if you can't give up your bad habits.'

Tom dropped his gaze, jaw stubbornly jutted. 'You're dead right. In fact, I'm one step ahead of you.'

'Have you rejoined AA?'

'I have and I won't miss another meeting. That last time I put on a turn in front of Bella's friend was my wake-up call. I really let Bella down.'

Kent gripped Tom's hand. 'That's great news, mate. Well done.' Now he was grinning widely. 'Doc King gave you plenty more years if you conquered the grog and worked on your fitness.'

'Yeah, so that's the plan. I want to be around to see my grandkids.' Tom gave Kent's shoulder a hearty bang. 'And your nippers, too.'

At the end of the day Zoe stood on the back veranda at Willara Downs, looking out at what had fast become her all-time-favourite view. She'd had a huge weekend and was almost dead on her feet, and Kent had insisted that she couldn't possibly drive back to Brisbane this evening.

So while he'd gone to talk to Tom Shaw, she'd prepared dinner—lamb baked with garlic and rosemary and lemon.

For an afternoon, she'd been living her fantasy—fussing about in a farmhouse kitchen, cooking a tasty dinner for the handsome farmer who belonged there.

Which only proved how foolish she was. It was time to put this episode behind her, time to forget about Kent.

The emotional connection she felt towards him and his beautiful home was out of all proportion to her true relationship. She was nothing more than Kent's former fiancée's *almost* bridesmaid.

OK. So maybe she'd promised Bella she would 'look after' Kent, but surely the kindest thing she could do was to leave quickly and without any fuss. Later she would stay in touch via email. Emails were safe.

Even though she knew all this…for now, she was enjoying her last look at this lovely view. Beyond the fence bordering the homestead's lawns and gardens stretched fields of sun-drenched golden corn and green pastures dotted with grazing cattle. Beyond that again, distant low hills nestled in a purple haze.

For Zoe there was something magical about it, especially now when it was tinged by the bronzed-copper glow of the late afternoon.

When she was small, she used to look out of the window of her parents' bus at views like this. At this time of day she would see farmers on their tractors, turning away from the chocolate earth of their newly ploughed fields and heading for home.

As the bus trundled down the highway she would watch the lights coming on in farmhouses, spilling yellow into the purple shadowed gardens. She'd watch wisps of smoke curling from chimneys into skies streaked with pink and gold and lavender. Sometimes she caught glimpses through windows of families gathered around kitchen tables.

Most evenings, shortly after dusk, her parents would turn in at a camping ground. Zoe and her mum would need a torch to find their way to the shower block, and they'd hurry back, damp and sometimes shivering in their dressing gowns. Her parents would cook a meal on their portable gas stove, and Zoe would do her homework, or read a book, or listen to the radio.

The bus was cosy enough at night, but oh, she'd coveted those warm, sturdy farmhouses. For Zoe, the simple ripple-iron-roofed dwellings surrounded by crops and fields were more beautiful and desirable than any fairy-tale castles.

Remembering those days now, she leaned on the veranda railing, drinking in details to keep them stored in her memory. The scent of newly cut grass. The deepening shadows creeping over the fields. The soft lowing of cattle. And coming from behind her, the fragrant kitchen aromas.

'I thought I might find you out here.'

Zoe turned, deliberately slowly, and smiled as Kent came to rest his arms on the timber railing beside her.

'Now everyone who needs to know knows,' he said. 'I had to leave messages for one or two folk, but at least they've all been informed.'

'How did Tom take the news?'

'Surprisingly well.'

'Wow. You must be relieved.'

'Very.' He turned, folded his arms and regarded her with a quizzical smile. 'Dinner smells good.'

'Yes, you have impeccable timing. The roast is due out of the oven right now.'

Together they went into the kitchen and Kent opened a bottle of wine. It felt incredibly domesticated and intimate to Zoe. But then, she was in full fantasy mode, while Kent was getting over a huge ordeal.

Nevertheless, he looked very much at home, pouring wine, wielding a carving knife, slipping a light jazz CD into the player. And he was lavish with his compliments for Zoe's cooking.

'I had farm-fresh ingredients,' she said. 'How could I go wrong?'

Across the table, Kent sent her a smile. 'Pity you're heading back to Brisbane tomorrow.'

It was silly to feel flustered, but there was a glitter in his dark eyes and a husky rumble in his voice that set Zoe's pulses dancing a crazy jig.

'So what are your plans for the rest of your week off?' he asked.

'Actually, I've been thinking that I might as well go back to work.'

Kent's eyebrows shot high. 'And waste the chance to take a holiday?'

'I'm not in the mood for a holiday now, and I can save this week for later. For when I go overseas.'

'Ah, yes. Christmas in Prague. Is it all planned?'

'No. I need to start booking my flights as soon as I get back.'

Kent frowned and dropped his gaze. A muscle jumped in his jaw.

'What about your plans, Kent? I know you had time set aside for a honeymoon. Are you still going to take a break?'

He shrugged. 'Not much point really. Besides, it's

the dry season and I need to keep the feed supplements up to the cattle. There's more than enough to keep me busy around here.'

Zoe was quite certain he was making excuses, but she understood. Under the circumstances, he wouldn't enjoy a holiday on his own. For her, getting back to work was about keeping busy and stopping her mind from revisiting endless if onlys...

It would be the same for Kent, magnified one hundred times.

Zoe left Willara Downs after breakfast the next morning. For the last time, she stripped the pink-and-white sheets from the bed in the pretty guest bedroom, and looked around fondly at the space she'd foolishly begun to pretend was hers.

Now it was time for reality. Back to the city. She needed to get over her silly crush on Kent, and the only way to achieve that was to stay well away from him.

Her car was parked at the side of the house, behind a hedge of purple-flowering duranta, and Kent insisted on carrying her bags, while she carried the bridesmaid's dress.

After laying it carefully along the back seat, she stepped back and took a deep breath. Time to say goodbye. *No tears, now.*

She offered Kent her best attempt at a smile.

But to her surprise he was staring at the dress, which was now a filmy river of coffee and cream chiffon on the back seat. 'You would have looked so lovely in that,' he said in a strangely choked voice.

Zoe tried to laugh. 'It's ridiculous how badly I wanted to be a bridesmaid.' She shook her head at her own foolishness.

'You've been perfect anyhow, a perfect *almost* bridesmaid.' He flashed a brief quarter-smile. 'Bella couldn't have had better support.'

'Nice of you to say so.' Zoe squeezed the words past the tightness in her throat. 'But if we talk about all that now, I'm going to make a fool of myself.'

Determined not to cry, she opened the driver's door, tossed her shoulder bag onto the passenger's seat, and slipped the key into the ignition. She was blinking madly, trying so hard to be strong.

'Zoe,' Kent said softly, and his hand closed around her arm.

She ducked her head, hoping he couldn't see her struggle.

'Zoe, look at me.'

He spoke with such convincing tenderness she couldn't bear it. She was swiping at her eyes as he turned her around.

'Hey…' With the pads of his thumbs, he dried her tears.

Electrified, she was zapped into stillness by his touch. He was so close now she could see the tiny flecks in his eyes—fine streaks of cinnamon combined with hazelnut—could see his individual eyelashes…

'There's something I need to give you,' he said and he produced from his jeans pocket a slim gold box.

'What is it?'

'Your bridesmaid's gift.'

Shocked, Zoe clapped a hand to her mouth. She shook her head.

'Come on,' he said, smiling as he pushed the box into her free hand. 'You've earned this, and I went to a lot of trouble to get the right colour.'

'Oh.' Her hands were shaking.

'Here, let me open it for you.'

She watched as Kent's big hands lifted the dainty lid to reveal a bracelet made of beautiful, translucent beads of every colour.

'They're made of hand-blown glass designed by a local artist.'

'Kent, they're gorgeous.' Each bead displayed a uniquely different rainbow of colours, but the overall effect was one of beautiful harmony. 'I love it. Thank you so much.'

Setting the box on the bonnet of her car, Kent took her wrist. Oh, the intimacy of his hands, of his warm strong fingers brushing her skin. A wave of longing and regret crashed over Zoe and she was in danger of crying again. She closed her eyes to hold the tears back. Then, to her utter surprise, she felt Kent's hands cradle her face, tilting it ever so slightly towards him.

Her eyes flashed open and for breathless seconds they stared at each other, and she saw surprise—the same surprise she was feeling—mirrored in Kent's eyes.

Surprise and disbelief...

And knowledge...

And helplessness...

And then he was kissing her.

Or Zoe was kissing him.

Or perhaps they simply flowed together, drawn by a potent, irresistible magnetism, as if by some miracle they shared the same aching need, the same unspoken longing.

Zoe's senses revelled in the scent of Kent's skin, and the dark taste of coffee on his lips, the thrilling strength of his arms wrapped around her. She was quite sure she'd never been kissed with such wanting, and she certainly knew she'd never returned a kiss with such fervour.

When they drew apart, at last and with great reluctance, they stood facing each other, panting and flushed and slightly self-conscious.

When Zoe spoke, she tried to sound a thousand times more composed than she felt. 'That was unexpected.'

'For me, too. But I'm not complaining.'

No. Zoe wasn't complaining either, but she felt compelled to offer reasons...excuses... 'It's been an emotional weekend. I—I guess I needed a hug.'

'I guess you did,' Kent agreed with a smile.

'And I—ah—should be going.' She turned back to the car again. Already the magic was fading, and the reality of their situation was rushing back. They'd both been under amazing strain and the kiss was an emotional finale to an incredibly emotional weekend.

Nothing more. Certainly nothing to weave dreams around.

What could she say now? *So long, it's been good to know you?* If she looked at Kent again, she might make a fool of herself, so she spoke without turning back to him. 'I'll let you know if I hear from Bella.'

'Thanks, and I'll pass on any news from my end.'

'Emails are probably the easiest.'

'Sure.'

Deep breath. 'Goodbye, Kent.'

'Bye.'

He took a step closer, and dropped another warm kiss on her cheek. Zoe's insides were doing cartwheels. 'See you later. Maybe,' she choked.

'Make that definitely,' Kent corrected quietly.

She didn't reply and closed the car door. He tapped

on her window with his knuckle, and they waved to each other.

Her eyes welled with tears, but she blinked them clear. *Enough of this nonsense.* They'd finished this story. This was...

The End.

She took off, watching Kent in her rear vision mirror. He stood with his feet firmly planted, his hands sunk in his pockets...watching her...and when she reached the end of the drive and was at last enveloped by the tunnel of trees, he still hadn't moved.

CHAPTER NINE

To: Zoe Weston<zoe.weston@flowermail.com>
From: Kent Rigby<willaraKR@hismail.com>
Subject: The Runaways
Hi Zoe,
I hope you had a safe trip back and that everything was fine when you got home. Just wanted to thank you once again. I don't think you truly realise how big a help you've been.

Also, I've had a text from Bella, and she and Damon are still on the trail of the grandparents. They're heading north—staying in Rockhampton tonight, I think.

Are you determined to go back to the office tomorrow?

Seems a shame you can't have a decent break.
Cheers,
Kent

To: Kent Rigby<willaraKR@hismail.com>
From: Zoe Weston<zoe.weston@flowermail.com>
Subject: The Runaways
Hi Kent,
Thanks for your email and for asking if everything

was OK, but I'm afraid I came home to a minor disaster. I asked my neighbour to take care of my goldfish while I was away and she overfed them, so my poor goldfish, Orange Juice, was floating on the top of a very murky tank. By the looks of it, Anita dumped half a tin of fish food in there.

I didn't think to warn her that you can't do that with goldfish. Thank heavens I wasn't away all week or I would have lost Brian and Ezekiel as well. As it is, they look a bit peaky.

I know you must be thinking I'm a screw loose to be so upset about a goldfish, but they're the only pets I can have in this flat, so they're important. Now, I've spent most of the evening cleaning the tank.

But, yes, to answer your question, I'll be back at the office in the morning.

Bella sent me that text, too. It's a weird situation they've found themselves in, isn't it? We can only hope it all works out happily.

Best wishes and thanks again for your hospitality, Zoe.

To: Kent Rigby<willaraKR@hismail.com>
From: Zoe Weston<zoe.weston@flowermail.com>
Subject: Thank You

Kent, you shouldn't have. Honestly. It was so sweet of you to have a goldfish delivered to the office.

The delivery boy caused quite a stir when he appeared in the doorway with a huge grin on his face and a plastic bag with a goldfish in his hand.

As if the office gossip wasn't already flying thick

and fast this morning. Quite a few of the girls were at the hen party, so of course the whole staff wanted details.

Luckily, when the delivery came I got to the door first, so no one else saw the docket and realised it came from you. That would certainly have put the cat among the goldfish, and everyone would have been jumping to the wrong conclusions.

But I'm very grateful, Kent. According to a magazine article on feng shui, three goldfish in a tank are always better than two, so your gift has restored my chances of inner peace and prosperity.

And I'm sure you'll be pleased to know that the new fish is very pretty, with lovely white markings and delicate fins. I've decided she's a girl and I've called her Ariel.

Brian and Ezekiel are very impressed.

Thank you again, and warmest wishes,

Zoe

P.S. I'm off to book my overseas trip tomorrow—with Christmas in Prague as a must.

To: Zoe Weston<zoe.weston@flowermail.com>
From: Kent Rigby<willaraKR@hismail.com>
Subject: Re: Thank You

I'm so pleased the delivery arrived safely. Sorry that it caused a stir in the office, but at least feng shui has been restored in your household. I hope you enjoy your new fish.

No news from the northern adventurers, but I'm assuming they're still hot on the trail.

Hope the travel bookings go smoothly. I'm jealous.
Cheers
Kent

The confession of jealousy was no lie. As Kent pressed send he could think of nothing he'd like more than to take off for Europe again. With Zoe.

He imagined showing her all the places he'd discovered—taking a ride on the London Eye and drinking a pint in a quaint old English pub. Dining out in Paris, or walking through the Latin Quarter. In Spain they would visit art galleries and sample tapas bars. They'd walk Italy's magical Cinque Terre. Experience Christmas in Prague.

Together.

He'd decided that Zoe would be a perfect travel companion. She was organised and yet easy-going, adaptable and fun. Sexy.

Yeah, if he was honest, he was utterly absorbed with the idea of kissing Zoe in every location. Their farewell kiss replayed in his head on an almost continuous reel.

He tried to tell himself that he was overreacting, riding on a tidal wave of relief now that he was no longer marrying someone out of a sense of friendship and duty.

So, OK, there'd been plenty of sparks. With Zoe he'd experienced the very fireworks that had eluded him and Bella. Serious sparkage that left him hungry for more than mere kisses. But Zoe was back in Brisbane now, and soon she'd be heading overseas. A man with a grain of common sense would look elsewhere.

Problem was, this man had experienced his fill of common sense. Now he wanted nothing more than to indulge in fantasies. And he kept remembering Zoe surrounded by dozens of smart little candles, kept picturing her on the bank of Willara Creek, her face soft with emotion and empathy, wanting to understand. He saw her on the road side struggling with a flat tyre. In the pub on the hens' night, in a sexy dress, bright as a flame. He remembered drying her tears just before he kissed her. Goodbye.

Zoe knew it was silly to keep checking her private emails at work and then to rush to her laptop as soon as she got home. Silly to be disappointed when there was no new message from Kent.

She wanted to move on and to put the entire Willara experience behind her, so Kent's silence was a step in the right direction.

Now that she was home, and had a little distance, she could see how dangerous her penchant for Kent had been. After her painful, harrowing heartbreak over Rodney, she was mad to hanker for another man who'd just called off his engagement.

Even though Kent and Bella's relationship had been very different from Rodney and Naomi's, the patterns were too close for comfort.

Besides, she suspected that Kent wasn't looking to settle down. She'd heard talk at the hens' night that he used to play the field, and, of course, he'd recently pulled out of commitment to Bella. It was true; he'd been gallant to the end. Just the same, he certainly wouldn't be ready to leap into a new, serious relationship.

Once and for all she had to move on. Kent's kiss had been nothing more than a spontaneous outburst of feelings at the end of an extremely emotional weekend.

And his thoughtfulness in sending the goldfish was just another example of his general niceness.

His email silence, on the other hand, simply meant there was no news from Bella—and it was a perfect opportunity for Zoe to move forward.

His silence was a desirable result. Honestly.

Very slowly, over the next twenty-four hours, the straightforward sense of this started to sink in. Zoe focused on planning her holiday.

It was going to be quite different travelling solo instead of travelling with Bella as she'd once hoped. Quite an adventure, really.

On Friday evening when Zoe arrived home from work, she was deliberately *not* thinking about Kent Rigby. She most especially concentrated on *not* thinking about him when she heard a knock on her front door.

Having just kicked off her shoes, she answered the door in stockinged feet—a distinct disadvantage when her caller was six feet two. No doubt that was why she blurted out inhospitably, 'What are you doing here?'

Kent had the grace to look a little embarrassed. 'I had business in the city and I was passing by.'

It might have been the lamest of excuses, but Kent Rigby in the flesh could obliterate Zoe's protests and doubts with a single warm smile.

One glance into the twinkling dark depths of his eyes and all her resolutions to forget him flew out of the window.

'So,' she suggested, trying to subdue her happy grin. 'I suppose you've dropped by to see how Ariel's settling in.'

'Ariel?'

'Your thoughtful gift. My new goldfish.'

Kent laughed—a lovely, sexy masculine rumble. 'Of course. I've had sleepless nights wondering. How is she?'

Zoe stepped back to let him through her doorway, conscious of his height and size and her lack of shoes and the supreme smallness of her living room. The fish tank sat rather conspicuously at one end of the low set of shelves that also held her television set.

With a wave towards it, she said, 'Ariel's the pretty one with the dainty white fins.'

Kent sent a polite nod towards the tank. 'She's a very fine specimen.'

'As you can see, she's quite at home now.'

'She is. That's great.' But he immediately switched his attention from the fish and back to Zoe. 'I know this is a bit last minute. I would have called at the office earlier today, but you were worried about wagging tongues.'

'You could have telephoned.'

'Yes.' His smile tilted. 'But I wanted an excuse to see you.'

Not fair. Zoe's resistance was melting faster than ice cream on a summer's day. Desperate to hang on to her diminishing shreds of common sense, she said, 'I haven't heard from Bella, have you?'

'Yes, she rang this morning.'

'So they're still heading north?'

'Yes, and there's an awful lot of coastline, so heaven knows how long it will take.'

Standing in the middle of her living room, Kent was watching her, unabashedly letting his eyes rove over her work clothes, her legs…

Self-consciously, she fiddled with the bridesmaid bracelet at her wrist. Unwisely, she'd taken to wearing it constantly. She rubbed one stockinged foot against the other.

He smiled again. 'So…how are you now, Zoe?'

'I'm—I'm fine.' What else could she say? She could hardly admit to feeling up and down and all over the place after one goodbye kiss. 'More importantly, how are you?'

'I'm OK. Surprisingly OK, actually.'

Memories of their kiss hovered in the air. Recklessly, Zoe thought how easy it would be to drift towards him again, to find herself in his arms, tasting that lovely, seductive mouth.

She struggled to remember all the reasons it was wrong. *He's free to play the field now. Don't get hurt. Remember Rodney!* She found refuge in her duties as a hostess. 'Would you like to sit down, Kent? Can I get you a drink?'

Instead of answering, he asked, 'Am I interrupting your plans for Friday night?'

'I—I was planning to have a quiet night in.' She'd been looking forward to a stress-free weekend for a change.

'So I can't tempt you to a quiet dinner out?'

Oh.

Zoe's mouth worked like her goldfish's. She'd spent the past week listing all the reasons why she must stop swooning over this man. Rodney the Rat had featured high on that list. Kent's own reputation as Willara's most dedicated bachelor was another point worth re-membering. But now—*shame on her*—now that he'd asked, she couldn't think of anything she'd like more than to go out with him.

Besides, she'd promised Bella she'd keep an eye on

Kent—and going out with him tonight was simply doing Bella a favour, wasn't it?

'Dinner would be lovely,' she said, trying to strike the right note between polite and casual. 'Why don't you make yourself at home while I change into something more—?' Zoe bit off the word *comfortable*... It was such a cheesy cliché and she didn't want to give Kent a whiff of the wrong idea.

'Let me get you a drink,' she said instead. Her kitchen led off the living area and she went to the fridge and opened it. Unfortunately, she hadn't been in the mood for shopping this week, so there was half a bottle of rather old white wine, the heel of an ancient block of cheese and a handful of dried apricots.

Thinking of the bounty at Willara Downs, she felt extremely inadequate in the hostess department.

'I don't need anything now. I'm happy to wait till dinner,' Kent said, watching her from the doorway. 'And you don't need to change. If you don't mind coming as you are, I think you look great in that outfit.'

'In this?' Zoe repeated, amazed. She was still in her work clothes—a dark green skirt and a cream blouse with pintucking and neat little pearl buttons.

Kent's eyes twinkled. 'Yes, in that. You have no idea how good city clothes look after a steady diet of jeans and Akubras.'

Given her own love of all things rural, Zoe had quite a fair understanding of how the trappings of a very different world might appeal.

So, five minutes later, having once again donned her high heels and given her hair and make-up a retouch, she was in Kent's ute and heading for her favourite suburban Thai restaurant. Fleetingly, she wondered if she should be wary or on guard, but such caution seemed impossible. She was ridiculously happy.

Apart from the huge fact that she was being escorted by a gorgeous guy who caught every woman's eye, she'd always loved this particular eating place. She loved coming through the swing glass doors to be enveloped by the fragrant and exotic aromas wafting from the kitchen. And she loved the sumptuous yet relaxing ambience—rich pink walls adorned with mirrors in dark, intricately carved wooden frames, and tables covered in cloths of peacock and gold.

She enjoyed the little rituals, too, like the basket of pale pink prawn crisps that came along with their menus. This evening, sharing one of her favourite places with Kent, she was filled with bubbling excitement.

They decided to choose exotic steamed fish, and chilli and ginger paste chicken. Then their drinks arrived—a glass of chilled white wine for Zoe and an icy beer for Kent—and they nibbled the prawn crisps and sipped their drinks. And they talked.

Wow, how they talked.

To Zoe's surprise, Kent did *not* bring Bella or the wedding into their conversation. He started by asking her more about her travel plans, and he told her about the places he'd enjoyed most when he'd been overseas. They moved on to movies and discovered they both loved thrillers. They talked about books, but Kent preferred non-fiction, so there wasn't quite so much common ground there.

They might have moved on to music, but their meals arrived in traditional Thai blue-and-white bowls and they soon became busy with helping themselves to spoonfuls of fluffy jasmine rice. The delicious fish had been baked in coconut milk with slices of ginger,

and the chicken had been stir-fried with masses of veg-
etables.

Everything was wonderfully hot and spicy and at
first they were too busy enjoying themselves to talk
about anything except the food, but then Kent asked,
out of the blue, 'Are you very ambitious, Zoe?'

Ambitious? Thrown by the question, she stared at
him. Her most recent goal had been to be a perfect
bridesmaid. Apart from that, she wanted to travel, but
her biggest ambition was to find the right man, to settle
down and start a family, which was the last thing she'd
admit to this man.

Fleetingly, she remembered her childish dream to
live in a farmhouse that sat safely and squarely in the
middle of green-and-gold fields. She hastily dismissed
it.

'Actually, I don't think I can be very ambitious,' she
said. 'I like my job and I want to be good at it, but I have
no desire to smash through glass ceilings.' She pulled
a face. 'Don't tell your feminist little sister.'

Kent grinned. 'Your secret's safe with me. Perhaps
you're content.'

No. Content she was not, especially since she'd met
Kent. Lately, restless yearning had been her constant
companion.

She doubted that Kent would want to hear her true
ambition—to settle down with the right man, to put
down roots, raise a family.

'My parents have never been go-getters,' she told
him instead. 'Lead the Way might have been a huge
success, if they'd had a bit more tooth and claw.'

'And you might have been the child of celebrity rock
stars.'

'Imagine.' Zoe rolled her eyes. 'Actually, I think my

parents would have hated all the celebrity fuss that goes with being famous. I can't imagine my mother being a diva, stamping her foot because the limo wasn't pink.'

She laughed at the impossibility of the picture. 'What about you, Kent? Are you ambitious?'

'I have big visions for the farm—projects like land management and tackling environmental issues. It's easier to try new methods now I'm managing Willara on my own. My dad wasn't keen to change and Tom's just as bad. They want to keep doing things the way they always have. Pair of dinosaurs, both of them.'

There was passion in his voice, which surprised Zoe. 'I must admit every time I was at Willara I was always so caught up with the wedding I didn't give much thought to the business and management of your farm. But it must be quite an enterprise. You're like a CEO of your own private company.'

'Yes, and it keeps me busy.'

'But you love it.'

'I do.'

Kent smiled that special way of his that launched Zoe into outer space. Yikes, she had to calm down. Tonight was all about friendship.

Sure, there were sizzles and sparks that zapped her whenever she looked across the table. And yes, there were dark flashes of appreciation in Kent's eyes. And, most certainly, she was aware of a deepening sense of connection when they talked.

But this wasn't a date. Kent hadn't once tried to flirt with her, or to touch her, or to offer her the over-the-top compliments that Rodney had trotted out on their first date. This evening was humming along at a nice, safe, just-friends level.

Reassured by this success, Zoe found herself asking

recklessly, 'Are there any other ambitions? Do you still plan to marry and have a family one day?'

Kent stiffened with obvious surprise.

Oh, good grief. What an idiot she was.

He concentrated on helping himself to a final spoonful of fish. 'Right now I can't imagine ever lining up for another wedding.'

'And who could blame you?' Zoe said fervently.

To her relief, her awkward question didn't ruin the night. As they left the restaurant and walked into the sensuous magic of the warm spring night the scent of frangipani and honeysuckle hung in the humid air. From a pub down the road a band was sending out a deep pulsing beat.

Kent reached for Zoe's hand, threaded his fingers through hers. 'Thanks for bringing me here. It was a fabulous meal.'

'My pleasure,' she said softly, while her skin tingled and glowed from the contact.

When they reached his car, he opened the passenger door for her, and she was about to get in when he said, 'Wait a minute.'

She turned and he gently touched her cheek. 'I just wanted to tell you—you look lovely tonight.'

Her skin flamed with pleasure. 'Thank—'

Her reply was cut off by his kiss.

Which wasn't exactly a surprise—all night she'd been teased by memories of their other kiss.

This kiss was different and yet utterly perfect. Beyond friendly—oh, heavens, yes—but not pushy. Just slow and sexy and powerful enough to make Zoe hungry for more.

She was floating as she settled into the passenger seat, and it wasn't till they pulled up outside her flat that she came to her senses. It was time for a polite, but hasty exit.

A kiss was one thing, but becoming more deeply involved with this man was way too risky. He might be the most attractive man she'd ever met, but tonight he'd admitted that his long-term goals were the polar opposite of hers. She wanted to settle down. He didn't.

It was all very black and white.

'Thanks for a lovely evening, Kent.' Already, her fingers were reaching for the door handle.

'Zoe, before I forget, I have something for you.' Reaching into the back seat, Kent picked up a brown-paper packet.

'Another gift? But you've given me a bracelet and a goldfish.' She hoped this wasn't going to be chocolates or flowers—the clichéd trappings of seduction.

'It's just a book,' he said. 'I thought it might come in handy.'

She caught the dark gleam of his eyes as he smiled at her through the darkness. A book, a nice safe book. Tilting the packet, she let it slip onto her lap. It was a hardback with a glossy cover. They weren't parked near a streetlight, but there was just enough light for her to make out the title.

'A book about Prague. Gosh, how thoughtful of you.'

Flipping it open, she saw beautiful, full-page co-loured photographs, but the dim light couldn't do them justice. It seemed rude not to invite Kent inside.

'I need to make you coffee before you tackle the long drive back,' she explained in case he got the wrong idea.

So they ended up on the sofa, poring over pictures of Prague while their mugs of coffee cooled on the low table in front of them. The pictures were gorgeous—

soaring cathedrals, fairy-tale castles, steep-roofed houses, a horse and carriage in the snow...

'It's so old world and so very civilised,' Zoe said.

'I know. I couldn't think of any place more different from Queensland.'

'I can't believe I'm going to see it all. I'm booked into a small hotel just around the corner from the Old Town Square.'

Kent was silent for a bit. Frowning, he said, 'I hope you won't be too lonely spending Christmas overseas on your own.'

Zoe wondered if he was teasing her, but he looked quite genuine, and if she was honest she *was* a little worried about being on her own. But now with Bella unavailable it was a matter of travelling solo, or not at all. She looked sideways to find Kent still watching her with a troubled expression.

'I'll be fine,' she said. 'I've been doing some research, and, from what I've read, solo travellers have a much better chance of meeting people. There's always someone to share a meal or a bus ride.'

'I dare say that's true.' Kent picked up her hand and turned it over.

At the unexpected contact, Zoe's breath hitched and her heart picked up pace. 'What are you doing?'

'I'm reading your palm,' he said calmly.

She should have resisted, should have pulled her hand away, but it was already too late. She was mesmerised by his touch, by the scent of his aftershave, by the inescapable fabulousness of having him so close beside her.

Instead of protesting, she found herself playing his game. 'And what do you see in my palm?'

His eyes sparkled. 'Travel to far away places.'

'Fancy that. How perceptive.'

'And romance.'

Her palm curled instinctively. The warmth of his hands and the mellow teasing in his voice wove silken threads of longing deep inside her.

Fighting the hot urges, she challenged him. 'I thought palm readings only told you how long you're going to live and how many children you'll have.'

Kent's eyebrows lifted. 'Is that right? I'd better take another look, then.'

OK…she really should stop this nonsense. She tried to pull her hand away, but Kent was holding her firmly.

'Yes, of course,' he said. 'I can see a very long and happy life here.' With his forefinger he traced a shiver-sweet line across the centre of her palm. 'And a whole tribe of children.'

'A tribe?' Her breathlessness was caused more by his touch than his words. 'How many children are in a tribe?'

'Oh, I'd say around ten or eleven.'

'Far out.' Zoe tried to sound appalled, but she spoiled it by laughing. 'I think you'd better give up reading palms and stick to farming.'

Sure that her face was glowing bright pink, she switched her attention back to the book, still lying in her lap. It was open at a double page, showing Prague in the soft blue light of dusk. Four beautiful, ancient bridges spanned the Vltava River, and the sky and the water and the distant hills were all the exact same shade of misty blue. Even the splashes of yellow from street-lights and windows were soft and fuzzy. So pretty.

'Willara Downs is as lovely as this at dusk,' she told Kent.

To her surprise, he closed the book and set it on the

coffee table, then he took her hands, enclosing them in both of his. 'Zoe, I have a confession to make.'

Her heart skidded as if she'd taken a curve too fast.

'Would you be shocked if I told you that I fancied you *before* Bella and I called off the wedding?'

'Yes.' Of course she was shocked. Her heart was thumping so hard, she could hardly hear her own voice.

'Believe me, I was shocked, too. But I couldn't shut off my feelings.'

'But you didn't—' She pressed a hand to her thumping heart. She was scared and excited. Confused. 'You didn't call off the wedding because of me.'

'No, I didn't.' Smiling, Kent tucked a strand of her hair behind her ear. 'You don't have to feel guilty. It was only afterwards that I allowed myself to think about what had been happening. By then, I realised that I fancied you like crazy.'

She closed her eyes, searching for the strength to resist him. Kent had fancied lots of girls. This wasn't a confession of love. But even though she knew this, his words were unfurling fiery ribbons of need inside her. His touch was clouding her thoughts.

When his thumb brushed gently over her lips, she couldn't think of anything but kissing him again, of throwing herself into his wonderful, strong arms, of climbing brazenly into his lap...the bliss of skin against skin...

'You're lovely,' he whispered.

'Kent, don't say that.' She dragged herself back from the magnetic pull of his touch. 'You mustn't. We can't.'

'Why can't we?'

Remember Rodney.

But Kent was nothing like Rodney. He wasn't up and down in his moods as Rodney had been. He'd been engaged to Bella for noble reasons and he'd been very considerate of everyone's feelings when he'd broken that commitment. He was a man who took responsibilities seriously.

Even so, by his own confession, he still wasn't the marrying and settling down type.

Maybe I can simply enjoy the moment?

In a few weeks she was going to Europe, and Kent knew that, so a liaison now could only be temporary. Temporary flings were safe. They couldn't break a girl's heart. She could look on her trip overseas as her escape route.

Besides…heaven help her, she wanted this man… wanted him to kiss her, wanted his kiss so badly she was trembling. Every nerve in her body was quivering.

Kent dipped his head till his lips were almost touching hers. She looked into his eyes and saw the dark urgency of her longing mirrored there. A soft gasp escaped her, an embarrassing, pleading sound.

His mouth brushed hers, slow but insistent. 'Tell me why this is wrong,' he murmured against her lips.

She couldn't answer. If there had ever been a reason to say no, she'd lost it. His lips caressed hers again, and the last warnings in her head crumpled like tissue paper thrown on fire. She couldn't think of anything but returning Kent's kiss. Already she was winding her arms around his neck…and she kissed him.

Kissed him and *kissed* him.

Somewhere in the midst of kissing him, she kicked off her shoes and wriggled into his lap. And this time it was he who gasped. Then his hands traced the silky shape of her legs encased in tights. He dropped a fiery line of kisses over her skin from her collarbone into the V of her blouse. Then their mouths met again, and

their kisses turned molten as they tumbled sideways—
a blissful tangle into the deep red cushions.

Out of habit, Kent woke early, but this morning, instead
of bouncing out to face a day's farm work, he lay in the
soft light watching Zoe sleep. She was on her side, facing him, her dark hair tumbling over the white pillow,
her dusky eyelashes curving against her soft cheeks, her
mouth pale and slightly open. She looked so innocent
and vulnerable now, so different from the fiery, sensuous woman who'd made love to him last night.

Last night…

When he'd knocked on Zoe's door, he hadn't known
what to expect. Hadn't dared to hope that he might end
up spending the night with her. And yet, he couldn't
deny he'd been on fire since their farewell kiss at
Willara.

Even so, last night had defied all logic. He and Zoe
had shared a mere explosion of passion and excitement,
but there'd been astonishing tenderness, too. The same
kind of emotional connection he'd felt before—over
dinner conversations or on the creek bank. An amazing sense of rightness. A certainty that some kind of
miracle had been set in motion.

Briefly, as he lay there, he wondered if such thoughts
were fanciful. But then Zoe stirred beside him, opened
her bright blue eyes and smiled, and he was flooded
with a wonderful sense of buoyancy. Perhaps his life
was taking a turn in a very good direction.

CHAPTER TEN

ZOE's new version of heaven was waking up beside Kent Rigby on a Saturday morning and knowing they had the whole, delicious weekend to spend together.

They rose late, and went out to have breakfast at a pavement café that served great coffee and luscious, tasty mushrooms on thick sourdough toast. Afterwards, they walked beneath flowering jacarandas on the banks of the Brisbane River, enjoying the sunshine, and sharing happy, goofy smiles.

In the afternoon they went to a suburban cinema to see a creepy thriller movie. Like teenagers they stole popcorn flavoured kisses in the dark, and on the way home they stopped off at a supermarket and bought ingredients for a pasta dish to make at home.

In Zoe's kitchen they sipped wine while they chopped and cooked. Every chance they had, they touched and smiled and hugged and kissed. They were, in a word, entranced.

Wrapped in a bubble of bliss, Zoe wouldn't let anything intrude. No negative thoughts, no questions, no doubts. If the slightest misgiving about history repeating itself reared its ugly head, she told herself this time was nothing like her disaster with Rodney. Rodney had moved in. Rodney had promised for ever.

With Kent, she was merely enjoying a fab weekend. At the end of two days he would go back to Willara, knowing that she was about to leave for overseas. For now she was trusting her instincts and her instincts felt *fantastic*!

Their pasta sauce was bubbling beautifully and Kent was stealing yet another kiss from Zoe when the phone rang. She grabbed the receiver and trilled 'Hello-o-o,' in a super-happy singsong.

'Zoe, how are you?'

'Bella?' Zoe shot a startled glance to Kent and watched his eyebrows hike.

Bella laughed. 'Don't sound so surprised.'

'Sorry. I wasn't expecting you, Bella, and I was—um—distracted for a moment.'

'Are you all right, Zoe?'

'Absolutely fine. Why?'

'I don't know. You sound—different somehow.'

'I don't think I'm different. More importantly, how are you?' Zoe flashed another glance Kent's way.

His eyes were more cautious now, as if he felt as awkward as she did. It would be so hard to explain this to Bella. A week ago, Zoe had been focused on being the perfect bridesmaid. Last night she'd slept with the bridegroom. Admittedly, those roles were now defunct, but how would Bella react if she knew they were together so soon?

And just like that, with Bella on the other end of the line, Zoe saw her wonderful weekend in a whole new light—as an outsider might—and her brain flung up words like *impetuous*, *cheeky*, *reckless*…

Bella said, 'I'm fine, thanks. I'm in Port Douglas with our grandparents. There's been a cyclone, would you believe? But we're all OK. Just garden damage.'

'That's really bad luck about the cyclone. How's everything…going…with…Damon?'

'OK,' Bella said in a sharp, *don't-go-there* tone. 'I was actually ringing to see if you've been in touch with Kent.'

'Oh?' Zoe was instantly nervous. She widened her eyes at Kent. Pointing to the phone, she mouthed, *'Do you want to talk to Bella?'*

Frowning, he shook his head.

She swallowed. 'Yes, I've had *some* contact with him.'

'I tried his mobile, but he's switched it off, so I rang the homestead and he wasn't there either so I rang his parents and Stephanie told me he's away for the weekend.'

'Did you want Kent for anything important?'

'Not especially. I guess I just wanted to make sure he's OK. You know the wedding would have been happening right about now.'

Oh, gosh. Zoe glanced at the clock on her kitchen wall and saw that Bella was right. At this very moment, Bella and Kent should have been exchanging their marriage vows. How on earth had it slipped her mind?

'I would have liked to make certain that Kent was OK,' Bella said.

'I'm sure he's fine. He's probably decided not to dwell on the wedding too much.'

'Yes, that would be best, wouldn't it? I hope you're right.'

On the stove the sauce began to boil and spit. Zoe gestured frantically, but Kent had moved to the window and was standing with his back to her, studiously looking out into her backyard. His shoulders were squared and his back very straight. Sure signs of tension.

Zoe tried to attract him with a stage whisper. *'Pssst, can you turn that sauce down?'*

'Do you have someone there?' Bella asked.

'Yes—just—a friend over for dinner.'

'Oh, that's nice. I won't keep you, then.' But instead of hanging up, Bella lowered her voice. 'Would this friend be male by any chance?'

Zoe made the mistake of hesitating for a shade too long.

'Zoe, it's a guy, isn't it? That's why you sounded so different—sort of bubbly and excited. Who is he? Anyone I know?'

'Bell, I'm sorry. The dinner's burning, and I've got to go. But it's been fantastic to hear from you and to know you're OK.'

'All right.' Bella laughed. 'I can take a hint. But if you hear from Kent, tell him that I rang and, apart from the weather, I'm fine.'

'I will, and I'll tell him you were thinking of him.'

Zoe hung up and rushed to rescue the sauce. Kent turned from the window, and she sank back against a cupboard, letting out a groan. 'That was awful. I felt terrible lying to her.'

'You weren't exactly lying.'

'No, but I was hiding the truth and that's just as bad.'

Zoe felt sick. Hands clenched, she paced across the kitchen. And to her horror, all the reasons she shouldn't be with Kent rushed back to taunt her. What was she doing leaping into bed with another man who'd just broken off an engagement?

Spinning around, she challenged him. 'Had you remembered that you should have been getting married right now?'

He looked uncomfortable. 'Is that why Bella rang?'

'Yes. She was worried about you. She tried the Willara Downs number and your mobile.'

Pulling his phone from his pocket, Kent thumbed a button or two. 'It's not that I don't want to talk to her. I didn't want to embarrass you. I'll call her back now.'

'Actually...I'm not sure that's a good idea. If you call back straight away, she'll probably guess you're with me. She's already figured I have a guy here.'

Grimacing, Kent stood looking down at the phone. It looked tiny in his big brown work-roughened hand. His throat rippled as he swallowed. 'I'm sure Bella will understand if I explain.'

Zoe gave a choked laugh. 'How are you going to explain that you ended up spending the weekend with her bridesmaid? It'll sound so—' she swallowed, grasping for a word '—tacky.'

'Tacky?' Kent repeated, shocked.

'Hasty, then. Indecently so.'

In two steps, Kent was across the room and grabbing Zoe's arm. 'Is that what you think? That last night was tacky?'

'No.' Suddenly, Zoe was trembling and fighting tears. 'Oh, Kent, you have to admit it might be viewed by many as indecent haste.'

He pulled her in to him, holding her against his broad chest, kissing her hair. 'Whatever's happening between us is *good*.' Gently, he tucked her hair behind her ear and kissed her brow. 'And it's no one else's business.'

Zoe closed her eyes and let her head sink against his shoulder. She loved being with this man so much— loved the way he smelled of sunlight and clean shirts, loved the hard strength of his body, and the warm reassurance of his arms wrapped around her. Loved who he was.

But she had loved Rodney, too. She'd adored him. She could never have believed he might hurt her.

'How did we let this happen so soon?' she asked Kent.

For answer, he hugged her closer, but even as warmth and pleasure seeped through her the impact of Bella's phone call remained, lifting the lid on all the difficult questions she'd doggedly resisted for the past twenty-four hours. And one thing was certain—she couldn't find answers to these questions while she was in Kent's arms.

With enormous reluctance she pulled away, went to the window and opened it, letting in a fresh breeze as if, somehow, that might clear her thoughts.

'I never meant this to happen,' she said. 'After that kiss goodbye last weekend I decided we shouldn't get too involved. It's all too soon. Too convenient.'

She looked down at her hands—rubbed the rough edge of a thumbnail. The real issue here was that Kent didn't want to settle down. He'd said so last night. She, on the other hand, wanted nothing more than to marry and start a family—to be the bride, not the bridesmaid. And Kent was exactly the sort of man... No, he was the *only* man she wanted to settle down with.

She couldn't tell him that. There was no point. 'I can't help worrying that this weekend has been a mistake,' she said instead.

'You mean you're feeling pressured?'

'Well, yes. I tried to tell you last night that we shouldn't...' She shot him an accusing glance. 'I'm sure you remember.'

'Oh, yes, I remember.' Kent's slow smile made her wince.

No doubt he was remembering the way she'd shamelessly climbed into his lap and kissed him as if there were no tomorrow. She was so hopelessly weak around him and last night she'd foolishly given in to that weakness.

Now she was determined to be strong. 'The thing is, I've been through something like this before, Kent.'

He frowned. 'How do you mean?'

'I fell for a guy who'd recently broken off an engagement. He was a work colleague and I'd known him for about twelve months. I'd even met his fiancée, Naomi, at parties. A few months after their break-up he asked me out, and I conscientiously tried to cheer him up. All went well. He moved in with me and we lived together for another six months. Until—'

Zoe paused for dramatic emphasis.

'Until he let you down,' Kent suggested.

'Yes. I came home one Friday evening and found him in *my* bed with Naomi.'

He scowled. 'That's a low-down act.'

'That's why I call him Rodney the Rat.' Zoe closed her eyes at the memory. 'He made me feel used and stupid and conned and hurt and angry. You name it—I felt it. I was devastated.'

And now…she wouldn't run the risk of being hurt again, surely? She'd been a fool to let herself fall for Kent so quickly and easily, when she'd spent the past week telling herself that it wasn't wise.

'Zoe, I swear I would never do anything to you like that.'

'I know you wouldn't hurt me intentionally, but I can't help feeling vulnerable.' Impatiently, she swept a lock of hair from her eyes. 'Maybe I'm jumping the gun. We haven't even talked about what we want from—from this. Are we having a fling—or—or—?'

'I thought we were getting to know each other.' He came to stand beside her again, and with his hands on her shoulders he turned her to look at him, trapping her with the dark, frank depths of his eyes. 'We were honest with each other when we made love, weren't we?'

Zoe couldn't deny there'd been a special openness and sincerity about last night. But that was the problem. To her, it had felt like so much more than a temporary fling and just thinking about it brought her to the edge of tears.

She took a deep breath. If she played this the wrong way, she would lose Kent, and live to regret it deeply. But her bigger fear was that she'd keep seeing him for several more weeks and *then* the novelty would wear off for him. To spend more time with him and then lose him would be so much worse. Unbearable.

The hard truth was that every moment she spent with Kent was dangerous. She'd been falling more deeply in love with him since the moment she'd met him beside the road side. If she didn't apply the brakes now, before she was in any deeper, she could end up *very* badly hurt. Again.

It was important now to list her extremely valid concerns.

'Kent, until last weekend, you were all set to marry my best friend. You were ready to vow to love her till you were parted by death.'

A muscle jerked in his jaw. 'But you know why we called it off.'

'Yes, I do. And I can understand why you want to move on with your life. But I'm not sure it's a great idea to move straight on to the bridesmaid, as if I was there, ready and waiting—like the next cab on the rank.'

Zoe knew it was a cheap shot, and a sound like a

growl broke from him. Anger flashed in his eyes and he looked so unlike his calm, easy-going self that she almost backed down and apologised. But then where would she be? In his arms with nothing sorted? Nothing solved?

Kent's eyes narrowed. 'Are you asking me to leave?'

No, no, no. That wasn't what she wanted at all. How could she let him go? She'd been so looking forward to this evening—to their shared meal, and the long night after—and then, all of Sunday still ahead of them. And their future…

She dropped her gaze to the floor. It was too hard to think when Kent was standing right there all gorgeous and frowning in front of her.

Be strong, Zoe.

She took a deep breath before she spoke. 'Perhaps we just need space to sort things out—a sort of cooling-off period.' She hoped she didn't sound as miserable as she felt.

Kent remained very still, and his dark eyes, usually so warm and sparkling, remained severe and narrowed. 'Cooling-off period? So what's that? Forty-eight hours? Four weeks?'

I don't know! she wanted to wail.

Kent, however, had made his decision. 'It's clear I should go.' Stepping forward, he dropped a light kiss on her cheek. 'I'll be in touch, then.' And just like that, he was heading out of her kitchen.

Zoe wanted to call him back.

Don't you want dinner? It's a long drive back to Willara. She shot a desperate glance to the sauce-spattered stove. They'd cooked all this pasta.

But what about your things? she almost called out, until she remembered that Kent hadn't brought any luggage. He'd slept naked, and used her spare toothbrush—because he hadn't planned to stay...

Everything that had happened this weekend had been wonderfully spontaneous and...

And now she'd spoiled it.

Stumbling behind him through the flat, she swiped at embarrassing tears. When they reached her front door, Kent turned to her again, looking so desperately stern and handsome Zoe could barely breathe.

'I guess I need to get this straight,' he said. 'While we're cooling off, what exactly are we sorting out?'

Zoe gulped. Her mind was swirling. What could she say? Was this the time for painful honesty? What else could she offer him? 'I'm worried that I'm not the right girl for you, Kent.'

He stood, wary-eyed, waiting for her to continue.

Now that she'd started, she had no choice but to confess. 'I'm afraid I'm very keen on you, keener than you realise. And I don't think you'd want to deal with that right now.' Taking a deep breath, she rushed on. 'To be honest, I'm in love with the whole picture of you and your farm and your country lifestyle.'

Kent didn't speak. Perhaps he was stunned, or simply puzzled.

And Zoe realised, now, too late, that it had been a mistake to mention any of this, but she felt compelled to explain. 'It started when I was little, living in a bus and always looking out of the window at snug farmhouses in the middle of neat, tidy fields. I thought they looked so wonderful and I developed this fantasy of marrying a farmer one day.'

'So I'm a fantasy?' he queried, looking uncomfortable. 'Along with a country wedding?'

Oh, God. Too much information.

'I'm making a hash of this,' Zoe said. 'I didn't mean that the only reason I like you is because you're a farmer.'

'OK.' He lifted a hand as if to put a stop to the conversation. 'This is getting way too complicated.'

'I'm sorry.'

'Don't apologise, but I take your point about a cooling-off period. I guess it's a good idea.'

Thud. It was ridiculous to be disappointed as soon as he agreed to the very thing she'd asked for. Zoe's throat was suddenly a scalding knot of unshed tears.

Already he was turning to leave, but she couldn't speak, was too busy keeping her lips pressed together to hold back embarrassing sobs.

'Take care,' he said gently, before he went swiftly down her steps to his ute.

Driving west against the fierce glare of the setting sun, Kent had never felt less like cooling off.

He was fired up. Burning.

Angry with himself.

Last week he'd been a step from marrying Zoe's best friend, and a week later he'd leapt straight into her bed. What was he thinking?

Of course it was a hasty, rash and thoughtless act. If one of his mates had behaved the same way, Kent would be wondering if the guy's actions were driven by a bruised ego, or by his brains dropping below his belt!

Zoe had every right to ask questions—questions he should have asked himself.

What did he want from this relationship? Was it a casual fling? Did he expect to follow his old pattern, to date her for a month or so, and then drift away?

He certainly hadn't been thinking about the long term.

After last week's close brush with the responsibility and permanence of matrimony, he'd been set free, so to speak. He was free to embrace his old ways and his plan was to prolong his bachelorhood for as long as he could.

But did he honestly expect a conscientious girl like Zoe to treat their relationship lightly? After her past weeks of hard work and dedication, shouldn't he have known better? After she'd made love with such breathtaking spontaneity and touching emotion, shouldn't he have known their liaison was already complicated?

Hell. Zoe had told him about her rat of a boyfriend, and he'd been so self-righteous.

I would never do anything to you like that. What a fool he was.

Selfish, too. He'd wanted a little fun after the tension and drama of the past weeks, and Zoe had been available. How had she put it? The next cab at the rank.

And yet—that wasn't how he thought of her. Zoe was special, amazing in so many ways—the kind of girl he could, quite possibly, marry one day…if he'd had plans to settle down.

Maybe he shouldn't have been so surprised by her confession that she had feelings for him and wanted to marry, that she'd always wanted to be a farmer's wife, for heaven's sake.

But he hadn't seen it coming, and now, instead of relaxing after a pleasant weekend, he had a lot to think about. Too much. Not a chance of cooling off.

CHAPTER ELEVEN

IT WAS ten-thirty when the delivery boy arrived at the office doorway. At least, Zoe assumed it was the delivery boy, although all she could see of him were his jeans and his grubby green and yellow sneakers. The top half of him was entirely obscured by the biggest bunch of flowers she'd ever seen.

As the flowers appeared there was a collective gasp from every female in the office. The girl at the desk nearest to Zoe stopped a phone conversation in mid-sentence. Someone else gave an excited little squeal.

Mandy, whose desk was closest to the door, got out of her seat and practically tiptoed in awe towards the mountain of blooms.

Zoe was as curious as anyone else as she exchanged smiles with her workmates. She knew everyone was trying to guess who the lucky recipient could be. Emily had recently announced she was pregnant. Joanne was turning forty soon. Jane had acquired a new and, apparently, ultra-romantic boyfriend.

At least, Zoe knew the flowers couldn't be for her. The only person who might send them was Kent and he'd embraced her cooling-off suggestion with depressing enthusiasm. It was three weeks now since she'd seen him. Three desperately miserable weeks.

In all that time, she'd made no attempt to contact him and he'd only been in touch once to report that, despite the terrible weather in the north, Bella and Damon were apparently OK. There'd been nothing personal in his message. Not a breath of romance.

The silence had been awful. At times Zoe had felt so miserable, she'd almost weakened and begged him to forget everything she'd said.

Fortunately, she'd restrained herself. She'd done enough damage last time when she'd talked about loving him. Of course she'd frightened him off.

If she'd handled everything sensibly, they would have continued to see each other on weekends and who knew what pleasing developments might have occurred?

Now, in just a few days, she would be leaving for Europe, so there was no point in even thinking about what might have been with Kent. Instead, she was hoping and praying that the exciting new foreign sights and experiences would cheer her up, and help her to put the whole Willara experience behind her.

At any rate, she could relax right now. There was absolutely no chance these flowers were for her.

At the doorway, the floral Mount Everest was handed over to Mandy, who had to turn sideways to see where she was going as she made her way carefully back into the centre of the office.

'Help, someone!' she called. 'I'm sure there's a card pinned on here, but I can't possibly reach it.'

Zoe jumped to assist her. The bouquet was so huge, it took a few moments to locate the small white envelope, but she finally found it pinned beneath a cascade of lavender orchids.

'Here!' she cried, triumphantly waving the small white envelope above her head like a trophy.

'Who's it for?' cried several voices.

All eyes in the room were on Zoe. She saw smiles of amusement, wistful faces filled with hope, others wide eyed with genuine tension. The air was shimmering with palpable excitement.

Suddenly the centre of attention, Zoe felt her heartbeats begin a drum roll as she deliberately took her time looking at the name on the envelope. Then she dropped her gaze to the white square of paper. And her heart stopped beating altogether.

There...on the envelope in clear blue ink...

Zoe Weston.

There was a painful thump in the centre of her chest, and then her heart began to pound savagely. She hadn't expected, hadn't dreamed... The paper in her hand was shaking.

Everyone was watching her.

'Oh, gosh.'

'Who's it for?' Mandy demanded.

Almost apologetically, Zoe said, 'Me.'

At first there was silence. Then a voice cried, 'Oh, wow! Congratulations!' But for Zoe this was almost drowned out by her thundering heartbeats.

Her hands were shaking so badly, she had a hard time getting the little card out of the envelope, but finally she was able to read it.

I'd like to talk. How about you?
Kent xx

A thrill burst inside her like fizzing champagne.

'Who's it from?' called Jane.

Zoe hesitated. Many of these girls had been to

Willara Downs for the bridal shower. 'Just a guy,' she said lamely. As you did.

The response was a predictable group groan.

'If a guy sends a bouquet the size of a house he must be asking you to marry him at the very least,' someone said.

'Or perhaps he's been a very, very bad boy and he's very, very sorry,' said someone else.

Zoe shook her head, but she wasn't about to tell them: *he just wants to talk.* She was still trembling as she took the flowers from Mandy and stumbled off to hunt for a bucket to put them in.

In a back room she found a metal waste-paper bin, and she filled it with water. With the flowers taken care of, she sank back against a filing cabinet and read Kent's note again.

I'd like to talk. How about you?

Every possible emotion raged war inside her. Joy. Hope. Fear. Uncertainty.

Kent was opening a door, trying to reconnect, and she couldn't think of anything she wanted more than to see him again.

But in a few days she would be flying to the other side of the world, and she'd be away for a month. Surely her sudden impatience to see him was foolish.

Just because he's sent me a bunch of flowers?

But I love him.

Did she? Really?

She'd had enough time to think about it, to try to work out if she was actually in love with the real man and not with an embodiment of her childhood fantasy.

She found herself asking how anyone ever knew for certain that they were truly in love. In three weeks her longing to see Kent had been agonising. Was that love?

Was love ever safe and certain, or was it always a great big gamble?

She reminded herself again, as she had so often in the past three weeks, of her headlong rush into love with Rodney. She'd been so certain he was The One.

She'd been such a diligent girlfriend, so anxious to please Rodney, cooking his favourite meals, hiring his favourite DVDs. She'd been so busy showing him how devoted she was, she'd never stopped to make sure he felt the same way.

Being dumped by him had awoken every one of her insecurities. Once again she'd been an outsider, without a best mate.

Lately, she'd even wondered if she had poor judgement when it came to men. Perhaps it would be much more sensible to wait to talk to Kent after she got back from her travels. Mightn't she gain a clearer perspective with the benefit of further time and distance?

At lunchtime, Zoe divided the flowers into smaller bunches and handed them out among her surprised work colleagues.

'There's no point in taking them home to my place,' she explained over and over. 'I'm leaving for Europe on the weekend. You may as well enjoy them.'

The only flowers Zoe saved were the lavender orchids, which she took home and placed in a vase on the shelf beside the fish tank.

That was the easy part. Deciding how to deal with Kent was the difficult bit. She had to ring him to thank him, and there shouldn't be any harm in a phone call. Just the same, she had to be careful not to say too much. Now, when she was about to leave, she certainly couldn't let on how much she'd missed him.

No, she would have to be very strong and in control

of this conversation. Most definitely, she mustn't allow
Kent to say or do anything to spoil her holiday plans.

The phone's shrill ring sent a jolt of adrenalin punching into Kent. He willed himself to stay calm. Almost
certainly, this would be yet another phone call from a
wedding guest, calling to cheer him up, or to invite him
over for a meal. There'd been many such calls during
the past month.

Even so, Kent knew the flowers must have arrived in
Brisbane, and he was picturing Zoe as he picked up the
receiver. He imagined her on her sofa in her Newmarket
flat, with her long legs tucked neatly beneath her, her
shiny hair a dark splash against the vivid red of her
sofa's upholstery. Her eyes the blue of the morning
sky...

He forced a smile into his voice as he answered.
'Hello. Willara Downs.'

'Hi, Kent, it's Zoe.'

Twin reactions—elation and alarm—tightened like
lassos around his chest. It was so good to hear her voice
and he couldn't believe how much he'd missed her. For
these past three weeks he'd spent far too much time
thinking about her, missing her smile, her touch, her
company.

But he couldn't believe how worried he was, too.
Worried she would read too much into this gesture. He
simply needed to see her again. From their first meeting, he'd been aware of a fatal chemistry, and he'd tried
his best to ignore it, but it was still tormenting him like
a constant ache.

He'd given in, sent the flowers and a request to make
contact, and now he forced a smile into his voice. 'Hey,
Zoe, it's great to hear from you. How are you?'

'I'm fine, thanks.'

She didn't sound fine. She sounded nervous, as nervous as he was.

'Your flowers arrived,' she said. 'Thank you so much, Kent. They're beautiful. There were so many of them.'

'Not too over the top, I hope. I ordered them over the phone and just named an amount. Anyway, I'm glad you liked them.'

'All the girls in the office were jealous.' After a small pause, she asked, 'How—how are you?'

'Fighting fit.' He swallowed a sudden constriction in his throat. 'But I've missed you, Zoe.'

'Oh.'

Oh? What was that supposed to mean? He needed to know if she was pleased or disappointed. 'I was wondering if you'd had enough of this cooling-off period.'

'It hasn't been much fun,' she said softly, but then added almost straight away, 'but I still think it's a sensible idea, don't you?'

'I'm not sure it's possible to sort out a relationship in isolation. I was hoping we could talk.'

She made a noise that sounded like a sigh. A sad sigh that chilled him. 'I'm leaving for Europe on Saturday, Kent.'

'So soon? But Christmas is a month away.'

'I'm going to London and Paris first. Ten days in each city, and then on to Prague.'

A curse fell from his lips before he could bite it back. He didn't want to wait another month. He'd had enough of waiting while his thoughts went round and round the same worn track. Solitary contemplation hadn't helped.

He couldn't make decisions about their relationship in a vacuum.

He wanted action. He needed to be able to touch Zoe, to share meals and conversations, to make love to her.

If they waited another month, Zoe would have all kinds of opportunities to meet suave, silver-tongued Continental Casanovas. Hell. Had she already dismissed him?

Surely she owed him another chance? He had to see her. 'I'll come down to Brisbane.' Kent glanced at his watch. It was too late tonight. 'How about tomorrow night?'

'Sorry, Kent, my parents will be here. They're coming up to Brisbane to collect the goldfish and my pot plants.'

Curse the goldfish. Why had he ever thought it was a good idea? 'What about Friday night, then?'

There was another, longer pause. 'I—I'm not sure that's a good idea. I'll be leaving early on Saturday morning. Maybe we should let this go till I get back.'

'Sorry, Zoe. That's not an option. I have to see you. I'll come to the airport. What's your flight number?'

'Honestly, there's no need to see me off.'

'You can't keep stalling.' He was bulldozing her, but he didn't care. He'd heard a quiver in her voice that hinted at her inner battle, and in that instant he'd decided there was no way he could let her leave for the far side of the world without seeing her.

'Just tell me the flight and I'll be there.'

'OK, but I'll need to make a condition though, Kent.'

'What is it?'

'Promise you won't try to talk me out of going away.'

'Agreed,' he said, with a reluctance that disturbed him.

* * *

Zoe's boarding pass was tucked into her handbag and her suitcase was already on its way down the conveyor belt as she scanned the international terminal, searching for Kent.

Despite her best efforts to remain calm, her insides were flapping like bait in a net. She couldn't wait to see him, couldn't believe he was driving all the way from Willara Downs to Brisbane airport to spend a few short minutes with her.

How amazing was that? She'd given him a chance to cool off and it seemed that he hadn't cooled.

Of course, she hadn't cooled either. She was desperate to see him. And yet she was scared. For three and a half weeks, she'd kept her feelings for Kent carefully tied up in tight little parcels, and now, when she was about to head overseas, she wanted them to stay that way.

This trip was important to her. She was looking forward to the exciting new sights and sounds and smells of foreign places.

More importantly, she was hoping that time and distance would offer her an excellent chance to sort through her emotions and get a new perspective on her hopes and dreams. It would give Kent time, too.

Right now, however, she was scared. Scared that seeing him again would unravel her tightly bound feelings. Scared that one look into the deep brown warmth in his eyes could too easily break her resolve. How awful if her emotions spilled out all over the airport, like luggage bursting from an over-stuffed suitcase.

I can't let that happen. I have to be strong.

It would be so much easier to leave now without seeing him. All she had to do was walk through the exit doors into the secure Customs area and Kent wouldn't be able to follow her. Then she could keep herself together until she was safely out of reach. Should she leave? Now?

'Zoe.'

His voice came from behind her, spinning her around, a smile already flooding her face.

Oh, wow! He looked even more wonderful than she'd remembered. He was so tall and broad shouldered and his skin was darker, as if he'd spent a lot of time outdoors.

They stood, just staring at each other. Not touching.

'I'm late,' he said. 'The traffic was insane. I was afraid I'd miss you.'

'It won't be long before I have to go.'

'That's OK. At least I'm here now.' He smiled.

Heavens, his smile was gorgeous.

Dangerous. Zoe wanted to lean in to him, to touch him, to smell him.

Instead she searched for safe conversation. 'How's everything on the farm?'

'All running along smoothly.'

'Who's looking after the garden?'

Kent smiled again, but his eyes were watching her with hawklike attention. 'I have my work cut out running the farm, and my mother's busy planting up her new cottage garden, so, for now, the garden's looking after itself.'

'That's a shame.' There would be so many weeds, and the roses would need dead-heading. All the lilies and irises would be out now, but there'd be no one to truly appreciate them.

'I might get someone in,' he said, still watching her.

Zoe nodded and told herself to forget Willara Downs.

Kent said, 'You're going to have a fabulous trip.'

She was grateful that he wasn't going to try to stop her from leaving. She hoped he had no idea how easily he could.

His eyes searched her face, again, worried now. 'You'll be careful, won't you, Zoe?'

'Of course. Don't worry. My dad's given me all the lectures about a girl overseas on her own... I have a long list of instructions. Use a money belt. Keep enough money for the day in my pocket. Stay away from the lonely spots.'

'All very good advice.'

'And I've scanned my travel documents and emailed them to myself.'

'Great. And remember to keep in touch,' Kent added.

'That, too.' She smiled. 'I have international texting on my mobile phone.'

'And you have my number, I hope.'

'Yes. I'll text you.'

'Promise?'

The dark intensity in his eyes made her heart stumble. 'I promise, Kent.'

His shoulders visibly relaxed, and it was only then that she realised how very tense he'd been. 'Text me as often as you like, Zoe. If you're having a great time, or—or a not so great time.'

'I will.' She smiled. 'Don't look so worried.'

'I can't help it. I'm letting you go.'

She didn't know what to say. She hadn't expected him to be quite so...so protective...and she was scared she'd start to cry. 'I should head off now.'

He touched her elbow. 'You can't rush off without a decent goodbye.'

It was a warning, Zoe realised, not a request. But

Kent gave her no chance to deny him. In a heartbeat, he'd gathered her in, and he was kissing her.

Not hungrily, as she might have expected after their three-week stand-off, but with devastating tenderness. And heaven help her, she couldn't even pretend to resist. He only had to touch her and her will power evaporated like mist in sunlight.

Now, he'd barely sipped at her lower lip and, already, she was trembling.

His lips brushed her top lip. A kiss, as teasing and as light as air. Heartbreaking in its sexiness. He pressed another kiss to the corner of her mouth.

Wherever his lips touched her, Zoe melted.

Her knees threatened to give away as he took the kiss dizzyingly deeper, and she had no choice but to cling to him, grabbing handfuls of his T-shirt to steady herself. Now she was truly melting all over. Melting from head to toe. Dissolving right there. In the busy airport.

The bustling crowds and the voices over the intercom faded as Zoe became lost in the deep, dark mystery of Kent's kiss. Her impending flight no longer mattered. The whole world was happening right here. In Kent's arms.

When he released her, she wanted to cry.

Gently, he tucked a strand of her hair behind her ear, and his eyes betrayed a mix of sadness and triumph. 'So, Zoe…about this cooling-off idea.'

Right now, the cooling off was quite obviously the most ridiculous idea she'd ever had.

Then again, this kiss only proved how very badly she needed a safety net. She was so susceptible to this man. She lost her head whenever he was near. His kisses made her want to cancel her flight, tear up her ticket and toss her passport in the nearest waste bin.

Snap out of it, Zoe. For heaven's sake pull yourself together. Now.

She squared her shoulders. 'I—I don't think we should change our current status before I get back.'

Kent was smiling, damn him. 'So I guess this fare-well kiss was an exception.'

Somehow, miraculously, Zoe kept her face poker straight. 'Under the circumstances, it was an excus-able infringement.' With deliberate brusqueness, she checked the time on her phone. 'I'm sorry. I really must go now.'

To her surprise, Kent nodded. 'Yes, you must. I hope you have a safe journey, Zoe.'

'Thanks.'

It was happening. Kent was letting her go. Why couldn't she feel relieved?

His eyes were burning and serious. 'Remember to stay in touch. Your messages can be as cool as you like, but keep them coming.'

'All right.'

She thought he might kiss her again. And he did. He dropped one last, sweet, too-tempting and too-brief kiss on her lips, and then he stepped away from her, his throat rippling.

He lifted his hand.

Zoe's vision blurred and when she tried to walk her shoes were filled with lead.

CHAPTER TWELVE

AT FIRST, Zoe managed quite well. In London and Paris there were so many famous sights she wanted to see, so many beautiful art galleries, and amazing, historic buildings. So many wonderfully enticing shops to explore. She managed to keep busy every day and she found each new experience thrilling and exciting.

She also discovered definite advantages to solo travelling—total freedom to decide what she wanted to see and where she should stay, or when and where she should eat. And she met lots of interesting fellow travellers from all over the world.

But of course, she missed Kent and thought of him often.

Too often.

No way could she pretend she didn't miss him. He was always there, as an ache beneath her breastbone, a tightness in her throat. Her solo travels would have been a thousand times better if he'd been there to share everything with her.

Even so, she was very disciplined. She restricted her text messages to Kent, allowing only one message every second day, and she kept them brief and cheerful. No mushy stuff.

Kent's responses were disappointing—often arriving much later than Zoe would have liked, even taking the time difference into consideration. And when he replied, his tone was cool and utterly lacking in anything even slightly mushy or romantic.

Clearly, he was taking her request to extend their cooling-off period seriously, and she knew she should be grateful for that. But there was always the chance that his interest in her was fading, just as she'd always feared.

Zoe hated how sick this thought made her.

She tried to cheer herself up by conjuring memories of their farewell kiss at the airport, but what an unhelpful exercise that was. She found herself missing Kent more and more every day.

It was dark when Kent got back to the homestead. He fed his dogs on the back veranda, then went into the kitchen to heat up a can of tomato soup for himself. He knew it was lazy, but it was already after eight, and he was too weary to bother about cooking a proper meal. Since Zoe left, he'd been working long hours, seven days a week, hoping that the self-imposed labour would act as a sedative.

It hadn't worked.

Nothing in his life felt right. Each night he fell into bed exhausted, but then couldn't sleep. His solitary existence, which had never bothered him before, was now suffocating.

He couldn't stop thinking about Zoe in Europe, wishing he were there. Worse, he kept reliving all the times they'd been together. Not just the lovemaking—all the everyday moments, like the evening she was here in his kitchen, making a salad while he flipped steaks, on another afternoon, preparing a roast, or sharing a sunset.

He remembered the meals they'd enjoyed on the back veranda, the conversations. Recalled Zoe's enthusiasm for the garden, remembered the morning she'd gone down to the creek with him to collect sand—the soft empathy in her eyes when she'd asked him about the accident.

Each small recollection had become painfully sharp and clear. So important.

Now that Kent had too much time to think, he realised that he'd been so caught up with the wedding plans that he'd never really noticed how perfectly Zoe fitted into life on Willara Downs. Now, despite his best attempts to ignore such dangerous thoughts, he knew that his plans for a lengthy bachelorhood were fast losing their charm.

It was not a comforting discovery. Small wonder he couldn't sleep.

For Zoe, things went from not so great to downright dismal when she arrived in Prague.

As her plane touched down she looked out at the banks of snow lining the cleared runway, and her first, her *only* thought was—*Kent should be here*.

Riding in the taxi from the airport, she couldn't stop thinking about him. She'd brought his beautiful book with her, and now the same gorgeous pictures she knew by heart were unfolding before her. She kept thinking about the night they'd shared dinner on the back veranda at Willara Downs, when Kent had first told her about Christmas in Prague.

If only he were here.

Impulsively, she sent him a text message.

1.30p.m.: I'm in Prague!!!!!!! My first glimpse of the fairy-tale skyline. Prague castle silhouetted against a winter-white sky. It stole my breath. So pretty and timeless.

She'd only come to Prague because Kent had told her about it, and now she was here, surrounded by its ancient, wintry beauty, she wanted him to be here with her. So badly. How could she enjoy the snow, the castles and the Christmas markets without him?

Loneliness descended like the snow.

She remembered all the overtures Kent had made before she left—the enormous bunch of flowers, the offers to visit her at her flat, the trip to the airport to say goodbye. Each time he'd tried to restart their relationship she'd blocked him.

Now, she had to ask why.

Why? *Why?*

Why had she been so fixated on keeping him at bay?

She was left with unanswered puzzles. She was surprised that he still seemed keen even though she'd spilled her dreams about settling down. Not that this meant he was ready to marry her. Perhaps he'd hoped to win her around to accepting a freer relationship. To Zoe, in her present lonely circumstances, that seemed to be a reasonable compromise.

However, her fixation with Kent annoyed her. She'd come away, hoping that distance and time would clear her head and her heart. But now, here she was in Prague on the far side of the world, and she still spent her whole time thinking about one man.

She missed his smile, missed his friendly brown eyes, the warmth and power of his arms about her. Missed his smell, his voice, his kisses, his touch...

And she had to ask why she'd insisted on an extension of their cooling off.

Her initial caution, so soon after the cancelled wedding, had been sensible. But was her request to continue it really such a good idea?

Suddenly, it made no sense to ration her text messages.

She had to make contact with Kent. If he couldn't be here, she needed to share her experiences by the only means she had. Opening her phone, she began to type.

4.15 p.m.: It's already dark and it's snowing and I'm wearing a new red woollen hat I bought in Paris.

5.45 p.m.: I'm in the Old Town Square. So many sounds. Church bells, a brass band playing carols, the chiming of the famous astronomical clock.

6.01 p.m.: Now I'm walking across Charles Bridge. There's a busker playing a violin. Magic.

7.10 p.m.: Goulash for dinner with five white dumplings to mop up the yummy rich beef gravy.

7.30 p.m.: Have just had my first drink of grog—a mix of rum and tea. Miss you heaps. Xx

By the time Zoe went to bed she'd had no reply from Kent. She told herself this was to be expected given the time differences, but it didn't stop her from feeling depressed and lonely and sorry for herself.

She knew it was pitiful, but she couldn't help feeling

down. She cried herself to sleep, and she slept fitfully, waking often to check her phone for messages.

There was only one, which arrived at 3.00 a.m. From her mum.

Next morning, Kent still hadn't replied, and Zoe found reasons—he'd risen early and taken off on his tractor without checking his phone. Or perhaps his phone's battery had needed recharging. She knew there were all sorts of logical explanations.

Just the same, she waited on tenterhooks. And to cheer herself up, she kept sending messages.

8.05 a.m.: From my apartment window, I look out at steep rooftops covered in snow and I can see Prague castle.

Don't you wish you were here?

8.35 a.m.: The cars are covered in snow. The statues have snow on their shoulders. The tree branches are sagging beneath the weight of the snow. There are children tobogganing.

What's it like at Willara?

9.15 a.m.: I'm trying to catch falling snow in my mouth. Can you tell snow's a novelty for me?

10.00 p.m.: Kent, I've been in Prague a whole day. Where are you?

At midnight, Zoe sat on her bed, wrapped in a warm quilt, staring forlornly at her phone. She'd written an-other message, but she wasn't quite brave enough to press Send. Kent's silence had made her desperate, but the message was so—*revealing*—and sending it was far too risky.

Heartsick, she read it again.

11.53 p.m.: Kent, I miss you so much. This cooling off isn't working any more. When I get back home, I hope we can talk.
I love you,
Zoe xxx

She'd changed the last part of the message a dozen times, had deleted and then rewritten those three telling words— *I love you.*

She knew this wasn't what he wanted to hear. How could she make such a rash confession? In the weeks since she'd left home, he hadn't given her any fresh reason to hope.

At twenty past midnight, Zoe was still huddled on the bed, but she decided she'd been too cautious for too long. What the heck? It was time to be brave.

Taking a deep breath for courage, she pressed the send button, and then she slipped beneath the covers, and tried to sleep. Her heart was pounding.

Next morning there was still no answer from Kent, and Zoe had never in her life felt as bereft as she did now.

She stood at the window looking out at the postcard-perfect scene of Europe's fairy-tale city. Overnight it had snowed again and all the rooftops and the streets were coated with glistening white. She didn't care. She didn't want to be in Prague. It was almost Christmas and she was alone and heartbroken and on the wrong side of the world.

How could she have been such a fool? How had she ever thought she could enjoy this alone?

But even if she paid the extra money to change her flights in the middle of the festive season, she didn't want to fly back to Australia if she couldn't be sure Kent would welcome her. That would be unbearable. Better to stay here in Prague and try to make the best of a bad situation.

She should try to put Kent out of her mind.

This morning she would go to the markets and buy Christmas decorations. She would school herself to live in each moment, to enjoy the ancient cobbled streets, and the old Gothic architecture, and the brightly decorated wooden huts selling handicrafts and wooden toys. Instead of dwelling on her misery, she would think of others. She would buy presents. Lots of presents. Her little brother, Toby, would love those cheeky wooden puppets.

But as Zoe walked from stall to stall she was painfully conscious of the small solid weight of her phone in her coat pocket. All morning, even though she knew it was the middle of the night in Australia, she remained on edge, waiting for the phone to vibrate against her hip, to tell her there was an incoming call.

In the afternoon, she joined a tour of Prague Castle and St Vitus Cathedral. The buildings were beautiful, and the history was epic and fascinating. The views of the city and the elegant bridges over the Vltava River were truly picturesque. Zoe soaked up the atmosphere and told herself how lucky she was to be having such memorable experiences. She told herself this over and over.

Her phone didn't ring.

By the time she'd finished the walking tour, darkness was closing in, but she didn't want to go back to her hotel room. She stayed out in the streets where the music and pretty lights were designed to lift everyone's spirits.

The air was thick with the warm smell of cinnamon and she admired the enormous, brightly lit Christmas tree which, according to the hotel concierge, had been brought down from the Sumava Mountains.

Every ten minutes or so, desperation drove her to take her phone out just to check that she hadn't missed a call.

She hadn't.

By now, her legs were leaden and aching from walking all day in the freezing cold. Her stomach was hollow with regret and self-recrimination. Her last message had been too strong. Kent didn't know how to answer her.

Or worse…

Kent had been in an accident. He was ill.

Stop it.

She would go mad if she kept this up. She should eat. The market stalls sold all kinds of wonderful hot food—corn on the cob, crumbed mushrooms and spicy sausages. Perhaps she should buy a cup of the hot mulled wine that everyone else seemed to be enjoying so much. The wine certainly looked and smelled yummy—spicy, with floating pieces of apple and orange.

At least it would keep her warm.

Slipping her phone into her coat pocket, Zoe gave it a small pat. Silently, she said: *That's it—I'm done with you for tonight.*

The thought was barely completed before she felt, through the soft kid of her glove, a gentle vibration against her fingers.

Her heart banged hard against her ribs. And then her phone began to ring in earnest.

This wasn't a mere text message. On the tiny screen she saw a name.

Kent Rigby...

Her hand was shaking as she held the phone to her ear.

Kent said, 'Zoe—'

And at that very moment a brass band struck up a noisy rendition of 'Good King Wenceslas', drowning out Kent's voice as it blasted the carol into the frosty night air.

'Sorry,' Zoe cried to him, running across the cobblestones with the phone pressed to one ear and her hand covering the other. 'I can't hear you. Hang on, Kent. Are you still there? I'm going to have to get away from this music.'

Around a corner, in a small, narrow street, she sank against a stone wall. 'Sorry,' she puffed. 'That's a little better. Are you still there?'

'Yes, I'm here.' His voice was rippling with warmth and a hint of laughter.

'Are you OK? It seems ages since I heard from you.'

'I'm fine, Zoe. How are you?'

'I'm OK. Everything's lovely here. But it's so good to hear your voice.'

'Are you homesick?'

'I am a bit, yes.' Nervously, she chewed her lip. 'Have my text messages been getting through to you?'

'They have.' There was a tiny pause. 'Thank you.' His voice sounded deeper, rougher, thick with emotion.

Zoe held her breath, wondering if he would explain his recent silence, or if he'd comment on her last message.

At least *I love you* hadn't frightened him away.

'It's beautiful here,' she said lamely.

'Where are you exactly?'

'I'm not sure. It's a little side street off the Old Town Square. Why?'

'I was hoping you weren't too far away.'

She laughed. 'Yeah, right. Like I'm just around the corner from Willara Downs.'

'I'm not at Willara Downs.'

'Where—?' she began, then froze as she heard the triumphant notes of a brass band. The music was coming from...

Inside her phone.

Surely she was mistaken?

No, she wasn't.

'Kent?' Zoe was so tense she was sure her skin had snapped. 'Where are you?'

'Right behind you.'

Heart thumping, she spun around.

And there he was.

On the street corner in a heavy winter coat, outlined by the bright lights from the markets.

She tried to lift a shocked hand to wave, but already Kent was coming towards her, and then, as fast as her shaky legs would allow, Zoe was stumbling over the snowy cobblestones.

Into his open arms.

She buried her face in his shoulder and he held her. She was crying, laughing and snuffling with happiness.

'What are you doing here?' she asked when she got her breath back.

'Looking for you, of course.'

'Kent, that's insane.' A huge sob burst from her. 'Oh, God, I've missed you so much.'

'And I've missed you.' Kent wiped her tears with a gloved hand. 'You wrote that you missed me on your first day here, and I jumped straight on the very next plane.'

Stunned, she pulled back to look into his face. His dearly loved, beautiful face. And in that moment she understood exactly why she loved him.

It had nothing to do with his farm, or his lovely homestead. Or his country shirts and his riding boots. She loved him for something else entirely. Something warm and powerful and steadfast and strong that she found shining in his beautiful brown eyes.

'Thank you for coming,' she said softly.

'Thank you for missing me,' he answered, kissing the tip of her nose.

Arm in arm and warmed by mulled wine and hot corn cobs, they walked through the snowy night to Zoe's hotel. Kent was insanely happy. *Insanely. Over the moon.*

They collected his backpack and went up the narrow stairs. In Zoe's room, they peeled off their gloves, hung up their woollen hats and coats, and removed their heavy, damp boots.

Zoe, looking all kinds of gorgeous in a soft crimson sweater and pale blue jeans, turned to him, her eyes shining with happy expectation.

He wanted nothing more than to scoop her in to him, but he remembered, just in time, that he had something even more important planned for this moment.

He said, with a rueful smile, 'Can you hang on a tick?'

'No, Kent, I can't.' Zoe was laughing and impatient,

rising on tiptoes to nuzzle his jaw. With her lips against his skin, she growled, 'I can't wait another second.'

OK, it was a whacky plan anyway, and Kent knew he couldn't wait either. He needed this. Now. Needed Zoe wrapped in his arms, needed her sweet mouth locked with his, needed the soft silk of her skin under his palms, needed her eager and hungry and loving...

Later...

Everything else could wait till later...

'So what was it?' Zoe asked much later as she lay with her head cradled against his bare shoulder.

Kent yawned. 'What was what?'

'Earlier tonight, when we got back here to the room, you asked me to hang on. What was that about? Were you going to show me something?'

'Yeah,' he said sleepily, and then he yawned. 'But it can wait.'

Gently, she ran her fingers over his chest. 'Poor Kent. You've flown all this way and you must be so jet-lagged.'

'Mmm.'

Kent slept, and Zoe lay awake. After the strain of the past few days, she should have been exhausted, but she was too happy and excited to close her eyes.

Kent had come to her as soon as she told him she missed him. How wonderful was that?

Faint moonlight spilled from the window across their bed and she watched him sleep and thought how amazing, how unbelievably perfect he was.

Her happiness was astonishing, as if she'd been living in a grey world that was suddenly flooded with colour.

Of course, in a deep corner of her heart there was still a niggle of disquiet. When Kent had swept her into his arms he hadn't promised love or marriage. But perhaps it was time to put her dreams aside. Time to put Rodney behind her and to take another risk. Didn't loving someone always involve a risk?

Bella had taken a huge risk when she dashed off to Far North Queensland with Damon Cavello. Kent had taken another big risk by travelling over here on the strength of a text message...

Anyway, why should she worry now simply because Kent hadn't actually told her in so many words that he loved her? He'd flown all this way to be with her, and he'd made love to her with a passion that made her blood sing.

Really. On a night like this, just having him here was enough.

Kent kissed Zoe awake. 'Morning, Sleeping Beauty. I've brought you coffee.'

To her surprise it was already past ten.

'Gosh, you're the one with jet lag. I should be bringing you coffee.'

Kent smiled and sat on the edge of the bed. 'Did you know you're at your most beautiful when you've just woken up?'

'I can't be.'

'But you are. I love the sleep-tumbled look.'

For a moment she thought he was going to say he loved her—no matter how she looked.

It doesn't matter. I don't need words.

Outside, the day was sunny, crystal clear and gleaming white, but they stayed in until lunchtime, making leisurely love. When they eventually went out, they ate food from a market stall, then took a train ride to Karlstejn Castle.

The castle was stunningly beautiful, and Zoe decided that Cinderella, Snow White and Sleeping Beauty had all spent time living within those spectacular walls at the top of a snowy mountain.

From the castle ramparts, the view was truly majestic. They could see for miles, and Zoe wondered—just briefly, as she had earlier that morning—if *this* setting might prompt Kent to tell her he'd changed, that he loved her and wanted to spend the rest of his life with her...

It didn't happen.

But that was OK. Nothing could spoil her happiness as they took the train back to Prague, or as they walked to Wenceslas Square to a café that served coffee and sensational apple strudel with home-made ice cream.

'Save room for dinner,' Kent warned her. 'I'm taking you somewhere special.'

So they walked off the strudel, then went back to their hotel to change. Kent had made reservations at the most gorgeous restaurant where the food was so divine it could easily have inspired a brand-new 'Bohemian Rhapsody'.

Over dinner they talked about Prague and what they knew of Czech history, and the whole time Kent's eyes were lit by a special light that kept Zoe's heart zinging.

All right, all right...

There was no talk of love. *But who needed words?*

Back at the hotel, Zoe took a long hot bath and told herself that she had to stop waiting for Kent to say *something*.

He was a farmer, a doer, a man of action, not words.

He'd bought her a bracelet and he'd sent her goldfish and flowers and given her a book. He'd rushed to the airport to farewell her. And he'd flown all this way from Australia. Why would he do all that if he didn't really care for her?

Just the same…tonight, she would pluck up the courage to mention her last revealing text message. She needed to know how he felt about it…

After drying herself, Zoe rubbed moisturiser all over her body, then slipped into the luxuriously thick towelling robe supplied by the hotel. She opened the bathroom door…

And gasped when she saw their room…

Candles…

Candles everywhere. Candles on the coffee table, on the bookcase, on the bedside tables, on the deep stone window sills. Candles on every available surface. Dainty, *little* candles.

Candles that looked strangely familiar.

Kent was standing in the middle of the room, watching her. In the flickering light, he sent her a shy, crooked smile. 'This was supposed to happen last night.'

'Wow.' Zoe pressed a hand to the jumping pulse in her throat. 'They look so lovely.'

The candles were more than lovely. They were gorgeous. Dazzling. The room danced and glowed with romantic light, while darkness hovered outside and white snowflakes fell soundlessly against the window pane.

Kent grinned. 'You probably recognise these little guys. I have to confess I borrowed your smart candles.'

Of course. Now she knew why they were so familiar. They were the same candles she'd planned to put in sand-filled paper bags for Bella's wedding. 'You brought all of them? All this way?'

'Yes. Four dozen smart candles in my backpack.' He smiled boyishly. 'I brought them to help me.'

Help him? Why? Zoe held her breath. Her heart began to thump.

Kent stepped closer and reached for her hands. 'I wanted to tell you how special you are, Zoe, but I wasn't sure I could convince you with words alone. The candles are my back-up.' His eyes shimmered. 'They stand for everything I love about you. They're bright and—'

'Wait,' she said. 'Please, don't rush over that bit.'

'What bit?'

'The—ah—bit you just said.'

'About loving you?'

'Yes.'

Kent smiled gorgeously. 'Darling girl, that's why I'm here.' His hands framed her face. His eyes shone. 'I love you so much. So much it kills me.'

She was so happy she was going to cry. But she still mustn't get her hopes up. She had to stay sensible. 'But—but this isn't a proposal or anything, is it?'

'It certainly is.'

Her heart almost leapt clear out of her chest. 'But you—you said—'

'I know what I said about long-term commitment, but that was before.' Kent's throat rippled and his eyes shimmered. 'Everything changed when you stepped on that plane, Zoe. I watched you walking out of my life, and it was like I was drowning all over again. Every moment I'd spent with you flashed before my eyes—from the first time we met by the road side and you had the flat tyre, and all those other times at Willara, and then in Brisbane.'

He took a deep breath. 'I've been falling for you from

the start, but I was planning the wedding to Bella, and I couldn't let myself think about you.'

Lifting her hands, Kent pressed them against his chest and she felt the thud-thudding of his heartbeats. 'I've missed you so much. And I've come to my senses at last. Of course, I want what you want, Zoe. I want your help with running the farm, and I want our own little family.'

It was too, too wonderful to take in. To Zoe's dismay, fat tears rolled down her cheeks and she had to blot them on Kent's shirtfront.

When she looked up again, his dark eyes burned with an intensity that made her tremble. 'Don't ever doubt that I love you, Zoe. You're exactly like these candles. You're beautiful and smart and you set me alight.'

'And you brought all forty-eight of them all this way to prove it.' Smiling, she snuggled closer and wound her arms around his neck. 'I do love a man of action.'

'So does that mean you'll marry me?'

Would she? Would she marry the most gorgeous farmer in the world and live in his lovely farmhouse set solidly and safely amidst spreading fields?

Would she embrace her most cherished dream?

For answer Zoe kissed him. 'Yes,' she said, and she gave him another kiss. 'Yes, please, I'd love to marry you.' Then she kissed him again while forty-eight candles glowed warmly in the midwinter night.

* * * * *

JUST ONE MORE NIGHT

CAITLIN CREWS

To all the Dare editors who worked so hard on these books, and to all my fellow authors who told such brilliant stories in the first place, it's been such a pleasure to be a part of this series!

And to my readers, thank you so much for going on these dark, delicious adventures with me.
It's been an absolute delight!

CHAPTER ONE

INDIANA MARCH, CALLED INDY by her loved ones and much filthier things by her lovers, landed in Prague on a gorgeous June afternoon, ready to face her destiny.

It had been two years since one night in Budapest had changed everything.

Two years since she had made a promise before flying standby back to New York, where she'd moved in with her far less free-spirited older sister—who never would have gone to Budapest in the first place and wouldn't have gotten into the trouble Indy had no matter where she went.

Bristol was the *good* March sister.

She had recently gotten her doctorate after a lifetime of endless, serious, and committed studying. Indy, on the other hand, was committed to having fun. And while she was at it, living up— or down—to everyone's expectations of the other March sister.

Not *bad,* she liked to say. But *better.*

Especially because when she said things like that, and vamped it up, it made her sister roll her eyes. And then laugh in spite of herself.

Indy and Bristol had settled on these designations for themselves when they'd still been little girls in small-town Ohio. And all these years later, Indy still thought she'd made the better choice. She'd decided school was boring in roughly the fourth grade and had decreed that she had better things to do, leaving Bristol to study away to her heart's content while she danced and partied and ran around just being silly, because she could.

Bristol would probably be off studying right this minute—because there were apparently *post*-doctorates for people who felt the one PhD wasn't enough—if it weren't for the little summer adventure Indy had sent her sister off on. *An opportunity to discover the parts of you that aren't all about your mind, at last,* Indy had told her—but that was another story.

Indy smiled at the notion of studious, killjoy Bristol getting her freak on out there as her plane taxied toward the gate, bouncing a little on the tarmac. She couldn't wait to see if her big sister finally loosened up a bit—and couldn't really imagine what a *loosened up* Bristol would look like. As the plane came to a rocking stop at the gate, she gathered up the small carry-on that was all she'd brought with her and held it on her lap, watching as all around her, people leapt to their feet and started dragging much heavier bags out of the overhead bins.

It always looked so unpleasant. And then the reward for all those heavy bags was that you then had to lug them around with you. Where was the fun in that?

Indy never troubled with much baggage, figurative or literal. After college she'd backpacked around for a couple of years, but never with one of those massive packs that some people toted across the planet that made them look like unfortunate tortoises. Their packs were always seventeen times their body weight, the better to mark them to all and sundry as a tourist, and barely fit in the narrow, often cobbled streets that they were always trundling along in. Not to mention, they might as well have worn neon signs inviting any predators to take a swing their way.

No thanks, she thought now, though she smiled nicely enough at the woman next to her and her two enormous, overstuffed suitcases.

That wasn't how Indy operated. She was less about neon signs that weighed her down and more about going with the flow. And she'd never had an issue with predators.

Well. She stood up from her seat when she could

finally step out into the aisle and considered. That wasn't *entirely* true, was it?

Indy had made up no itinerary, back in her world-traveling backpacker days or even today. Because *itineraries* were boring. They nailed you down to a time and a place and a *schedule* and Indy was all about never, ever being boring, nailed down to anything, or, God forbid, the kind of person who couldn't grab a drink without consulting seventeen sticker-laden planners and her phone's calendar app. She'd watched Bristol—whose whole life was about schedules and responsibility and tedious meetings about any number of inane things—whittle away her life in tiny little recorded increments on hundreds of planner pages, but Indy had never wanted any part of that kind of nonsense. She had barely made it through college. Not because she was dumb, but because there were always so many more delicious things to do than study. Or sit in a yawn-worthy lecture. Or write dreary essays that were never about the things that interested her.

Those being, in no particular order: life. Sex. Fun.

Indy wanted to squeeze every last bit of the good stuff out of every single day, then roll herself around in it until it became who she was. On a cellular level. What else could possibly be the point?

Sadly, that was not, it turned out, the kind of

mission statement the average employer liked to see on a résumé. Or the average landlord liked to hear about when rent was due, so it was a good thing for Indy that Bristol was always so dependable.

Still, Indy never had too much trouble finding work. Or getting laid, for that matter, and the two often twisted together in ways she was sure she could probably hashtag about—if she weren't too busy living to live tweet. She didn't have any particular airs and was perfectly happy to take a waitressing job here or a temp job there. Just as she was happy to roll under one man in the morning and ride a different one that night. Jobs and men were an endlessly renewable resource, in her experience. There were always, always more when a girl was game for whatever came her way.

Her sister and her perfectly lovely parents back in Ohio did not understand Indy's approach to life—and only Bristol knew the more salacious details, thank you. All her parents knew was that Indy *had trouble settling down.*

Her mother thought she needed a man. Indy had to bite her tongue every Christmas to keep from saying things like, *don't worry, Mom, I've had many.* She didn't think that would shock the unflappable Margie March. Nothing could, in her experience. But it would open up her personal life to conversation, and Indy always figured that was a bad idea all around.

Particularly these past two years when, she could admit, her usual carefree, hedonistic attitude had become something a good deal more...manic.

It was true. She'd had something to prove, hadn't she?

Indy shivered a bit in the cab that drove her from the airport down into the old city. Prague spread out before her like a fairytale, but not the kind of fairytale that warmed the hearts of wannabe Disney princesses. Bristol had been the one who loved those happy ever afters when they'd been girls. She'd always longed for the Prince Charmings and the perfect kisses.

But Indy had been far more intrigued by the Big, Bad Wolf. She'd seen no reason for Little Red Riding Hood to waste her time swinging an axe or even getting a passing huntsman to do the same on her behalf.

Not when there were so many other things to do in the dark.

She shivered again, even though it was warm in the cab. The truth was, Indy had been aching like this since she'd left Budapest. It had only gotten worse over time. Her nipples were always so tight they hurt. Her pussy was always *so* wet. Sometimes she could simply clench her thighs together and make her clit throb, or even get herself off sometimes, but none of it was enough.

None of it was near enough.

No matter how many cocks she rode or took deep in her mouth, none of it had made her feel the way today did. Just here, sitting in a taxi, was already hotter and better than all the sex she'd had since she'd left Budapest.

Combined.

Because today she got to keep her promise.

Indy didn't let herself imagine, even for a moment, that he wouldn't be here.

He would. She was sure he would.

He had to be.

His instructions had been simple and clear two years ago. He'd given her the address, a time, and a key. The same key she could feel tucked between her breasts now, because she'd hung it from a chain when she'd gotten back to New York. The key she'd never taken off, no matter who she was fucking or what other adventures she might have had since.

Sometimes she'd gotten off more to the memories the key kicked up in her than whatever—or whoever—she'd been doing. She wrapped her hand around the key on its chain now and sighed a little, feeling her whole body hum in anticipation.

She'd never been one for waiting. But she'd waited for this. Some days she'd been sure the waiting might kill her—but it hadn't. And now here she was. Alive after all.

The waiting was finally over.

Or almost over. Indy had a few hours before the agreed-upon meeting time, so she didn't go to the address she'd been given. She had the taxi drop her off on the cobbled street ringing Prague's Old Town Square and dodged armadas of tourists as she walked around the looming statue of the fifteenth-century martyr that dominated it. She peered up at the great Gothic church that always made her sigh a little and got a glimpse of the famous Astronomical Clock over the inevitable crowd waiting for its next show.

It felt good to walk. The last time she'd been in Prague she'd been so exhausted after far too much clubbing in Berlin that she'd hardly been able to feel her own feet, much less fully register where she was. She knew she should have been jet-lagged today, but she wasn't. Or if she was, it was buried so far beneath her excitement and the adrenaline of finally being here that it didn't affect her at all. She hadn't slept on the overnight flight from New York to Zurich. She hadn't nodded off in the Zurich airport where she'd caught her connection. And she'd been good and wired on the plane into Prague.

When she sat down at a table in the crowded,

open-air café, she waited for a wave of weariness to take her over.

But it didn't come.

She was *amped*.

Indy settled back in her café chair and blew on her coffee when it arrived. She was hardly able to believe it was only a matter of hours now. She checked her phone. Less than two hours.

And she could still remember that night in Budapest far too clearly. As if it had happened last night instead of two years back.

Indy had been with some friends she'd hooked up with in Croatia. She'd been two solid years into her world traveler phase and hadn't seen any end in sight, at that point. These particular friends were the sort she picked up wherever she went. A hostel here, a club there—there were always like-minded people about. Always another party, always another adventure. A new city, a new face, a new story to tell. Indy hadn't been able to come up with a single good reason why she would ever return to what waited for her back in the States.

That being the hum-drum little lives that all her friends lived in the various places they'd settled down. Nine-to-five desk jobs, paycheck to paycheck, dreary cubicles, and boring conversations about *the property ladder*.

None of that was any fun at all.

You need to make some real decisions about

your life, her father had told her after her college graduation, which everybody liked to say had been a skin-of-the-teeth kind of deal for the not-so-good March sister. *Serious decisions.*

Indy had felt that she was full up on *serious.* She had taken a fifth year to get her degree and might have taken a sixth if she hadn't been so deeply bored by the whole thing. Still, she'd paid her way—meaning there had been no letting anybody down if she made academic decisions that didn't suit them, like failing a class because she'd forgotten to attend it, or accidentally going off to a music festival instead of taking her exams.

Disappointing them, sure. But not actually letting them down or spending their money. Indy had some standards, thank you. And she had never felt the need to let her father know *how* she'd paid her way through college. Or why it was she had such a robust savings account come graduation.

There were things a father didn't need to know.

I know what I want to do with my life, she had told him, wrinkling up her nose in his direction as they'd sat down by the river near her childhood home, fishing.

Or in Indy's case, pretending to fish while doing what she did best. Lounging.

Okay, what she did second-best.

Nothing *is not a good answer,* Bill March had replied. He'd shot her a look she knew well, filled as it was with laughter, love, and that particular gleam that made her think, sometimes, that her father knew exactly how free-spirited she really was.

I'm going to live*, Dad*, she had said. *Deep and hard and wild. Isn't that what you're supposed to do with a life?*

Everybody's hard and wild until it's time to pay taxes, her father had said with his typical calm midwestern practicality.

I'm going to be just fine, she had told him, smiling wide. *I promise.*

And she had been.

She had taken a certain delight in sending her raciest photos to her sister, because Bristol was so easily scandalized. Indy had sent postcards to her parents from every new place she went. London to Bali to Perth to Rio and back again. She'd worked when she needed money, went on marvelous adventures as the spirit took her, and followed her pussy wherever it wanted to go.

The club in Budapest had been one of the underground ones she'd developed a taste for over time, on all continents. She loved the inherent mystery of these pop-up events. A warehouse or a field somewhere, often in a sketchy part of town to make the whole thing feel more edgy and exciting. There was never any possibility of planning for these things, there was only waiting for the text to come and then racing off—no matter her state of inebriation—to dance and howl and party until the sun came up.

That was why a wise woman didn't have a plan. All the good stuff happened outside those lines.

The night in question had been like all the other nights in all the other cities and fields and beaches she'd discovered on her travels. The DJ had been particularly good and Indy had lost her friends somewhere in the crowd, but that was never something she worried about. She liked to let the universe take a hand in such things. She would either find them again or she wouldn't, but her experience, everywhere, was that there were always new friends to be made.

You have a low bar for what you call friendship, Bristol had told her. More than once.

Or you have a ridiculously high one, Indy would retort. *You can make a friend, Bristol. It's not a lifetime commitment unless you want it to be. It also won't kill you.*

Bristol, as ever, had remained unconvinced. And also lonely, by Indy's reckoning, though she would die before she admitted it.

But Bristol hadn't been on Indy's mind that night in Budapest. She'd danced and danced. At some point she'd decided she needed a little bit of fresh air after all that dancing and she'd wound her way through the crowd, buzzing along nicely on the music and the beat she could feel deep inside her.

Indy had slipped out the side of the warehouse, and never knew, later, what made her wander away from the groups of people doing the same thing she was. Either taking a breath from the party inside or carrying on their own festivities out in the summer dark. She'd wandered away from the clusters of them, half wondering if she could see the stars in this part of Budapest. If she got away from those party lights and all the lit-up cell phone screens. If she'd had another motivation, she couldn't remember it.

She hadn't known what she was walking into until it was too late.

Scary men arguing in a dark alley. A gun in her face.

Then Indy on her knees on the pavement, hard, her heart pounding so wildly it had made her feel ill.

In that moment, she'd been certain that every warning she'd ever been given was about to come true. With a vengeance. Every dire prediction anyone had made about the way she lived, the way she *was*, was about to happen to her after all.

You don't think before you act, her sister had said a thousand times.

I hate to think of you getting yourself into trou-

ble, her mother had said more than once, *and all because your head is always in the clouds*.

And her father had frowned at her, the day he had dropped her off at the airport. Looking far more serious than he usually did. *The world isn't a magical place just because you want it to be, honey. Be smart out there.*

Indy had not been smart. She had been the opposite of smart, in fact, and had reveled in how little care she'd taken because it made for a better experience and then a better story to tell. And she had known, then, that she was going to pay for that in some out-of-the-way alley where no one would ever find her if they left her for dead.

Assuming they left her.

But that wasn't what happened.

She shuddered now, her hands cupped around her coffee. Far away from Budapest in a crowded café in lovely, fairytale Prague, two years later.

Still, Indy shuddered, because she could remember too well her first sight of him. That face of his, so beautiful it was cruel as he'd stared down at her in disbelief. She'd noticed that *face*, like the blade of a hatchet, piercing and inevitable. She'd had the impression of a tall, well-built, dark-haired man, but he'd had the eyes of a poet, intense and yet almost dreamy as he'd gazed at her there on her knees.

Their eyes had met down the length of the gun he'd held, pointed directly at her forehead.

And she'd had no doubt whatsoever that he knew how to use it.

He asked her something in a language she didn't understand. Hungarian, she'd thought, which would make sense as she had been in Hungary. Indy had shaken her head, almost smiling in an out-of-body sort of way, because at least if she was going to meet a brutal end it would be at the hands of a man who looked like an angel.

A fallen one. And fallen hard.

That he was dangerous, brutal and powerful at once, would have been obvious even if he wasn't holding a gun. Right in her face.

Even with those too-blue eyes.

What are you doing here? he had asked her in English, after trying a couple of other languages and getting nothing. His accent had made the words seem like liquid, swirling around her and washing through her. A new, potent heat.

I have no idea, she had replied, honestly.

And for a long moment, possibly a lifetime, she had been aware only of him. That look on his overwhelming face. That gaze of his that made her want to cry. The electric *something* that arced between them, even with concrete digging into her bare knees and her hands in the air.

For that little while, nothing else existed.

Nothing.

He had muttered something she'd understood was profane, even if she hadn't understood it.

And then everything got fast.

Indy remembered it like a blur, though she knew that each action had been precise. Surgical.

He had looked at her. She'd seen something in his gaze, something that had made her breath catch.

Something that had gone through her like an earthquake.

Then he had turned and taken down the other three men standing there with him. She had hardly had time to gasp, to shake, to react. She'd thought of poetry again, all of it lethal, as he'd spun around with blistering speed and laid all three men out flat.

Two kicks, one punch.

Like he was an action star.

Come, he'd said to her when they were all slumped on the ground. *You cannot be here.*

He'd reached down to pull her up to her feet with a possessive grip on her arm.

And Indy had gone willingly.

More than willingly. Because he'd saved her, that she'd had no doubt—even though it hadn't been clear if he was one of the things he'd saved her from.

But there was something about his grip on her

arm. The way he'd moved them both out of that alley. Quickly, but with that same liquid grace she'd already seen used with lethal intent on his friends.

It had occurred to her then that she ought to have been more scared than she was. As scared as she'd been when she'd first understood what was happening to her. As scared as she'd been before she'd actually caught his gaze and everything had…shifted.

If you're just going to kill me in a different location, she'd said as he led her away from the alley, *I have to tell you that it will be very disappointing.*

They'd made it out into the street by then. She could hear the pumping sound of the club she'd so foolishly wandered away from, though she couldn't see it. Had she wandered into the alley from the other side? And yet Indy hadn't really cared, because there had been a streetlight and she could *really* see him then.

He was built like a weapon far deadlier than any old hatchet. His beautiful eyes were breathtakingly blue, and he had a set of lips that should have made him a courtesan—and might have made him pretty if his face wasn't drawn in such harsh, male lines. She'd thought she would happily pay the whole of her life savings, and then some, to have that mouth between her legs.

But those were the only two soft things on his body.

Everything else was muscle. Thick and honed at once, so that he fairly hummed with power. With threat.

She remembered thinking how odd it was that she had been with so many men and had always happily explored all the various ways they used their power. Physical and intellectual alike, but nothing like this. Like him.

This man was darkness personified and his body showed it.

Indy had noticed a tattoo rising from the neck of his T-shirt, the same T-shirt that strained to contain his biceps. The same T-shirt that seemed unequal to the task of his hard, ridged abdomen. He wore dark jeans and the kind of dress shoes men wore on this side of the Atlantic because trainers were frowned upon for nightlife purposes in so many European countries.

She had been fully aware that he had that gun tucked in the small of his back. But looking at him, not only did she also know that his hands were weapons all by themselves—not to mention the feet that she'd seen in action with her own eyes—but that he likely had other things stashed around on his body, as well.

His profession seemed pretty clear.

I'm not going to kill you, he had said in that

accented voice of his that lit the night on fire, low and gravely with that impossible blue gaze behind it.

Or maybe the fire was only in her, making her wet and hot and something too close to desperate.

When she had never been desperate in her life.

She had tipped her head slightly to one side as she regarded him. *You sound surprised.*

I should have killed you the moment I saw you. His voice was matter-of-fact, suggesting that roaming about *killing people* was an ordinary occurrence for him, and yet his hand was still on her arm and she'd felt the heat of his grip. And she still hadn't been afraid. *That's what happens when foolish girls stumble into business meetings in the wrong part of town. Would anyone have missed you?*

Not tonight. Why had she said that? She might as well have knelt right down again and invited him to use that gun of his. Worse yet, she had kept talking. It was something about that faintly arrested look on his face, like he didn't understand what he was doing, either. It was that grip on her arm. It was her certain knowledge that something had *happened* between them in that alley. *Eventually, people back home would miss me, but they wouldn't know where to look. Most people think I'm still in Croatia.*

He had gripped her arm harder, though not hard

enough to hurt. He'd pulled her closer to him then, his poet's eyes blazing with a distinctly unpoetic fire as he'd gazed down at her—and she still hadn't been afraid.

She'd been *exhilarated*.

I fucked up my life for you, he'd gritted out at her. *I don't ever fuck up my life. For anyone. The kind of life I have, fuck it up too much and you lose it.*

Indy hadn't understood anything that was happening. All she'd known was that it was happening to both of them—and it was as intense as it was impossible.

They should never have met. She should already have been a statistic.

None of this should have been happening, but she'd been wearing red and he was clearly a wolf and somehow, it had all made sense. She had felt the sense of it everywhere, like fate.

Indy had reached up with her fingers and spread them over those beautiful lips of his.

Careful, he'd warned her.

But Indy had only smiled. *Too late*, she'd said.

Then she'd surged up on her toes and kissed him, like the dark little fairytale she'd always wanted to come true at last.

CHAPTER TWO

SITTING IN THIS bustling café in Prague all this time later, Indy could not only remember how it had felt to kiss him like that.

She could feel it still.

Kissing him on that deserted street in Budapest had been foolhardy at best. She'd had two years to question her behavior, and she had. Oh, she had.

But she couldn't regret it.

Kissing him had been like nothing she'd ever experienced before.

It was a shock—and it was no fairytale.

Because he'd kissed her back and there was nothing least bit tame about him. His lips alone were a revelation. He didn't use his hands to hold her head in place, because he'd managed to do that with his mouth alone.

And Indy had *ignited*.

She'd melted into him so that her nipples, already so hard and so greedy, were crushed against that stone chest of his.

He'd angled his jaw and thrust his tongue against hers and she'd come from that alone in a shimmering, shuddering rush.

He'd torn his mouth from hers, muttering filthy-sounding curses in languages she couldn't identify.

Damn you, he said then, his English sounding tame in comparison.

She knew, somehow, that he wasn't cursing her. Not specifically.

Then he'd picked her up, swinging her into his arms while she still had all those delicious waves of pleasure moving through her. She had only been half-aware at that point. He'd carried her down the street to a dark and gleaming SUV waiting at the curb and then he'd climbed inside, pulling her over his lap as he went.

I'm surprised you can park here, she'd murmured while he tossed his gun in the glove box, because she'd been loopy and her clit had still been pulsing and she felt like maybe what had actually happened was that she had died. That this had all been some kind of extended death scene in her head. It was the only thing that made sense. *I'm surprised no one stole this while you were off... doing whatever you do.*

She'd been straddling him and that had meant she could look down into that astonishingly beautiful face of his and see it when something like amusement flickered there.

Nobody would dare steal from me, he told her.

Then his hand was on the nape of her neck and he'd brought her face down to his, so he could take her mouth once more.

And Indy stopped worrying about *parking.*

He'd shoved her skirt up and out of his way, wrapping his big hands around her thighs to pull them even further apart so she was mashed down against the thick bulge of his cock, a glory against her clit. And his fingers had slid beneath her thong in the back as he'd skated past her ass to find her wet folds. He'd opened her, then penetrated her with one finger.

Then another, finding her wet and hot and crazy for him, writhing to get even closer to him—his cock, his fingers, whatever worked.

He'd let out a long spate of swear words again, but that time, it had sounded like a song. Then he'd shoved her tank top up, securing the fabric beneath the strap of the little backpack she'd forgotten she was wearing, so he could get his mouth on her breast.

God. His mouth. On her breast.

In Prague, remembering, Indy felt herself flush all over.

Back in Budapest, she'd arched back as best

she could between the steering wheel and his hard body, letting her head fall back into sheer bliss.

Indy had been lost somewhere between his mouth on her nipple as he sucked, hard, and the way she rocked her own clit against his cock. He was shockingly huge, and his fingers were blunt and too clever as they plunged inside her from behind.

In her head, it had gone on forever, but she doubted it had. Because she couldn't take it and came again, clenching hard on his fingers.

You are a witch, he'd muttered.

Indy had felt like a witch. Sex was always fun… but this was something else. It was like every single part of her had been made for every single part of him. As if nothing he could possibly do to her would feel anything but amazing. Because they'd been built for this.

She'd looked at him and been his. Their eyes had met over a gun, for God's sake, and there they were—and all Indy had wanted was *more*.

Reality couldn't intrude. It hadn't.

He'd reached between them. Indy had sat back as best she could, aware of the steering wheel digging into her in a way that should have been unpleasant, but wasn't. She'd liked the little spear of not-quite-pain, because that had meant it was real. It had really been happening.

This liquid heat, this glorious, endless explosion had truly been happening.

And his cock was a thing of glory.

He'd pulled it out, wincing because he was so hard. Indy's mouth had actually fallen open as she'd gazed down at where he rose between them. She'd felt her clit pulse and her core go molten.

You know what to do, he'd told her, and though his voice was quiet, there was that roughness to it, that command, that made her entire body break out in goose bumps.

But she'd felt that she did know what to do. That her entire life had been a dress rehearsal and that night in that SUV on an empty street in Budapest, of all places, had been the show, at last.

Indy had thought that very distinctly: *At last.*

She'd felt like crying. Like weeping with joy that she'd gotten to kneel up, even though her knees were still scraped—and that should probably have bothered her more. She'd felt emotional and beautiful and so connected to him it had hurt. It had *hurt*, when Indy was all about her fun and her orgasms, but even the hurt of it felt good.

And that was before she'd braced herself with one hand on the headrest behind him. Then reached between them so she could guide the massive head of his cock to her pussy at last.

At last.

Because it had felt like she'd already waited a lifetime and she hadn't even known his name.

But Indy had known it was true, even then. She'd been looking for him, for that wildfire connection between them and his dangerous saint's face, for a lifetime already without realizing he'd been her goal all along.

Something she couldn't have realized until she'd seen him, could she? Because only then had it been clear.

His hands had not been gentle. He'd shoved one into her hair and the other had gripped her ass, hard.

Indy had known many things then. That he was not a good man in the way she'd previously conceived of that phrase. That what she was doing was not a good idea, no matter how it felt. And that no one would ever understand how this had not only happened—but why she had *made* it happen.

But she had never been the good sister.

Because she also knew—as their gazes had clashed again, as she had notched the wide head of his cock at the mouth of her pussy—that this man was her fate.

That she had always been meant for this.

Right there. With him.

Now, he'd ordered her.

She hadn't understood until then that she'd been waiting for that, too. For him.

It had felt like running to the edge of a terrible cliff and then throwing herself off. And not caring at all, in the final moment, if she would fall or fly.

Indy had slammed herself down, impaling herself on him.

And she'd screamed out as she did it because he was so big that it hurt, so big that it was wildly, astonishingly uncomfortable to take all of him like that, and so *fast*.

But she'd known there was no other way to do it. It was like a kind of virginity because it was him. Them. It was *theirs*, the agony she was prepared to put herself through for one staggering beat of her heart. Then another.

And it had been entirely worth it when his mouth crooked up in one corner.

Foolish girl, he'd said in that quietly dark way of his that made everything in her sing. *I like that you want to suffer for me.*

Then he'd moved.

And any suffering she'd felt was gone that easily.

Because he'd fucked her like he'd known all the same things she did.

Like his cock, that big, battering ram of a cock, had been specifically designed to hit everywhere she'd needed it. He'd kept his hard hand on her ass, lifting her and slamming her in time with his thrusts, so that all she could do was melt into it. Become part of it.

His other hand, tangled in her hair, had kept her arched back so he could get his mouth on her throat, her lips. Down to her breasts and back again as he liked.

And he'd liked.

Indy had lost track of how many times she'd come. Again and again. Over and over. Because it turned out that what he liked, she liked, too.

And on he'd gone anyway, because he'd been making them one.

It was some kind of magic, fusing them together. Imprinting them on each other, because this was fate.

Maybe it might look like a simple fucking, but Indy had known better.

He was making them real. He was making sure the both of them knew that neither one of their lives would ever be the same.

Because how could anything have been the same after that?

When he came she could feel him inside her, scalding her, and she'd loved that, too.

And then, for a while, they'd had to stay like that. Slumped into each other in the front seat of his SUV because neither one of them was breathing too well.

He'd recovered first. He'd lifted her, muttering

another curse when she'd made a little sobbing sound at the loss of his cock. He'd set her in the passenger seat beside him, then winced as he'd folded his cock back into his jeans.

I am Stefan, he'd told her in that growl of his that had made her think of wolves again. She'd smoothed her red skirt down toward her thighs and shivered. *Stefan Romanescu.*

Indy, she'd replied. *Indy March.*

Indy? He'd sounded as if he was tasting her name the way he'd tasted her nipples. *What kind of name is this?*

Short for Indiana.

Indiana, he'd murmured, another long, deep taste.

Indy had nearly come again, just from that.

He'd looked around—out to the street and in his mirrors—in a way that told her more things about him. That he had some kind of military background. That he was just as deeply dangerous as she'd thought he was, if not more, because he wasn't anything so simple as a *thug*.

But none of that had changed the fact that he was hers.

Nothing ever will, a voice in her had intoned, solemn and sure.

She'd curled her knees up beneath her and hadn't cared where her skirt fell. The thong she'd simply moved to the side made her pussy feel even more wet and swollen, because it kept grabbing at her. Reminding her.

Not that she'd needed reminding.

We didn't use a condom, she had pointed out.

You American girls are all on the pill. He hadn't even looked at her as he started the car, then pulled out, roaring away from the curb and into the dark Budapest streets in a manner that told her he knew them well. *And if you give me something, eh. Then we both have it. A memento, maybe.*

She'd laughed, then shrugged when he'd shot a dark look her way. *I don't have anything. Yours is the only cock that has ever been inside me without a condom.*

His gaze had caught at her, intense and too blue. *The only one that ever will be, Indiana.*

And she'd accepted that, because she'd felt it, too.

Fate.

Stefan had driven her straight to the airport.

I don't know what your travel plans are, but they must change, he'd told her, another command. It came easily to him, she'd understood. It was who he was, maybe. *You must leave here. Tonight. And do not return.*

But—

I need time, he'd said with an urgency that she'd felt inside her like her own heartbeat. *Two years. Then I will deal with this. With you. Do you understand?*

Two years? She'd blinked the unexpected emotion away, not sure what was happening to her. Not sure words existed to describe what had already happened, much less what had still been happening. *Stefan...*

He had taken her jaw in his hard hand. *Keep that pussy greedy for me, foolish girl. And enjoy as many inferior fucks as you can with my blessing. I want you limber.*

He had given her the key, told her a time, made her memorize the address.

And she hadn't heard from him since.

Indy blew out a breath at her café table in Prague. She drank down the last of her coffee.

She hadn't told anybody what had happened to her in Budapest. Because what could she say? Instead, she'd flown back to the States. She'd surprised her sister and moved in with her when her latest disappointing roommate had moved out.

She had cried when her skinned knees healed, because it had felt as if the loss of those scrapes took Stefan away from her. And she'd spent the last two years in New York because she'd lost the thirst for it. She'd been everywhere. She'd seen everything. And she'd found what she'd been looking for without knowing it—but she couldn't have him.

Yet.

Yet, she would whisper out loud in her bed at night, holding on tight to that key. *Yet*.

For a while, she hadn't wanted to bother with sex—for pretty much the first time since she'd discovered it in high school—because what was the point? When you'd had the very best, why backslide into less than that? The first time she'd let a cute boy in a Brooklyn bar take her home, it had made her feel as close to empty as she'd ever been.

But when she thought of sex as keeping herself fit enough to be worthy to fuck Stefan again, that changed everything.

Indy had impatiently waited out her two years. She had kept herself limber.

And now she was ready.

She left the café with only twenty minutes to go before the meeting time. The gorgeous old city gleamed bright in the summer sun, but all she could think about was the house up in the hills that she'd stared at on Google Maps a thousand times.

Indy took a cab out of Prague proper, crossing the river and scaling the hills into a neighborhood she'd read a lot about, these past two years. Upscale. Quiet. Wealthy.

Her heart was going wild in her chest and she pressed the heel of her palm hard against it, feeling something like giddy that this was finally happening. She knew that if she'd told anybody what she was doing, they not only would have told her something was wrong with her, they would have tried to talk her out of coming here today. They certainly would have tried to impose their grubby reality all over what she knew was her destiny.

Her older sister in particular, bless her.

The cab dropped her off in front of the correct address, a house that sprawled over a sizable piece of property right on the road. Indy pulled out her key and walked toward the door, unable to hear anything but the way her blood rushed through her. She thrust it into the lock on the front door, held her breath, and turned it.

The bolt clicked open.

Indy pushed her way inside, having absolutely no idea what to expect, but aware that she was no longer holding her breath. Because the key worked. *It worked.* She hadn't let herself think about what she would do if it hadn't. She slipped it back over her neck as she shut the door behind her, taking comfort in the familiar weight between her breasts.

Inside, the house seemed light and airy—or possibly that was just the foyer she stood in that soared upward to a set of skylights. She could hear music playing, something smoky and instrumental, and her impressions of the house seemed to shudder into her from afar. Clean. Nearly stark, were it not for the odd pieces of intriguing art set here and there. Or the surprisingly ornate banister of the grand stair directly in front of her.

She followed the music through a sitting room on the same floor that opened into another, nearly blinding her with all its great windows that looked down over Prague and the Vltava River that cut through it.

But the music wasn't coming from those rooms or the bright gallery beyond, so she kept going. She wound her way down a hall until she came to a study at the end of it, drenched in the same sunlight.

And froze, because he was there.

Stefan sat in an armchair next to a bookcase, far more beautiful—and brutal—than she'd recalled. His poetic blue eyes came to hers. Held.

And she was sure she heard some kind of thunderclap in the distance.

It still felt like fate.

Better still, that gaze of his on hers felt like a command.

Indy only realized then—as she started moving toward him, unable to tear her gaze from his— that she hadn't been afraid that he *wouldn't* be here. That hadn't really worried her. But she had been afraid that he *would* be here—but that she wouldn't feel this again.

That she wouldn't feel all this heat and glory, greed and longing.

This sense of coming home in a strange place.

And through it all, fate making them one.

The way she knew they had always been meant to be.

As if she'd been built for him alone.

Indy kept moving until she stood before him. She shrugged off the small backpack she wore and tossed it aside. Then she sank down on her knees, there before his outstretched legs, and smiled up at him as if he'd given her the world.

Maybe she thought he had.

Already.

"Finally," she whispered, gazing up at him.

"Finally," Stefan agreed, with a voice like gravel and a hard, bright light in his gaze that made her feel like she might be shimmering. Inside and out. "We can begin."

CHAPTER THREE

STEFAN ROMANESCU WAS not a man of faith.

In anything.

But he had seen a vision in a shitty back alley two years ago. And even though he would have said he believed in visions even less than in the dour Orthodox god of his childhood, long since happily renounced, he had immediately known one thing above all others.

A man should never turn down a vision, no matter how inconvenient it was.

Though the word *inconvenient* was a mild way indeed to describe how he'd spent the past twenty-four months.

None of his former associates—because a man like him didn't have friends—had understood. But then, how could they? All they'd seen was Stefan systematically dismantling a network he'd worked hard to put in place, removing himself completely, piece by piece.

For no good reason, he was sure they would have said if he'd encouraged such conversations. Because his network made money and for a long while, that was the only thing he'd cared about. It was the only thing that mattered to most of his associates, as it had to him, too. Before.

Only people who had always lived safe and secure—and rich—ever imagined that money wasn't power.

But he'd met her in Budapest and everything had changed.

He couldn't have explained it himself. He'd seen Indy March, bright with a fresh beauty though it had been the middle of the night. And no one who was wandering around that particular neighborhood at such an hour could possibly have been *fresh* in any sense of the word. Still, she was such a tiny little thing, with glossy dark hair and a heart-shaped face. Picking her way through the rubble and ruin of the world he lived in as if she hadn't noticed the state of it.

She'd looked at him the same way.

His heart, that useless organ, had stopped. Then kicked back in, hard.

She had looked like an angel, and what fallen man could resist?

He couldn't. He hadn't.

And now here she was on her knees again, only this time Stefan had no gun aimed at her head. No collection of associates he barely tolerated himself. This time, she appeared before him of her own volition. Not because she'd wandered down the wrong alley in the wrong part of the wrong city.

Not to mention, she'd had two years to think better of the whole thing.

These were all important distinctions.

His cock might have been rock hard, the way it always had been every time he'd thought of her since he'd dropped her at the airport in Budapest, but he was in no rush now. Not now.

Because she was here. And Stefan could see from the expression on her face that her hunger was as fierce as his.

"Welcome to Prague, foolish girl," he murmured, settling back in his chair and regarding her almost lazily. "Why don't you tell me, at last, how you ended up in that alley?"

Her chest moved, telling him she was breathing too hard. He liked it. And though he saw a kind of dismay on her face, or possibly impatience, she didn't argue with him. She settled back on her heels, giving him the opportunity to miss that flowy little red skirt she'd worn before that had fueled any number of fantasies since. She shoved the silken mass of her hair back from her face and smiled at him.

As if this was a proper dinner date in whatever squeaky-clean world she came from.

Though he knew what her world was like. All its fresh, bright, happy details. A man might trust a vision all he liked—but a wise man verified it.

Only wise men survived the kind of life Stefan had built for himself, then destroyed.

"I was at a club," she told him, and her voice was as lovely as he remembered it. Sweet and sultry all at once, with that American Dream accent of hers. "It was just down the street in some crumbling-down warehouse I couldn't find again if my life depended on it. I wanted a breath of fresh air and a little walk and then there I was. In the middle of your... Situation."

That was significantly less celestial. He studied her, the laziness giving way to a frown. "You wanted to *walk*. At that hour. You didn't notice what kind of neighborhood you were in?"

Indy shrugged, and his eye was drawn to how delicate she was. She was such a little thing. He remembered, vividly, picking her up. Holding her against him, his imagination wild with all the ways a man of his size could indulge himself with a tiny little creature like her—but he'd urged himself to be careful.

He might not have been a good man, but he didn't break his toys.

Then she'd proved herself more than his equal. She'd showed him a libido to match his and better still, the ability to take his cock even if she hurt herself doing it.

Men changed their lives for far less.

That night had been warm, as he recalled. She'd worn a strappy little tank top, a tiny little back-pack like the one she'd tossed aside here, and that filmy red skirt that had haunted him ever since. And loads of necklaces and bracelets that marked her as one of the carefree backpacker set who pol-luted most of Europe—and the world—with their vast privilege wrapped up as wanderlust. Today she wore skinny gray jeans that seemed pasted to her and a flowy sort of T-shirt that did as much to expose her midriff as cover it. She still wore a ton of bracelets, but the only necklace she wore today was the key to his villa.

Back in the alley, his first thought had been *angel*. His second thought had been bohemian—in the sense of a certain beach culture style popu-lar with both Californians and those who aspired to look like Californians. Not in the sense of the Bohemian region where they currently sat that had nothing at all to do with Californian anything.

When she'd spoken, he had not been surprised to hear that she was an American, though he hadn't known how to feel about that. And then he hadn't cared, because it made his path clear.

He had practically been able to see the white picket fences of her people stamped all over her.

"Those kinds of clubs are always in terrible neighborhoods," she was saying, almost dismissively. As if he was being...silly. Something Stefan had never been in his life. "I never got into trouble before."

Stefan leaned forward. He rested his elbows on his knees and got his face close to hers.

She was even more perfect than he'd recalled. Flawless, really. That pretty face of hers, eyes like chocolate and that sweet and dirty mouth. She looked soft and breakable, but he knew better, didn't he? His Indiana was wild, and a little crazy, and her pussy was voracious.

God, she was perfect.

Even if, right at this very moment, he was pissed at what could have happened to her if he hadn't been the *situation* she'd stumbled into.

"Do you know how much trouble you were in?" he asked quietly. "Do you really know?"

Her melted chocolate gaze glittered. "I think the gun to my head was a clue."

Stefan reached over and slid his palm over her jaw, her cheek. Not sure if he was holding her there...or assuring himself that she was real.

That he had not simply lost it in that alley two years ago, as many had claimed since. That there had been a reason and it was her.

That she was *here*.

"The man who held a gun to your head no longer exists," he told her, making no attempt to keep the darkness from his voice. "But he was a very bad man, Indiana. You should have been terrified of him. Why weren't you?"

She smiled and pressed her cheek deeper into his palm. "I don't know."

"I gave you that key and an address. You could have come here any time you liked, but you didn't. You could have forgotten all about one strange night in Hungary, but you didn't. You waited two years. You came to Prague. You showed up tonight at precisely the right time and now look at you, down on your knees with your skin already flushed with arousal." He shook his head, his gaze all over her. "Why?"

"I trusted you." When his scowl deepened, her smile widened. "And it didn't occur to me to come here any sooner. I guess I could have come straight to Prague after Budapest, but I went to New York instead. And by the time it occurred to me, much later, that I had the key and could come over here and see if it fit in anytime, I was too busy... Recovering."

He searched her face intently, something in him going still. "You were hurt?"

She shook her head. "No. But it was..."

Stefan nodded. Because he knew. "A beautiful catastrophe."

Indy's eyes glowed. "Yes. And then I thought I

might as well wait. You had been so certain about the time period. Why was it two years? Why not two months? Or five years?"

He could have told her. That he had always had an exit strategy, because longevity was not a feature of the life he'd chosen after he'd left the army. He'd been planning his escape almost from the day he'd started. Meeting her had simply expedited those plans.

Instead of sharing any of that, he lifted a shoulder. "There were things I had to do."

It was her turn to study him for a moment. "Like... A divorce?"

Stefan had not been expecting that. He laughed. "A divorce? What makes you think such a thing?"

Indy let out a small sigh, once again nestling her cheek a bit deeper into his palm. "It seemed like the kind of thing you might have had to get out of your way. I've never slept with a married man, to my knowledge, but then we didn't do much talking."

"I have never been married." The very idea was ludicrous. "Have you?"

"Never."

"And no unpleasant diseases," he said, finding his thumb moving over her cheekbone. "Or I would have known soon enough."

"Right back at you. And yes, I'm on the pill."

"I suspected these things. I am happy I was right."

"You strike me as the kind of man who's usually right." Her eyes were big, but she smiled. "Or usually thinks he's right, anyway."

He was a lot more than that, but Stefan saw no reason to share that with her. Not until this all felt like less of a dream.

"You are even more beautiful than I remember," he found himself saying, almost as if it wasn't up to him. As if the words simply came out of their own accord. "How is that possible?"

Indy let out another sigh, her cheek in his hand and her gaze bright with heat. "Do we really have to do all this talking?"

She leaned forward, sliding her hands up along the inside line of his thighs. And still Stefan couldn't quite believe that she was here. Right here with him. That he hadn't made her up as he'd thought he must have over these last dark months. Even though he could remember her taste. And that fierce grip of her tight little pussy on his cock.

He still couldn't believe that she could possibly be real.

But he took her hands before they reached his cock and held them away from him, smiling a little as he gazed down at her.

"I like it that you are still so greedy, my foolish girl," he said. "But there are things we must discuss."

"Can't they wait?" she asked, her gaze between his legs in a hungry way that almost made him think, *what the hell*.

The way he had in Budapest.

Almost.

"You flew all the way to Prague for this, Indiana. You can wait a little longer."

Her eyes were a little bit wide as she looked up at him, and he could see the hunger there. The same greed that burned in him.

"I would have flown even farther," she told him. "But why make the anticipation even worse? It's been two years in the making for one night. What if it's not worth it?"

He regarded her for a moment, taking that in. She thought this was one night. That felt a lot like a blow.

But the flip side of that surprising notion was that she'd waited two years and flown all the way to Prague for that one night.

"It will be worth it," he assured her. "But you should know something about me, Indiana. I am... Bossy."

"A lot of men are bossy," she said softly. She smiled. "Not all of them have your cock. So... I'm okay with it."

"Excellent."

And then, Stefan thought, it was time to reacquaint themselves.

He settled back in his chair and inclined his head, not surprised that she understood his command immediately. Watching the change in her made him even harder. She flushed, swallowed hard, and then reached for him again with hands that trembled slightly.

Because she continued to be perfect in every way.

Indy angled herself closer to him and this time, when she ran her hands up the inside of his thighs, he let her. He looked down the length of his torso as she knelt there between his outstretched legs. Her glossy dark hair flowed down her back and her heart-shaped face looked fierce as she concentrated on unbuttoning his jeans. Then that ferocity turned into something far hotter as she reached into his jeans and pulled out his cock.

She made a soft little humming noise, wrapped both her hands around the base of him, and leaned in.

Then she licked him, swirling her tongue around the broad head. She took her time learning his length before she tried her best to suck him into her mouth.

Stefan thought he could die happy, watching this tiny, impatient woman—his woman, whether she knew it or not—try to suck him off.

She returned her attention to the head of his cock and began to move her hands up and down his shaft, not exactly gently. That mixed with the hot suction of her mouth, and the way she used her clever tongue, and that fire in him began to build.

Indy took her time, teasing him. Swirling her tongue around and letting her hands play him like he was nothing but her instrument. Something he should have hated, but he didn't.

Not with her.

The fire grew higher, more intense. So did she.

Until the marvel of it took him over.

Because this was already better than all his expectations, and his expectations had been extreme.

He let his head fall back against the chair while he gripped her hair with one hand, holding her head to his cock and feeling her as she worked.

And when he came, it was with a roar.

Stefan wasn't at all surprised to find she drank him down, then sat back on her heels and smiled up at him as if he'd given her a gift.

This woman was going to kill him.

He was going to let her kill him.

"Take off your clothes," he told her, doing nothing to soften his voice.

She shivered a little, still smiling, and stayed where she was as she stripped her shirt off, then tossed it aside, without a word. Her small, perfect breasts weren't contained by any bra, so he could see her hard nipples immediately, and he liked that. Then she knelt up higher on her knees, unbuttoning her jeans and shoving them over her hips, with another one of those thongs that he vividly recalled from Budapest. Tonight it was hot pink, a detail he suspected would live within him always.

He hoped it would.

When she sat back, she rolled back so she could stretch her legs out in front of her and pull her jeans the rest of the way off.

So smooth, so easy.

"You take your clothes off well," he said. "Almost as if you have done it before. For money, perhaps?"

He knew she had. But would she admit it? It wouldn't ruin anything for him if she lied on this, their first night. Stefan knew too well the risks of oversharing, or even the faintest attempt at transparency. But if she lied, it would give him an insight into her. And her relationship with shame.

Indy's smile was wicked. And completely shameless. "You should see me on a pole."

"Is that what you do when you're not roaming about bad neighborhoods in Europe? Strip?"

She shook her head. And she knelt so easily before him once more, he was already hard again. "You know how all the girls like to say that they're stripping to get through college, right? I actually did. It was fun."

"Then why did you stop?"

She considered him for a moment while she knelt there, perfect and naked and within reach. After all this time, he could simply extend a hand and touch her as he wished.

Part of him still couldn't believe it. Not even now, after she'd sucked him good with that wicked mouth of hers.

"I think that stripping is the kind of thing that could quickly become pretty much the opposite of fun, if it went on for too long and became about, for example, paying rent. And here's something about me that you should probably know, Stefan." Her gaze was steady on his. Her voice was quiet. "I don't want to do it if it's not fun. Whatever it is. Because what's the point of that?"

"Life is not always fun, foolish girl. I would say it is very rarely any fun at all. How have you never learned this?"

She was so young, he thought. A product of the country she came from and the splendid life he knew she'd lived there, white picket fences and shiny dreams and all the rest of that New World crap. While he had been born into the ruins of the very, very Old World, had been raised dreamless and dark, and knew better.

But when she smiled, she seemed neither young

nor naïve. "Whether life itself is fun or not isn't the point, Stefan. How I choose to live is fun or I don't choose to do it. Do you understand?"

"I understand that you are a privileged American girl, no? So maybe it is easier for these things to be fun for you while for others, living is not so delightful. It is merely the better option."

"Maybe," she said, and though he studied her expression he could see no indication that she took any offense at his words. He couldn't tell if he liked that or not. "Or maybe I don't think that we all need to be *quite so* serious all the time. Really. We don't. No one does."

"And if I tell you that I'm a very, very serious man?"

Another flashing smile and something like wisdom in her gaze. "I like how serious tastes. And I'm guessing you like how fun tastes, or you wouldn't be here either. Would you?"

He laughed at that and then he stood, leaving his jeans unbuttoned. And enjoying the look of her there, still kneeling at his feet.

His beautiful, foolish girl.

Stefan reached down and picked her up, but he didn't set her on her feet. He lifted her even farther, liking the way she laughed a little and melted against him. Making it the easiest thing in the world to lift her so high that she was kneeling on his shoulders.

Indy laughed. "You aren't really…"

"I would hold on," he advised her. Sternly.

Then he gripped her ass, made sure he was holding her securely, and brought her pussy directly to his lips.

He licked his way in, finding her wet and sweet and hot and in the next moment, coming against his mouth.

Just as he remembered.

He teased her clit, sucking on it and raking it gently with his teeth. He saw how many more times he could make her come as she gripped his hair so hard it hurt and arched her body there where she knelt on his wide shoulders. She tossed her head back, writhing against him and showing him that she fully trusted he would not drop her.

Her trust made his cock so hard it nearly hurt.

And only when he was satisfied with the way she screamed and rocked against his face did he lower her down his body, handling her with an ease that made him ache, to finally slam his way inside her.

This time, her whole body formed a perfect bow. She wrapped her legs around his hips, her mouth wide open as if the scream was trapped inside her, and he could no longer tell if she was coming or about to come again.

He didn't wait for her to accommodate him, because she was molten hot and so sweet it almost burned. Instead, he moved her, using her to fuck himself, loving the feel of her in his hands. That tight fist of her pussy, wetter and hotter with each stroke.

The longer it went, the more she moved into it, letting her back arch once more. Letting her head fall. Closing her eyes and once again trusting him to hold her where he wanted her, to move her as he liked.

Taking all of him and making low, greedy noises as if she loved every inch.

And when he felt her pussy clamp down on him once more, she sobbed wildly, another orgasm taking her over. Stefan found his own release, emptying himself into her with a few hard, deep, glorious thrusts.

Then he held her there as she collapsed against him, her mouth wide open in the crook of his neck as she fought for air.

He was still inside her and carried her that way, enjoying the little noises she made when he took the stairs up to the second floor. He carried her to the loftlike master suite and into the bathroom, where he set her down outside the massive shower stall. He reached in and turned on the water, smiling with deep satisfaction when she made her way in a moment or so later, but had to hold on to the tiled wall as if her legs weren't quite steady.

He stripped, then followed her into the hot spray, already steaming up the room.

"Oh," she breathed, gazing at him in what looked like awe. His cock certainly thought so, and stood proudly. "I've been wondering what you look like naked."

She reached over and traced the tattoo that took up the better part of his chest, then wrapped around his back. It was a phoenix etched in bright colors and utilizing all his scars, its tail ending in the small of his back. And Stefan had always loved his tattoo, the story of how he always rose from any ashes, but never so much as now. Because Indy moved closer and began to trace it with her fingers. Her soft little hands. That hot, dirty mouth of hers.

"What are these?" she asked softly, finding his various scars concealed in the lines and swirls.

"Knives and guns." He grunted as she found a different ridge. "The odd boot."

Her dark eyes rose to meet his, then dropped. But she kissed his scars a little bit longer.

After the shower he dried himself, then took her towel from her and amused himself with drying her, too. She combed her tangle of hair with her fingers, then braided it, letting the damp mass of it fall over one shoulder.

"I left all my clothes downstairs," she told him when he pulled his jeans back on.

"You don't need clothes." He studied her. "Are you hungry?"

She considered, and then her face lit up. "Ravenous, as a matter of fact."

He had her walk before him down the stairs so he could watch her move. So he could contemplate the sweet line of her spine and the flare of her hips as he imagined taking her from behind.

Would his hunger for her ever end?

Once on the ground floor, he settled his hand on the nape of her neck and steered her into the kitchen at the back of the house that looked over the terraced grounds, green by day. Tonight the pool gleamed turquoise and beyond, down in the valley, the city of Prague lay like ribbons of light.

"Tell me about this place," she said, jumping up lightly to sit on the counter as he moved around the kitchen, assembling a simple meal of savory pancakes, a Romanian staple his grandmother had always made him when he'd visited her. "This villa. The art on the walls, the air of old-school elegance mixed in with all these modern lines... None of this seems to go hand-in-hand with an alleyway in Budapest."

"I think you would call this *layers*, no?"

"Are we naming all these layers?"

He glanced over at her, but she didn't look avid in any way. Just... Interested.

In him.

Not what he could do for her. Not what she could get. Just him and whatever story he might tell.

It felt like a new kind of magic. He remembered he'd called her a witch, and it fit.

Stefan cleared his throat. "My father was a hard man. When I tell you this as a Romanian, you must understand that I do not mean hard in any American sense. I mean the real thing. A real kind of hardness that went deep inside him. He should not have married, but then, even monsters get lonely. After my mother died he stopped pretending to be a father, not that he had ever taken to the role. He was a jailer. I mean *hard*, you understand." He moved his shoulders to do something about the tension in them, not sure why he was telling her this story. There was a reason he wasn't much for sharing. But he didn't stop. He couldn't. "It was a relief to escape him when I joined the army. But then, the army takes all men and makes them hard. I think this is true everywhere. Afterward, I found other ways to fight. And learned to live by my own laws."

"Meaning outside everyone else's laws."

He nodded. "But my grandmother left Romania a long time ago and settled in Old Town. Far away from her troublesome son-in-law and her memories of the daughter she lost. I visited her here in Prague as a boy. And I bought this house early in my…career, let us call it. Maybe as a monument to her. I always knew that someday I would retire here."

"You don't look old enough to retire."

"The kind of business I was in…" Stefan shrugged. "If you are lucky enough to retire, you do it young. Or not at all."

For a while she didn't say anything, and he finished preparing the meal. He brought a stack of the savory pancakes over on a plate that he set down on the counter next to her, and then stood there himself, watching her as she ate. Eating himself, until it felt as if that, too, was a kind of sensual act.

Simply being with her was a sensual act.

He was going to have to find a way to get used to it.

And for more than *one night*—but he did not intend to argue that with her. Not when there were far more interesting ways to make the same point.

"You still have not told me how you ended up in Budapest." He shook his head. "Did you travel the world, finding dark alleys to wander down alone?"

She paused in the act of licking her fingers and smiled at him. "As a matter fact, I did."

"You were a backpacker."

"Yes, though I always traveled a bit more lightly than proper backpackers. If I needed something I would buy it or borrow it. And then when I didn't need it anymore, I'd gift it to someone else. I didn't tote around a mobile office or anything. I just had my phone."

"And who funded all this aimless wandering?"

"If I didn't have money, I worked." She took another bite of her meal and chewed happily, then smiled when she swallowed. "Budapest was a stop along the way, though I didn't really have a destination in mind. I've never been one for itineraries. I was thinking that I was going to head back toward Australia, to keep the summer going, but then you happened."

He liked that. "As if I am some storm?"

"I didn't see the point of traveling anymore when all I wanted to do was come here." That almost sounded like a confession, but she looked so casual that Stefan thought he must have misunderstood. "So I went back to New York instead, where I've been living with my sister ever since."

"Is your sister like you?"

"Bristol? Oh no. No, not at all." Indy laughed. Almost too hard, in his mind. "She's a very serious person, like you. She finds me... Delightfully trying."

"But what is it you *do*? You must do something. Everyone does."

She lifted her chin, and though her voice stayed light when she answered him, her gaze was not. "I thought I told you. I do whatever makes me money and if I don't feel like doing it anymore, I don't."

"Indiana." He sounded severe, but he didn't modify his tone. "That is playtime. Not real life."

She sighed. "Everybody says that. A lot, actually. But none of them are particularly happy, are they? So why would I listen to them?"

"Does this mean you did not work in New York?"

"I worked in a lot of different jobs in New York." Indy shrugged. "I like temporary positions. Right when they get boring, you move on to the next."

He studied her, sitting so carelessly on his counter, eating food he'd made her with his own hands. Naked and unselfconscious. Perfect in every way.

The ways he wanted her should have horrified him, but they didn't. They never had.

Still, he wanted to know her. Not what he could dig up on her, but *her*.

"Surely you must know that the kind of life you lead is only possible because you're young and beautiful." He tugged on the end of her braid. "It cannot last, this wandering here and there with no thought to your future. That is the thing about the future. It finds you, always."

"All the more reason to enjoy it then," she replied with maddening calm. "While I can."

"You must have some kind of dream. Some ambition."

"Must I? Ambition is for people who don't like what they have. But I do." She frowned at him. "And if I have a dream, I go after it."

He didn't believe her. But he didn't press. She wanted one night, so that was what he would give her. Because there were a lot of things a man could do in the course of one night that might just teach his foolish girl how to want a few things she couldn't possibly be sure she could get.

And to learn how to long for them, like everyone else.

"Lie down on the counter," he told her then, all command and heat. "Face down."

The heat in her eyes kindled, but she still took her time licking her fingers. Then stretching sinuously, like a cat, so he had no choice but to watch the way it made her breasts bounce. She rolled herself over, sliding herself across the countertop until she was stretched out before him.

"Enjoy the stone on those greedy little nipples," he invited her.

Stefan gripped her hips, pulling her back toward him so her legs hung down over the edge of the counter and he could line her up with his cock again.

He slid inside, sheathing himself fully. She made a cute little grunting sound, wiggling this way and that because he filled her so completely and she needed to make a little space. He had the notion then that no matter how many times he took her, she would always be this tight, always gripping him just like this, always precisely this perfect.

This time he went slow, because he wanted to enjoy looking down at her the way he'd imagined so many times before. Feeling her cute little butt against him as he plunged deep, then drew back. The line of her spine, the swell of her hips, the soft nape of her neck.

She stretched her arms up so she could grip the other end of the counter, giving herself a little bit of leverage as he worked.

Slow. Deep.

Relentless.

He watched as her skin reddened, everywhere, and listened as her breathing changed. She came differently in this position, one wave into the next, an easy kind of roll. But Stefan wanted more than waves, so he reached beneath her to find that eager little clit and played with her until her intensity skyrocketed.

On and on he went, drawing out her responses, learning the difference between those light little climaxes and the wilder, deeper ones that made her whole body seem to shatter around him.

The ones that made her sob. Real tears.

And only when he thought he could read her well enough did he build her up to one more bone rattling, screaming finish.

Then follow her.

But he still wasn't done.

Because she thought this was only the one night.

And Stefan knew full well that one night wasn't going to be enough.

CHAPTER FOUR

INDY WOKE UP with a start instead of her usual sweet ease. There was sunshine all over her face and she had no idea where she was, but that wasn't particularly unusual in and of itself. Normally she stretched, smiled, and happily looked around to see where she'd ended up the night before.

But then she didn't normally wake from dark, erotic dreams, unsure what was real and what she'd imagined. She blinked in the bright light, the contrast to the cascade of images in her head making her feel almost lightheaded.

Then the night came back to her in a rush, far more erotic than any dreams she might have had. Her body reacted as if it were happening all over again. She was dizzy and molten, hollowed out with longing, and a little bit drunk on all that sensation within her.

She sat up slowly, gingerly, and looked around the room, half expecting to find Stefan watching her from some or other vantage point.

But she was alone.

And when she took a breath or two, she decided she was glad of it.

Because clearly, she needed to take stock of... this.

Of what had happened to her here.

What she'd wanted, so desperately, last night and now...

Thinking about all the things she'd done last night—all night—made her flush, everywhere. Her nipples pebbled into twin aches and between her legs, the rush of sheer longing made her squirm against the soft sheets. She pressed her hands to her cheeks and found them hot, and that, too, made her shudder.

Inside and out.

Indy hardly knew who she was, sitting upright in a shaft of Czech sun, her hair falling all around her in abandon, adding to the shocking sensuality of the morning. Since when had she ever been *embarrassed*? Or even this affected, the morning after and alone? She'd meant what she'd told him last night. She only did things that were fun. She followed that fun wherever it led. The more people who told her she couldn't dance her way through life, footloose and fancy free and whatever else they liked to call it, the harder she kept on dancing.

And sex had always been the sweetest and best

dance of all. Fun from start to finish, every time and everywhere.

But Stefan had switched things up last night. She knew exactly when he'd done it. When he'd taken that electricity between them and jacked it up to high. It was when he'd had her spread out across the kitchen counter like a dessert, and suddenly, without warning, it was as if he'd thrown a switch.

That suddenly, everything had been far more... intense.

Until she'd felt scraped raw and needy in a way that had nothing to do with laughter. And it was still with her this morning, as if he'd peeled off a layer or two of her skin and left her naked in a new way.

A lot like that night in Budapest, but this time, there had been no dark alley or scary gun in sight.

It had just been...him. Stefan.

He had carried on like that throughout the night. Until she'd found herself sobbing, in a frantic, mad frenzy to find her release—so she could start all over again, ripping herself wide open and giving him things she hadn't known she had it in her to give.

Indy was not used to intensity.

That night in Budapest, sure. The situation had been intense.

She'd come here for the connection, but on some level, Indy had figured nothing could *stay* so intense. One night of intensity was one thing. She didn't want to repeat it.

You avoid intensity, a voice inside her pronounced and she couldn't say she cared for that, either. *Like the plague.*

Intensity left a residue, she found. She felt stained with it.

She rubbed at her face, waiting for that flush to fade from her cheeks, and wished the unsettled feelings churning around inside her would go away with that heat. Then she sat there in the sunlight and took her time re-braiding her hair.

As if curbing its wildness would settle her, too.

But it didn't help as much as she wanted it to. And eventually she could see no other choice but to get up and face…whatever there was to face on the other side of a night like that. At least after Budapest, she hadn't had to face Stefan. She'd imagined facing him, but that was different.

Everything about this was different.

Indy suddenly found she related to all those stories other women had told her over the years. The ones she'd laughed at, but there was no laughter in her now. Instead she had a strange flutter in her belly. She had *feelings*. And an emotional hangover that made her bare feet against the distressed wood floor feel both sensual and unsteady.

The truth of the matter was that she had no idea how to feel anything less than perfectly confident when it came to sexual politics or bright mornings after dark nights. Much less how to navigate the unexpected wallop of all this *emotion* churning around inside.

She remembered crying over her healed-up skinned knees, curled up in a ball in the closet that passed for her bedroom in the Brooklyn apartment she shared with Bristol. Actual tears for her own healed flesh.

Why did she feel like that again today?

Indy looked around the stark yet somehow welcoming bedroom, dimly recalling that she'd left her clothes on the floor she'd first knelt on. Downstairs. She opened the first drawer she found, something inside her lurching a bit at the discovery that Stefan was…neat. She pulled out a T-shirt and tugged it on, because she didn't want to be naked.

Or maybe she'd wanted the softness of the fabric against her sensitized skin, so soft it told her he cared about the things that touched him. And the faint hint of whatever laundry detergent he used that teased her with a part of why she wanted to bury her face in his neck and inhale that scent. Forever.

"You need to get a grip," she advised herself

then. And avoided looking at her reflection in the mirror as she left the bedroom.

Another new thing she couldn't say she liked.

Then she slowly walked down the stairs, her bare feet silent in the quiet house that loomed around her. It was too bright everywhere, and slowly, it dawned on her that it wasn't actually *morning*. The sun was overhead. Had she really slept that hard? Maybe it was the jet lag she should have had yesterday, catching up to her at last.

Because it certainly couldn't be a deep reaction to what had happened between them. Indy didn't have reactions. She moved on.

She always, always moved on, like a flickering flame never quite committed to any one fire. She burned on and on without burning out.

Indy padded through the house, appreciating it all the more now that she wasn't in such a rush of anticipation, wondering if he'd actually be here. Today she wasn't bristling and wild with two years of pent-up need. Now she could take her time with the surprising art gracing the walls and the quiet, understated elegance of the rooms she peered into. This wasn't a designer's take on a rich man's house. This was a home of modern lines and a crisp aesthetic, run through with an old-world undercurrent.

Not unlike the man who lived here.

But she didn't want to think too much along those lines. It made her feel even more unsettled than she already did.

You need to find him to say goodbye, she told herself sternly. Because their night was over and it had been as overwhelming as the first, if different. Maybe she'd need three years to recover this time.

Maybe more like five.

She found herself rubbing absently at the gap between her breasts, as if that could do something about the ache inside.

Indy headed for the kitchen, but it was empty, and she could admit—if only to herself—that she took it as a reprieve. She helped herself to a glass of water, drinking it down hungrily. When she was done, she rinsed it out and set it on the drying rack, then drifted over to the big glass doors that looked out over the slope of the hill. There were gardens rolling down the slope of the yard on the far side of the gleaming pool, green trees almost concealing the other houses tucked away on this hill, and in the distance, the silvery ribbon of the Vltava carving its path through Prague.

That was where she found him. He was sitting out on the terrace off the kitchen with Turkish coffee and a laptop before him on the table, though he was looking at a newspaper, turning the pages with a kind of efficient crispness that indicated he was a habitual reader.

The June sun adored him. It cascaded all over him, lighting him up and making him seem made of some kind of melted steel. Gleaming and lethal in a pair of loose, casual trousers and a T-shirt much like the one she was wearing. And something shifted in her as she looked at him. Because she'd really never imagined Stefan, her dark and dangerous man, who'd been there in that alley and had haunted her dreams ever since…sitting at a table in the sunlight, looking edgily domestic and burnished with heat and light.

While *reading*.

Indy didn't understand why something so unremarkable should sit on her the way it did, like a set of heavy weights. She only knew she could hardly breathe through it.

Stefan glanced up at her, a glimmer of blue that seared through her, but he said nothing. He only picked up the small pot at his elbow and set it in front of the other place at the table. That was when she noticed that there was a plate waiting for her with the traditional Czech breakfast she recalled from her last visit here. Slices of thick bread with a choice of butter, honey, and jams. And a selection of cold meats and cheeses.

He returned his attention to the paper, leaving Indy to sit down and pour out the thick coffee Stefan had prepared. She sipped at it to find it smooth and silky and still hot, with a hint of sweetness and other spices that gave it a richer, deeper taste. Even that struck her as sensual today.

The same feeling she'd had upstairs returned to her with a vengeance, slapping at her and then sinking in deep, though she did her best to fight it off. She concentrated on the coffee with its texture against her tongue, glad it was sweet and savory and strong. Just what she needed.

Maybe it would clear her head. And wash away whatever cobwebs these were, cluttering up her chest.

It felt a lot like baggage, this intensity hangover, and Indy didn't do baggage. She always had much, much better things to do. She found herself scowling down at the plate of food before her as she thought about that. And this electric reunion between them that was not how she'd anticipated it would be at all. It was all supposed to be that rush of wonder and dark joy she had experienced in Budapest. That *certainty* that had changed her so profoundly, down on her knees in that alley. The sudden clarity like a punch, telling her she was exactly where she was meant to be and with the man she was meant to be with, above and beyond everything else.

Not this...*unrest*.

"Is something the matter?" he asked, his voice mild.

She lifted her scowl to him, but he was still

reading. *Reading*, of all things. "What could possibly be the matter?"

"If you do not wish to eat, do not eat," he said in that practical yet jaded way of his that made her think of the house rising behind her that represented him all too well. Functional with that old-world spin. "You surely don't have to look at it as if it is plotting your death."

"You don't know," she replied. "Maybe the honey is looking at me funny."

He put the paper down then, shifting all that intense blue to her. Was that what she'd wanted? Indy felt a different sort of sensation shiver all the way through her. It took her a moment to recognize it.

Uncertainty.

She rarely felt such a thing. And it hadn't occurred to her, until just now, what a gift it was to always feel she knew her place. Her sister liked to tell her—sometimes laughing, sometimes not—that she was filled with unearned confidence. Indy had never understood that as a criticism. Why should confidence need any earning? Bristol had always believed that a person gained things like confidence—and self-worth, and bragging rights while she was at it—by accomplishing things.

But that meant there was a measure and others might assess it differently.

Indy had always felt real confidence was innate. It was about being open to anything. To being fully prepared to say *yes* to whatever came. She had done that in spades, always.

The only other time she'd felt *uncertain*, this man had held a gun to her head.

"Do you still have a gun?" she asked.

But she regretted it, instantly, because that was exactly the kind of question that she prided herself on not asking. It wasn't that she didn't *care*, she'd explained to her sister once. It was that there was no point digging in deep to things she couldn't hold on to. Better by far to accept what was given and make do.

And okay, she acknowledged internally. *There might also be some power wrapped up in* seeming *not to care about the things people usually care too much about.*

The power thing was especially clear now. As she'd just given hers away.

She watched as Stefan took in that question. His expression changed as he sat with it, growing unreadable as he gazed back at her. Not quite like armor, she thought. More like the suggestion that he could, at any moment, produce an entire armory.

"Not that particular gun," he replied, and something jolted in her because he didn't pretend he didn't know which gun she meant.

Or maybe it was all the implications about his relationship with guns wrapped up in that succinct statement.

"And are you…the sort of person who spends a lot of time pointing guns at people's heads?" Again, she didn't know what on earth she was doing. Or what she hoped to gain. This was why she never asked questions like this. She preferred to let people tell her their stories as they liked, the bonus being she never felt so *messy* while they did. But now that she'd started actually asking him questions she wanted the answers to, how could she stop? "It was a while ago now, but if memory serves, you were holding it pretty confidently."

"I was in the army for some time. I hold all guns confidently."

"Are you really not going to answer me? We met up in Prague after what certainly couldn't be called a *meet cute* Budapest. Two whole years ago."

"Thank you." His dry tone and all that gleaming blue made her…edgy. "I had forgotten all of this."

Indy plowed on because she'd never skidded over this particular cliff before and she didn't have the slightest clue how to stop herself. "There has been no communication in all of that time, yet here we are. Surely that means, at the very least, we owe each other a little bit of honesty. Don't you think?"

"I live for honesty." And it occurred to her that that little undercurrent in his voice, the one that matched the gleam in his eyes, was amusement. "Why don't you tell me why you're so nervous?"

Nervous. Indy wasn't *nervous.* She was never *nervous.*

And yet, as wrong words went, that one seemed to hit her in all the places she felt raw.

"I'm just wondering if I've flown across an ocean to shack up with the Big Bad Wolf," she said tartly. "Maybe this wasn't my smartest move."

"I thought we were being honest." Stefan shook his head, though his hard blue gaze never left hers. "We met in a dark alley with my gun in your face. That didn't stop you from fucking me blind not ten minutes later. And it didn't stop you coming here for more, years afterward, knowing nothing about me except that alley. Are you afraid of me, Indiana? Or are you afraid of yourself—and the fact that you don't care what I am?"

She felt caught by that, in a hard, tight grip. As if the honesty she'd demanded was choking her—but Indy forced out a laugh anyway. And maybe she gripped her coffee cup tighter as she settled back in her chair, wishing she'd come down naked.

Because that would have been a distraction. And a distraction was obviously better than... whatever this was.

Indy opted not to acknowledge the uneasy sort of knots that drew tight inside her at this unwelcome awareness of how she operated. Almost as if she wasn't the carefree, fun-loving creature she'd always been so sure she was.

"This is getting pretty heavy for a morning after," she said as her laughter faded. "And besides, aren't conversations like this better during sex? To spice it all up a little."

She expected the usual reaction when she said even the most nonsuggestive things, as long as sex was implied. Explicitly stated, she expected his eyes to drop where his T-shirt rode up on her thighs. She expected his hands on her, touching her like he couldn't bear not to for a single moment more…

But Stefan remained as he had been all along, lounging in his chair and regarding her far more closely than was comfortable. Not as if he wanted to jump her bones. More like he wanted to forensically examine them, then jump them.

Indy didn't like it.

"Do you have discussions when you're not having sex?" he asked, with entirely too much *mild amusement* for her taste.

"I'm having one right now."

"Are you?" There was a hint of a smile on his hard, sensual mouth, but only a hint. "Because it seems to me that *discussions* are not something you wish to do. Most people reveal themselves in sex, Indiana. But you? You hide."

That felt a lot like a terrifying mirror shoved straight in her face. And after she'd gone to the trouble of avoiding that actual, nonmetaphoric mirror upstairs.

She made herself laugh again, though she didn't love the sound of it in the summer air. Had she always felt so forced? "I have sex when I'm having sex. I don't put any extra, weird weight on it. I don't understand why people do."

"Do you not?"

The way he said that felt a lot like an accusation. Or maybe a dare.

Worse, it butted up hard against all those raw and hollow places inside her.

"I keep forgetting we're strangers," Indy said, and laughed again. Longer this time, because the *summer air* could bite her. She drew her legs up onto the chair, pulling the T-shirt down over her knees, then resting her chin on the little shelf she'd made. "Let me give you the story of Indy March. First and foremost, I'm not like other girls."

Stefan considered her. "I have lived in many places, you understand. Not only different countries with different languages, but in many conditions. Rich, poor, and many shades between. And I have never met a person who introduced themselves to me by telling me how special they were who was, in any way, special."

But this was where Indy sparkled. She didn't take offense. She didn't glare at him. She only laughed. Because where everyone else went intense about their identities, she went effortless.

It felt as if she'd been treading water since she woke up this morning, and suddenly she'd found the bottom. And could finally stand.

"I don't attach to things the way most people do," she told him with a shrug. A smile. "That isn't to say that I don't have feelings, because of course I do. But some people make feelings their whole life. To me, feelings are just experiences. I have them, I put them aside, and then I move on. Sex is supposed to be fun. Not an opportunity to dredge up the dark and let it take you over. Because where's the fun in that?"

"You're talking about run-of-the-mill, boring sex," Stefan said dismissively. "Anyone can have this kind of sex. With any person they happen to meet. With their own hands, even. It is not so thrilling, this kind of sex, but it gets the job done."

"I wouldn't call the sex we've had boring or ordinary." She wrinkled up her nose at him. "But it's been fun."

"Fun." It was his turn to laugh, and Indy found she *really* didn't love it when he did it.

Not like that. Not *at* her. "Is this what you tell yourself?"

"Fun is what matters to me," she told him. "Or I wouldn't have come here, would I?"

"Indiana."

He still didn't lean forward. She didn't understand it. This was a perfect opportunity for him to reach out and put his hands on her, so they could both feel the kick of that wildfire connection and get lost in that for a while. But he didn't do it.

And yet, somehow, she still felt caught tight in that gaze of his. It was too blue and far too knowing. She had the shocking notion that he could see straight through her.

For once in her life, a man's dick wasn't getting in the way of his gaze. Indy would have sworn that wasn't possible.

Her heart began to gallop. And his gaze only seemed to pin her to her chair.

"The first time we've fucked you had just had a near-death experience. The sex was many things that night, but not fun." Stefan's mouth did something, some near-curve, that made her feel lightheaded again. "It changed you. I know, because it changed me. And now here we are, two years later, and nothing that happened last night was *fun*. It was intense. Provoking. It also only scratched the surface. Because this thing between you and me?" He did that thing with his chin, indicating the two of them. "This is not fun. It's too big. Too dark. And you are terrified of it."

She tried to make herself laugh, because she always made herself laugh, but she couldn't quite get there. "You have me confused with someone else. I don't get terrified."

"You like to fuck your way across this planet," he continued, in that same too quiet, too confronting way. "You like your little candy-coated orgasms, like sugar. But you and me? It's blood and fire, my foolish girl. This is life or death. Do you think I didn't notice that the more intense it got, the less experienced you seemed?"

"That's me." Indy's voice was rough. She told herself it was Czech allergies, nothing more. "A born-again virgin, just for you."

He was really smiling now, no question, and it burned through her. "What are you afraid of? Don't you ever ask yourself what the point of it all is if you're always too scared to truly strip naked?"

Indy's heart was pounding at an alarming rate inside her chest and all the rest of her was in a knot. She wanted too many things, most of them at odds with each other. *What if you picked one?* something in her asked, but she ignored it. And switched tactics.

Anything to disrupt the steady way he looked at her.

"I know I can't be understanding you correctly," she said, and the light tone she used was a struggle. But she did it. "Do you really mean to tell me that this is how a man like you rolls around? Ranting about intensity to every girl he touches?"

"Not every girl I touch." His smile made his lean, almost-cruel face a kind of portrait, painted in the light all around and her own rapid pulse. It made her think of poetry again. "This is how I know the difference. If I wanted a quick fuck, Indy, I could get that anywhere."

She was pretty sure it was the first time he'd called her by her nickname, and there was no reason she should dislike it. But she did.

And she hated that she'd even noticed. "Wait, wait. Are you telling me that despite your snide commentary on the number of countries you've lived in and the number of times people have claimed to be special only to prove that they were not... I am, in fact, not like the other girls?"

He leaned forward then, but for emphasis. Or so she assumed, because he didn't reach across the table to her.

"This is what fascinates me," he said in that same mild tone that was completely belied by the fire in his eyes. The fire that matched hers, and that was what was going to kill her. She knew it was. "Why would you fly all this way, two years later when anything could have happened in the meantime, only to pretend you did such a thing for *fun*?"

There was the knotting inside and the way each little snarl pulled painfully tight. There was the clatter of her heartbeat, the din of her pulse. And now Indy found her throat was dry, which would tell him all the rest if he heard it, wouldn't it?

"What else would it be?" she asked, in a vain attempt to sound lazy and unbothered.

But Stefan only smiled.

That damned smile of his that made her melt where she sat.

"You had better eat before you go," he told her, sitting back again and resuming that *lounge* of his, as if a man as lethally built could ever look truly languid. "Regardless of whether or not you hate the meal that had you scowling so ferociously, you expended a lot of energy last night. For all that fun we had."

She stared at the meal in question as if she'd never seen it before. Then lifted her gaze to his again. "Where am I going?"

"We agreed on one more night." He shrugged, looking entirely unbothered. "The night is over. I assumed you would be in a hurry to get away. After all, Indiana, the world is stocked full of the kind of fun you claim to love so much, is it not? Why would you waste your time here?"

Indy knew that this was a part of the game he

was playing and clearly, she'd walked right into his hands. Because even though she'd been planning to leave when she woke up earlier, had been very nearly eager to get away and settle herself down, she'd gotten sidetracked in all this…light and heat.

It felt like a gut punch.

She wanted, more than anything, to pull out a measure of that effortlessness that usually came so easily to her. An airy laugh. A languid hand. She could stand up, stretch, and grin mysteriously down at him as if she already had six more lovers lined up for the next twenty-four hours. Because both of them knew she could make that happen. She could pile her hair on top of her head, because it was rare that she did that in front of a man without him itching to get his fingers in it.

Indy had never considered these things games of her own, but she could see now—with uncomfortable clarity—that they were. That she'd been playing all kinds of games for a long time. The difference today was not only that Stefan could see through her.

The difference was that she could, too.

And it didn't matter anyway, because she couldn't seem to move.

"One night," she managed to say, fighting to sound anything but thrown. "Yes. That's what we agreed."

"Are you not satisfied?"

That darkly mocking note in his voice should have been all she needed to hear. It should have sent her running for the door—or in her case, sauntering with purpose while doing her best to look as unbothered by this as possible.

But sure, a voice inside chimed in, as mocking as Stefan. *You're not a game-player at all.*

"It's not a question of satisfaction," she replied. And even managed a smile. "This is what I'm trying to tell you. I'm always satisfied."

He didn't actually call her a liar then. He didn't have to.

"Terrified," he said softly, instead.

"Maybe," she heard herself say, filled with a wild, dizzy sensation that was certainly not *terror*, "I'd like to renegotiate the one night we agreed on."

"Because you want to see?" His voice was so rich. A dark ember, already lodged deep inside her, yearning to catch fire. "What can be?"

"Not at all." Because she didn't. Did she? She couldn't. "To prove to you what it is."

He took a long time to smile at her then, though his poet's gaze gleamed bright. Like everything else where he was concerned, it pierced her. She was sure he could see straight through her as if she were glass.

Indy had never thought that she was trying to

fool anyone, but she knew without question that she wasn't fooling him.

"Very well," Stefan said. He inclined his head slightly. "Convince me then. Show me how much *fun* you're having, Indiana. You have one night."

CHAPTER FIVE

STEFAN EXPECTED HER to crawl directly onto his lap to work her magic the way she knew best, but she didn't.

Instead, Indy seemed to relax, though he didn't believe it for second. Still, she sat differently, still curled up in the chair opposite him. His T-shirt seemed to grab at her, or *almost* let go to show more skin… And he suspected there wasn't a lot his Indy didn't know about the way her body moved, how it looked from all angles, and what those things meant.

She shook her hair out of its braid so that it fell all around her in a silken, heavy mass of dark waves. The smile she aimed at him rivaled the summer sun above them. And then she dug into her breakfast at last, looking for all the world as if she was totally unaware of the pretty, sexy picture she made.

Stefan knew better.

He would wager that Indy March knew exactly

the effect she had on him. On anyone and everyone, but right now, just him. She sat there naked with only his T-shirt on, her hair wild from the last time he'd had his hands in it, eating with such relish it became a sensual act when she licked her fingers. Looking totally unselfconscious, though he knew better.

It wasn't that she was calculated. He wouldn't accuse her of that. She was far too generous with her body, her responses, her need. It was more that she was *aware*.

The thing was, he liked it. His cock liked it more.

She had slept in late, which wasn't surprising after her travel the day before—not to mention the night they'd had. He had gotten up with the sun, as was his custom no matter what kind of night had gone before. It had long been a way he had exercised control over a life that had sometimes seemed to be forever careening where it wished.

One of the only things life with his father had taught him.

He had gone for a long, looping run through this quiet neighborhood, the kind of place he couldn't have imagined well enough to dream about back when he thought his father was the whole of the dark, unkind world. Stefan had pushed himself, trying to clear his head of all that need and passion...if only to prove he could.

As always, he had failed.

Indy had still been asleep when he'd returned, curled up in a soft ball in the center of the bed he'd put to use in a hundred different creative ways, all night long. Her face had been hidden by a thick curtain of her hair, so he had brushed it back, sighing a little at the curve of her cheek. The way she looked so serious as she slept, a far cry from the laughing, flickering creature she was by day.

Mi-ai intrat în suflet, he'd said, because he knew she couldn't hear him. And even if she could, he would not translate the Romanian phrase for her.

Because she did not need to know that she had entered his soul. Become a part of him.

No matter what happened.

His chest had ached enough that he'd found himself tensing, and he'd left her there as he'd showered and dressed, then had gone about his day as if it were any other. As if he hadn't been aware that she was finally here, in this house, where he'd pictured her a thousand times.

Stefan had never trafficked much in imagination. His father's backhand had taught him the folly of expectation early, a lesson he had taken to heart. But when it came to Indy, he found himself indulging in the kind of *what-ifs* that he knew better than to entertain.

The man he'd been two years and one day ago would not have recognized him now.

He chose to take that as a good thing.

A very good thing, as men who lived as he had often found themselves dead.

Whatever else happened, he told himself now, he would always be grateful that an unexpected vision in the form of this foolish, beautiful girl had appeared before him in that alley. Then led him out.

Because it had been in the dismantling of his various operations that he'd truly seen how much the cancer of it all had spread. It was possible that had he not pulled out when he had, he would have found himself incapable of it later.

That would mean, among other things, that this house would have stood empty. That he would never have discovered what it was like to wake up in a place he loved, a place where no one would show up at his door uninvited, bringing their ugliness and violence with them. That he would never have known what it was to sit high above Prague on a summer afternoon, across from a beautiful woman with the wind in her hair.

That he would never have known *this*.

It would have been a loss worth grieving, though he never would have known what he'd missed. Somehow, that made it worse.

He sat back in his chair. He enjoyed the sun on

his face. He waited to see what his Indy would do next.

After she finished with her coffee and breakfast show, she sat back and stretched. Stefan noticed with great appreciation how her hard nipples showed against the soft fabric of his shirt. As if she knew it, Indy pulled the T-shirt off, shooting him one of her liquid, sparkling glances as she got up. Then she sauntered over to the edge of his pool, pausing for a moment at the edge.

Appreciation wasn't a strong enough word to describe his reaction to seeing her there above the deep blue water, naked and lush and perfect, a better monument to Prague than all the statues on the Charles Bridge down below.

Indy tossed back her hair, then dove in deep. He stayed where he was, watching as she swam beneath the water, sleek and sure.

She surfaced, slicking her hair back, and then smiled at him as she floated there, another vision. This one drenched in light.

"Don't you want to join me?"

He only smiled. "I prefer to watch."

And he got why she'd said she wasn't like other girls. She didn't pout as many would. She didn't try to cajole him. She shrugged as if it didn't matter to her if he did or didn't join her, then turned and went back to her swimming as if that was what she'd wanted all along.

Stefan understood why she had a trail of lovers behind her, a battalion or two at least, each and every one of them determined to pin her down.

But he wasn't concerned about that. Because he knew what all of them didn't. He knew the truth of her. He'd seen it.

And even if he hadn't, she'd come back to him.

Proving, whether she cared to admit it or not, that the intensity between them had wrecked her the same way it had him.

Stefan almost felt bad for her. Because he had changed his entire life to make it here. To find himself sitting on this terrace today. He had the feeling that she'd spent the same two years frozen, waiting, which meant she had yet to change the way he had.

He couldn't wait to taste it.

And he meant it when he told her he would rather watch her move through the water, slippery and sure. That was what he did, settling back in his chair and enjoying the sun, the sky. Prague below and the scent of flowers in the air. It had been a long road and yet if this was the reward, Stefan thought he would walk it again a thousand times.

Indy took her time, floating for a long while in the clear blue water of the pool. Sending the message that she'd forgotten he was there, which he assumed was the point. When she was done she swam to the side and lifted herself up, displaying that easy grace of hers that he found spellbinding. Still. Then she made her way toward him, fully and unapologetically naked. And she smiled as she walked toward him.

"You don't look like you're having fun," she said.

"Do I not?"

She didn't answer him with words. She shifted to kneel down before him, dripping wet and gloriously naked, her hair in a sodden tangle as she reached forward and helped herself to his cock.

Stefan was only too happy to let her have it.

And as she set to work licking all around the thick head, then wrapping her hands tight around his shaft—one on top of the other—he wondered, idly enough, if she actually knew how manipulative she was. Or if she truly believed that this was all in aid of the kind of *fun* she thought she liked. Most men would be putty in her hands at the spontaneous skinny-dipping. Much less after she got finished turning him inside out with that wicked mouth of hers.

But then, Stefan doubted very much that she'd ever met a man like him before. That was why she was here, wasn't it? He was perfectly capable of coming down her throat with a groan and still being just as much of a problem for her when he tucked himself away again.

"You keep staring at me," she said mildly when they were back in the kitchen some time later that afternoon. She had gone upstairs to shower off the pool and to dress in another flowy, shapeless sort of dress that made him think of fairytales. It allowed her to pad around the villa in bare feet, her hair around her like a cloud, looking ethereal and making him long to eat her up in one bite. "As if you're waiting for me to turn into a frog right before you."

"Not at all," Stefan replied. "I would prefer you stay in your current form. Frogs are not so appealing."

He had poured them both a small glass of *țuică* and had tossed his back as he set about frying eggs to put on the bowls of his grandmother's *tochitură* for a late lunch, a thick pork stew that reminded him of her few visits when she would command the kitchen, ignore his father, and cook. Indy was sipping at hers, not his favorite way to consume his favorite plum brandy, imported from Romania with his own two hands. But he noticed she avoided the counter where he'd laid her out the night before and tucked that away as a little bit of ammunition. Maybe she *should* make sure to keep her wits about her.

"I'm thinking about the way you handle men," he said as she took another sip. "It makes me wonder where you learned this. Was your father a man you felt you needed to handle?"

She laughed, as he'd expected she would. "This sounds like another one of these very deep conversations you always want to have at the strangest times."

He watched as she tossed back the rest of her *țuică* and hid his smile. "If it is too painful for you, I understand."

"My father is the most decent man in the world," she told him, her dark eyes flashing. "There's nothing painful about it. He's solid. He loves my mom and his daughters and that's that. He works hard, fishes whenever he can, and still dances cheek to cheek with all the women in his life. That being the three of us. He didn't require handling. He doesn't."

"Who then?"

He took the bowls over to the table that sat in the small nook off the kitchen, sunny like the rest of the house, this one with windows that let in the green and the gardens. And he was not surprised that she trailed after him.

"Is this because I sleep around a lot?" she asked, sounding ever-so-faintly bored. "I have to have daddy issues?"

"You're not *required* to have daddy issues, no."

"Good. Because I don't. And to be honest with you, I don't really have any other issues. It's amazing how easy life is when you make the conscious decision to…make it easy."

He waved her to a seat and took his. "It is not that you have a lot of sex. It's the rest of this thing you do. All day I have been debating whether it's a deliberate manipulation or, instead, an innate understanding of how to smooth over a moment with sex." Stefan studied her response to that, but indicated the food he'd made. "Eat."

She did not eat. She stared back at him, looking thrown, which he found he enjoyed. "I don't think I do either of those things."

"Do you not? And yet if I were to take a poll of people who know you, what would they say?"

"I live in the moment, Stefan. I don't spend a lot of time calculating possibilities or manipulating people. Or worrying what other people think about me. That's all gross. I just do what feels right."

"Innate it is, then. Fascinating."

"I'm sorry if this is disappointing for you." Indy sounded sweet then, yet the glittering light in her gaze was anything but. He liked her fierceness. He wanted to bathe in it. "I realize that men really, really want me to have some kind of deep inner wound only they can heal. With their penises. And I hate to break it to you but I really just like a lot of fun and a lot of sex. The end."

Stefan could have told her that while that might

have been true in her past, it wasn't now. Because if it was, she never would have showed up in Prague. She never would have come back to him.

Because what happened between them in Budapest was the most intense thing that had ever happened to Stefan. And his whole life had been intense. None of it, before her, in a way he would call *good*. If what Indy said was true, her life had been a monument to avoiding intensity—meaning, she could have continued doing that. She could have very easily stayed in New York.

But she hadn't.

And if she didn't understand that yet, all he could do was sit back and enjoy the show while she came around to the truth. He intended to do just that.

"Tell me how you lost your virginity," he said, picking up his utensils. "Let me guess. It was *fun*."

"Yes, it was fun," she said, her soft eyes gleaming. "He was an older boy, scandalously. I was a freshman in high school and he was a senior. Do you have freshmen and seniors here? Or… In Romania, I guess?"

"We have American television, Indiana," he said dryly. "So it is all the same."

"We dated a long, long time," she said with a laugh. "Meaning, most of the fall semester. He wanted to do it and I finally told him it was fine as long as it felt good. And it did."

"In the backseat of a car, I can only hope. What could be more American?"

"It *was* the backseat of a car!" She sounded delighted. "A Chevy, no less. It didn't really hurt—he made it fun as promised, and that, I'm afraid, is how I began my downward spiral into the fallen woman you see before you today."

He waited as she tucked in happily to her meal, but the silence dragged on.

"Do you want to know how I lost my virginity?" he asked.

"Not really." She glanced up at him, her dark eyes laughing. "It doesn't have the same resonance, does it? When and how girl gives away her V card is a *clue*, isn't it?"

"Or a story."

"Don't be naïve, Stefan," she said, waving her hand in the air so the spoon she held gleamed in the light. He tried to remember if anyone else had ever called him that. But of course they hadn't. But his pretty little bulldozer charged straight on. "For men, who cares? The only reason it would be relevant would be if you were still a virgin. Otherwise, it's assumed that men shed their innocence the way a caterpillar sheds its skin, then carry right on."

"I am not a virgin," he said, not sure if he was amused or…something else. "In case you wondered."

"I didn't. Now you think you know things about

me, don't you? When what you know is that I gave it away when I was fourteen. But that's not the shocking part." Indy paused, waiting for him to ask. When he didn't, she rolled her eyes. "The shocking part is that I don't regret it, and it wasn't a horrific experience. Maybe I was always destined to be a whore."

"The sounds like a lot of baggage, does it not?"

"It's not my baggage," she said, with another one of those light, airy laughs. "I slept with Jamie Portnoy in the backseat of his father's Chevy because I wanted to. And even then, there were people who wanted to shame me for that decision. Because it turned out Jamie was a bragger. So I broke up with him and then I told even more people than he had. Why should *I* be embarrassed?"

And he thought he understood, then. She wasn't pretending. It was all unconscious. She hadn't needed to handle her father, maybe, but an older boy who had bragged about her and the people he'd told. She'd taken what could have been shame and called it fun, and he believed she felt that. It wasn't a put-on.

It wasn't quite real joy, either.

But this was about fun, he reminded himself. Or her attempt to convince him that *fun* was what they were having here. What he really wanted from her could wait.

After they ate, she played music from her mobile and danced around the kitchen. She made him laugh and once she did, she climbed into his lap, reached between them, and worked his cock deep inside her. And then sang along to the song that was playing as she rocked against him, until they both came in the same swift rush.

That was how it went. Light, airy.

She took a nap in the early evening, flushed and warm in that bed upstairs while he tended to business concerns that couldn't wait. Later, after she woke, he drove them down into Prague so they could walk through Old Town and sit in one of the restaurants opened up to the summer night. In public, where there was no possibility that she could revert to nakedness or sex when she wanted to change the subject.

That it also tortured him was worth it, because he could see—as the color climbed her cheeks and her eyes got brighter—that being forced to simply sit there and *talk to him* was driving her crazy.

"Have you been to Prague before?" he asked sedately when she looked as if she might be considering starting a scene to divert his attention.

"I came through twice during my two years of travel," she said, squirming in her chair. Stefan knew full well that she was wet and ready. And more, that the prospect of this long dinner stretching before them was sending her over the edge.

Good. He hoped it did. He doubted Indy would be any quieter than that famous movie scene.

"Only twice? Some people would stay here forever if they could."

"I would always think I'd found the perfect place," she said, her smile taking on a slight edge. "Every place I go, I'm sure it's the one. But then I go somewhere else. I meet someone else. And I fall in love all over again."

He opted not to take the bait. "So nowhere is home, then?"

She squirmed again, taking a long pull from her water glass. "I guess when I think of home I still default to Ohio, but it's not really *my* home. It's my parents' home. My sister and I vowed we would get out as soon as we could, and we did. And I haven't lived there in a million years. I complain when I have to go back, the way I do every Christmas. But still. You say home, and that's still what I think."

"What makes it home?"

Indy sighed, and he thought he could see the very moment she remembered that she didn't like to share anything but her body. "Do you have a home?"

"No," he said. "I grew up in various Romanian cities. Bucharest, mostly. But none of the places I lived were *home*. I don't fall in love with places."

"That makes me sad." She was tracing patterns on the side of her water glass. Around them, tourists talked loudly, languages blending together on the warm night air. "That's the whole point of travel, as far as I am concerned."

"But I did not travel as you did." His smile was harder, then. "Flitting about the globe, finding myself in questionable pop-up clubs in dark, dangerous cities. This was not available to me."

"Budapest isn't all that dangerous."

"There is no place in the world that is not dangerous if you are a pretty, careless girl," he retorted. "As you discovered."

But she only rolled her eyes at him. "The world is the world. I refuse to live in fear. If you assume goodness, most of the time, goodness is what you're going to get."

"That or guns to your head when you walk down the wrong alley."

Indy shrugged. "That's my case in point. A gun really was to my head and yet here I am, wined and dined in beautiful Prague for my trouble."

"I think you know better."

"What about you?" she asked, her dark gaze on his with more heat than he thought she meant to show him. "If the world is so dangerous, surely you should be walking around with an armed guard."

"Not in the Czech Republic. It is not necessary." Stefan didn't quite smile. "There are some places it would not be wise for me to go, and so I will not go to them. But I am the reason pretty young things should not venture into alleys in the first place. I am not afraid of the world so much as it is afraid of me. And rightly."

She studied him. "I can't decide if you want me to be afraid of you or if you just like boasting about how mad, bad, and dangerous you are."

"I think you should be afraid of me, Indiana," he said quietly. "And I do not boast."

"You've never seemed particularly dangerous to me. Sorry. I feel like I would have seen it by now."

"But that is where you are wrong," Stefan told her. "It is you who are in the most danger."

For a moment, her gaze clung to his.

But then she waved her hand, picked up her menu, and let that roll away too, as if what he'd said was sheer nonsense. Maybe she wanted it to be.

He knew better.

After they ate and left the restaurant, she took his hand. She linked her fingers with his in a gesture that he told himself felt as foolish as the rest, but he didn't disengage. Then she led him out into the cobbled streets of Old Town Prague, tugging him along through the crowds until they became a part of the same great energy of the ancient city on a clear summer night, like so many before them. Like everyone around them.

"Should we pretend to be tourists?" she asked, smiling up at him outside Prague Castle.

"I have never been a tourist."

He looked down at her, still holding his hand like they were anyone. As if he were a regular person like all the other men he saw around him tonight. Soft, unwary. Was it that simple? Change his life, shed his old skin, and become what he had never let himself imagine he could?

With her fingers threaded in his, he almost believed it.

He wanted to believe it, and maybe that was worse.

"Then there's no time like the present," Indy declared. "We can be tourists right here."

Stefan let her tote him along with her, walking the length of the Charles Bridge and then back again. He posed for the inevitable photographs. He even smiled winningly as they took them, which made her nearly cry with laughter.

"What? Even I know you must smile in these things."

"Yes, Stefan," she murmured, standing on her tiptoes to adjust the angle of her mobile. "You're a regular old selfie-taking fool like everyone else. It's obvious."

And she was still laughing, later, when instead of following him back to where he'd parked his car so they could drive back to his villa, she tugged him into a dark alley. Then let her smile go wicked as she melted against him.

"Is this the real truth?" he asked her gruffly as he leaned back against the nearest wall and let her sprawl against his chest. "You cannot keep out of alleyways?"

"Let's call it symmetry," she whispered back.

And she wanted it fun and light. Flirty and fun. But he didn't.

Stefan kept it slow. He lifted her up and wrapped her around his body, then pinned her back against the wall so he could hold her there and take his sweet time.

He drew it out, teasing and tempting her, so that by the time he moved between her thighs she'd been shuddering on the edge instead of tipping over into her sugarcoated orgasms.

That was why he eased inside her, slow and sure. Filling her but never quite giving her what she needed to make it over that cliff.

And he fucked her like that, slowing down every time she tensed against him, until she was beating at his shoulders with her fists. Glaring at him, her eyes damp with her sensual misery.

"This is supposed to be fun," she hissed at him.

He smiled and slowed down even more. "Maybe this is fun for me, Indiana."

By the time he finally let her come, she had to bite her own fist to keep from alerting half of Prague to their illicit behavior.

When she tried to put a little distance between

them as they walked back to the car at last, he didn't allow it. He pulled her tight, wrapping his arm around her shoulders, and kept her close. Making sure she could feel the heat in him just as he could feel it in her.

As if it marked them both.

When they got back to the villa he did the same thing all over again, but this time stretched out in that wide bed upstairs until she was nothing but a sobbing, writhing, begging mess.

And in the morning when she wouldn't meet his gaze he fed her, fucked her again, and when she made a move to leave once more, only smiled at her.

"Surely not," he said. But lazily, as if he didn't care one way or the other, which made her eyes darken, there where she was sitting cross-legged on the bed. "You had your fun. Surely it's time I had mine."

"You already had your fun," she flared at him, pausing in the act of braiding her hair again to glare at him. "Ruining mine in the process."

"You seem ruined," he agreed. "But not in the way you mean, I think."

"Whatever. I told you, this is supposed to be—"

"Fun, yes." He lifted a brow. "I never thought I'd see my foolish girl, unafraid to walk into dark alleys and take her chances with questionable men... Afraid."

"Is that… Are you *daring* me?"

Stefan shrugged. "If you are too afraid to play with a little intensity, Indiana, I cannot help you with this. I have learned to live with other disappointments."

He saw a series of emotions move over her heart-shaped face. Temper. Dismay. And then, more interesting, that amusement she usually wore so easily. He had never seen her put it into place in quite that way before. Like she was settling into a mask.

She laughed, because she always laughed. Because he thought she'd decided that made her seem exactly as fun—and as bulletproof—as she thought she needed to be.

"You're reading this all wrong," she told him lightly. Always so lightly. "I'm not afraid, I promise. I'm just not an intense person. It's not how I'm made."

He thought of the way she'd sobbed beneath him last night, her gaze slick with hunger and need, every part of her so tuned into him it was like its own, sweet agony. He thought of the way she had kissed her way over his scars, finding them in his tattoo and taking her time. Making sure she found every last one of them.

And he knew that she was used to controlling things this way. Her carelessness. Flitting from place to place, lover to lover, to the endless soundtrack of her own laughter.

But Stefan knew she was a liar.

All he did was study her until she flushed. And she did, bright and red.

"Bullshit," he said.

And he made sure that when he smiled this time, it was a weapon.

CHAPTER SIX

HE WASN'T EVEN touching her and yet Indy felt splayed wide open like they were back in that alley.

She'd thought she'd made such a good choice after playing tourist. After wandering around in the summer night, making them part of the crowds doing the same—and therefore not strung out on their connection and all that electric, breathtaking need—she'd thought she could pull him into a dark alley to reframe the admittedly intense beginning of their relationship.

The joke had been on her. Because he'd wrecked her.

Indy felt turned inside out. She didn't like it.

"It's not bullshit," she said, frowning at him.

It was another beautiful, breezy summer's day in the Czech Republic. Everything outside the endless sweep of windows was green and lush and beautiful. She could see the bridges spanning the Vltava and the spires of Prague Castle from the center of Stefan's bed, where he'd ruined her fun. Repeatedly and deliberately, all night long.

Last night she'd been so sure that she had this situation under control. She'd been convinced that she could simply *be herself*—because she didn't accept what he'd said, that she was manipulative or unconsciously trying to handle anything—and he would somehow start behaving in a way that made sense to her.

Yeah, she thought now, finishing up her braid while holding that gaze of his. *That didn't work.*

Today she was a little bit wiser, maybe. And dressed, thank you. Because she certainly had no intention of prancing around naked in front of him when he was far too good at using her own body against her. One more thing she'd never experienced before, she could admit. Normally she was the one who used her body. And she'd never met anyone who was better at it than she was...until now.

But that didn't make her afraid. And it didn't make him right.

"It is bullshit," he said again, his voice implacable.

And God, the way he looked at her. That hard and steady gaze that left her in absolutely no doubt that he could see straight through her. That he saw everything. Maybe even things she didn't know about herself, a notion that made her feel far too trembly deep inside.

That and his marvelous accent, that made her think of the taste of that plum brandy on her tongue.

"I understand you like to play this carefree, languid character," he continued in the same way, all steel and certainty. "But even your orgasms tell the truth, Indiana. You like the easy way out. You don't like the commitment of anything more. You don't even want sex if it demands too much of you. You tell yourself you're made that way, when as we have proven, what you're made for is me. This." His blue eyes gleamed, brighter than the sky that stretched on forever outside the windows. "Us."

Indy told herself she was tired of the earthquakes he kept setting off inside her. The fault lines she hadn't known were there, tangled and fragile and *shaking* while her heart beat too hard. In parts of her that her heart shouldn't have been.

"You don't actually know me at all, Stefan."

She knew that sounded more defensive than she wanted to sound in his presence. Why not bare her throat to his teeth and see if he really was the wolf she thought he was? She knew he would read too much into it. She knew he would take that tone as *proof.*

But she couldn't seem to help herself. There was something beating in her along with her wild pulse, feeling far too much like panic.

She smiled. Politely. "The fact of the matter is, we had a lot of sex. And I don't know how to break this to you, Stefan, but that doesn't make you special."

"If you say so." His blue eyes gleamed, but not with the fury she'd wanted. It was something far more like amusement. Only hotter. She could feel it connect to all the shaky places inside her.

She waved her hand in the air, a dismissive gesture she hoped he would find insulting. But he didn't look insulted. He looked hard, everywhere, as he stood near the windows, his expression something like indulgent. And mouthwateringly hot. And gloriously wicked while he was at it. He wore only the pair of athletic shorts he had tossed on this morning when he'd left the bed, heading out for a run while she was left limp and soft and wheezing for breath. And she had so dearly hoped that he would somehow be diminished by rolling around in the kind of clothes that any random guy would wear. By doing mundane things like *running*, meaning that body of his wasn't simply his by chance...

But not Stefan. There wasn't a single part of him that wasn't commanding or powerful. He wasn't a *guy*. He was a man, all man, and he was so far completely impervious to her fervent wishes that he might magically, suddenly, have less of a hold on her.

"I'm not trying to be mean," she began.

"Are you not? That must be a bit of your kind of fun, yes?"

She ignored that. "We met under bizarre circumstances. There's no denying that. And we both like sex, clearly. A little rough and spicy, maybe. We spent two years apart after only being together for a few hours. And now, what? It's been two nights?"

"I applaud your ability to count."

"Basically, Stefan, we've shared a weekend stretched over years. We're still strangers no matter how many times you've made me scream in the course of that weekend. That's just the truth. And so when I tell you who I am and what I'm like, I think you can trust that I'm the expert in the room on that topic."

"Indiana. Please." Everything was the blue of his gaze, then. Too hot to bear. "Do I strike you as the kind of man who leaves things to chance?"

That panicky thing inside her seemed to pick up speed, or maybe it was simply that she couldn't catch her breath. *Maybe you need to stop trying.*

"I don't know what that means," she threw at him, panic and all those other dark and nameless things pulsing too hard inside her. While, even then, her pussy melted, as if the way she wanted him was hardwired into her. "You left a thousand things to chance. Whether or not I would show up.

Whether I might just take the key you'd given me, come to this address, and rob you blind at some point over the past two years. I could pick a thousand ways this could have gone that did not involve me showing up here, desperate for another taste of you." She sniffed as if she were above all this, hoping the sound would steady her. And if that was impossible, the way it sure seemed to be, at least let her pretend. "Sounds like a gambler to me."

Stefan laughed. "I gave you a key, yes. There is also a security system. If you had attempted to access this house with your key alone at any other time you would have found that further security measures are required to get inside. They were waived because I was here. So no, there was no gambling involved."

"You didn't know if I'd even show up," she argued.

"Maybe not." But he didn't look unsure in any way. It made her question why she was nothing but. "I built a certain life for myself—you know this. And after I cleaned up the mess I made in Budapest that night, I had a choice. Continue with the madness I began in that alley or go on as if it had never happened. Continue my life as it was. Maybe show up here on the time and date I'd given you, maybe not. That was something I could worry about two years later, if I chose that route. But before I made a decision, I studied."

Something in her hitched at that, though she frowned at him. Ignoring the way her heart fluttered.

"What do you mean, you studied?" She heard the panic in her voice and made herself laugh. "Between you and me and the college I attended, I was never much for studying."

"You, Indiana. I studied you."

Indy felt as if she was coming apart. She found her hands in fists as she stared mutely back at him while all the implications of what he'd just said pounded through her.

And made her pussy ache all the more.

"Don't be silly," she managed to say softly. She wished she weren't sitting on the bed, wearing nothing but cutoff jeans and a tank top. She wished she was swaddled in protective gear and far, far away—*where you would only wish you were here,* a voice inside chided her. "This is shallow water, Stefan. No need to study a puddle. It is what it is."

His gaze seemed to sharpen on her at that but he stayed where he was, lounging there with his back to the windows, the very picture of a certain insolent ease. If a person ignored the heft and majesty of his body, that was. Which Indy didn't think she would ever be able to do.

"What fascinates me is not that you would say such a thing, which of course is false," he said after a moment. "But that you appear so invested in me believing it."

Her heart was starting to *hurt* her. "You don't have to believe it. But I wouldn't want to disappoint you any further. Because that's where this is going. You know that, right? You can imagine me to be anything you want, Stefan. I can't stop you. But that doesn't make it real."

Stefan considered her for a moment, and she wanted to *do* something. Anything. But she felt pinned into place by that gaze of his. "You are so dedicated to performing this party girl persona. Even when it doesn't suit you."

"It's not a performance. It's my life."

"You're very easy to track, Indy." It was official. She hated when he called her that. Though she refused to ask herself why. "You put it all out there, all over social media. This party, that party. Hints of new lovers everywhere you go. Suggestive photos in dark clubs. Naked flesh on sunny, topless beaches, all of it calculated to show off your beauty and your inability to stay in any one place for long."

She forced herself to uncurl her fists when her fingers began to cramp. "I am who I am. I post what I feel like posting. You could always not look at it if you don't like it."

"And yet, if all of this were true, surely you would have developed a drug habit to go along with it as so many do. How else to fuel all those late nights and erotic dances? It is common enough. Yet instead, though you spent more time committed to your strip club than your college, you graduated a year late with suspiciously average grades. And with a hefty savings account and investment portfolio. These things do not match."

"How are average grades suspicious? They're just average." But her mouth was dry. "I'm not embarrassed by that."

"Your bank account demonstrates that you are not average. You were able to not only save, but invest to a profit. It suggests you deliberately downplayed your abilities in the classroom. I cannot be the only person who has noticed this, surely."

But no one else had ever looked at her this closely. Indy had made sure no one could. And she felt as if he were clawing her open. As if he were digging his hands deep into her chest and pulling her wide. She had to look down at her own front to make sure that wasn't really happening.

It wasn't. Of course it wasn't. Indy sighed as much in relief that she was still in one piece as anything else. "I'm good at being naked, Stefan. But as I said, not so good at studying."

"Then why didn't you fail out?" He sounded so calm. So reasonable. It was maddening. "Why did you continue your studies at all if it meant so little to you?"

"Now you sound like my father." She managed a frosty sort of smile. "Which is not hot, by the way."

He didn't laugh at that, but the look on his face felt about the same. "You are the one who said you did not have daddy issues. Or was that another lie?"

She made herself laugh to try to break the tension. Before it broke her. "I'm not a liar, for God's sake. I was a middling student. I was a much better dancer. I had some regulars who gave me great tips and suggested I bank what I could. It's not a mystery, Stefan. It's not a clue to my wounded inner child. And as I already told you, I stopped doing it because it stopped being fun. Or I thought it would stop being fun eventually, whatever."

"What is this 'whatever'?" he asked, sounding irritatingly *patient*. "I have known many strippers over the years. Very few of them *invest*. This is what you did while paying for the school where you were pretending to be terrible student."

"I don't know what part of me not liking school you're not getting."

His blue gaze was bright then. Knowing in a way she not only didn't like, but felt rush through her like a cold chill.

"Is it that you don't like school?" he asked. "Or is it that your sister is the scholar and that means that you cannot be?"

It would have been better if he'd hauled off and

CAITLIN CREWS

123

hit her. It would have shocked her a lot less than…
that. Indy moved then. She crawled over to the
side of the bed, wishing her head weren't spinning. Wishing her belly weren't knotted up tight.

Wishing this had stayed as simple as it had been
that night in Budapest.

Live. Love. Leave.

"My sister?" She could barely get the words out.
"Why are you talking about… How do you even
know about my sister?"

"I know everything about you," Stefan said,
mildly enough, which only made it worse. Because
it was so matter-of-fact and everything inside her
was a mess. Knots and shivering and what was he
doing to her? "I made this my business. Because
when I choose a path, Indiana, I expect to commit
to it totally. Or I do not do it."

Foreboding settled in her, making her bones
ache.

Indy stood up abruptly, holding her palms up
as if trying to ward him off—though he made no
move toward her. He looked as if he was relaxing,
in fact. Standing by his windows while the summer breeze blew in. Enjoying the lovely day, not
eviscerating her.

Not turning her inside out with every word.

"This has all gotten way too intense for me,"
she told him, fighting with everything she had to

keep her voice from shaking. "And I told you, I'm not about that."

"I am unsurprised to hear this." Stefan shrugged in that way of his that was not, in any way, a gesture of uncertainty. Somehow, when he shrugged it was aggressive. A decisive critique—of her. "Maybe you should ask yourself why dark alleys do not scare you. Why men with guns do not stop you. But intensity makes you run."

Her lips felt blue. She couldn't feel her own face. But she still tried to fight. "Maybe you should ask yourself why you think it's okay to dig around in someone's life without permission. Then use it as bait."

"I have never pretended to be a good man, Indiana." His voice was harsh. But something about the way he was looking at her was kind, and it made her want to give in to the sobs she could feel inside, threatening her ribs. "I never promised you anything at all, except a time and place. This is not a redemption story. I do not require your forgiveness. Did you believe that you might meet me as you did and I would be anything at all but this?"

"I've never given any thought," she managed to say.

His blue eyes lit up with an unholy glee. "Liar. But it is not me you lie to, I think. It is yourself."

Indy had never been so grateful that she packed light as she was then, with all that emotion surging around inside her, making her feel misshapen with it. Because all she had to do was pick up her little pack from the floor and shrug into it, then gaze at him almost sadly.

"I get that there's this big movement for everyone to act as if what they really want from life is to be known," she said. "To be wide open and vulnerable so that any passing stranger can take a glance and see exactly who they are. If you want to talk bullshit, that's what *that* is. You think you know me because you looked through some social media posts and hacked my information? You don't. *You don't.* I don't perform, but I also don't think that the sum total of a person is a collection of photographs. Carefully curated photographs at that."

Stefan didn't look particularly impressed with that speech. "I'm not following. First you were a puddle. Now you cannot be discerned through the pictures that you post. Surely both cannot be true."

"I have no interest in being psychoanalyzed," she bit out. "If I wanted a therapist, I'd get one. And knowing me, I'd probably sleep with him. That's how I roll."

"I know how you roll, Indiana. I know you use sex to hide from your life, not to embrace it." His smile lanced through her. "I told you—I know everything."

"Then you already know what I'm going to do, don't you?" She was finding it hard to stand still when she wanted to run. But she made herself do it. "That's handy. It means I have no need to tell you myself."

"You will storm out." Stefan sounded almost bored—unless she looked at the way his eyes blazed at her. "Though I expect you will do it slowly. An easy, carefree little walk so I'm not tempted to jump to the wrong conclusions. So that no one could suggest that you are having an emotional response. And off you will go. I expect to a bar, where you will surround yourself at once with men who do not challenge you. Who will fawn all over you, buy you drinks, tell you that you're pretty. And if you let them, give you those empty sugar-high orgasms you like so much. But not for long, because there's always another cock to ride, is there not?"

Her whole body jolted with every word he said. Indy could hardly see past the strange heat clouding her gaze. She had given up on her breath. She either seemed to be panting, or holding what air she could inside her, and either way, she felt… Unhinged.

"Do you think that you're the first person in my life to try to run me down so that I'll do what they want me to do?" she managed to ask.

"I'm not trying to influence you one way or the other," he said with a laugh. Still lounging there as if he not only didn't have a care in the world, but as if none of this was getting to him. She was falling apart, but none of this was touching him at all.

"You can't really believe I don't know what I want, can you?" she demanded, though she knew she should have already made her exit.

Again, his shattering blue gaze moved through her like a storm, making her wish that he would shout, flip a table, punch a wall—do *something* to indicate that this was as ruinous for him as it was for her. That it mattered to him that he was ripping her apart.

That I matter to him, a voice inside said, and she didn't want that. She didn't want to feel these things. She didn't want to *feel.*

"I imagine you want any number of things," Stefan said with all that quiet intensity that had ruined her from the start. "But I know what you need. And so do you, I think, which is why it scares you so much. When you are ready, you will come back. And we will do this dance as many times as it takes, Indiana. Because in the end, there is nothing you want so much as the things you are afraid to need. Deep down, you know this."

"Goodbye, Stefan," she managed to bite out.

And then she turned, his words heavy inside her as she did exactly as he predicted. She made sure she kept her stride little more than an amble as she left the bedroom and headed for the stairs.

She moved through the light and airy house, the

sunshine pouring in from all sides feeling like an affront. She wanted it dark and moody to match what she felt inside, but Prague wasn't cooperating.

But she didn't need it to rain to do what she needed to do.

She threw open the front door and walked away from Stefan Romanescu and all his simmering *intensity*, telling herself she had no intention of ever going back.

No matter what.

Because she, by God, was going to have some *fun*.

CHAPTER SEVEN

THOUGH *FUN* WAS NOT her first thought as Indy stood there outside the house, breathing in the summer morning while she tried to take stock of what had just happened.

What she'd just done.

A part of her wanted nothing more than to turn around and race back inside. She'd waited two long years for this and she was bailing already? Surely it made sense to just go back to him and see if she could salvage this somehow—

Salvage what? asked a caustic voice inside her. *You know what you're good at and it's not this.*

She blew out a breath, and started down the road, thinking a nice long walk would suit her perfectly, thank you. It would settle her down and let her think.

Prague glimmered there in the distance as she made her way down the hill, dance music in her ears to remind her that she liked her mood light and her parties never-ending. And it was the beautiful fairytale city it always was, but she hardly saw it. Because she was too busy going over every single thing Stefan had said to her.

Indy had always been a mediocre student. That wasn't a question. Why had he made it a question? And why now, years after she'd finally graduated, when it didn't matter what kind of student she'd been in the first place?

Her sister had been the student in the family. And it wasn't that Indy had set herself up in opposition to Bristol. It was that there was no point competing with her sister for a crown Indy didn't even want. She'd always thought that Bristol had become serious about her studies to put herself in an unimpeachable place where studying was all she did. Because Indy had been much better at flitting around their small-town schools, doing the popular thing.

There was no point doing things you weren't good at, was there?

No one's good *at paying bills, Indy*, Bristol had cried in exasperation at one point during their time as roommates. *I'm not* good *at being responsible, I just don't have an option not to be. Why don't you understand that?*

Maybe you don't have a choice, Indy had replied, hugging Bristol even though her sister tried to shrug out of it, even batting at her a little because Bristol didn't feel like *not* being frustrated.

But you maybe also love it a little bit at the same time, don't you?

Bristol had given up. But Indy had taken it as confirmation. She gravitated toward the things she was good at in life and that was why her life was a delight. Bristol might claim to enjoy what she did, but she had sure seemed endlessly stressed out about all of it while she did it, didn't she? Her grades in high school. Her GPA and course load in college. Her masters and then her doctorate—it was all *stress stress stress*.

One thing Indy had avoided, as much as possible, was stress.

She couldn't understand why anyone would want the kind of intensity Stefan had showed her. That just seemed like a whole lot of stress in all the places where life was supposed to be the most fun and she wanted no part of it.

"I'm fine the way I am," she muttered out loud as she left his street behind.

It took her a while to walk down into the city and when she did, she found herself wandering through the city streets until she found a shop that sold newspapers and magazines in English.

And stopped dead, because there was her sister on the cover of several. Front and center.

Go Bristol, she thought.

She found a place to sit down by the river and read them all through. Then she got her sister on the phone, the way she did as often as she could while Bristol was off adventuring in tabloid splendor. If only for a few moments.

"Did you know that you're on the front page of every single tabloid there is?" she asked when Bristol answered.

"What do you mean by every tabloid?" Bristol sounded annoyed, but Indy was looking at a whole series of pictures of her face. Soft and open and splashed across the papers—and Bristol was an academic, not an actress. Something in Indy turned over at that. "I'm not comfortable with *one* tabloid."

"Then I have some bad news for you," Indy said merrily. "They're comfortable with you. And you do know you have a little something called the internet at your disposal, Bristol."

She laughed, picturing the annoyed expression her sister was certain to be making, off in her Spanish island paradise with one of the richest and most famous men alive. *Nice for some*, she thought, though she knew she didn't actually envy Bristol. It was that look on her face in all these pictures, though. It made Indy wish she were different, inside and out.

But she wasn't. "You can access this exciting new invention with the newfangled handheld computer you're using to talk to me, in a totally different country, *right now*."

"I access the internet all the time, asshole," Bristol replied in her typically snooty way. All big sister bossiness and the suggestion, right there beneath her words, that Indy was wasting her life. It was oddly comforting today. "And yet, oddly enough, it's not the tabloid newspapers I look for when I do."

"Well, good news, then," Indy said brightly. "You look amazing. What else matters?"

Bristol let out her trademark longsuffering sigh, but Indy could hear that her out-of-character adventure was already changing her. Because Bristol was doing the exact opposite of the things she normally did. She was celebrating finishing up her doctorate and not knowing exactly what to do with the rest of her life by doing something completely outside her normal range. That was how she'd ended up on the arm of Lachlan Drummond, one of the most eligible billionaires in the world.

She even sounded happy.

And as Indy sat there glaring at the river after the call ended, that felt like yet another jolting sort of indictment inside her.

Stefan's breakdown of what she was going to do once she walked away from him seemed to simmer inside her, taunting her, because she knew he was right. Wasn't that what she always did when she found herself on her own? Maybe after a long night. Maybe after an adventure where she'd lost track of her companions. She could walk into any bar, anywhere. She often didn't even have to walk into a bar. A few suggestive glances and she was sure that she could have a man eating out of her palm no matter where she was. But to what end?

She could hear Stefan's voice in her head. *Those empty sugar-high orgasms you like so much*, he'd said, and she was very much afraid he'd ruined them for her. Because who wanted hollow junk-food sex when there was…him?

Meanwhile, despite her *Bristol-ness*, her sister had sounded happy.

Happy.

And for all that Indy had spent her life pursuing fun at all costs, had she remembered to make sure that she was happy while she was doing it?

Do you even know what happy is? asked another voice inside, this one sounding a whole lot like her father.

She called home, smiling when she heard her father's grumpy voice on the other end.

"Do you know what time it is here?" he asked, instead of saying hello. "Don't tell me you forgot to look at the time change. I think we both know you do it deliberately."

"Hi, Dad," she said, affection for him racing through her and warming her. "You sound deeply stressed out. Isn't it a Saturday?"

She heard his laugh and could picture him easily, back in that house where she'd grown up. It was a little after six o'clock in the morning, Ohio time, but she knew perfectly well he hadn't been asleep. Margie liked an extra few hours to catch up on her beauty sleep every weekend, but not Bill. He worked all week, as he liked to say, and therefore liked to be up and at it on the weekends to squeeze out every drip of leisure time available.

"It's a fine Saturday," her father said. "I have big plans. The hardware store, a little project in your mother's vegetable garden, and I'm going to fire up the grill for dinner. Did you call to hear my itinerary? You're not normally the itinerary sort, are you, Bean?"

Bean. She couldn't remember why he'd started calling her that, only that he always had. And that something inside her would break forever if he ever stopped.

"I want to ask you a life question, Dad," she said, and though her voice was pleasant enough, her heart still hurt. Walking down from Stefan's hillside villa hadn't helped at all.

"You're the one gadding about in Europe. Mysteriously. Seems you have it figured out."

She hadn't told him—or anyone—where, precisely, in Europe she was. Because everything concerning Stefan had seemed too private. Too personal.

And because if she told them what she was doing, she would have to tell them why. Which could only lead to explaining things better left un-explained. Or, worse, coming back after a night or two and having to explain that instead.

Better not to risk any of that. "What is *gad-ding* anyway?" she asked. "No one ever says, *oh, I think I'm up for a* gad. *Come join me in some* gadding."

"Is this one of your internet games?" She heard sounds she recognized. Her father puttering around in the kitchen. The cabinets and the fridge opening and closing as he made himself the English muf-fin he liked to eat every morning, getting out the honey and butter to use when the toaster made it the exact shade of tan he preferred. "You know I don't like being recorded."

"That was only the one time. I told you I wouldn't do it again. And besides, you were amaz-ing. You still have fans on my page."

"Then my life is complete," Bill said dryly. "Every man needs fans on a webpage."

"Are you happy, Dad?" Indy asked before she lost her nerve. "I mean truly happy?"

There was a small pause, and Indy screwed her eyes shut. But when she did, all she could see was her dad at the kitchen window half a world away, staring out at the backyard and the woods, his brow furrowed in thought.

"Are you in trouble, Bean?" her father asked, his gruff, joking tone changed to something quieter that made the knots in her seem to swell to twice their size. "Because you know that all you have to do is say the word and your mother and I will be on the next plane. No matter where you are. Or what you're doing."

And something flooded her then, bright and sweet, because she knew he meant that. Her parents, who had always seemed so deeply content to be exactly where they were—who didn't take the kind of trips their daughters did, or even their friends did, and never seemed all that interested in far off places—would think nothing of racing to her side if she needed them.

Shouldn't she be happy with that? Why did she need more? Why did anyone need more? There were a whole lot of people who didn't even have what she did.

"I'm fine," she hurried to assure him. "I was just thinking about what happiness really is. And you and mom always seem so content, I figured you must know."

"You always said contentment was a fate worse than death," her father reminded her, though he laughed when he said it. "When you were thirteen, you and your sister made solemn vows to leave this town and never come back, because neither one of you had any intention of *settling*. You were very sure of yourselves."

"I'm always sure of myself, Dad." That was true enough, but saying it out loud gave her pause. Why was she so sure? That she was bad at school. That she was shallow. That she only wanted what she knew she could get, and even then, only for a little while. She found herself rubbing at her chest again, though she already knew it wouldn't keep her heart from aching. "But that's why I'm calling. I'm asking what you're sure of, for a change."

She expected him to shrug that off. Make a little joke, maybe. Keep things light and easy.

"I think that a happy life is earned," her father said instead, sounding…thoughtful. "Because life itself isn't one thing or another. It's not happy or sad. It just is. Like anything, it's what you make of it. Your mom and I have had some hard times and we've had easy times. But the hard times are better, and the easy times sweeter, because of the work we put in."

"That's something people like to say," Indy whispered. "Putting the work in. But they don't ever say what it means."

"It means you don't let your life just happen to you, Indy," her father said, not unkindly. "You have to live it, good and bad, boring and exciting, one day after the next. It's not meant to be fun all the time. That isn't to say you can't enjoy it, but a life that's only one thing isn't much of a life."

And though she changed the subject then, even talking to her mother for a while when her father passed the phone on because Margie was actually up before nine for a change, it was that part that resonated with her.

A life that was only one thing wasn't much of a life.

She couldn't let it go. She tested herself, finding her way into a bar, and, sure enough, letting a few men flirt with her while she sat in it. But she did not take them up on any of their invitations.

Or their candy-coated anything.

Because her life had been only one thing for a long, long time.

And she hated that Stefan had seized on the reason for that being Bristol, because she loved her sister. Adored her. Supported her, cheered her on, and wanted nothing but the best for her. That didn't change the fact that way back when they were kids, Indy had decided that she was going to go a different way.

Maybe *because* it was different.

Was it that easy? If you made a decision when you were young were you doomed to repeat it ever after?

But no, she thought as she found herself in Old Town Square again. She watched the statues of the apostles appear in the famous Astronomical Clock, doing their thing while the crowd cheered and took pictures. The statue of death waved. And Indy felt a kinship to the funny old thing. Because the clock put on its show at the top of each hour, and it was wonderful. But the rest of the time, no matter how beautiful and old, it was just a clock.

Maybe, for the first time in her life, she didn't want to be the same old thing she'd always been.

And she could admit, then, that Stefan was right about this part, too. Intensity terrified her. The things that Stefan said to her, and all the implications, terrified her even more.

But maybe she'd come all the way to Prague to be terrified. Maybe it was good for her. The fact was, if she paid attention to her orgasms alone, the man knew what he was talking about. Everything with him was dialed up to one hundred or more. Everything with him was *more*. Longer. Deeper.

Better.

What did it say about her that all she'd wanted was to finally come to Prague, to meet him here, and yet she'd run off the minute it got to be too much for her? Was she really that person? Deep down, she knew she'd woken up scared silly that first morning and had been running ever since. Because he'd touched things in her she hadn't known were there.

Over the past two years she'd convinced herself that she'd imagined the intensity. That it had been the circumstances, not the man.

But the truth was, Stefan still felt like fate.

Like destiny.

She might like to tell anyone who asked that she was shallow and silly, but deep down, she didn't think of herself that way. And Stefan was the only person she wasn't related to who didn't take her at face value. Who looked at her and saw depths. Who saw more than her body or her face or what she might look like beside him.

And she knew she should have been horrified that he'd treated her like a research project, but she wasn't. Who else had she ever met who wanted to know *more* about her when they'd already had sex with her? Who refused to accept what they saw?

Even though she'd run off from his house and even though she hadn't been faking her outrage while she'd been there, Indy knew the real truth was she liked it. All of it.

She *liked* how intense he was, little as she knew how to handle it. He'd been that intense the first night she'd met him. Despite what she'd told herself since, she hadn't imagined that part. And she liked what he seemed to be suggesting, that he'd been as shaken by her as she'd been by him. Maybe she just needed time to acclimate to that. To him.

To fate.

Maybe she'd needed to know that she could leave so that she could return.

Because that was what she did, climbing out of a taxi at his front door once again, and this time noticing the security pad on the wall. She let herself in with the key that still hung around her neck, finding the house as bright and sunny as she'd left it. She wandered through the beautiful rooms, amazed that a man she'd met in such a dark and gritty place had made himself a sanctuary like this one. Amazed that he felt the same way, impossibly bright when he should have been something else entirely.

She saw him standing out on the terrace, looking out over the pool toward the city in the distance with his mobile to his ear. He'd changed his clothes, putting on jeans and what looked like a well-loved red T-shirt that made the muscles in his wide back enough to weep over.

He was talking in what she assumed was Romanian when she opened the glass doors and stepped outside. He turned around, his blue gaze coming to her and staying there.

Bright and hard.

He finished his call and shoved his mobile into his pocket, then did nothing at all but regard her where she stood.

"Yes," Indy said, as if she was making proclamations. "I'm back. I went to a bar, just as predicted. Are you happy?"

"Ecstatic."

"I did not have sex with the numerous men I could have had sex with." She studied him for a moment, that face carved of stone that had haunted her for years now. "I think you should take that as a statement of my intentions."

The light in his blue eyes changed. Like a lightning storm. "I will make a note."

"I don't know how to do intensity, Stefan." That sounded a little more uncertain, but Indy didn't let that stop her. "I don't know how to do any of this. This is not the kind of thing I do."

"But you do, foolish girl. You have from the start."

She blew out a breath and then crossed her arms, as if that could help her. "That's very opaque, thank you. Anyway. Here I am. You get your night of wild intensity."

His smile made everything in her seem to stand at attention. "No. I am afraid that is no longer on offer."

"It's not?" And she was… Crushed. There was no other word for it.

But he was still holding her gaze. "A night will not do it. I'm tired of these one-night games. You will give me a month, Indiana. And then we will see where we are."

"A month?" She thought her teeth actually chattered. "I don't know if I can."

"You can," Stefan told her, and *he* was sure. He was commanding and certain in all things. She liked that, too. Maybe too much. "Because it is a month or nothing. Which will you choose?"

And when he put it like that, it was simple.

CHAPTER EIGHT

JUNE FADED, TURNING into a sweet, golden July that seemed to stretch on into forever.

Maybe he only wished it could.

Stefan had never spent much time contemplating the seasons. They marched on, one after the next, and what mattered was surviving what they wrought. Summer had simply been warmer than the bitter winters, but life had carried on the same. The less said about his childhood the better. Ditto the army. And since then, he'd been far too busy catapulting toward his dark future to spend any kind of deliberate time in the light.

But this summer he was in Prague. The only place on the planet that he had ever viewed not just as an escape, but as safe. It was where his grandmother had showed him that there was more to life than his father's heavy fist.

And now, fittingly, Prague was where he and his Indy were finally coming to terms.

I'll give you a month, she'd said that first afternoon. When she'd left him but come back, looking jittery and wide-eyed and still somehow stubborn.

Still stubborn, even as she'd surrendered.

Even as she gave him what he wanted, she did it her way.

He'd thought again of a splash of red in a dark alley. And how quickly, how irrevocably, this woman had happened along and changed everything. It was a good thing he had always been a practical man, or he might have been tempted to tear down a wall or two. With his bare hands, just to feel them fall.

Anything to feel as if he could control the things he felt for this woman. As if he could control himself the way he always had before her.

But he had a month. And Stefan intended to use it.

Let me guess, she'd said that first afternoon, when all he'd done was gaze at her, victory and something that felt too much like relief pounding through him. *You require nudity at all times. Blowjobs morning, noon, and night. Is that the kind of intensity you have in mind?*

It is never a bad place to start, he'd said, already amused. *As I think you know.*

She had already told him that not indulging in her usual behavior, out there where she could have lovers eating from her hand with a single glance, was a statement of her intent. But Stefan didn't think he was the only one who thought that really, when she crossed the terrace to kneel down at his feet, then held his gaze while she took him into her mouth again, that it was a new set of vows.

And for the first few days, it was enough to simply have her near. To know that there would be no renegotiation come the dawn. That she had promised him a month and that meant she wouldn't sneak out when he was on his run or while he was dealing with the inevitable phone call.

Not that she struck him as the type to *sneak* anywhere. But then, before her, he hadn't been the type to worry about what a woman might be doing. Or about anything at all save getting richer and staying in one piece.

"I thought you walked away from your business," she said when he finished one of those calls, standing out in the dusk and testing himself. Not looking back into the house to see what she was doing. Not checking to make sure she was where he'd left her.

He supposed that was trust. Or a gesture in its direction. And in him, trust was a muscle that had atrophied long ago—but for her, for them, he would work on it.

Stefan had been cooking Indy a traditional Romanian dinner when the call had come in. He walked back in now, something in him shifting—

not quite uncomfortably—at the sight of her standing there at his stove. The kitchen was warm and bright, filled with the scents of his childhood, and Indy there in the middle of everything. She was barefoot, wearing those cutoff shorts that he had become a little bit obsessed with. Her hair was tied in a big knot on the top of her head, letting him look at her elegant neck and her shoulder blades beneath the airy tank she wore. Her bracelets sang small, happy songs every time she moved.

He felt his heart beat harder in his chest, the way it did now.

And he knew that two years ago he would have called what surged in him then a kind of horrifying neediness. He would have found it unpardonable. A weakness. He would have tried to excise it with his own fingers, if he could.

But that had been before. Before she'd walked into his world and knocked it straight off its axis.

"I walked away from my major business, yes," he replied. "The part that would be frowned upon by any number of law enforcement agencies."

"Then why are you still taking business calls?"

Once again he was struck by the fact she simply sounded interested. Not trying to score any points. Not building toward some kind of agenda. Just interested in him as a person.

And only when he acknowledged how rare that was could Stefan also admit that he liked it. That he wasn't sure how he'd lived without it all this time.

"I always intended to retire from the more dangerous part of my business eventually," he told her, and opted not to share how difficult that had turned out to be. It was clear to him that if he'd stayed in any longer than he had, exiting would not have been possible—and he didn't like that at all. He'd always imagined himself in control of the things he did. "I only expedited the process. I am sure I told you this."

She looked over her shoulder at him, laughter in her gaze. "I guess I didn't realize you had a legitimate arm of whatever had you gun slinging in an alley in Budapest."

Stefan went over to the stove and took the wooden spoon from her hand, nudging her away from his pot. "My money is perfectly legitimate. And as you know, money invested wisely makes more money."

"That's what you do? Invest?"

"Isn't that what you do?"

"I travel all over the globe, wherever my mood takes me," she said airily. "My investments fuel that lifestyle, sure, but so do the jobs I take when I want some cash. But what about you? What do you like to do?" She lifted up a hand when he started to answer that. "Don't say me. You had a whole life before you met me, Stefan. And in the years since. What is it you actually *like*?"

Another question no one had ever asked him. A question he'd hardly dared ask himself some years, because how could it matter what he liked? He had needed to focus on surviving, like it or not.

"Art," he said, without letting himself brood about it.

And he cautioned himself against putting too much weight on the fact that he'd never told anyone that before. His grandmother was the only person in his life who might have been interested in such things—but she had been a stoic, stern woman. It had never been her way to chatter idly.

Still, he found himself looking sideways to see what Indy's reaction might be. Would she laugh? His heart kicked at him. Would she laugh *at* him?

He had never put himself in this position before. Where another person's opinion could hold so much weight.

The truth was, he did not care for the feeling.

But all she did was nod, looking off across the room. When he followed her gaze, he saw that she was looking at a bold piece he'd bought years ago in Cluj, known for an avant-garde art scene to rival Bucharest's claims of being Romania's artistic capital. He'd had it installed here in this house, his cathedral to what could be.

What could be—and now was.

"All the art you have in this house is beautiful," she said, moving that dreamy look of hers to him. "Interesting and confronting and lovely. Is that why the rooms are so airy here? So that the art is what's seen?"

"I spent most of my life in dark, desperate places," Stefan told her, and his voice was rougher than he would have allowed it to be for anyone else. But this was Indy. And he could hardly demand her vulnerability if he wasn't prepared to share his own, could he? "My mother did her best to make the places we lived feel more like a home, but my father always ruined it. Any extra money we had went to his debts or his drink. After she died, there was no point bothering."

"I'm surprised you remembered art existed at all," Indy said softly.

"Art is not something a person forgets." He scowled down at his pot, this sentimental meal from one of the few good moments of his childhood, as if only just noticing that there was no part of what he was doing here tonight that wasn't emotional. But he couldn't seem to stop himself. "The perfection of a finely drawn line. A pop of color that changes everything. I saw pieces I liked over the years and had them sent here, telling myself that one day I would come here, live here, and have them all around me all the time. But that day never seemed to come any closer. Then I looked up from an ordinary evening of the typical darkness in my life, and there you were. All your fine lines and a splash of red in the night. I knew you were art, too."

He snuck a look at her and found her gazing back at him, her lovely eyes filled up with tears.

Stefan could tell that she was trying out this intensity thing, as he'd asked her to do, because she didn't dance away. She didn't start singing, or change the subject, or move closer so she could put her mouth on him and distract them both. He almost wished she would. Instead, Indy let him see her respond. React.

All those emotions he knew she would have said she didn't possess. Right there in her eyes like the finest chocolate.

"My grandmother left me her flat down Old Town when she passed," he told her, because he couldn't seem to stop. Maybe he didn't want to stop. "It was filled with art. Maybe she was why I never forgot the power in it. I bought this house before she was gone, but it wasn't until then that I began to make it mine. Even if I only made it here once a year, if that, I knew it waited here. I knew that I could come, walk these rooms, and let the art I'd chosen make me believe I was a different man. A better man. I told myself it didn't matter how far off *one day* was. For a long time, knowing this was here was enough."

Indy drifted close and bumped him with her shoulder, a kind of unconscious gesture that about laid him flat. Because it was the antithesis of any of the ways they touched. It wasn't sex. It wasn't the prelude to sex. It didn't have anything to do with sex at all.

But it was intimate.

And even though Stefan was the one who'd confidently thought he'd already done all the changing necessary, he felt something in him crack wide open.

"It seems like you do have a home after all, then," she'd said quietly, her eyes shining. "That's not a small thing, is it?"

And he didn't know how to tell her than nothing that happened between them, or because there was a *them* at all, had ever been small.

But later that night, after he'd tied her up so she didn't have access to her usual bag of tricks, then made her sob and scream until he was satisfied that she didn't have a single thought in her head without his name on it, Stefan lay in the dark with the soft weight of her in his arms and wondered what he would do if a month was not enough.

Because he did not think that any place would soothe him now, not when he knew how much better it was when she was here. Lighting up already bright rooms with that smile of hers, making the world stop again and again while she did it.

He knew it did no good to worry about the future. There was only now.

July continued on.

Some days he bossed her around, because he could. Because it made both of them hot.

"I think, foolish girl, that I will have you naked today," he would say.

Sometimes she grinned wickedly and looked thrilled at the notion. Other days she had different reactions, not all of them positive. One morning she scowled at him, blinking the sleep out of her eyes while she did it.

"Why do you call me that? Maybe I should call you *foolish man*. Would you like that?"

"You can call me whatever you like," he told her. "But you will always be my very own foolish girl, who wandered into the dark and brought me out into the light."

And he watched, sprawled there beside her in the bed they shared, while she melted at that.

"Well." Her voice was grumpy, but her eyes were bright and shining. "I guess it's okay then."

"Naked," he reminded her.

Because naked days were all about power and surrender and all the marvelous things a man with his imagination—and the wicked delight she could never repress for long—could build between them.

"I thought you'd be like that all the time," she panted one night, after the kind of naked day that

CAITLIN CREWS 155

left her so limp and boneless that he'd had to carry her upstairs, bathe her with his own hands, then put her to bed.

He did not mind these tasks, to be clear.

"Like what?" he asked.

"You know. The way you are on naked days. All the rules. All the kneeling. I assumed you'd demand to be called Master Stefan or something and go crazy with nightly spankings and all the rest of that stuff."

He was amused. He was stretched out, propping himself up on one arm, toying with a strand of her hair while he looked down to that heart-shaped face of hers that only grew more beautiful. When surely that should have been impossible. "Is that what you want?"

"Sometimes," Indy replied, grinning up at him. "And sometimes not."

"You do not like a steady diet of anything, Indiana," Stefan said in a low voice, because he knew. And sometimes she was not in the mood to hear all the things he knew. He tugged on the lock of her hair, gently enough. "You thrive on variety. But then, so do I."

"You're the one with a big house full of art. You must like some steadiness in your diet."

He smoothed his hand over her face, her soft cheeks, where heat from her bath still lingered.

"I like you, foolish girl," he said, though he

knew he should not have. "Have I not made that clear?"

She smiled at him, though he thought he saw shadows in her gaze. "I'm not really a dietary staple. I'm more of an occasional dessert."

"I like dessert, too," he offered.

But she laughed and ran a hand over his chest, then down over his ridged abdomen. "*Do* you?"

The days passed. Stefan watched her, closely. He expected her to show signs of claustrophobia. To act as if it was sheer torture to stay in one place, with one man, for so long. He wasn't sure she'd ever tried before. He anticipated that she would make it clear she was *doing him a favor*.

And yet, as one week became another, and another, if Indy was restless she failed to show it.

"I asked my father about happiness," she told him one afternoon. "I wanted to know if he was as happy as it seems he is."

They sat in the shade outside, beneath a trellis draped in blooming roses. He was working on his laptop while she curled up beside him, reading a book in between her dips in the pool. Not naked, sadly. It seemed the tiny little bright yellow bikini she wore was, apparently, one of the surprising number of items she'd managed to roll up and stick in that tiny pack of hers.

"I never needed to ask my father such a question," he had replied, not looking up from his screen. "I already knew the answer. It was his fist, preferably connecting with my face."

"I guess I can understand that," she said with a quiet ferocity. "Because I'd very much like to plant my fist in his face. And imagining it makes *me* happy."

He looked up then, entertained and touched in equal measure that his carefree, relentlessly non-judgmental Indy had it in her to sound so blood-thirsty. Much less on his behalf.

"He died as he lived, never fear," Stefan assured her. "As we all must."

Indy had her book open in her lap and she turned it over then, frowning at him. "In a way, that's what my father said. But how can you tell if you're living life the way you should be?"

"There is no *should*. There are only the choices you make in each moment, strung together to make a day. A week. And sooner or later, a life that is the sum of its parts."

There was the sound of the breeze rustling through the trees. Lawn mowers growled in the distance while up above them, birds sang and bees hummed. But Indy didn't return to her reading.

"The thing is," she said after a moment, halt-ingly, "I never saw myself in competition with Bris-tol. It was so important to her that she be the smart one. And if she was the smart one, then I got to be the pretty one." She blew out a breath. "For a long time, that was all I really wanted."

"I've seen your sister," he said, though Indy knew that already. She called her sister daily and had told him, with glee, that she was responsible for her sister becoming girlfriend to Lachlan Drummond, the billionaire who couldn't seem to keep his face out of the tabloids. The same tabloids that featured Indy's sister, now—and that she liked to brandish at him. "Whether she is smarter or not, I couldn't say. But she is also pretty. Surely you both know this."

"She's gorgeous, obviously. Hello. She's my sister." She smiled while she said that, but it faded. She toyed with the spine of her book. "It seems silly now. But for some reason, back when we were kids, it seemed absolutely crucial that we choose. We had to make sure that there was always a critical and obvious distance between us. Bristol disappeared into her books. And I…"

For a moment it seemed as if she didn't intend to go on.

"And you?" Stefan asked.

To his surprise, she flushed slightly. "I did what I always do. I flitted around from group to group. I was everybody's best friend, but they were never mine. I kissed all kinds of boys, even before my fateful relationship with Jamie Portnoy." She shook her head. "If anyone had asked, I would've sworn on a stack of Bibles that I was a born extrovert."

He had a sense of where this was going now, but he only waited, sitting back to better watch her lovely face as she spoke. And to enjoy the way she used her hands as emphasis, drawing pictures in the air.

Stefan wanted to tell her that already, she had bloomed here. That the frenetic edge to her was gone, because she didn't have to plan her quick escape. Because living as they were, only the two of them in this house, it was impossible to maintain any kind of performance. He had seen her in all kinds of moods. The ones she would cheerfully admit as well as the ones she pretended she didn't have. He'd held her when she sobbed at a movie, then pretended she hadn't. He held her when she sobbed out her pleasure, then gave it back to him tenfold.

They woke every morning tangled around each other, as if in sleep they instinctively wanted nothing but to get closer.

Indy had not retreated from any of this. She had not run.

"But for weeks now," she was saying, frowning at the roses, "I've been here. With you and all these books. I think I forgot how much I like to read. And how, if things had been different, I might have liked to disappear into books, too."

"I'm glad," he said, and meant it. "You should."

She shifted, turning her body so she could hold his gaze. "But I was really good stripping, Stefan."

He laughed. "This I believe."

"It was fun. And I mean really fun. Maybe partly because I was actually paying for college, *and* saving, *and* doing something illicit at the same time. You may not know this about me—" and her eyes sparkled as she gazed at him "—but I really do kind of love it when people try to shame me for the things I enjoy."

"Shame does not sit well on you, Indiana." He wanted to reach for her, but checked himself. Because once again, this was not a sexual moment. He felt something more like sacred, and he was determined that he would honor it. "I am glad of that, too."

And she didn't have to tell him that they were only his, these moments that were all the more intense because they were not about sex. He could feel it in his bones.

"I stopped going to classes in college because I liked them too much." Her voice was solemn, then, as if she was making a painful confession. Her eyes lost some of that sparkle. Stefan still waited. "I was getting an A in one class, so I made sure to skip out on the final because it was half my grade. And I had already made my choice, hadn't I?" She searched his face for a moment. "How did you know that? Because you knew that, didn't you?"

"I suspected."

"No one else has ever thought there was anything more to me than a good fuck," Indy said, her voice hardly above a whisper. "Not even me."

He picked her up then. He hauled her into his lap and held her there, smoothing one hand over her damp hair and then holding her face tipped up to his so there could be no evasion. No hiding.

"There is much more to you than that," he told her, his voice nearly a growl. He reached between her legs, beneath the damp scrap of her bathing suit, and found her molten hot. Swollen with need, as always. "Your pussy is one of the great wonders of this world, Indiana. But it is only an addiction because it's yours."

He stroked her, playing with her slippery folds and circling her clit until she moaned.

She bucked against him, her breath feathering out. "I've spent my whole life hiding, but you saw right through me. I still don't understand how."

"You understand."

Stefan held her clit between his thumb and forefinger, pinching it in time with her pants. When she moaned again, he twisted his wrist and plunged two fingers deep inside her clinging heat.

"You called me into the light," he growled. "But I found you in the dark. We fit together, two halves of a whole. There was no possibility that you could ever be anything but exactly who you are, not if this was to work. Beautiful, yes. Uninhibited and remarkably sexy, always. I will never get enough of you but even if this—" and he sped up the rhythm of his thrusting fingers, loving the way she clung to him, her fingers digging into him, her eyes half closed "—went away, even if I could never fuck you again, it would change nothing."

"Bullshit," she whispered.

He pulled his hand away, then laughed when she glared at him.

"Who do you want to be, Indy? It's no longer a choice you made as a child. It doesn't matter how you spent your years. We are here now. What do you want to be here?"

She was breathing heavily, her gaze something almost like hostile as she stared back at him—but Stefan knew that had more to do with the fact he hadn't let her come.

"I will tell you what I know in only these short weeks," he said. "You have spent no time at all maintaining your online life. I never see you huddled in a corner, scrolling through your phone, certain you've missed something. You seem genuinely happy. Maybe the trouble is that you don't believe it."

He saw her sit with that. And saw, too, that she didn't like the weight of it.

"The trouble," she said solemnly, "is that you are not inside me."

"You know how to fix that," he growled at her.

And when she went to straddle him, he turned her around. She pulled her bikini to one side as she wriggled against him, arching her back as he pulled out his cock so he could slam himself inside her.

For a moment the sheer wonder of it swept over him. Her too, he knew. They both paused, reveling in that impossible fit.

She might think it was this house. His art collection, or this new, pretty life he'd made for himself. But Stefan knew the truth.

His home was her.

But that wasn't something he intended to tell her. Not yet. He wrapped one arm around her middle, holding her as he began to pound into her. He turned her head so he could take her mouth, because there weren't enough ways to taste her.

There never would be. Not in a lifetime.

Maybe more.

And then he showed her what he could not put into words, and fucked them both home.

CHAPTER NINE

"I'M TRYING TO DECIDE what my great passion in life is," Indy announced one morning into her mobile, and wasn't surprised when Bristol, off in some or other city on her world tour with Lachlan Drummond, laughed.

"I thought that was obvious," Bristol said. "Isn't it?"

Indy had been on her way toward the kitchen when she'd been sidetracked by her current favorite room in Stefan's house. She'd left her book in here yesterday and when she'd come in to retrieve it, had sat down and called Bristol. Her favorite room in the house changed by the day. This one was arranged around a white-bricked fireplace, with only a few throw rugs and a deep red painting to break up the color scheme.

It appealed to her sense of drama.

"Thank you, asshole, but I like sex for fun, not for profit." She let out a theatrical sort of sigh because she knew it would make her sister roll her eyes. "Believe me, if I felt otherwise, I've had ample opportunity to take up sex work."

That was all too true. She'd been offered all kinds of fascinating positions. Some people wanted her to be a dominatrix. Others thought she should lean into the erotic dancing. Or try the yacht-girl thing at Cannes and see if she could make that into an enterprise. One of the women she'd met in the South of France had told her frankly that these days, the internet made it so easy to conduct a personal escort service without having to cut anyone else in, that any woman who *didn't* make money that way was a fool.

Indy had found all of these offers and suggestions fascinating. Surely it said something kind of fabulous about her that so many people thought she could make money from an act she would have done anyway—and for free?

Anyway, she had always chosen to take it as a compliment. No matter how it was meant.

"I would ordinarily express dismay at that sentiment," Bristol said, sounding... Not happy. Not sad either, but almost... Rueful. "But you know. Pot meet kettle and there I am in the middle."

"Signing a contract to be somebody's girlfriend isn't sex work," Indy said loyally. "Not really."

"I think you'll find it is."

"Not at all." Indy waved a hand at Stefan's

white fireplace, as if her sister could see her. "It's nothing more than a prenuptial agreement for a relationship that isn't a marriage. Totally socially acceptable."

"I'll let Mom know then. She'll be so proud."

"Sometimes," Indy said, in a confiding way, "I'm pretty much positive that Mom and Dad might just be bigger freaks than we think. We had to come from somewhere. And maybe there's a reason they've always been perfectly happy to stay home and settle in to that Ohio life. Why bother going out when you have everything you could possibly desire right there with you already?"

"Ew. What? No."

"I'm telling you—I think they have a rollicking—"

"Anyway," Bristol said loudly, cutting her off. "Why are you interested in finding a passion? I thought you always had all the passion a girl could need or want. I thought you liked it that way."

"Men are a passion of mine, it's true," Indy said lightly, because it was expected.

But a bolt of something far more complicated than need went through her as she said it, because when was the last time she'd thought about men in a general sense? She only thought about one man now. And for the past two years, really. *Only and always*, something in her whispered.

Even as she thought that, she was aware that

it wasn't how she operated. She would have said she didn't have that kind of possessiveness in her, but she held on to it anyway. As if it was something precious.

Only and always didn't scare her.

Which, really, was the scariest thing yet.

"Your passion was always academics," she said to her sister, trying to shake that off…whatever it was. But her hand found its way to her heart and stayed there. "I don't really think that a meaningful life is built on an unquenchable thirst for socializing. We can both agree that I've tried."

"You tell me, Indy," Bristol said. "You've had a million temp jobs in the last year alone."

That shouldn't have stung. She told herself that the fact it did meant only that she was tired. And who wouldn't be tired? The kind of demands Stefan liked to make could take whole nights to work out.

Especially because he liked to take it slow.

She shivered. "Yes, yes," she said into her phone. "I can never settle down. I'm not serious. Lack of responsibility, careless and undependable, blah blah blah."

"I didn't mean that as a dig." Bristol's voice was even, and again, faintly rueful. "In a way, I'm envious. You've had the opportunity to try on a hundred different lives without having to commit to any of them. Did none of them appeal to you at all?"

"I guess I didn't think of them as trying on lives," Indy said, considering. "Maybe I should have. They were just jobs that I could leave whenever I wanted. It never occurred to me that someday, I might want... I don't know. A career. Or at least a purpose."

There was a long silence. Indy found herself sitting up straighter, her heart pounding. Because she'd just admitted something, hadn't she? Whether she meant to or not.

Something she hadn't admitted to herself before.

"And what exactly has prompted all of this fascinating speculation?" Bristol asked after a moment, sounding far more intrigued.

Bristol was stubbornly refusing to ask what exactly Indy was doing, and where, despite Indy breezily saying things like *I'm summering on the Continent, Bristol. As you do.*

That meant, as a matter of sisterly principle, Indy could not tell her.

"We all come to these crossroads, Bristol," she murmured. "One way or another."

And though she'd meant to sound mysterious, the words landed in her as if they'd been carved in stone.

"I can't tell you what to do," Bristol said, and again, there was that note in her voice. Maybe it wasn't *rueful*, necessarily. Maybe it was a kind of *aware* that echoed a little too sharply inside Indy just at the moment. "I wouldn't dream of trying. But I can tell you that I've always admired your fearlessness."

Of all the things her older sister might have said, she hadn't been expecting that. Indy had a sudden flashback to a particular day of playing games of make-believe with Bristol in their backyard, running around and around the old oak tree that had stood there for hundreds of years. They'd decided it was their castle.

I'm going to be the princess, Indy had announced, though really, she was looking for Bristol's permission. As the oldest and the bossiest, it fell to Bristol to make the decisions. *I'm always the princess.*

Bristol had looked back at her with all the bone deep weariness a ten-year-old could muster when faced with a younger sister.

That's actually because you decided *to be the princess, Indy,* she'd said loftily. *You could decide to be a wizard instead. Or a warrior. You know it's up to you, right?*

Indy could remember that moment so clearly, which was funny, given she hadn't thought of those games they'd played in a million years. Eight-year-old Indy had stared back at her older sister, a part of her desperate to leap out into the unknown. To take on a role she'd never played before and *decide* to be whatever she wanted.

But she hadn't.

Was it really Bristol deciding to get serious about her studies that had sent Indy down this path? Or had she been the one who'd chosen it all along?

Because she'd chosen the part of princess that day, out there playing make-believe. It had been familiar. It had required nothing of her. She could have played that role in her sleep.

In a way, she'd been playing it ever since.

"My fearlessness?" she echoed now. Then laughed. "I guess I fooled you, then. I don't think I'm fearless at all."

"Maybe that's not the right word," Bristol conceded. "Maybe it's that no matter if you're afraid or not, I've never known you to let that keep you from doing something. Even when we were kids. You always jumped in, no matter how deep the water was. No matter if everyone and their mother told you not to do something, you wanted to see yourself. And you did. I admire that, Indy. I always have."

"I love you, too," Indy whispered.

And then they'd mutually hung up on each other as quickly as possible, so there would be no sniffling.

But her sister's words stayed with her when she

got up from her white chair in the white room with its powerful splash of red. They haunted her as she wandered through the house, looking for Stefan the way she did more times every day than she would have imagined possible. Given that she'd never been one to *look for* a man before.

He isn't just a man, a voice inside her chided her. *And you know it.*

She knew that he'd come back from his run this morning because he'd woken her up then. He'd flipped her over on her belly and had her digging her fists into the mattress and moaning out her pleasure before she'd even opened her eyes.

Indy had never been the kind of woman to claim she didn't like morning sex. She'd never understood the complaint, because what wasn't to love? A hard cock moving deep inside her before she was awake, so she fell out of sleep and into an orgasm without having to do anything at all. It was like a gift.

But she'd never loved it more than she did with Stefan, who made it something far hotter and deeper than any mere *gift*.

Sometimes he used the gym he'd installed on the lowest level of the house after his run, but he wasn't there when she looked. She trooped back up to the kitchen, eying the ibrik that sat by the stove—the correct name for the pot he used to make Turkish coffee, as he'd informed her when she'd called it *that thingie*—and even though he'd showed her how to make it herself, she didn't. Because she liked it better when he made it for her.

She looked around outside, down by the pool and in the gardens. His laptop sat closed on the table in the shade of the rose trellis, but Stefan himself was nowhere to be found.

Maybe you'll just have to sit here with your thoughts, she told herself wryly. *Instead of hoping he'll distract you.*

Indy sat there at the table, because that felt a lot like a challenge. She frowned out at the view, telling herself that she was *fearless*. Bristol had said so. And surely, if she thought about that enough and didn't try to avoid it in the heat of another orgasm, her heart would open up wide and give her a passion.

A purpose.

A life she wanted, not the one she'd chosen when she was a kid who didn't know any better.

And that was where Stefan found her sometime later. With his usual disconcerting telepathy, he set a cup of Turkish coffee before her, as if he'd been standing about invisibly in the kitchen and had watched her decide not to make her own.

"You look distressed," he observed, his accent washing over the way it always did, like a caress. "What could possibly have happened since I left you, limp and moaning out my name?"

"Many things, Stefan. Many important and exciting things, none of which I'm going to tell you if you're going to keep bragging about your sexual prowess. It's so unattractive."

His blue eyes gleamed. "Is it?"

She laughed as he sat down beside her.

"I like that," he said.

"What?" she asked, though she was already distracted by his proximity. Indy had never been into the drugs that, he was right, had been a huge part of a great many of the scenes she'd frequented over the years. Strip clubs and all kinds of other parties, in all different countries.

But Stefan was far more potent than any party.

It was amazing what all this time with him was doing to her. Day after day of this. Of them. It made everything seem to take a different shape. Though the way she wanted him only seemed to increase, it was different now. Because she knew that she would have him.

Sooner or later, she would have him again.

It made the waiting hotter.

It made the wanting deeper.

"When you laughed now, you mean it," Stefan said quietly. "I like it."

And he didn't wait for her to react to that, the way he sometimes did. He didn't study her, tracking every stray emotion as she had it. This time it was a matter-of-fact statement. Then he picked up his laptop and cracked it open.

Leaving Indy there beside him with the sweet and rich taste of his coffee on her tongue, and a new ache in her heart.

It took her some time to compose herself. To gaze at the roses, let their scent fill her, and remind herself that she'd fooled at least one other person into believing she was fearless.

"How did you know that you'd be good at…what you used to do?" she asked.

The look Stefan shot at her was amused. "I did not know. I did it and did not die. Again and again. This is how I decided it was good." The corner of his mouth kicked up, and she knew by now that it was his real smile. She could see the way it made his eyes gleam. "Also I made money. This was also good."

"Some people have a calling, you know." Indy sighed. "Is something wrong with us that we don't?"

"If you want there to be." He reached over and tapped her on the nose. "Yes, some people have a calling. But everybody has a life. You are not required to choose your path once, long ago, and never deviate from it again. Maybe those who live that way are lucky. But then again, maybe not. Maybe it is better to try many things, so that when you choose, you know you chose well."

"Says the gangster who's made himself an art dealer."

His smile sharpened. "All art dealers are gangsters, Indiana. Ask any artist."

That night, everything seemed hotter. Brighter.

She knew by now that the kind of intensity she'd been so afraid of was both better and worse than she'd feared. Better, because it didn't wreck her and it made everything sing, in and out of bed. But it did ask more of her than she'd ever given before. It was the intimacy of this month together. It was staying put and more than that, letting herself enjoy what that was like. To relax into the time. To do it without daydreaming where she'd go next.

It was the conversations they had, rambling and endless, picking up and carrying on from one hour to the next. From one night into the next afternoon, making her think things like *forever*.

It was Stefan himself. This wild thing they'd built between them.

And it was worse, too, because it had an expiration date.

But Indy didn't like to think about that.

It was a long night. Stefan woke her again and again, taking her in every way he could, almost as if he was marking her. Imprinting himself on her and inside her, making her body his so that there would be nothing left of her that wasn't his.

A thought that made her come all around him, screaming out his name.

The next morning he was there when she woke, looking down at her with a stark expression on that beautiful face of his.

She blinked, then moved closer, searching his gaze as she fit her palms to his jaw. His beard had come in and scraped at her skin, but she loved it. She loved the heat. She loved—

Careful, she warned herself. *Be very careful.*

"What's the matter?" she asked him.

"Today is a naked day, foolish girl," he said, darkly. And she remembered, vaguely, that she'd once complained about that endearment. When now it was like a song inside her, sweet and long. "And it will be intense."

"Isn't it always?"

But she had hardly recognized the smile he gave her then. It didn't make it to his eyes.

"This will be different," Stefan told her. "Because this will be the last."

CHAPTER TEN

"Stefan..." Indy began.

But he didn't want to hear it.

Because their month was up tomorrow and the only thing she seemed to want to talk about was how to find her passion.

Meaning, clearly, it wasn't him.

He was going to have to find a way to be okay with that.

Tomorrow.

"Quiet," he said now, his voice low. "Today will be a day of silent reflection."

Indy laughed, and not in the genuine way he loved. "I don't think that it will."

"If you are not quiet," he continued in the same tone, feeling the anticipation in him surge, "I will find a way to encourage you. You do like it when I spank you, don't you?"

"You can do whatever you want," she said. "But first—"

"No," he said, cutting her off. "No *first*. On your knees, foolish girl. There's much to do today."

Indy looked a little surly, but she obeyed him. Because she knew by now that when it came to naked days and power exchanges, he meant what he said.

And she loved that he did. She told him so, but even if she hadn't, the way she melted in his hands would have done the trick.

"You might want to do something about the insolence in that gaze of yours," he murmured as she sucked him in deep. "Or you can be sure I will."

She lowered her lashes immediately, but he knew full well that he would have the opportunity to express himself as the day wore on.

Because Indy loved to play sex games, but she was only submissive when she thought it was hot. It wasn't a lifestyle.

Too bad, he thought, because if it were, he would simply order her to stay with him and that would be the end of it.

But that wasn't who he was, either.

He came with a roar, his hands deep in her hair. And he watched, feeling himself heat up all over again as she swallowed him down, then smiled as if she was the one in control.

Sometimes he couldn't tell either.

And this was the last day, so he knew this was going to go, didn't he? The only mystery was how she would leave. He didn't think she would creep away in the night. He thought she would put on one of her performances. A lot of laughter, probably some sweetness, and then she would dance away into what was left of the summer, leaving him here with whatever was left of him.

He would have to find a way to accept that.

Because this was the tyranny of wanting things he couldn't simply take. This was the problem with the intensity he demanded from her. For the first time in his life, he had something to lose. He would have to live without her, knowing what it was like to have her.

He hated it.

And he took it out on her delectable body.

They both liked toys, so he fitted her with one of her favorites, then made her walk down the stairs with it in. He made her keep it in, so that even the act of standing with him in the kitchen while he calmly made coffee made her blush and shift from foot to foot, moaning a little.

"Do not come without my permission," he said as he poured the Turkish coffee into two cups and then carried them outside. Where he had her sit in the sun, letting the light dance all over her skin while she squirmed in her seat and looked at him like he was the best kind of monster. "Or you will regret it."

"I already regret it," Indy retorted, her voice

rough and greedy, just the way he liked it. "It's torture."

"It is not. But it could be. Is that what you would like?"

"I would like to talk—"

"A spanking it is, then."

Stefan pushed back his chair and patted his lap, lifting one brow.

Indy stared back at him, naked but for the way her hair tumbled down over her shoulders. And oh, he loved to watch the expressions that moved over her lovely face. At first she looked mutinous. He saw the distinct flash of her temper. And then, almost despite herself, the heated awareness that became a flush. Her nipples hardened. Her lips fell open.

She muttered something beneath her breath but she got up, crossed to him, and draped her naked body over his lap. Deliberately making it awkward when he knew how graceful she was, as yet another level of protest.

"I'm not really into this, you know," she told him as he widened his legs to keep her where he wanted her. But could feel the way she melted into him, no matter what she said. "Not when you seem mad. Which, by the way, you do."

"Yes, I can see how not into it you are," Stefan murmured, his hands playing between her thighs. He gripped the base of the toy and fucked her with it until goosebumps broke out all over her back and the sweet curve of her ass.

He was not mad. But he did not wish to tell her what he was.

Maybe he didn't know where to begin.

"Stefan..." she started. Again.

"I told you to be quiet," he reminded her. "But there are some lessons you do not want to learn, Indiana. Maybe today, you will."

He removed the toy. And then he paddled her. He didn't go easy on her, either. He spanked her until her ass was red and she was sobbing with a mixture of outrage and pleasure. And the more she sobbed, the slicker and hotter she got between her legs.

When she melted against him again he pulled her up to bend her over the table before him, fumbling with his trousers before he thrust himself inside her.

Inside her, where he belonged.

Stefan pounded into her, making sure he smacked up against her reddened ass with every thrust.

Then she was coming, sobbing out his name. Then he was too, and it was all heat and intensity and how could she walk away from all this?

Because she was Indy. That was what she did.

He pulled out of her, but she stayed where she was, looking thoroughly debauched, tossed across the table.

"Will you make it?" he asked her dryly.

She didn't open her eyes. He bent over her, wiping away the moisture beneath each eye, and found himself tenser than he ought to have been—at least until she smiled. Sleepily, but smugly, as if she'd gotten exactly what she wanted.

"That's almost as good as your Turkish coffee," she murmured.

Stefan didn't keep her in the sun too long, but he did keep her naked.

He took her back inside and commandeered one of his sitting rooms. He let her recover from their first round, but when she was awake again and sitting up—if gingerly—he started all over again.

And this round, he really took his time.

Indy finally screamed out her release and shattered. He followed, but recovered far more quickly. He brought her a tall glass of water and some crackers, setting them down near the couch where he'd left her, seemingly dead to the world.

Then he watched her as she slowly came back to life.

First she opened her eyes. Then she slowly pulled herself up to sitting position. She gazed back at him for a time, almost without comprehension. Then she looked a bit more like herself, and reached out for the water. She drank deep, ate a few crackers, and frowned at him.

"I get that you like intensity, Stefan. But this seems over the top." She considered him for another long moment. "Even for you."

"Then let us make it more intense," he suggested. He was already sitting across from her, so he settled into his seat. Then waved a hand. "Make yourself come."

"Now? Really?" She sputtered a little. "When we just…?"

"Now," he ordered her quietly. "It may take some time. And I do not want you to close your eyes, Indiana. You will look at me. The whole time."

He could see what she thought of that. Not much at all. Her cheeks were almost as red as her butt as she shifted around on the sofa. She shoved her hair back from her face, then stared at him as if she didn't have the slightest idea how to find her own pleasure.

That was no problem. Stefan was happy to tell her.

"I want you kneeling," he said. "Right there on that sofa. Thighs apart, breasts thrust toward me, and your hands between your legs. Go on, Indiana. I won't ask again."

She shivered, and he knew her too well now. He knew she wanted to fight him. He knew she was even now weighing whether the punishment might well be more delicious than the obedience.

And he saw the precise moment she decided not to test his will.

Not then, anyway.

Indy knelt up on the couch, arranging herself just as he'd ordered. He heard her breath leave her in a little sigh as she ran her hands down her thighs, then tracked her way up again. Then, holding his gaze again, she trailed her fingers up the length of her torso until she found her own nipples.

He expected her to say something. Something racy, no doubt, but all she did was hold his gaze.

Just as he'd demanded.

Then she played with herself, her hair tumbled all around her and her eyes big, wide, and hot on his.

And Stefan was hard. He was always hard when she was around, but that wasn't the worst of it.

The worst was his heart. This last month had made it grow in ways he would have thought impossible had he not lived through it.

Now it beat, didn't it. For her.

Only and ever for her.

And she was still the most perfect thing he had ever beheld. There wasn't a single part of her he hadn't tasted, touched, studied, and made his own. She was his in every possible way. He'd seen to that.

But she was the only one who didn't seem to know it.

Slowly, still obediently holding his gaze, she let her hands move down her body again, settling them between her thighs.

And then, slowly, she began to rock. She thrust her hips into her own palms, again and again. Stefan thought it was the hottest thing he'd ever seen. He saw as she stopped worrying about him and tuned into her own need.

Because she began to pant, her hands moving faster and her hips thrusting, while her wide brown eyes became glassy.

But still she worked, until her skin began to glow from her exertion, and it took everything in him to stay where he was. To stay seated, watching her put on a show.

A show just for him.

Stefan knew that in the days to come, this is what he would hold on to. Indy, so wild and so abandoned, doing as he asked because he'd asked it. Because she wanted to do it. His beautiful Indiana, finding her own heat. He loved the flush on her cheeks and, as she got closer and closer, the way that same flush rolled down her neck until even her breasts looked rosy.

He loved the unmarred perfection of her flesh, when, if asked, he would have said that not only did he generally prefer a woman with tattoos but that Indy seemed the type to have a vast selection of them.

But she didn't. As if she knew, somehow, that no matter how depraved or debauched she might become of an evening, she would always look untouched.

It was mouthwatering.

He loved the way her hair moved with her, and his fingers itched to bury themselves in all that dark silk.

His beautiful girl. His perfect match.

And when she came, she tilted her head back, letting her scream come out like a song.

He let her sob. He fought to catch his own breath. And when she lifted her hands, still shaking everywhere, he crooked his finger at her.

She was still gasping for breath as she moved, coming over to stand before him, shuddering again when he pulled her into his lap.

Stefan was painfully hard, but he did nothing about it. He only held her there, licking her fingers clean as she nestled into him.

And then trying to control the thunderstorm where his heart should be as she drifted off into sleep.

He knew, intellectually, that the day was no longer or shorter than any other. It was a day; that was all. Yet still he would have sworn that this one was the fastest that had ever been.

He cooked as night fell, because it was the only thing he could do. He fed her, then fucked her, but as the night wore on he took her upstairs, spread her out on his bed, and held her to him.

She fell asleep almost instantly. But he refused to give in to any slumber. Not tonight.

He knew that he could have woken her at any point, and that they were so attuned to each other by this time that no matter how tired she was, her body would answer his. With that same joy that marked each and every time they'd come together.

His cock was hard and ready, and more than willing.

But still, Stefan only held her close. And stayed awake, because he wanted to remember every breath. Every small little noise she made as she burrowed deeper into him.

He thought of all things he'd lost, one after the next. His mother and grandmother. The father he should have had, who he'd seen glimpses of now and then, which it only made the reality of his father he actually had worse.

He thought of the things he'd given away, and more, the many things that had been taken from him.

All of it, all the things he'd considered *his whole life* before her seemed to fade away. He would live without her, because he would have no choice.

But he didn't fucking want to.

Stefan knew that living without her, waiting for

her, was the only possible way to win her in the end. Because he knew her now.

And because he knew her, it wasn't surprising in the least that she'd decided she needed to pursue whatever passion she wanted. Or that she would use that passion, whatever it was, as a way to put space between them. The truth was, he'd expected her to fight more against the intimacy he'd asked for here.

Instead, in true Indy style, she'd given him everything.

Was that worse or better, in the end? He couldn't tell. Maybe he would be better suited to handle her departure now if he didn't know how perfectly they fit together.

"I will remember this," he promised her sleeping form. "I will remember everything."

She had not merely become a part of him, as the overwrought Romanian phrase would have it. She was far more than that.

Because if he knew anything, it was this. A man was not meant to hold on too tight to a vision. The vision itself was the gift.

He had made this house of his beautiful. Inviting. A place where a woman like Indy could be comfortable, and stay a while. But she had made it home.

Stefan had already changed the way his world revolved for her. What was waiting a little longer?

Because he knew that chasing this woman of his, filled as she was with wanderlust and that stubborn streak, would only chase her away.

So he held her close as the dawn crept ever closer, settled in, and talked himself into setting her free.

Because that was the only way she would ever come back.

For good.

CHAPTER ELEVEN

INDY SHOULDN'T HAVE BEEN surprised to wake up the next morning to find Stefan gone from their bed.

He had taken intensity to whole new levels yesterday. She sat up carefully, and could feel her body, tight here and a twinge there, in case she'd forgotten. She hadn't.

Good thing it made her feel a little too hot all over again.

She made her way into the shower and stood there a long while, letting the hot water revive her. When she got out and toweled off, she realized that everything inside of her was clear. At last.

Their month was over. He had chosen to end things with that endless, sensual-intensity marathon that made her feel shivery and molten just thinking about it.

She could picture his face, looking somehow more cruel as the day wore on. Even as those hard hands of his took such care with her, though they were the same hands that had spanked her. They'd moved over her body, coaxing her to just one more peak.

Then one more after that.

The man was a sorcerer.

But the thing about his kind of magic was that, here on this most momentous morning after, Indy finally felt swept clean.

All the muddling around, all the *wondering*, was all gone. Everything clicked into place.

She felt it hum through her, like awareness. Like attraction.

Like certainty.

Like fate, a voice inside her whispered.

She let her hair do what it liked, shoving it behind her ears as she walked back into the bedroom and slipped on her flowy dress. The one she'd been wearing when she'd tried for symmetry in that alleyway, only to have Stefan teach her a lesson about intensity.

A lesson he kept teaching her.

But because she'd learned that lesson, maybe too well, she knew what he'd been doing yesterday. It had been different from what had come before. She'd understood that while it was happening, but it made even more sense now.

Stefan had been saying goodbye.

She padded her way down the grand stairs, running her fingers along the smooth length of the banister as she moved, as if she needed the sensory input. When, maybe for the first time in her whole life, she felt full up.

Indy never liked to think of herself as having a wound that needed healing, or an empty hole inside her, as she'd been accused of more than once. But she couldn't help noticing how different she felt here on the other side of a month of intense intimacy with Stefan.

Her whole life there'd been a kind of edginess in her that skittered over her skin and made her bones feel itchy in her limbs. The urge to keep going. The need to always leave where she was and find something new. But no more.

She'd always been preoccupied with seeing and being seen, but not because she had anything to prove. Indy had discovered early on that when she was feeling lonely—or feeling anything, really—the best cure was to go out somewhere and pretend she was happy.

Until she was.

And when that wasn't on offer, there was always social media, which could amount to the same thing.

At the bottom of the stairs, she slipped her mobile out of the dress's deep pocket, and pulled up her favorite personal account. She took a quick scroll through, on the off chance she'd forgotten what was there. Because she hadn't posted anything since she'd come to Prague.

But the evidence was there before her. It was curated joy.

It wasn't that it was fake. She'd taken all those pictures and had posted them, too. But she understood, in a way she wouldn't have month ago, that while she might not have been trying to prove anything to anyone—the account existed so that any time she felt any emotion she didn't like, she could scroll a little bit and feel like herself again. *Fun*, first and foremost. She collected pictures of the fun she had so in less fun moments she could look at it, remember it, and get back into that space.

And then somewhere along the line, she'd decided fun *was* happiness, and had built her life around it accordingly.

But happiness wasn't a screen of pretty pictures.

Happiness was what happened when there were no screens around to record it.

Indy shoved her phone back into her pocket and wandered toward the kitchen, her feet bare against the smooth floor. It was another bit of input, all of it like whispers next to a shout when she walked into the kitchen and found Stefan there at the counter where he'd once spread her out like a dessert, then feasted.

He didn't seem to move or acknowledge her

presence. He was looking down at his laptop, but she knew. Indy knew full well that he knew she was there.

That it was possible he'd heard the moment she sat up in bed upstairs.

She wouldn't put it past him.

"Am I allowed to speak today?" she asked, coming to stand on the opposite side of the counter, as if they were facing off with each other.

Stefan closed his laptop with a decisive click. His blue gaze pierced through her, lighting her up and leaving scorch marks.

She liked it that way.

Even if his expression was about as closed off as she'd ever seen it.

"You can do as you please," he told her, his voice perfectly even. "You kept your promise. The month is over. The world is yours, Indiana."

"I do love when the world is mine." She smiled. "But surely I can get a little coffee first."

To her delight, or maybe that wasn't the right word for the way her heart leapt in her chest, she saw a muscle move in his lean jaw.

Very much as if Stefan Romanescu was not as in control of himself as he usually was.

As if maybe, just maybe, he was finding this as overwhelming as she did.

She really hoped he did.

He stalked over to the stove, and set about making her the Turkish coffee she was pretty sure she was addicted to now. There were spices, fine coffee, a bit of sugar, and then the boiling. Three times, and all the while, she stood on her side of the counter and took the opportunity to study him.

Because maybe he was the real addiction.

She'd spent two years imagining and reimagining the little bit of time they'd spent together in Budapest. Now she'd had a month and two days. She knew him far better. The sex seemed to get more fantastic every time he touched her. She hadn't been anything like bored.

And it still wasn't enough.

There wasn't a single part of his powerful body she hadn't explored. Her mouth watered just thinking about it. Today he wore jeans and T-shirt, and as usual, elevated both to the kind of art he liked to hang on his walls. A study of a powerful man, she might call it, though the only kind of painting she wanted to do involved her fingers on his skin.

He turned back when the coffee was done, sliding the thick brew into place before her. And his eyes were still poet's eyes, brooding and emotional and all the things he acted as if he wasn't. His mouth was still sensual, and she knew how it felt at her breast, and all the other places he liked to put it.

He was a dream come true, but he was real.

This was *real*.

And she reminded herself that she got to decide what she made of this. Of them. Of her life and what was in it.

She picked up the delicate little cup and sipped at it, sighing a little bit at the first taste of the coffee she never could seem to get enough of.

"Stefan," she began.

But a flash of blue cut her off again.

"Stop," he ordered her. "I know already how this will go."

Indy put her cup down on the counter between them. "Do you?"

"I changed my whole life after that night in the alley," he told her, not sounding quite so even any longer. "This is not figurative speech. I am not exaggerating. I was one thing, then I saw you and I became another. There are some parts of some countries that will remain forever closed to me because of this. I accept it."

"Will people come after you?" she asked, momentarily diverted from the fact this was the end of the month they agreed upon, and he was acting... the way he was acting. "Are you safe?"

Something glittered there in all that blue. "I would never have risked meeting you here if I was not." She saw that muscle in his jaw again. "I would never have risked *you*. That part of my life is over. It is not merely a closed door, you understand. I set it on fire. It is better that way."

"Stefan, I really want—"

"You will listen to me, Indiana."

His voice was a command, but she could see he wasn't as in control of himself as he usually was. And the longer she looked at him, the more she began to suspect that this—that hectic glitter in his gaze and that muscle flexing in his jaw—was Stefan's version of messy.

Of wild.

Once again, she felt her heart swell to three times its size. All the parts of her that had been knotted tight loosened in a rush.

But she was still holding her breath.

"I have never worried about emotion," he told her, his eyes too bright and his voice too dark. "It is not a factor. I like sex. I like women. I like them when they come to me and I do not miss them when they go. Then there was you." He shook his head, as if he was trying to clear it. As if he was the one muddled now. "Nothing about that night made sense. Why were you there? Why weren't you afraid? How was it possible that I could meet a creature such as you over the barrel of a gun?"

"I asked myself a great many of the same questions."

"There is only one thing that makes sense," he continued, his voice gruff. "I fell in love with you the moment I saw you, Indiana. It was that fast, and that mad. This isn't intense between us because I'm an intense person. I never was before. Not with any other woman. It's only you."

Indy understood, then, that this was him stripped naked. That she could see so much in his gaze, he was telling her these things—this was how Stefan Romanescu ripped himself wide open.

"I love you," he said in the same way, as if he was delivering terrible news. "And I will tell you, I did not want to."

She smiled, though her heart was thumping at her. "How flattering."

"I wanted nothing to do with any of this," he growled at her. "What place is there in a life such as mine for a creature as soft as you are? You are too little, too breakable. You clearly have no sense of your own peril. You are American, of all things. And yet I knew that you were it for me. Instantly."

She blew out a breath, shuddery and long. "Why are you telling me this as if you're saying good-bye?"

And the way he smiled then changed him. He made her want to cry.

Maybe she did.

"I fell in love with *you*, Indy," he told her, almost hoarsely. "And I don't want to change you. I don't want to tie you down. I threw out my entire world so that I might try to deserve an angel in an alleyway. How could I pluck off your wings?"

An angel in alleyway. It sounded like a poem,

and even though Indy still felt as if she might cry, there was something laced through it. Something so beautiful it hurt.

"It doesn't take much to deserve me," she told him, though her voice was thick. "I think you've already cracked the code."

But Stefan shook his head again, looking down at where he had his hands braced on the counter. "You have spoken a great deal about how you want to find your passion. I want this for you. And I know who you are, Indy. I know you are not a girl who stays put."

"Stefan—"

He ignored her, lifting that blue gaze to hers. "But I will. I want you to understand that I'm not afraid of anything you might find out there, or anything you might do. I have never been a patient man, but for you, I will wait." He managed to indicate the house with one of those shrugs of his. "I will be here. And I know you'll come back. Maybe more than once. And maybe one day, you will stay."

Indy stared at him, stricken. That look on his face was doing odd things inside of her. He looked so stoic. So resigned. And yet here he was, making this sacrifice, when she knew there was not one inch of this man who was at all good with either waiting, letting go, or sacrificing himself in any way.

She knew it.

She knew *him*.

Maybe what she knew most of all was the two of them, together.

"This is what you think will happen?" she asked softly. "You think the passion I want to find involves going back out there and continuing to do what I've always done?"

That muscle in his jaw twitched, but his gaze remained steady. "If that is what you want, I won't be the one to stop you."

Indy wanted to throw something at him. She wanted to throw herself at him. Hug him a little and maybe shake him while she was at it.

But she didn't do any of those things.

"Well," she said. And maybe made a little meal out of the word. "Look at that. You don't know everything."

Whatever response he'd expected, that clearly wasn't it.

Stefan blinked. His head tilted slightly to one side. And she watched those impossible blue eyes change once more.

Taking on a shade she recognized.

Danger, not sacrifice.

Which was to say, *him*.

"I woke up this morning and everything made sense." It was her turn to look at him steadily. To hide nothing. "Yesterday was so intense it's like it was a key in a lock. You wouldn't let me speak and so I couldn't make excuses. Not even in my own head."

"You don't need to draw this out. You can simply leave. I told you this already."

"And in the middle of all that intensity, the whole world boiled down to this," Indy said, ignoring him. "I didn't think that I was searching for anything, but then I found you. I think you know I've had a lot of steamy nights. I don't normally pay them any attention. They fade away as soon as the sun comes up, and I go on to the next. It was different with you."

"Maybe it was the gun," he suggested, with a glimmer of that dry humor she loved.

She smiled at him, and even she knew that it was a real smile. Because it was for him.

"It was you, Stefan. I thought of nothing else for two years, and then I came here to find that you're everything I had imagined and so much more." Her heart was thundering at her. She felt almost shaky standing still. But she looked at him and none of that mattered. "You were right—there was part of this that terrified me. I walked away, but really, I think I only did it to see if I could. To see if you'd let me. And you did."

"I'm doing the same thing now," Stefan gritted out. "But I should tell you, I was never much of a martyr. The longer you stand here, not leaving, the less I can remember why I'm not convincing you to stay."

"You can't convince me to stay," Indy said softly. "No one could ever convince me to stay. Because a long time ago, I decided that I needed to be a rolling stone. That I could never stay in one place too long. That it would take something from me if I did. Do you know what I think that was?"

Another hint of dryness. "Not daddy issues, I understand."

"Because I thought I had to be different from how I started. Just like I decided I couldn't do well in school because my sister did. I had to distinguish myself." She pulled in a breath. "I took something that might have cut a different girl off at the knees, a dumb older boy taking private things and making them public, and I owned it. And do you know what, Stefan? It felt good. Powerful."

"As it should."

"I tasted that at fourteen and all I wanted was more. So I had whatever sex I felt like having. I was a stripper because why not? I liked taking off my clothes, and more than that, I liked people's reactions when they found out that's what I did." Indy had never talked about these things like this. She had never laid out her life, not like this. But it didn't feel like *her* life any longer, did it? She focused on him. "And ever since then, I've done exactly as I pleased. I've gone wherever I wanted, taken lovers and friends as I liked and left them, too, without a qualm. You're the only man I've ever come back to. Twice."

"This is how I know you will come back again." His voice was a low, rough sound. "As I have told you, I will wait for you."

"But yesterday taught me something," Indy said, as if he hadn't spoken. "It taught me everything. I already know what my passion is, Stefan. I finally figured it out."

She watched him gather himself, as if he expected a blow. And she could tell that he was a man used to taking blows, and returning them in kind. Those hands might curl into fists but she knew, deep inside, that he would never strike back when it was her.

"It's you," Indy said softly. "My passion is you. And with you, Stefan, I can do anything."

He let out a sound she didn't recognize, because it was low, almost animal.

And she didn't wait. She vaulted onto the counter, and then crawled across it until she was kneeling there in front of him, her face to his. Then she took the jaw that had given him away in her hands, and held him there.

Fully aware that he allowed it.

But this would be their life, she understood then. He would always allow her to leave, and so she would stay. And she would have this power over him, because he let her—and because she would never abuse it.

"You need to be sure," he said, his voice a mere scrape of sound. But his gaze was loud. "Very, very sure. Because if you choose me, this, now… I will not have it in me to be quite so forgiving as I might have sounded."

"I don't want forgiving," Indy told him fiercely. "I want you, Stefan. I'm not afraid of your darkness. I know all about the light and I think deep down, beneath everything, it turns out I've been a jealous, possessive, dark kind of woman all along. Can you handle that?"

His smile was a long time coming, but when he finally surrendered to it, it took over his face. "I can handle it. Can you?"

"You and me," she said. "No one else. I dare you."

He was picking her up, holding her in his arms and then lifting her up above, as if he needed to look at her in the sunlight. She gazed down at him, aware only when her cheeks began to ache that she was smiling so hard, so wide, she might as well have been the sun herself.

"I will never understand where you came from that night," he said, his voice as intent as his gaze.

"All that traveling. All those adventures. All of them were leading me to you." Indy wrapped her legs around his waist when he let her slide down his body, smiling even brighter when they were face to face. "I love you, Stefan. I thought love at first sight was a myth, but then there you were."

"I love you," he replied.

And she kissed him, or maybe he kissed her, and everything was a tangle of heat and need and better still—best of all—love.

When he pulled away again, neither one of them was breathing steadily.

Indy hoped they never would.

"Now," he murmured, his bright blue eyes turning wicked. "About that dare."

Then he showed her how he met a challenge, right there on the counter again. How he would always meet a challenge, especially if it was her.

How they would always find their way back to each other, to that perfect fit that was only theirs.

Their hot, sweet, life-altering love, that was worth changing a world or two.

So they did.

CHAPTER TWELVE

TEN YEARS LATER, Indy shivered in the cold on the front porch of a sweet little old farmhouse she and Stefan had spent the last six months renovating.

Right there on the outskirts of the same little Ohio town where she'd grown up. The town she'd been so certain she would never return to, ever.

She reached down and slid her hand over her gigantic belly, feeling even bigger beneath all the layers she was wearing, smiling. Because life, it turned out, did what it wanted.

Especially when a person finally wised up and stopped living it all in one way.

Her parents had thought that when Indy called home at the end of the summer to announce she'd met a man and *oops*, had accidentally married him on a beach in Bali, it was more evidence of her well-documented *flightiness*.

Then they'd met Stefan that Christmas. It had been a banner holiday in the March family. Bristol had come home with Lachlan Drummond, and it had been a strange few days of too many men in a house that had never had that problem.

Lachlan and Stefan had bonded. Bristol and Indy had realized, too late, that this was a potential cause for concern.

"We are brothers now," Stefan had said, a wicked light in his eyes, there in her childhood bedroom.

Where he'd proceeded to wash away all the ghosts of Jamie Portnoys past.

But quietly, so as to be respectful.

Indy's parents had been instantly impressed with their new son-in-law. Bill had a few beers with him. Margie had taken Indy aside and told her, with great confidence, that a man like that would settle her down. Eventually.

That wasn't quite how things had worked.

She and Stefan had followed their passions, whatever they might be. They didn't need to work, or wander off into think tanks like Bristol and Lachlan, so they indulged their whims instead. And over time, their whims tended to shift back and forth—something worthwhile for every selfish bit of hedonism. Art appreciation and buying trips all over the world. A year of volunteering in the rain forest. A summer scuba diving off the Great Barrier Reef. A season in Antarctica on a research expedition.

There was no need to waste her time on silly

love affairs with men not worth remembering. Not when she had everything she could ever want, and more, in Stefan.

Indy had never wanted to settle. She and Stefan had attended Bristol and Lachlan's wedding a few years after theirs, and while she'd loved watching her sister so happy, she was even happier that she and Stefan had married in private.

Because that kind of happiness, to her, was real.

And it made settling fun. Even the most domestic, hum-drum activity in the world was fun if she did it with Stefan.

"Are you ready?" she asked when she heard him come out of the house behind her. "Christmas morning waits for no one, Stefan. You should know this by now."

She turned to look at him, this beautiful man of hers. He still looked as dangerous as ever. He still had the bluest eyes she'd ever seen.

"For you?" Stefan grinned. He did that a lot more now. "I am always ready."

"You know we Marches take our holidays seriously." She smiled when he moved his hands over her belly, too. This baby they'd made, a little boy she was already madly in love with, would be joining them at any time. "Just wait until he comes. He's going to be worse than all my sister's kids combined."

Stefan's hand settled at the nape of her neck,

possessive and perfect. The snow had come in last night, but he'd been up early to clear off the steps and the walk to their car. And now he helped her navigate her huge, unwieldy body down the wintry steps.

"My son will be properly reserved and contained," Stefan told her. "I will teach him myself."

"You're not reserved at all, foolish man," she said softy.

His gaze seared through her. "Not anymore."

He helped her into the car and she sat there as he rounded the hood, looking at this place they intended to call home, at least for part of the year. So that Indy could be near her mother and the child could be near his grandparents. And they would always be close enough to Columbus that they could fly away at a moment's notice.

Because she liked to spend a good chunk of her summers in Prague, where they'd become them.

That was what she'd learned. Life was what she made it. It was never all one thing. She and Stefan got more solid by the day, happier and better, and none of that prevented them from playing the kind of games they liked best.

Give and take, year after year.

Carrying their home with them wherever they went, because the two of them, together, were what they needed. That was the passion that made life worth living.

Together they were rooted deep and tangled up in each other.

And yet, when the mood struck—and it always struck—they could fly.

Out of that alley in Budapest into a bright future, laced through with the most delicious darkness, and all for them.

"I love you, foolish girl," Stefan said when he climbed into the car. He turned the engine over, but didn't move. He was too busy studying her face.

"I know you do," she replied. She frowned. "I love you, too. But I think we need to head to the hospital instead of my parents' house."

"The hospital—?" But he cut himself off. "Now?"

"I'm pretty sure my water broke."

They stared at each other. Then both of them grinned, so big and wide it was brighter than the snow outside.

And they might have stayed there forever, but the little contractions she'd been ignoring changed into something she couldn't have ignored if she'd tried.

"Okay?" Stefan asked, searching her face, when it passed.

"Intense," she panted at him.

Then she strapped in, because Stefan drove like a man on the run when he liked. She opted not to ask him how or when he'd learned to do that.

Two short hours later, Indy beamed up at him from a hospital bed as he held their son. Stefan looked at her in wonder.

And together, plus the brand new love of their life, they started their greatest adventure yet.

* * * * *

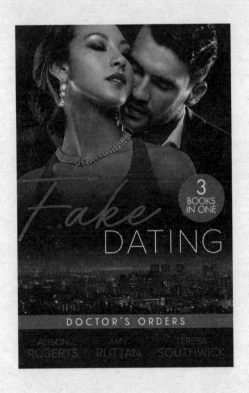

MILLS & BOON

THE HEART OF ROMANCE

A ROMANCE FOR EVERY READER

MODERN — Prepare to be swept off your feet by sophisticated, sexy and seductive heroes, in some of the world's most glamourous and romantic locations, where power and passion collide.

HISTORICAL — Escape with historical heroes from time gone by. Whether your passion is for wicked Regency Rakes, muscled Vikings or rugged Highlanders, awaken the romance of the past.

MEDICAL — Set your pulse racing with dedicated, delectable doctors in the high-pressure world of medicine, where emotions run high and passion, comfort and love are the best medicine.

True Love — Celebrate true love with tender stories of heartfelt romance, from the rush of falling in love to the joy a new baby can bring, and a focus on the emotional heart of a relationship.

HEROES — The excitement of a gripping thriller, with intense romance at its heart. Resourceful, true-to-life women and strong, fearless men face danger and desire - a killer combination!

 — From showing up to glowing up, these characters are on the path to leading their best lives and finding romance along the way – with plenty of sizzling spice!

To see which titles are coming soon, please visit

millsandboon.co.uk/nextmonth

MILLS & BOON
HEROES
At Your Service

Experience all the excitement of a gripping thriller, with an intense romance at its heart. Resourceful, true-to-life women and strong, fearless men face danger and desire – a killer combination!

Eight Heroes stories published every month, find them all at:

millsandboon.co.uk

GET YOUR ROMANCE FIX!

Get the latest romance news,
exclusive author interviews, story
extracts and much more!

blog.millsandboon.co.uk